To Speak of it Again
My Journey from Innocence
By Dina Redmon

Thanx 4 seeing me :)

To Speak of it Again
By Dina Redmon
Published by Dina Redmon
Copyright © 2013 Dina Redmon

This is a work of fiction. Names, characters, places and incidents are either works of the author's imagination or are used fictitiously, and any resemblance to actual persons, living or dead, business establishments, events or locales are entirely coincidental.

Dedicated With Love To:

The children of my heart: Amanda Carlenberg, Idril Faith, Cynthia Peterson, Spring Johnson and Darius Bentley.

Parents of my heart: Karolyn and Tom Miller

My "sister" and friend: Angelique Luzader

And finally to all of the amazing friends I've made along the way! You have all been the inspiration that filled these pages.

<3 I love you ALL... Always. <3

With Special thanks to:

Editors:
Aimee Koenig and John Homer, Thank you for making sense of my sometimes erratic ramblings.

Cover Photographer:
Layla Beth Munk, Thank you for working your creativity and for putting up with all of my many changes. You are incredible.

Cover Model:
Chevelle Noir Munk, Thank you for gracing the cover with your beauty and innocence. I am honored by your presence.

PROLOGUE

I won't insult your intelligence by using these opening words to say something frivolously exciting to try to catch your attention. Nor will I drone on and on describing some epic scene or deep, dark secret. I simply don't see the point in it.

You may be asking yourself then, "Why would she start the arduous task of writing her story, and what's so special about her that I would want to use my precious time reading it?" Well, the short answer is… Nothing. This isn't just my story. Here, let me explain.

Have you ever been sitting around with a bunch of people and someone gets all over animated, jumps up and yells, "This would make a great book!"? Well, I'm the friend that took notes. I mean REALLY took notes. I write in my journal daily, and sometimes even multiple times a day. Over the years, I've collected quite a few interesting stories. You know what? I'm about to tell you all of them. Yep, every juicy detail of everything I've ever written, heard and lived through. Well, okay, you busted me. Of course, I'm not going to write every one of the stories because, quite frankly, it would just be too much, but I did pick what I think are the best ones.

My people, as I like to call my very close friends, support me 100% in this endeavor and have even offered up some story ideas for this book. I honestly don't know what I would have done without the people that support me through my life's decisions. They are my therapists, my confidants, my shoulders to cry on and voices of reason when I need them the most. For that, I will always love them to the deepest depths of my soul.

I am sure there are people, that at this very moment, are cringing at the thought of being mentioned here. I have to ask, "Why are you so worried?" After all, we are all responsible for our own actions. If you've said or done something you don't want made public, well, I think that says more about you than it does me. Hell, it's my book, and I don't even come across as a good person all the time.

This is not just a tell all book about people you don't know. It goes much deeper than that, or at least I hope it does. It's a story about human interactions, relationships and my journey from innocence to personal growth. It's a story about everything, nothing and all that is in between.

So again, why did I choose to write this? The truth is, this book had to be written. I mean, it absolutely had to be written. No, not because it's some epic tale. Hell, at this point, I don't even know if anyone, other than me and my people, will ever read it. It had to be written because if I hadn't, my people would have ripped out my larynx and shown it to me. You see, I've talked about turning my journals into a book for years, and they are tired of hearing about it. So, for my own safety and well being, it simply had to be done.

I suppose, this is the part where I should tell you who I am. It's easy in its complexity. I'm not so conceited as to tell you how I think you should see me. Instead, I would rather tell you the facts as I see them, as I lived them and let you come to your own conclusions. I cannot promise that I will not throw in any personal commentary. After all, this is my story and the story of the people I've met. With that said, I think it may be time to introduce myself.

I was born under the midnight stars. Naw, I'm just kidding. I screamed my way into this world somewhere in the 1970's in northern California. Shortly thereafter, my family and I relocated to Minnesota, where I lived, until I returned to California later in life. I have lived all over the United States, California, Minnesota, Colorado, New Jersey, New York, North Carolina and Oregon. I am a gypsy, a care giver, an artist and a human. Everything that makes up this package has been labeled as Maggie. Hello, it's nice to meet you.

CHAPTER ONE

I hope, as you read my story, you will discover I am a hopeless romantic. I believe in a "white picket fence" kind of love. You know, the kind of love we read about in romance books? The type of love that is played out on the big screen when the actress is scooped up, kissed and her foot pops off the floor. I dream of the kind of love that is sung about in real love songs and the love that is promised in the fairy tales read to us as we fade away to dreamland.

I do not need the tangible white picket fence. I want what I believe in most, unconditional love. Real love is about forgiveness and knowing yourselves so completely you are able to trust in the love you have for one another. When it is real, you live and thrive in that love. I believe real love is waking up every morning and falling in love all over again. I believe we choose who we are going to love and how we are going to love them.

I blame my infatuation with love on my parents. The story of how they met is so sweet that it drips with syrupy goodness. Before we get to that, let's get to know them a bit, shall we?

Susan, my mother, was born in a tiny town in central Minnesota. Now, when I say tiny town, I mean tiny. There was a gas station that also served as the local grocery store, a feed store that supplied grains for the farmers, two churches and five bars.

Susan lived there with her three brothers, two sisters, mother and alcoholic father. She was the oldest of six children. When she was just eleven years old, her mother left them to go live with another man. That left the responsibility of raising her siblings and taking care of a drunk father solely on her shoulders.

They lived in a ramshackle of a house that was built as if it were a jigsaw puzzle with missing pieces. It was constructed on top of a cement slab with salvaged scraps of barn wood. The cracks were filled with mud because it had no insulation to speak of whatsoever.

The shack consisted of three rooms. The largest area served as a living room and bedroom for all of the children. There was a small, makeshift kitchen with a sink sitting in a single counter top, a propane stove which seldom had fuel and a refrigerator that had seen better days. There was a bedroom, in the back, where their father resided. The only bathroom was an outhouse that was hand dug by Susan. Before that, they used buckets and dumped it in the wooded area behind their house.

A potbelly stove sat in front of the only window in the living room and was used to heat their entire home. Susan and Kerry, the eldest brother, would spend a couple of hours a day clearing trees from their property and cutting wood for that stove. Their only tool was an old ax that had been given to them by a concerned neighbor.

I understand many people have had a much harder life than my mother. However, this is not their story; it's mine. I believe that my mother's upbringing, or lack thereof, was a major factor in the decisions she made later in life.

So, here's a bit of the personal commentary I mentioned earlier. How does a mom just up and leave her children in that type of situation? Talk about a selfish waste of a human. I could never do that to my children... Never. Anyway, let's continue.

Susan was barely five and a half feet tall. She had long, light blonde hair, blue eyes and very tanned skin from working outside so much. She was extremely slim as her lifestyle would not allow for weight gain.

Susan did whatever it took to make and keep her family happy. She made a dollar a day working in the rutabaga fields pulling weeds and harvesting the vegetables until her hands bled. Nightly, she scrubbed her family's tattered clothing out with those same bleeding hands and would hang them on a twine rope over the wood stove to dry.

Each of the children had two sets of clothing, one for school and one for work or play. As her siblings outgrew or tore up the clothes, Susan would sit by the fire and hand sew them to either repair them or modify them for the next child to wear. Any new clothes that were needed, were either donated from the church's thrift store or from a neighbor.

Water was heated nightly on the wood stove and poured into a small, metal wash tub in order for the children to bathe. Old material was torn into strips that she used to wrap her sisters' hair in rag curls. She spent an absurd amount of time, every night, cleaning up the whiskey bottles and vomit her father left around their shack of a home.

Susan cooked all of their family meals, to include squirrel, by herself. She trapped, bled, skinned and cleaned the animals. She would put them in a stew pot with whatever vegetables she was able to scavenge from work and her own little garden.

When she turned eighteen, after graduating from high school, Susan moved to southern Minnesota to become a live in nanny. She had seen an ad in the local newspaper and wrote to them with her qualifications. I don't know if the family thought she was qualified or if they just felt sorry for her.

Moving from a town where there are more bars than sidewalks, into a city that had skyscrapers, highways, office buildings, stores of all kinds and more people than blades of grass was a lot for her to take in. Susan was overtaken with culture shock. She muddled through as best as she could.

Though she felt free, guilt filled her heart because she had left her siblings to fend for themselves. She knew if she wanted a better life for them, she had to start with making a better one for herself. Susan felt as if she could show her siblings, through her actions, there was more to life than what they knew in their tiny hometown.

It was summer, and the family she worked for decided to go on vacation to California. She was completely excited and looked forward to the trip.

Bianca, the mother of the children Susan took care of, asked her to pack the necessary things. Susan did as was requested and packed a bag for herself as well. She was thrilled to be included.

As they drove across the country, Susan was glued to the window like most people these days are attached to their televisions. Having no camera, she took mental pictures of everything she saw. The flat plains of the badlands, the mountains in Montana and the bright lights of Nevada all became painted memories in her mind.

Richard, my father, lived in Northern California. He stood six feet four inches tall and was a slim, muscled man. He wore his thick, black hair cut short to the sides of his head with a 60's trademark flip on the top. He always carried a rat-tail comb with him just to keep his hair in place. He was the type of guy that changed the oil in his motorcycle more often than the oil in his hair.

Richard rode with a local biker gang called "The Hardened Ones." He was a bad boy with a heart of gold. He had dropped out of high school in the eighth grade and never looked back.

In his early twenties, Richard did some time in San Quentin. When released, he became a truck driver and drove for a local trucking company on day trips. He loved what he did and continued to do it for quite a few years.

My parents came from two different worlds and are proof that opposites attract. I realize that is not always the case, but it worked for them. Here's their story.

When Susan walked into Bianca's mom's house, Richard, Bianca's brother, was sitting at the table in the kitchen. He looked up at Susan, and she smiled a shy grin at him. His first words to her were, "I'm going to marry you." Eleven days later, they were married at "The Chapel of the Palms" in Las Vegas. No shit, that's exactly how it happened. Of course, she stayed in California when his sister and her family returned to Minnesota.

Richard and Susan rented a tiny apartment near his family's home. During the day, Susan would clean, cook and work on crafts. They spent their evening's painting and decorating. They were in love, so it didn't matter that their first home had more cockroaches than carpet fibers. They told me a story of how they had been out for the evening, and when they returned home, their blue velvet bedspread was almost black with roaches. I cringed whenever they told me that tale. They made the best of what they had until they were able to move on.

They saved their pennies, along with whatever else they could live without, for three years and were finally able to purchase their first house. They were so excited. It was a dusty blue color, and when looked at, at just the right angle, it would almost disappear into the sky. Little, white shutters framed the windows on the front of the house to match the white door that marked its entry. It had two bedrooms, an eat-in kitchen, living room, bathroom, large front porch and a mud room off the back. It had a large enough yard for Susan to plant a garden and a garage where she opened a ceramics studio. She was truly in her element here.

Standing in the front yard, wrapped in each others' arms, they talked about the life they would have there. They spoke of the children they would raise, the Christmas parties that would be hosted and the love they would share. They were content in the love they were creating.

My parents struggled to have children. Susan had five miscarriages in the first three years of their marriage. She had almost given up hope when she became pregnant with me. Ordered to complete bed rest, she was not allowed to do anything except the things needed for personal care. Mom and Dad called me their "little miracle." That is, until they took me home, and my nickname changed.

Why the nickname change? Well, Dad was sitting in his black, leather recliner, holding me above his head and talking baby talk to me. As he tickled my sides, I shit all over him. Yes, you read that correctly; I shit all over him. Hence, the new nick name, "Little Shit."

Can you guess what my first word was? Yep... Shit. I think I heard that word more in my first few years of life than any other word. Maybe that is the reason I can curse like a sailor to this day. * laughing *

The first four years of my life, I was spoiled beyond spoiled. If a new toy came out, my dad bought it for me. I was always at my mom's side no matter what she was doing, be it working in the garden, painting ceramics in the studio or cooking for my father. I have been told so many stories from that time in my life, but I don't remember much of it myself.

Have you ever thought about your first, true memory? I mean YOUR memory, not one that was planted in your brain by someone else. It's harder than you may think.

I had just turned four years old when Mom gave birth to my little sister, Brianna. We were all in the recovery room oohing and awwing over her. She was so tiny; born with jet black hair and a wrinkled, little, red face. I was afraid to hold her because she looked so fragile, but Dad sat me in a chair and placed her in my lap. I held her for a little while, watching her tiny fingers wrap around mine and the expressions on her face. I spoke to her, "Hello Sissy, I'm your big sister Maggie, and I promise I'll always be here for you."

After a few minutes, Dad took her from me and held her close to his chest. I saw tears fall down his weathered, tanned cheeks. He then sunk to his knees and lifted her into the air with both hands. His voice, soft and deep, lifted to the heavens, "God, I asked you for a baby boy, but in your infinite wisdom, you have blessed me, once again, with a beautiful, healthy daughter. I am grateful and promise to take care of her to the best of my ability." His voice now became a bit louder,

"But I am putting in my order RIGHT now. My first grandchild had BETTER be a boy."

Guilt filled my heart as I heard him speak those words. I wanted my dad to be happy. I decided, right then and there, I was going to do my best to give my dad the son he deserved, the son he wanted. It was that day that I began my journey to becoming a tomboy.

Brianna and Mom had just come home from the hospital, and our home was full of people. Some I recognized, but most of them were strangers to me. A few relatives flew in from Minnesota to help Mom with the new baby.

Grandma dressed me in a pretty, little, pink dress with white ruffled socks. She tied my long, curly, blonde hair into pony tails on the sides of my head with little, pink ribbons. I was adorable, and I HATED it.

As soon as no one was paying attention to me, I snuck into my bedroom and changed into a pair of black and white, striped, bibbed overalls with a white t-shirt. I pulled out the ribbons from the pony tails and put a baseball cap on with my hair tucked up under it.

When I went back to the living room, Grandma yelled at me to put my girl clothes back on. I started to go do as I was told when I felt my dad's huge hand on my shoulder. I froze in my tracks as I heard him say to my grandmother, "There's nothin' wrong with what Maggie is wearing. She likes to be comfortable, and I love my children to be who they are. Now quit fussing over what she is wearing and start fussing over the new baby." He looked down at me and smiled. He became my hero that day.

Personal thought here... This was the same woman who had abandoned my mother with the drunk father and five siblings to take care of. Who the hell was she trying to fool?

While everyone visited with Mom and Brianna, Dad busied himself out in the part of the garage that he had set up for his workshop. It wasn't as big as the ceramic studio, but he made do with what he had. I was at his side as much as I was allowed.

Dad loved to work with his hands. He was quite talented when it came to things like that. He had built my entire bedroom set, to include a bunk bed, a dresser, a toy chest and multiple shelves. He also made a play kitchen set that consisted of a double sink with a cabinet above it, a stove and a table with two benches.

Dad spent the entire weekend building a new bookshelf for Mom. When everyone left, he presented it to her and set it up in the hallway. He was very proud of it.

I remember how nice the fresh wood smelled. I had just learned to print my name, and I wanted to show my dad how well I could write it. I proceeded to print my name on the side of the bookshelf with a pencil.

When Dad saw it, he became irate. I was so scared that I tried to blame it on Brianna. He picked up the pencil I used and tried to put it in Brianna's hand. She couldn't even grasp it, let alone use it.

"She can't even hold the pencil. How are you gonna stand there, lie to me and try to get your little sister in trouble? What the fuck is wrong with you? Weren't you raised better than that?" He picked me up and swatted my butt three times. I wouldn't cry. He spanked me harder. I still wouldn't cry. Finally, after spanking me a third time, a single tear fell down my cheek.

He sat me back down on the floor and told me, "It's your job to take care of your little sister. You're supposed to make sure she stays out of trouble and always has what she needs. Now, go to your room and think about what you've done." I did as I was told and spent the rest of the night in my room without dinner or companionship.

I need to interrupt the story again. Is it just me, or is that a lot to put on the shoulders of a four year old? I took that seriously, and I made it my life's mission. I provided for her almost to a fault. She never had to ask for anything, just point, cry, and I would get it for her.

Mom had to spend most of her time taking care of Brianna. That left me to fend for myself a lot. I loved to play in the little bird aviary in our back yard that Dad had converted into a sandbox for us. I spent hours, almost every day, out there playing in the sand. I would pile it up and carve it down with sticks to form reproductions of different things I had seen in my short lifetime. My favorite things to sculpt were animals. They interested me like nothing else.

One day, I was playing in the sandbox, when I noticed something hanging in the corner. There were bugs flying around it, and I got very curious as to what it was. I repeatedly threw my shovel at it until I knocked it down. The moment it hit the ground the bugs began to swarm around and sting me. It hurt like nothing I had ever felt before. I managed to stand up, run to the side door of the house and scream for my mom.

Mom came running to the door and saw what was happening. She grabbed a glass of water from the sink in the mud room and threw it at me through the screen door. Yeah, through the screen door.

I don't remember what happened after that, except to tell you, I ended up in the hospital, and the doctors told my mother that I was lucky to be alive. I had been stung over one hundred times. She explained to the doctor that she had been taking care of Brianna when she heard me screaming. She had to put her down safely before she could tend to me. When she got to the door and saw what was happening she did the only thing she knew to do, because she was afraid to open the door. Geez, thanks Mom.

When Mom was working in her garden, Brianna and I played in a cage in our yard. The people, who owned the house before us, had built it for their birds. Our parents turned it into a play area for us. Well, they really didn't turn it into one; they just called it our play area.

It stood ten feet tall and was eight feet wide by twelve feet long. It's frame was made with six large, metal poles that were sunk into concrete in the ground. The walls, along with the ceiling, were covered with chain link, and it had a grassy floor. There were multiple shelves and perches throughout the cage and a narrow door, on the southern end of it, to allow for entrance.

Brianna was almost two years old. She was much more fun to play with now. While Mom worked in the garden, we had our dolls and our little tea set spread out on a blanket in the cage.

As I poured tea for Brianna, I noticed her face frozen in a horrified stare. Looking behind me, I saw a very large dog digging under the side of the cage. I quickly stood up, screamed for Mom, lifted my sister to the highest shelf I could reach and told her to keep her eyes covered. Turning around, I closed my eyes, bracing myself for the inevitable, as the dog came into the cage. His snarling growls were silenced. Slowly opening my eyes, I saw Mom lying over the dog's lifeless body. She had opened the door to the play area, slammed herself over the dog and slit its throat with her spade. In shock, I turned, lifted my sister down and took her into the house. After laying her down for a nap with her favorite doll, I returned outside.

Mom was digging a hole near the side of the garden. When she saw me, she handed me the shovel and told me to finish digging it. I did as

I was told. When the hole was over the top of my head, I crawled out using the shovel as a ladder. I pulled the dog over to its grave, dumped it in and buried it. Mom planted marigolds over it, and we never spoke of it again. That's what my family did best. When things got out of control, we took care of it and then swept it under a rug like nothing had ever happened.

Sorry to interrupt the story again, but I just had another adult thought. Is this what happened to my mother when she was growing up? Is that why no one rescued them from the life her mother had left them to? Was it all just swept under a rug only to be whispered about in the anonymity of shadows? That would explain a lot.

We spent a lot of family time at a small, local theme park. We would ride the kiddy rides, play with the animals at the petting zoo and fish in the little pond at the park. Mattie, Dad's youngest sister, and her family would join us there at least one weekend a month. She was married to a nice man named Glen. They had two children, a girl named Rhea and a boy by the name of Rob. They were almost the same age as Brianna and myself. It was delightful.

Dad taught us how to fish. He told us to sit very still and watch our bobber float in the water. He explained that when the bobber went under the water, it meant we had a fish. He was not a very patient man and would often yell at us because we were not following his instructions.

Our parents also belonged to a local skin diving club. We often traveled to the northern coast of California with the group of people that formed the club. Brianna and I would hang out with the other children, picking shells, while our parents practiced their diving skills.

I remember, one specific occasion, when the divers had caught one over their limit on abalone. One of the women in the club slid the shellfish down the front of her swimsuit to conceal it from the game warden. It sucked on to her stomach, and she was rushed to the hospital to have it surgically removed.

The divers had huge barbecues where everyone chipped in what they could. There was always a ton of food and drinks. No one ever went without. People stood around the campfire, sang, talked and laughed. I always hated it when those weekends would come to an end.

I wish I could tell you more detail of those times, but the truth is I simply do not remember them. I believe that those memories were pushed aside and replaced with the darker ones that haunt me still to this day. It's sad what we remember and what we forget.

I had just turned six years old and Anna, my little friend, had come to visit. She lived up the block from me and was my best friend in the whole world. We used to play in the sand box for hours. Anna loved animals almost as much as I did, and she would bring over story books with pictures of little animals in them for us to try to recreate.

Anna and I played all afternoon in the sand box. Around 3:30, Mom yelled out to us from the ceramic studio, where she was teaching a class, that it was time for Anna to head home as her mom had instructed. We gave each other a hug, performed our secret hand shake and said goodbye.

On her way home, Anna was kidnapped. There were over sixty people looking for her including the Lodi police department and Lodi REACT team. Other authorities and members of the citizen band radio operators club were looking for her over a three county wide area. Though everyone searched desperately, it was too late. They discovered Anna's little, lifeless body, beaten and dismembered, in a suitcase, in the back yard of the man thought responsible for her death. He lived on the same block as we did. I never saw Anna again.

I personally do not remember any of this, but I do know the stories I heard growing up. Later in life, I did my own research and found a newspaper clipping about it on the internet. I think there was more to this story than what I had been told. I can't explain the feeling I have about this, but I do know that I feel the wrong person was blamed for her murder. Every once in a while, I dream of her on that day, and the alleged events just don't add up. I wish I could bring those distant and dark memories into the forefront of my mind and put it to rest once and for all.

Our parents were terrified and quickly made arrangements for us to move to Minnesota. They borrowed money from Aunt Mattie and Uncle Glen, rented a moving truck, packed us up and we were on our way. There was no looking back, no remembering. There was barely time to say goodbye. Are you feeling like this ended too abruptly? Yeah, me too.

CHAPTER TWO

The journey to Minnesota was uneventful. So much so, that I have dug through the deepest recesses of my mind and have yet to find a single detail to share with you. My personal feelings are that we as a family, were so disturbed by the events that put us in that moving truck, that we traveled those dark, long, twisting and turning roads in silent thought.

I do remember, a few days after being on those aforementioned roads, we pulled into a long, gravel driveway that marked the entrance to Aunt Julie's property. We had arrived at Mom's sister's home, home sweet hillbilly home.

To our right was a vast, wooded area bordered only by a small garden and wooden fence. To the left sat a house? At least I think it was a house... Yeah, it was a house or at least a resemblance of one. Did people really live like this?

The wood shake siding was falling off, and there was tar paper covering what was left of the roof. A single, blackened chimney pipe extended out of a hole in the roof and thick, black smoke billowed into the air, happy to make its escape from the torture chamber it had been created in.

The shadows of a barn, cast by the early morning sun that was beginning to rise into the sky, loomed before the front of the truck. I could see little pigs, like the ones in the story books that Anna used to bring over, playing in the mud. There was something that looked like sheep with very short hair, kicking up their heels in a small fenced pasture. I later learned they were goats.

As I sat there attempting to take in this new environment and all it had to offer, gun shots filled my ears. I almost jumped out of my skin as they continued to echo across the open land. I put my hands over my ears, in an attempt to block the sound, but it didn't help. Dad sat there, laughing hysterically. His laughter seemed almost wicked as it escaped through his smile. That is when I noticed he was throwing rows of firecrackers out of the window to announce our arrival. Mom just sat there, shaking her head in utter disgust, while Brianna slept soundly, curled up in a ball, on the floor of the truck. How did she do that and why couldn't I?

The door to the house opened and three sleepy children filed out with their parents in tow. The eldest son began to pick up the remains of the firecrackers. The middle son and younger daughter clung to their parents legs as if it offered them protection from the sounds still hanging in the air.

After waking Brianna, we stepped out of the truck. I watched as Mom and Aunt Julie hugged each other tightly in a tearful embrace. At the time, I thought the tears were because they were so happy to see one another. Looking back at it now, I understand the tears were because Mom realized her efforts were in vain. Aunt Julie lived now just as she did as a child. I guess it's true when they say, "the apple doesn't fall far from the tree."

Introductions were made and more hugs, kisses and handshakes were exchanged before we headed into the house to have breakfast. The front door of the house led directly into a large eat-in kitchen. To the right was a small bathroom, and I noticed as I walked by, that it smelled like something evil had died in it.

A large, black, wood stove made its presence known with the sounds of burning wood and the heat that emanated from it. Aunt Julie added more wood to the stove, and Mom began to dig through the cupboards. She found everything needed to make pancakes for this brood of people that had now filled the little kitchen.

Dad and Uncle Pete sat at the kitchen table, punching each other in the arms and talking shit like men did. We children sat on the floor, in silence, for we knew that children were to be seen and not heard. We stared at one another as if we were trying to telepathically communicate. It didn't work, of course, but it was not for lack of trying.

Uh oh, I had to pee. Did I just get up and use the bathroom, or did I ask for permission first? Better to ask I guess. I stood up and tapped Dad on the shoulder, "Dad, may I use the restroom?" The next thing I knew, I was flying across the room and slammed into the oven door of the wood stove. As it came down and hit me in the back of the head, silence filled the room. A single tear rolled down my cheek. Mom picked me up and carried me to the bathroom, but it was too late. I had wet myself as I sat there wondering what had just happened. Pops had backhanded me so hard that it knocked me almost senseless.

Mom went out to the truck and got me fresh clothes, helped me clean up and told me to never interrupt the adults again when they were speaking. Lesson learned.

When breakfast concluded, the children were ordered to go outside, do the chores and to find something to occupy our time. Chores? What were chores? I was soon to find out.

We headed toward the barn when Timmy, the middle child, stopped dead in his tracks. "Hey, ain'tcha gonna change into old clothes first?" Timmy turned around as he spoke. "Maggie, ain'tcha gonna change first?" Timmy repeated his question.

"These are my old clothes." Timmy's jaw dropped with a look of awe when I answered him.

"Wow, you must be rich." Timmy shook his head in complete amazement, took Pam, his little sister, by the hand and followed Gary, their older brother, to the barn. I followed their lead and took Brianna by the hand, trailing behind them.

We threw hay to the beef cattle and dumped buckets of household slop to the pigs. We tied out each goat to a tree in their yard, so they could eat the grass that was growing there. The rabbits were fed from the buckets of clover we picked for them. I thought it was so cool that they had pet bunnies... Until they told me they ate them. I didn't believe them when they told me that. I think I was just too young to understand. We then brought fresh water to all of the animals and collected eggs from the chickens.

Chores were now finished and understood, so we did what we were told and found something to busy ourselves with. Brianna and I were obviously very new to this lifestyle, so we just followed along with our cousin's lead. We all headed out to the wooded area on the other side of the garden to play Hide-N-Seek and Tag until we could no longer breathe through our laughter.

"Let's build a fort." Gary's suggestion seemed popular enough... But what was a fort? The two boys began to grab large branches and pile them along a downed tree that was high enough we could all walk under it. Oh, a fort is like a wooden tent.

The boys asked us girls to gather pine boughs and pile them next to the structure. They tied branches to the downed tree with twine they had been carrying in their pockets. When the pile was big enough, the boys laid the pine against the branches to form solid walls. Our fort was really starting to come together, and we were pleased with our little creation.

I used one of the boughs, stripped it, except for the very bottom, and formed it to look like a broom. When the others saw this, they began to forage the area for other things that could be used in replacement of household items. Pam found a large mushroom, growing on the side of a tree, and broke it off. She brought it to me and said we could pretend it was a bowl. Timmy broke off some small, bare branches and announced we should use them for forks to go along with the bowl. Gary discovered a few hollowed out pieces of dried wood that we used as glasses.

Brianna, feeling left out, sat on the ground crying. I couldn't stand to see my little sister upset. I quickly thought of something for her to do to make her feel like a part of the group. I stepped over to her, knelt down on the forest floor and put my hand on her shoulder.

"Hey Sissy, do you know what our home needs the most? Some wild flowers to make it pretty. Do you think you could pick some for us?" I smiled as I spoke to her.

I loved her beyond even my understanding of what love was at the time. She scampered to her feet, wiped the tears and ran off. A few minutes later, she presented a handful of blossoms to me with the biggest smile I had ever seen on her face. I used one of our glasses as a vase and sat them in the middle of the floor space we had designated as our table. I was so very proud of that little shit. * smile *

Timmy brought some birch bark into our "home", ripped it into pieces and told us that we should use it as our money, which we happily did. We played all day and even built two more small structures to use as our store and a school. I played the school teacher and taught the kids how to count in Spanish. I also showed Brianna and Pam how to use dandelions as make-up. They would pick them and rub them on their cheeks. Happier children could not have been found that day. That is, until we returned to the land of the adults.

We heard Pops whistle while we played out in the woods. It was our signal to return home. We marched in single file as if we were in the Army and chanted a military cadence, "Sound off, 1, 2... Sound off, 3, 4... Sound off, 1, 2, 3, 4... 1, 2."

When we marched into the yard, Uncle Pete and Pops were sitting on the front porch drinking beer and, once again, acting like men did. Well, maybe not men but neanderthals. They were crushing the empty beer cans against their foreheads and slamming the next ones back to see who could finish them first. I had never seen Pops act like this before and it concerned me. It was as if an alien race had swooped down from outer space and replaced him with someone else.

"Gary, what did I tell you about playing Army?" Uncle Pete's voice echoed loudly across the yard. I didn't understand the problem, though later learned that it was because they were Jehovah Witnesses and did not believe in being in the military.

Unaware that Gary had quit marching, I bumped into him. That is when I noticed the look of complete and utter fear on his face. Uncle Pete stood up and walked toward us with giant strides. As he did, he picked up a piece of water hose that was lying in the yard. Unintelligible words escaped his throat. All of us, except Gary, scattered to the corners of the yard. I, with Brianna in tow, headed towards Pops.

Uncle Pete proceeded to beat Gary, with that piece of hose, until his skin bled. I stood there, in absolute horror, not believing what I was seeing. Was this a pattern that was only seen in this part of the country? Is that why our father had backhanded me earlier that day? Was he just fitting in? If so, please Lord, let us leave soon.

When it was over, we were ordered, once again, to take care of the chores and then get washed up for supper. Even though I was only six years old at the time, I remember thinking that no one tended to Gary's wounds before he was sent out to the dirty barn. Again, we all did as we were instructed, without question, because we lived in fear of what would happen if we didn't.

The same chores were repeated that we had performed earlier in the day, except the goats were brought back to the corral next to the barn. It seemed like a lot of work for children that were all under the age of eight, but we did it without question or thought. It had already become second nature.

Supper was served, and we children ate in silence on the dirty floor of the kitchen. The adults sat at the table telling stories and comparing lives. It was as though they had to constantly one-up each other. I now call that "comparing dick size," but back then I didn't even know what a dick was. I just knew I was witnessing odd behaviors and it scared me. I guess I was a pretty observant child now that I think about it, or maybe it's my adult thoughts mixing with my childhood memories. Either way, I knew something wasn't right.

When supper concluded and was cleaned up, Aunt Julie and Mom ran a bath. Each of us kids took turns in the tub, and yes, we shared the water... Icky. We were bathed according to our age, starting with the youngest. Pam and Brianna were bathed together and then myself, followed by the two boys. I was so happy we didn't start with the eldest first. That would have been completely gross.

When the baths were completed, we dressed in our pajamas and were sent upstairs to the attic.

The staircase entered into the middle of it. The girls were to sleep on one side of the stairs and the boys to the other. There were holes in the ceiling big enough that I could see the tar paper that protected the roof.

We were instructed to make our beds. Um, beds would have been nice. There were no beds to speak of. Instead, pallets made from piles of hay, covered with homemade blankets, were stacked on the floor. Our cousins seemed reluctant to share what little they had, but they did as they were told.

As we lay there, my mind played a slow motion movie of the day's events. Was this real? Did we really leave our beautiful home in Lodi to move here? Though we had fun, it wasn't the kind of fun I had grown accustomed to. It also felt like even more of a responsibility to take care of Brianna. There were so many more dangers to keep her safe from, the biggest, now being our father.

I fell asleep listening to the sound of the tar paper flapping against the roof. It became a lullaby to sing me to sleep. I dreamt of our lives in Lodi, playing in the tomato field next to our house and picking the fresh, red, ripe tomatoes. I saw myself helping the elderly lady across the street with her vegetable garden. Visions of playing in the sandbox with Anna haunted my dreams. Oh, how I missed Anna. I fell asleep that night with crocodile sized tears streaming down my cheeks. I let myself be a girl, and I cried a silent cry.

Mom and Dad bought a mobile home within days of us moving there and placed it in the back field on Aunt Julie and Uncle Pete's property. The electricity and plumbing were quickly connected, making it possible for us to move in the same day. We hurriedly unpacked the moving truck and put each box in the room for which it was labeled.

Once the truck was emptied, Uncle Pete jumped into his pickup and followed Pops into the next town over to return the moving truck and bring him home.

Home... Even at six years old, I knew and recognized the difference between the place we used to call home and where we were now. It probably wasn't as bad as I remember it with my childhood eyes. I'm sure that the suddenness of the move had a way of coloring my views on the events leading up to it and the way I chose to deal with it once we got there. Okay, so this is home now, suck it up and deal with it.

Pops started driving a truck for the same company that Uncle Pete drove for. This meant that he was gone for several weeks at a time. Mom worked harder than I had ever seen her work before, but she appeared to be in her element again. She made things seem so easy and natural.

Aunt Julie needed help expanding her garden, so it would produce enough for both families. Mom stepped right up with ideas and a plan to do it. She walked right into the big sister role like she had never left. They started it right away.

Mom loved being a homemaker and spent her nights turning the trailer into a home for the four of us. She crocheted throw rugs and hand sewed curtains from old clothes that she ripped down and pieced together. She picked wild flowers and dried them to make wreaths and bouquets. She framed pictures she found in magazines and even painted some herself to hang on the walls. I swear, there was nothing this woman couldn't do. That is, until she fell and hurt her back.

The doctor said that without surgery, Mom would never walk again. She spent three months in bed recovering, but refused to have the surgery. She was a very strong willed woman. Through her direction, I learned to cook simple meals and took care of our family as best as I could. Tomato soup and grilled cheese sandwiches became my specialty. I took her place in the garden and performed both her's and my share of the chores. Aunt Julie helped when she could, but she had her own family to take care of and had very little time to help.

It was now the middle of autumn. The time had arrived for us to harvest, can and freeze the bounty of the land that we had worked so hard to grow. I had no idea what I was doing and Mom knew it. She did her best to help me with whatever she could.

Ryan, Mom's youngest brother, made her a small cart with wheels on it. She used that cart to pull herself up and down the rows of the garden on her stomach. I worked at Mom's side doing everything she asked me to do. Brianna sat at the head of the rows and played with her dolls because she was just too young to be of any help. Quite honestly, I wanted her to stay a child as long as she could.

When the harvest was complete, Mom taught me how to prepare the vegetables for canning and freezing. She taught me how to boil the jars in preparation for the hot vegetables and how to place the lids and rings on the jars in order to form a tight seal. She sat in her wheelchair and aided me with what she could reach. We smiled as we worked, and she told me stories of her childhood. I had never felt closer to her.

When Pops came home from the road that autumn, he was thrilled to see all we had accomplished. The hallway closet had been turned into a small storage pantry for our homemade canned goods. There were six shelves, from floor to ceiling, each about six square feet. Colorful jars of vegetables, jellies, pickles and different flavored syrups and juices lined the shelves. Each shelf was labeled with the type and quantity of canned goods that could be found there. Every time we took one down, we changed the number on the label. It looked like a rainbow of canned goods.

It was now hunting season. Pops and Uncle Pete headed out to do what they thought was needed in order to take care of their families. I remember playing out in the yard when I heard the first and then the second of two gun shots. It wasn't much later that I saw the men carrying a deer, tied to a tree limb, over their shoulders. I was absolutely mortified. That memory is still so vivid in my mind that I can remember the look on the deer's face.

They hung the deer, upside down by its hind legs, in a tree in the yard and bled it by slicing its throat. Once it was bled, Pops and Uncle Pete began to skin it to prepare it for butchering. They had no concern about the children witnessing this. I couldn't watch. My heart broke for Bambi.

Winter seemed to come out of nowhere. Mom had made a full recovery from her back issues. We played out in the snow as much as we were allowed. It was our first, real experience with snow, and it is something I will never forget.

Our cousin Timmy had been teasing us, for what seemed to be the entire winter, because we had never experienced this much snow before. It had only snowed a couple of inches, one time, in Lodi and even then it lasted only a few, short hours.

I told Gary how upset it was making me when his little brother teased us. It made Brianna cry, with hurt feelings, every time Timmy said something. He told me to leave it up to him, so I did. After all, he was the oldest and had lived here longer than I had.

We were all playing out in the cow pasture, making snow angels, snow forts, having snowball fights and pulling each other around in our sleds when Timmy said he had to go to the bathroom. He started to run up to the house but knew he wasn't going to make it. He began to pee in front of us when Gary stopped him. He told him that no one wanted to see him do that and to go over by a tree instead.

Timmy went over to where Gary told him to and started to urinate. Out of nowhere, we heard a girl scream the most blood curdling, horror movie worthy scream, ever heard to this day. We all ran over to where Timmy was and saw him lying in the snow. We found him with his pants around his ankles, his hands over his genitalia and crying like a baby.

Gary couldn't stop laughing, but in between breaths, he told us that Timmy had peed on the electric fence and it zapped him. We all started laughing at him too. Gary told him that's what he got for teasing Brianna and I. He never teased us again the entire winter.

As soon as spring made its wet, muddy appearance, we began to break ground for an even larger garden. In our free time, our cousins taught us how to play football in the mud. Aunt Julie and Mom would spray us down with the water hose before allowing us into our separate homes. The memories of Lodi were beginning to fade, and I was enjoying living in the moments that had become our life.

Uncle Ryan worked for a paper mill. He brought us boxes of wooden doughnuts from the paper roll ends to help with starting the fires that heated our homes. Boxes and buckets of them littered our yard, the storage sheds, our porches and anywhere else there was spare room.

One spring morning, Brianna and I were watching cartoons, and we heard Aunt Julie yelling at our mom. All of a sudden, Mom burst through the front door and slammed it behind her. She was cursing at the top of her lungs, and I remember how shocking it was to hear because she never cursed, except when she called me her little shit.

Glass shattered around us. I grabbed Brianna and sheltered her from the flying shards. I took her by the hand and ran down the hallway to our room. Pushing her onto the lower bunk, I covered her with a heavy blanket and told her to stay there until I came to get her. I ran out to the living room where I saw Mom picking up the wooden doughnuts that Aunt Julie had thrown through our windows. She threw them back at Julie, screaming louder with every throw.

I stood there in wonderment as I watched Mom pick up a bunch of the doughnuts and cradle them in the front of her t-shirt. As she headed out the door, she began to hurl the wooden doughnuts directly at Aunt Julie who would then pick them up and fire them right back at Mom. Looking back at it now, it was quite humorous, but at the time it was scary.

Later in life, when I asked Mom what happened that day, I was told that the two of them had gotten into an argument about how to raise their children. Aunt Julie thought Mom was too easy on us. She said we watched too much television, and Mom dressed us like little princesses. This started a feud between them that turned into a wooden doughnut hurling contest. I guess Julie grew tired of being the poor little sister.

When Pops returned home from the road, arrangements were made to move our mobile home into a trailer park in the next town over. I believe this was the best plan of action at the time. Had we continued to share that homestead, there may have been bigger problems to follow.

Goodbye little country home, and hello city life. Okay, not actual city life, but as close to it as we could get. At least here, we didn't have to be bussed into school because it was in the same town to which we had moved. There were also grocery stores, a library, a museum, churches, gas stations and a park.

Life in the trailer park was wonderful! Mom opened a daycare in our home and had thirteen children in it. There was always something to do and someone to do it with. We used to hike up to an abandoned train depot and play house for hours. We had it all set up with things we would sneak out of our own homes like dishes, a broom, blankets and art we had drawn or painted ourselves. It was quite cute in it's humbleness. I even got my first kiss in that little building. * smile *

We rode our bikes around the trailer park, played Tag in the playground and Hide-N-Seek in the woods surrounding it. There was never a dull moment with so many children to play with. Mom bought a swimming pool for our yard, and in the summer almost every child in the park would come to play while the moms sat around drinking iced tea. I still think there was liquor in that tea. They would start out pretty quiet, and as the day progressed they would get loud and silly.

Pops was driving a lot more now and would be gone for two or three months at a time. We didn't see him as often as we would like, but when he did come home it was always an incredible time. He would bring us gifts from every state he had been in, and each of us girls had a spoon collection from those states. He brought my sister and I lavish dolls that sat on shelves in our bedroom and books for me to read to Brianna.

One day, while we were playing outside, we saw a huge truck pulling a beautiful, golden colored mobile home up the road that circled the trailer park. We watched as it was carefully placed in the empty lot directly behind us. It was fun to watch the big truck slowly backing the new trailer into its spot.

Right away, Mom started talking about how it must be nice to have that kind of money. She went on to say how she hoped that the new neighbors were not snotty and stuck up. Mom rolled her eyes in disgust as they placed the trailer and then a gorgeous, wooden porch at its front door. She always seemed to have issues with people that she perceived to have more money than we did.

Oh my goodness, Pops is home! We saw his truck coming up the road of the trailer park and then watched as he carefully parked it in our driveway. Our thoughts immediately switched from the new addition in the trailer park to our Pops being home. He got out of the truck, and we all ran over to him and hugged him.

"I see we have new neighbors moving in." He smiled as he spoke.

"Yep, seems like they have money too. They probably won't fit in around here." Mom stood there with her hands on her hips, surveying the new trailer.

"Let's go take a look at it." Pops took Mom by the hand and we followed them over to the new mobile home.

"We can't go in there, Richard." Mom stopped at the front door.

"Yes we can. We own it." Pops couldn't hold back the surprise any longer. He had secretly purchased the new trailer and had made arrangements to have it placed without telling Mom. What a magical surprise.

Adult thought here... I wonder if Mom ever regretted her words about the "new neighbors" and how much money they had or how they wouldn't fit in. Somehow, I doubt it. I believe she was just happy to still be the big fish in the little pond. She had changed so much since that fight with Aunt Julie and us moving into the park. She was the stuck up and snotty one after that.

We all ran through the door to look around. Right away, Brianna and I chose our bedrooms without argument. We were so happy to have our own rooms that we didn't care about the size or location of them. Brianna took the one nearest to our parents' room, and I claimed the one closest to the front of the mobile home.

We started moving in that day. Mom had opened all of the doors and windows to air out the "new trailer" smell before we moved in. It took all of us a total of four days to get everything cleaned and moved in, but it was worth it.

After everything was situated, Mom talked to Pops about how nasty the old furniture looked in the new place. It took no time at all, and the four of us were on our way to the store. Mom chose wooden framed furniture with off white cushions that had a country print on them. There was a new couch, a love seat, two chairs, a coffee table and three end tables. It was absolutely lush. Pops spoiled Mom so much.

The furniture was delivered the next day. Aunt Julie and Uncle Pete came to retrieve our old stuff. It was a step up for them, and they were pleased to receive it. At least, that is what I overheard Mom say to one of the mothers from her day care.

We lived in that trailer for two years. I was now nine years old, and wouldn't you know it? Just as I started getting used to life there in the mobile home park and set in a routine, Mom and Dad announced we were moving again. This time, we would be moving about eight miles away to some property Mom inherited from a distant relative. At least we would still be in the same school and with our friends.

The construction started immediately. Trees were cut down to make room for a driveway, an area for a yard and for the mobile home to be placed. A septic system was installed and a water well drilled. There was gigantic machinery everywhere, and we had to be really careful when we were out there watching all of the happenings.

Our parents decided to have a walk out basement built for the mobile home to sit on. It was the same length as the trailer but twice as wide. Pops said, eventually, we were going to build on an addition and double the space of the house. For now, the extra space was covered with wood and tar paper. An entry porch was built at the front door to usher people into our new home. Pops also had a small porch constructed over the back door, with a ladder into the basement, so we could access it from the inside of the house.

Brianna and I stood at our parent's side to watch our home being moved on to the freshly finished basement. We all held our breath as the giant hunk of aluminum was hoisted on to its new home without issue. It was a sight to see.

When all was said and done, we had a beautiful new location for our home. Now was not soon enough to start unpacking and getting settled in. There was so much to do. Berry patches, vegetable gardens and flower gardens all needed to be put in. Of course, before we could plant them we had to break ground.

Pops bought a tractor, a plow and a disc from one of our neighboring farmers. He set out right away to begin to break ground for our gardens. He often invited me to sit on his lap while he plowed the earth. It's how I learned to drive.

We cleared five acres behind the house to plant a garden. Before we could plant, we had to pick all of the rocks out of it. Ugh... Talk about hard work.

We hooked up a trailer to the tractor, and I would drive it out into the field and park it. We then began the lengthy, back breaking task of picking up the stones and throwing them into the trailer. Once it was full, I would drive the tractor and trailer back to the head of the driveway where we would unload them. Mom used the stones to build a rock wall around the border of the parking area of the driveway. It really was quite lovely.

It took us nearly a month to completely clear that field, and the drudgery didn't stop there. We spent all of our spare time pounding stakes into the ground and tying twine between them to mark our rows. Seeds went in next. We grew almost every kind of vegetable you can imagine.

Mom was an organic gardener even before it became the popular thing to do. She never used man made pesticides. She taught us how to plant marigolds with the tomatoes as they would keep the bugs away and how to use ashes from our wood stove around other plants to work as a pest deterrent. She would pay Brianna and I a penny for each of the potato bugs we would pick from the plants. As part of our payment, she asked her mother to take us into town, so we could use our money to buy ice cream. Mom never learned to drive, so she was dependent on others for transportation.

The minute the plants began to sprout, Mom would take us to the garden and teach us how to identify the different vegetation. We spent many long days under the hot sun picking weeds, tending to the plants and enjoying each other's company. Our gigantic garden was thriving and so was our little family.

CHAPTER THREE

Mom had a lot to do, and I think that it sometimes interfered with her parenting. She didn't always make the best decisions, like allowing me to start dating at the young age of twelve. Of course back then, I didn't think like that. I was excited to be able to go out.

There was this really sweet boy in my shop class. His name was Chad, and he had the cutest dimples. We were working on a project together and became good friends. Well, you know what they say about friends...

Chad asked me to a movie. Mom said I could go as long as his parents picked me up and brought me home. Chad and his father picked me up at seven o'clock on a Saturday night. He dropped us off at the theater. We held hands and smiled as we watched the movie together. It was completely sweet and innocent.

After the movie, we went to the sub shop across the street and enjoyed a late night snack. We talked about school and then split a dessert, one milk shake and two straws. * swoon *

Chad's father picked us up and drove me home. Chad got out of the car and walked me to my front door. I knew this was the moment I had been waiting for, my first real kiss. Nope, instead he reached up and shook my hand. What a little gentleman.

I used to ride my bike eight miles, into town, to hang out with him and his family. His sister was a couple of years older than us, and she was so cool. She taught me how to wear my eye make-up and how to line my lips. She was like the big sister I had always wanted.

Chad and I dated for a few months. We decided, for whatever reason, we were better off as friends. We must have been right because we are still friends to this day. He's still a sweet guy even though he has his odd moments. * wink *

Pops never knew about Chad, and it was probably better off that way. Pops had started driving for a different trucking company and would still be gone in the upwards of three months at a time. He drove the mid-west to west coast hauls. We always missed him when he was away, but we did the best we could to keep our little farm moving forward.

Something snapped in my father when we moved to Minnesota, and it got worse when we moved out to the farm. He was not the same man I had known and loved when I was a little girl. Please, don't get me wrong, I always loved my father. I just didn't like him much anymore.

Pops was gruff and angry so much of the time I had forgotten what it was to see him smile or hear him laugh. We seldom hung out anymore. There was no longer any fishing, no family game nights, no more big dinners unless it was a holiday and absolutely no more feeling of family.

I believe our parents coped with their extended time away from one another by drowning themselves in their individual lives. Mom's was the farm, crafting, our home and raising Brianna and I. Pops' consisted of driving those very long and lonely roads for months at a time with only his mind to keep him occupied. When he returned home, instead of being able to relax and spend time with his family, he had to tackle his "honey-do" list. There were always buildings that needed repairing or constructing, fences to mend, sap to collect and cook into syrup, wood to cut, trees to plant, gardens to be tended, animals to be slaughtered, lawns to be mowed, leaves to rake or snow to be plowed and shoveled. Their perfect family was suffocating under the pursuit of the American dream. There just wasn't time for it any longer.

The only time Pops seemed to be his old self was when we were entertaining company. I think that is what he missed the most. He loved having people around all the time and with our new endeavor, there was seldom time for it except for special occasions.

It was Mom and Pops' wedding anniversary, and they planned a huge party to be held in our back yard. We had two barbecue grills set up next to rows of picnic tables and a couple of kegs of beer sitting in metal wash tubs full of ice for the adults to enjoy. Pops set up a horseshoe pit, near the end of the garden, so the guys could play when they were drunk enough.

The children were to be entertained with volleyball, badminton and a giant horse watering trough that had been cleaned and filled with fresh water for us to use as a swimming pool in the front yard. Except to eat, we were never allowed to be around the adults during these parties. They always made sure we had enough to keep us busy though.

The tables were covered with blue and white checkered table cloths that Mom had sewn by hand, and upon the tables, sat matching paper plates, cups and plastic ware. Mom went all out for these occasions because it was her way of showing off for the rest of her family. She always said she was the "black sheep" of her family and this was her way of saying "Fuck you."

Pops drove a refrigerated truck and hauled a lot of produce. He always got his hands on some, one way or another, so there were large bowls of fresh fruit in the middle of each table. They were surrounded with plates of fresh veggies from our garden. Mom really knew how to make food look beautiful. I always admired her artistic eye.

There were blue and white Christmas lights strung through every tree in the back yard and around an area that had been cleared to be used as a dance floor. The house stereo and records sat on a table near it, waiting to be played. Seen through a young girl's eyes, it was very pretty. I loved how the lights twinkled under the heaviness of the shade provided by the trees even in day light.

Family and friends started arriving, and the party was off to a huge success. The children played happily while the adults got drunk and talked. It seemed as though we could never host an event without major amounts of alcohol.

The men of the clan gathered around the grills and talked about the right way to cook the meat. "You're gonna wanna spray that meat right 'der or it's gonna dry out." "No, ya don't spray it down, you turn down the heat and keep flippin' it." It went on and on until it ended with the typical, "This is damned good meat." (By the way, go back and read that part with a heavy Minnesota accent. Yeah... Even funnier. I wasn't even sure how to spell some of that.) To this day, I believe that each of my family members must have an entire beef steer's worth of meat stuck in their colons.

Estrogen oozed from the females that had now congregated around one end of the last picnic table near the stereo, listening to music and comparing lives. Looking back at it now it was really quite sad. I noticed the heavier women of our family always sat at the tables while the more slender ones stood. They usually had one hand on their hip and a drink in the other.

A couple of hours into the party, while all of the children were happily playing volleyball, Brianna disappeared. I knew, if I didn't keep an eye on her, there would be serious consequences to pay. I called a time out to the game, and we all started looking for her.

The children began running around and calling her name while I walked over to the swimming trough. She loved the trough because there was a stabilization rail across the center of it, and she would flip around it splashing into the water. She was in there every chance she got. I thought maybe she had decided to take a break and swim. As I approached the trough, I saw Brianna floating face down. My heart stopped.

I didn't even think as I jumped into the water. After flipping her over, I pulled her from the trough and laid her on the ground. I had taken some first aid, through gym class at school, so I did my best to remember the lessons. I called for help, turned her head and made sure her mouth was clear. I bent to listen for her breath, but there was none there. I performed chest compressions... Nothing. Plugging her nose, I breathed into her mouth three times. I stopped and waited for what seemed like an eternity... Nothing. I repeated what I had just done. I know, it wasn't exactly what I was taught, but I was panicking and did what I could remember. Brianna began to cough and spit water out of her mouth. I cried with relief.

Cries of joy rang out and were then immediately silenced. A huge hand reached down and pulled me up by my ponytail, lifting me off the ground. It was my father, and before I knew it, he was literally beating me with a closed fist.

The first few shots landed on my rib cage. The next to my chest and stomach. I was a human pinata, except there was nothing but blood coming out when I got busted open. The final blow, that I know of, hit me square in the head and knocked me out.

I woke on the lawn a little while later with the women of our family surrounding me. They were putting ice packs on my neck, head and rib cage. As I slowly came to full consciousness, I saw the men of our family sitting at a table drinking shots. It was at that moment I realized we were no longer living the dream. It felt like I had slipped into a nightmare. Oh wait, that's because I had.

After I was able to get up and walk, Pops approached me much more calmly then he had before. He explained to me why I had been punished. He said I was supposed to be keeping an eye on my sister and because of my lack of supervision of her she had almost died. He went on to repeat almost the exact same words he had told me when I had written my name on the book shelf. "How many times do I have to tell you that it's your job to take care of your little sister? You're supposed to make sure she stays out of trouble and keep her safe. You are supposed to protect her, dammit."

Lesson learned… Once again.

The party went on until the wee hours of the morning. The kids were all camped out on the living room floor. We had our sleeping bags, movies, popcorn and ghost stories to keep us happy. The adults continued on until they passed out on the lawn or in the tents that had been set up around a huge campfire in the back field. It was a grand ol' celebration… For the most part.

We worked hard, the rest of the summer, to keep our farm running smoothly. We harvested the garden and canned everything we could. What we couldn't can was frozen or sold. The animals, that were ready, were butchered and frozen. I hated that part of living on the farm the most. Brianna and I butchered one hundred chickens that year. Have you ever done it or seen it done? It's pretty nasty. I could spare you the details, but I feel it is important that you know.

First, I held the chicken by the head, and my sister held it's feet. I then used a small hatchet and chopped off it's head. It would flop around in Brianna's hand as she handed me the chicken, and it would spray blood everywhere. I would dunk it into a tub of scalding water that was kept hot over a fire. Brianna and I then proceeded to pluck all of it's feathers from it's skin. I would repeat this a few times until the skin was as feather free as possible. Pin feathers were removed before we split open its underside, removed all of the innards and washed it in a different bin of cooler water. We then cut off the lower part of it's legs and tossed them over to the dogs. The gizzard, heart and liver were all plucked out from the pile of once living organs laying on the chopping block. They were then cut open and washed before being placed in a bucket of water with the cleaned chicken. We repeated this process through all one hundred chickens.

Mom came out to gather the finished chickens. She took them in the house to rinse them in the sink and dry them on the counter before wrapping them to freeze. We had been doing this for four years at this point. It affected us both in very unique and different ways.

The adult women handled the slaughtering of the other animals like the rabbits, goats, pigs and larger fowl. They said it was too gruesome for children. As if slaughtering one hundred chickens wasn't gruesome! * rolls eyes and laughs *

We did, however, help with the slicing and packaging of those meats. It was all set up like an assembly line in our basement. After Mom sliced the meat, she would hand it to me. I wrapped it in plastic and white freezer paper before I passed it to Brianna. She would label it, using a big black marker, with the contents and date and then place it in a box. When the box was full, one of us took it to the root cellar and stacked it in the freezer according to what type of meat it was.

That was not all the three of us did in preparation for the winter either. We also cut, split and ranked thirty cords of wood in our basement and next to the barn. We had to make sure we had enough wood to not only heat our home but the barn as well. It was our duty to keep the animals warm through the long and cold winter months. It was very productive and grueling at the same time. There was seldom any time for us to play, and I longed for my childhood as I watched it blow away with the autumn winds.

September was finally here. That meant school was starting again, and I had an escape from the hell that had become my life. This may have been what Mom and Pops wanted for their lives, but I had turned thirteen earlier that spring and had no interest in being a farmer.

Mom let me go to a back to school campout. Some of the parents in our community were hosting it to celebrate the end of summer. It was to last the entirety of Labor Day weekend.

Did I mention that I lived on a small farm with a lot of chickens on it, and one of my many jobs was to gather the eggs every day, twice a day? I can't remember, but if not... Well, now you know. Every day, I would stick some eggs away in the back of the shed that housed the feed for the animals. I did this through the entire summer. Why would I do this? HA!

I was not a popular girl in my own school. I did, however, have a handful of friends from other cities that I had met through family members, speech competitions, or friends of other friends. Anyway, there was this small group I hung out with, and we had come up with a plan.

Obviously, the aforementioned "adult supervised back to school camp out" was a total and utter lie. Okay, now that I read it, it might not have been so obvious. I'm sorry about that. It's kind of hard to write in all of the hand gestures and eye rolls I would be doing if I were telling this to you in real life. Okay, back to the story...

There were a total of nine of us in our little group. We often referred to ourselves as "Karma's Chaos". We were so cute in our teenage, idealistic understanding of Karma and all that it entails. * Giggle *

Judy had just graduated last year and had her own car. I looked up to her. She had long, black hair with really pale skin and wore a blood red lipstick with thick black eyeliner framing her pretty, dark blue eyes. She said she hated the sun because it depleted your inner self of its harmony. She believed the moon filled you up with all of its softness and glow... Or something like that. Her clothes were always layered and torn up but her car, purse and bedroom were incredibly clean. It was the yin and yang that made Judy who she was. She was light and dark, messy and clean, enlightened and learning and dedicated and aloof. She was my idol.

Mike and Jill were brother and sister. Jill was my age and Mike was a year older. They, along with myself, were considered "the smart ones." * eye roll *

All three of us had long blonde hair, blue eyes and pale skin. Jill and I both wore our hair ratted up with bangs as tall as we could make them. I still think our hair spray use contributed greatly to the holes in the ozone layer.

Mike wore 5 spikes of hair down the center of his head in a mohawk fashion. He had the coolest pickup that he had decked out himself. Now that I think about it, he was kind of a walking oxymoron. I mean no offense by that. It's just that he lived on a farm, loved being a farmer, drove a pickup and had a mohawk. He was so cute! (I would pinch his cheeks right now if I could.)

Erin and Karen were cousins and two years older than me. Karen would often talk down to the younger kids in our little group... Like me, ugh. Anyway, they were both brunettes with deep brown eyes. I remember the way they used to chew and pop their gum constantly. Why they hung out with us, I will never know.

Then there was Emily. She had just moved to our little town at the end of our seventh grade year from Los Angeles, California. She was mysterious looking with dyed, deep red hair, dark green eyes and the black lipstick she wore on her full lips.

Emily and I became best of friends. I slept over at her house all the time. It was just her and her dad living there. He pretty much left us to raise ourselves. He would throw some money at us on his way to the bar, and we would go from there. He never kept a good eye on his liquor cabinet either, so it was easy for us to get into. We would just explain away the vanishing booze with, "We're worried about you Dad. Don't you remember? You drank it last night."

We came and went as we pleased because there was no one there to answer to. We didn't ever cause any real trouble. Never any trouble with the law, at least.

Speaking of the law, I guess I should introduce you to the last two members of our group. I had been dating a guy named Dave for a while. He was the sheriff's son. Emily was dating his friend Greg. They were both three years out of school and lived in their Mom's basement (did you do the math there? Yeah, they were both eight years older which made them twenty-one, and somehow Mom thought that was okay.) They were the coolest. *teenage swoon* * Adult eye roll *

So, we're back to Labor Day weekend, and the nine of us went camping. The campsite was in the backwoods of Karen's dad's farm. They had so much acreage that it was easy for us to hide out and have no worries of local law enforcement or anything else.

We took the vehicles as far up an abandoned logging road as we could. We then unloaded the four-wheelers to take the rest of the way in. We had to do seven trips because we only brought 4 quad runners with us, and there was a lot of beer to haul in. Oh yeah, and the nine people, tents, coolers full of hard liquor (Apple, peach and root beer schnapps, cheap vodka, even cheaper rum and a bottle of Goldschlager. Don't laugh, you know you thought it was cool back then too.), food, sleeping bags, pillows, bags of clothes, female necessities, bug spray, batteries, boom box, tapes (yes, tapes.), matches, fire starting logs, cartons of the aforementioned rotten eggs, folding chairs, air mattresses and a couple bags of cooking utensils, paper plates, cups, silverware, paper towels, napkins, wet wipes, aluminum foil and starter fluid. We really were roughing it. * laughing *

It took us a couple of hours to set up camp and then we headed back into town. We snuck in through the back roads because we didn't want to be seen. Not just because we were suppose to be out camping with some kids and adults from school, but because we were about to do something amazing.

We snuck to the top of a train trestle that was the border between my home town and the next town over. We parked the cars on the side of a road by a lake near the snowmobile trail that ran very close to the top of the trestle. The nine of us sat up there drinking beer and watching the cars traveling beneath us. You couldn't see us from the road because the sides of the trestle were made almost completely solid with only small slits in between the panels of heavy wood.

Here's where the cartons of rotten eggs come into play. Now remember, I had been saving these for months. Some of them were so rotten that when you shook them you could hear powder inside of them. HA! * evil grin *

We drank beer as we watched the sun set over the cemetery to the other side of the tracks. The moment the sun faded completely into the night sky, we started chucking those rotten eggs at the cars traveling under our feet. We waited for jeeps and convertibles and would throw a dozen eggs at a time into their cars. We didn't make it every time, but after a couple of practice shots, we were getting to be pretty good at aiming.

People stopped and tried to see us, but they couldn't have caught us if they tried. There was no way up to the trestle from the street except to climb a very steep, grassy hill and then up at least ten feet of solid concrete. Since the walls on the sides of the tracks were solid, as long as we stayed low, we could run back down the snowmobile trail to our vehicles before anyone could have caught us.

When we ran out of eggs, we returned to the two trucks and the car, laughing the entire way. On our way back to the campsite, we re-lived the events of the memories we had just created. Okay, yes, it was not very nice of us, but when compared to today's youthful antics... Not so bad, right?

We made it back to the campsite with one trip because we put two people on each of the four wheelers and then attached a plastic snow sled to the back of the last one for Mike to ride in. We went slow... For the most part. Poor Mike. Sorry dude.

Food... Yes, we needed food. Hotdogs, buns, chips, ketchup, pickle relish, mustard, well, you get the picture, right? Oh yeah, and more beer, a lot more beer.

Deeper thoughts were never thought by anyone before this night. We were all laid out under the stars, around the campfire, drunk and young. We talked about the possibilities in life such as the human race being a giant doll house with living dolls controlled by a ruling alien nation. We painted vibrant word pictures of our beliefs such as the simple fact that we are all of God. We talked about how energy cannot be destroyed; it can only be changed. Rambling on, we discussed how our energy must simply join the larger collection of energy when we die. Well, that meant we really didn't die then. Since there was no such thing as death, we were actually all immortal. That must mean that we can be reborn too and that meant we've done this before. Yep, it was time to pull out the hard stuff... Yeah, the hard stuff. What were we thinking? * wink and a smile *

We poured and passed around shots like it was water in the hot desert. With the amount of beer we had in our system, it didn't take long for the liquor to take effect. We were pretty wasted when Dave stood up, took my hand and led me off to our tent.

We hung out the rest of the weekend laughing, drinking, talking and just being young. Monday afternoon arrived, we packed up and went home. No one was ever the wiser, except for us maybe. I think those days in the woods helped us to take the next steps in growing up. It was a celebration of what we were leaving behind as we walked into our futures.

CHAPTER FOUR

Mom and Grandma took us school shopping. The clothes were nice, but I truly loved the new notebooks, pens and pencils. Mom always allowed me a couple of extra ones as she knew that I loved to write. Sometimes, it was just a few words to capture my thoughts for the day, but most of the time I wrote about what I dreamed for my future.

I was in the eighth grade, and I couldn't wait to learn. I got to pick my own schedule, for the most part, and I made sure I signed up for every English class I could get into, including communications. After all, I was going to be a writer and live in New York.

Physical education was my first period class. Ugh, how I hated that. Nothing like getting ready for school just to get sweaty and have to shower again. There was never time to do my hair and make-up, that really bothered me. I had outgrown my tomboy phase and loved being a girl. I loved everything I thought it took to be feminine. I loved make-up, hairstyles, clothes, jewelry, panty hose, playing dress up, manicures, pedicures, perfume, purses and shoes. Oh... My... Goodness, I still love shoes! *AHEM* Oops... Sorry, I get a little excited when it comes to footwear, but then again, is there a woman alive that doesn't love shoes?

Anyway, I loved the process of it all and felt that it was like painting a pretty picture. I always felt cute, but when I had my make-up and hair done I felt beautiful. We all know there is a difference in those two things. I know ya feel me there ladies.

In between classes, I would rush into the bathroom and apply whatever make-up I could. I spent part of my lunch hour, a couple days a week, buffing my fingernails and applying nail polish. I created a lot of my own colors by dumping the powdered pigment Mom still had from the old ceramic shop into bottles of clear nail polish. There was no sense in wasting it. Some of my classmates teased me for having such odd colors, but I didn't let it get to me. It's not my fault they weren't as creative as I was.

Communications was my last class, and I raced to it every day. I didn't want to miss a single minute of it. Mrs. Hart was incredible. She read and critiqued anything I asked her to and was always so encouraging. I believe, to this day, that she is why I never gave up on my dream, nor will I ever. I owe that woman a debt of gratitude and hope that she knows just how very much she meant to me.

My favorite part of that class was the week we spent watching "Pink Floyd, The Wall". When the movie ended, Mrs. Hart asked us to write our opinion on what it was about. I had identified deeply with the main character. I wrote how I believed the lack of love he felt and the neglect and abuse he had suffered as a child led him to be the adult he was. I went on to explain how it frightened me that the same thing would happen to me. Of course, there was much more to it, but that's the gist of it.

Two days after I turned in my final paper, Mrs. Hart asked me to stay after class. I told her I was worried about not being able to catch the bus home. Informing me she had already spoken to my mom and had received her permission to keep me after school, she said she would be more than happy to give me a ride home when we were finished.

Mrs. Hart asked me if I would like to go out for ice cream and talk. I accepted her generous offer, and we headed out. I'll never forget how excited I was to sit there and share ice cream with my teacher. I had wanted to pick her brain for so long, and I did just that.

After asking her a barrage of questions about what it took to become a writer and the appropriate way to go about it, she reached across the table and held my hand. Mrs. Hart started by reassuring me that she had my best interest at heart and that anything we talked about was strictly between us. She then proceeded to ask me how things were at home. I remember the look in her eyes when I started crying.

Knowing there would be consequences, I did not tell her how I had been beat that past summer. I did tell her that things had changed since we had moved from California. I told her how I longed to be a child again, and how I felt that I carried too much responsibility. I cried about how hard it was to do the work that I had to do at home and still keep up with my school work as well. I just let it all out.

She stood up, came over to my side of the booth, wrapped her arms around me and just let me cry. It was as if everyone else in the restaurant had disappeared, and it was just her and I there. I don't know how long I cried, but I do know when I finished, I felt better.

Mrs. Hart told me that I was a very strong, young woman and my strength would take me far in life. I believed her and found in myself a new source of that strength. Someone believed in me, and I wasn't going to let her down. She drove me home, and we never spoke of it again.

Easter vacation was upon us. We had an extra long weekend off from school, and Pops was supposed to be coming home. Mom, Brianna and I spent the first night cleaning and preparing for Pops' arrival.

We were all in Mom's room, cleaning, when the phone rang. Mom answered the phone and handed it to me. It was Dave. He was leaving for Texas, and it was over.

I sat on Mom's bed as she took the phone from my hand and laid it back in its cradle. She asked me what happened and I spit the words out. I just couldn't stop.

I told her how I felt used because I had given my virginity to him. I told her everything. I told her about the camping trip, about how Dave and I used to sneak off to the woods to have sex, about how we were caught in the back of his dad's squad car, but there was no trouble because I was under age, and that wouldn't look good for the Sheriff or his son... Everything. What was I thinking?

She just looked at me and shrugged. She told me that's how life goes sometimes. We never wasted much time on emotions.

Pops had come home just as we were going to sleep. We had enough time to hug him, tell him we missed him and kiss him goodnight. We wandered off to bed and left Mom and Dad alone to spend some quality time together.

I guess Mom wasn't in the mood because instead of loving up on Pops, she told him everything I had told her that night. Fuck. I was in SO much trouble now.

I felt the vibration from his heavy footsteps before I heard them. They got louder as he stormed through the living room, dining area, hallway and toward my room. My bedroom door flew open as if it had been knocked off of it's hinges. As he stepped into the room, he reached for his belt, unlocked the buckle and with one hand pulled it from his belt loops in one swift motion. He said in a deep, scary, monotone voice, "You wanna fuck someone..."

I awoke from that part of my living nightmare in the bathtub. It was full of cold water and someone was dumping more ice into it. My eyes were so swollen that I could not open them enough to clearly see who it was. As the person stepped toward the door, I could make out the size and shape of my father. The demon had been banished for now, and Pops was back.

Warm, dressed, medicated with expired pain pills from Mom's back issues, fed and pampered, I was then tucked very gently into bed. The blankets were so heavy on my bruises and cuts that it was hard to breathe. I rolled onto my left side, tucked a pillow under my arm to help hold my body up and tried to sleep. My body felt three times its size, from all of the bruising and swelling, so it made it very difficult.

I woke as the sun was beginning its appearance in the lower horizon. My face, arm and side were stuck to the bed sheet with dried blood. I heard the cotton tear from my skin as I struggled to sit up. The pain pushed the air from my lungs, and I collapsed back onto the bed. I laid there, staring out the window, as tears flowed down my cheeks. I watched the sun make itself more known in the morning sky. At first, it looked like it was shy and innocent, afraid to come out. I noticed that it peeked out more and more as if it were learning it's own self worth before finally standing proudly in it's place in the middle of the daylight sky.

Taking a deep breath, I slowly but steadily pushed myself into a sitting position. I moved my legs to the side of the bed and twisted myself around, so I was sitting upright and facing the bedroom door. My ribs felt like they were on fire. I walked into the bathroom and fulfilled my morning needs... Barely. When I was finished, I opened the door to find Mom standing there with a couple more pain killers and a glass of water. I happily took them and struggled my way back to bed.

Meals were served to me, and I stayed in bed reading for the remainder of Easter break. I was waited on hand and foot. Pity? Sorrow? Yeah... Guilt, that's what I thought too.

Getting ready for school proved harder than I had anticipated, but I achieved it. I did not, of course, put the same effort into it that I normally would have. Make-up only concealed so much.

There was NO WAY I was going to participate in gym. I had a note from my mom to excuse me from class. She had written that I had been bucked off of a horse over the break and had gotten banged up. I gave the note to the gym teacher. She had me sit in her office and write a short report on why team sports were beneficial to students.

When she returned from class, she read the essay I wrote. Sitting the paper down, she looked at me and asked if I had really gotten thrown from a horse. She said the black and blue marks on my face looked more like a fist than a horse hoof, and anything we talked about was just between the two of us.

I couldn't take it anymore, and I let myself cry. My body trembled as the tears flowed from my eyes. I could barely breathe, and I had to concentrate on slowing my breathing in order to calm myself. I told her everything, every detail of every blow, of every pain and of every word screamed at me.

She sat there listening with an understanding look on her face. I think she knew what I was telling her already. I was sure she wasn't the only one either.

After cleaning myself up, I headed back to class. I received many odd looks throughout the day, more so than usual. I suspected that people knew what had happened and were whispering about it behind hands and locker doors. Over the years, my family had become characters of legend and lore. We were the people you heard about in the stories from the elders, the ones that were told to forewarn you of the consequences of making the wrong choices. We were the great white trash. I always thought that was funny because of Mom's view of herself. One man's trash and all that I guess. Oh well, anyway...

About half way through social studies class, the door opened and the school's secretary entered. She whispered to the teacher, and they both looked at me. The secretary motioned for me to follow her, so I did.

We entered the office of the high school guidance counselor. He was sitting there with the sheriff and a woman that I did not recognize. Nope, it wasn't me... I didn't do it. I didn't know what was going on.

I was told to come in and shut the door. Amy introduced herself, saying she was a social worker with the Department of Child Protective Services. She asked me questions about my family and what the bruises and lacerations were from. I had to tell her.

After answering a few more questions, I was asked to go with Amy to the hospital, so I could be examined. I did what was asked of me; it's not like I had a choice.

I was escorted into the doctor's office where I sat with him and Amy while she explained what had happened. They came to an agreement about the tests that were needed before they left me there alone to undress and prepare. I was scared.

When the blood draws, x-rays and other procedures were completed, I was told to wait patiently. After what seemed like hours, the doctor and Amy came back in. The doctor said I had some broken ribs and needed to be wrapped up to help with the healing. Oh... My... God was that painful. Amy let me squeeze her hand as they wrapped me up with a wide, stretchy bandage and secured it with a few small metal clips. Amy then helped me to get dressed, and we left.

Driving out to the farm, Amy explained she did not feel it was a safe place for me, and she had received permission from her boss to have me removed. We were going out to gather some of my things and tell Mom I was being placed in temporary foster care. I faded into a hazy place and could not even begin to repeat the rest of her words.

Mom met us at the door. I walked right past her and went to my room to pack some of my belongings. I had a difficult time deciding what I should take. My journal, a few changes of clothing, my make-up, a copy of "The Scarlet Letter" and a couple of pictures made their way into my bag. Amy knocked on my door, asked if I were ready, and we left.

Mom sat at the end of the table in the dining room, smoking a cigarette, as we walked past. I looked at her, needing to see her eyes, but she kept her head down and didn't say a word. Brianna was at Aunt Julie's house. Thank goodness because I don't know how I would have found the strength to say goodbye to her.

I was transported to a crisis shelter about thirty miles north of my home. After a ton of questions and my belongings being searched, I was escorted to a bedroom in the upstairs of the shelter. I was thankful to have my own room because I was still in a fog.

Although I was in a stupor, I made it through the next few days. I ate three meals a day, watched a little television and talked to different therapists. Other than that, I spent most of my time sitting in my room alone, writing in my journal and reading my book. I was simply waiting for whatever was going to happen to just happen. I had no idea what to expect.

The weekend came and went. The counselors took us to a museum over the weekend and to get some take out food. I didn't really talk to anyone unless I had to. I felt like the sun just starting to peek over the horizon.

Sunday evening, after dinner, I was told to be dressed and ready to go to court by two the next afternoon. I nodded in recognition of the given information and went to my room to read.

Amy picked me up and took me to court. It had been less than a full week since I was taken from my home and placed at the shelter. My father could not make it home in time for court, so it was ordered that I be placed, as soon as possible, in a temporary foster home.

I was placed, two days later, with a family in the same town as the shelter. They were a very religious couple and had two young daughters of their own. Pat and John seemed to be nice enough, at least, I hoped they were.

I unpacked and laid down on my bed to look around. There was a light knock at the door. I told the person that was knocking to come in. The door slowly opened and in walked someone I went to school with from my hometown. It was a girl named Tammy. She was a year younger than me and had been placed here about a year ago. Though I didn't know her well, it was a relief to see a familiar face.

She came in and explained how things worked around there. Pat and John did not want to be bothered with us. We were not to disturb their family in any way, whatsoever. Our meals were prepared for us, placed on a specific shelf in the refrigerator and on a lower shelf in a cabinet in the kitchen; we were only to eat what was left for us. Every Sunday evening, money would be taped in an envelope to our bedroom doors, and we were to use that money to take care of our personal needs. We were to supply all of the things needed for hygiene, clothing, school supplies and transportation on $20.00 a week.

I realized Pat and John were not what they appeared to be. I had been told horror stories, by some of the kids at the crisis shelter, about the evils committed by foster parents. At the time, I thought they were just trying to scare me. I was told there were foster parents that were only in it for the money. It sounded like these two were some of them.

Tammy taught me how to get what I needed without spending any money on it. There were quite a few stores in the area, and we found it easy to shoplift from them. We layered new clothing under our own. We shoved bottles of shampoo and boxes of tampons into our purses when no one was looking. We were even so bold as to wear new shoes right out of the stores. We didn't like having to do it, but we knew of no other choice.

It was ordered that I live in the foster home until my father completed all court ordered classes and served five days of jail time. Five days? Really?

I lived there for just over three months. School was done, and I was being sent home.

Walking into that house again made my skin crawl. I knew, from family therapy sessions, nothing had really changed. My parents played along with the game, but that's all they did. I think my father felt, since we had talked about it right away, there was nothing left to discuss. Remember, we were the family that never spoke of it again, and that's just the way things were.

My bedroom had been emptied of everything important and personal to me. It was set up like a guest room now. The bed stuck out from the corner of the room, most of the books had been removed from their shelves and replaced with pretty, little trinkets. The curtains were pink lace and cascaded down the windows to pool on the floor. The bed was covered with a matching spread and pillow shams. All of my rock posters had been removed and were replaced with paintings of children and animals. It looked like the bedroom of a small girl and not the room of a fourteen year old.

I put my suitcase on the bed, opened it and started to put my things away. Right away, Mom came in, pushed me aside and did it for me. She told me there was a new way of doing things in her house, and I had better learn it quickly. I thought to myself, "then why is it only my room that is any different?" The rest of the house was a cluttered pig stye.

Again, I did my chores daily, helped with everything that was needed and spent a lot of alone time in my room. I had no interest in spending time with my so-called family and being a farmer. I was going to be a writer, and it was just that simple. I needed to read and write, as much as I could, to prepare myself for my future.

I was consistently ridiculed for my choices in life. It didn't matter what I did. I was teased by my family or made to change it. After months and months of this, I finally had enough. On my fifteenth birthday, I shaved the left side of my hair, dyed pink and blue stripes in it with food dye and pierced thirteen holes into each ear. How ya like me now?

When Mom saw what I did, she started to freak out and call me insane.

She told me I was no daughter of hers, and the family would shun me until I went back to "normal." I just shrugged my shoulders and walked away.

I fell into a spiraling depression. I no longer fit in with my family. I wasn't allowed to see my friends, and the kids at school didn't think much of me. There had been so many rumors spread around that no one knew the truth, and no one bothered to ask. They just stared and whispered as I walked by.

Cutting became my security blanket, and I did it for months without getting caught. I never did it deep enough to hurt myself and only on the top of my left arm, but I did it nonetheless. It made me feel alive.

I had developed an entire ritual for it. I would tear the plastic from a new, disposable razor until just the blade was left. I then held the blade with tweezers, burned it and laid it on a white cotton cloth. I poured a cap full of rubbing alcohol and placed it next to the razor blade. After wiping my arm with alcohol, I began with small scratches across my arm. My feelings grew with every scratch, and every scratch became deeper. Once I reached a place where I felt no pain, I would cut across the scratches much deeper. I felt peace as I saw the blood run from my body. It somehow proved to me that I was alive, and eventually I would be able to escape this hell.

There was one particular afternoon that I was exceptionally moody and decided to cut. I usually waited to do that at night because I didn't want to risk getting caught. I should have stuck to that part of the ritual. Mom walked in and caught me. Again, instead of talking to me, she freaked out, and before I could explain anything, she was on the phone calling 911 for help.

Amy was called as well, and she showed up with the police about an hour after the call. Mom had wrapped a piece of twine around my bedroom door knob, tied it to a bureau that sat in the hallway, and locked me in my room. She was great with dramatics. There was no need for any of it. I was calmly sitting in my room, with the razor blade still in my hand, waiting for the inevitable.

After a couple of questions, I was deemed suicidal, even though I wasn't. I've always believed my life was not mine to take because I was here to help others. It was decided that I should be placed in the Minnesota State Hospital in our hometown. Wow, talk about overkill. (Ha! Pun intended.)

I was kept in the hospital from Wednesday afternoon until Monday morning. After a lot of tests and talking with Psychiatrists, it was decided that I was not suicidal. I guess Amy didn't know as much as she liked to think she did. So, what do they do with me then? Why lock me up in a juvenile jail, of course. I mean, isn't that the right thing to do? Take someone, who is obviously hurting emotionally to the point of self mutilation, and lock them up with criminals their own age, after spending time in an adult state hospital. Yeah, that's what they did.

I was strip searched, deloused, given a set of gray sweats to put on and was then led to a small cell. A tiny window, framed inside a stainless steel door, marked the entrance to it. It was constructed of four steel walls and held a steel bed frame that was attached to the wall. There was a thin, plastic covered mattress on the frame. A steel toilet and a steel sink finished off the cell.

I was given a set of bedding, a pillow, a roll of toilet paper, a bar of soap, a towel, a toothbrush, toothpaste, pencil, notebook and a giant rule book. I was to spend the next four hours reading the rule book and sitting alone in my cell.

There is no need to go into great detail here. Needless to say, it was an experience I will not soon forget. Through the stories of the other kids, I learned tips on how to survive in this new world. Staying invisible seemed to be the most important one. I was good at being invisible.

I spent ninety two days in there before the court decided what to do with me. It was as if I had been forgotten. I was now to be placed in a work camp for girls south of where I grew up. What the hell did I do to deserve this?

CHAPTER FIVE

The sides of the interstate were lined with fully grown pine trees that provided privacy for the people living on the other side of them. It was as if the trees pointed the way to the next destination in my travels. Geez, thanks trees.

We pulled off the interstate and started down a long, dirt road. I swear the trees were following us. After a few more twists and turns, we arrived at "St. Louis Camp for Girls." I was turning sixteen in just three short months, and I kept reminding myself that I only had two years to go after that.

Again, I was strip searched, and my belongings were gone through. Most of it was confiscated, labeled and put away. What little I was able to keep, was handed to me as I was instructed to dress and to follow a very tall woman.

We walked out of the main building, across the court yard and into a large cabin. Bunk beds sat in neat lines along the four longer walls, and there were bathrooms centered at each end of the structure. There were gym lockers on the walls directly outside of the showers. I was shown a bed and was told it was my bunk. I was then shown a locker, told to put my things in it and follow her again.

School? Really? I get to go to school here? What a relief. I thought I was going to have to do nothing but work. This was awesome. I walked into my class room and was introduced to the teacher, Miss Dalent. I looked around at the other eleven girls in the classroom and met their stairs eye to eye.

We each had our own desk and spent the rest of the day taking tests. Their tests were about what they had been learning, and mine were to show my teacher what grade I should be placed in. I guess they didn't trust the public school system.

The school day ended, and it was now time to do our chores. I was assigned to laundry duty, and I loved it. The smell of the clean linens, the crispness of the sheets, and the perfectly folded corners were a wonderful escape. I turned it into a math game. Each sheet was folded six times to form the perfect rectangle. I couldn't help it; I loved math. In my life, numbers were the only thing that remained constant and never changed. I'm still kind of a math geek to this day.

When chores were completed, we found our way to the dining hall and took our seats at a long table. Our meal was served by some of the girls from other groups in the camp. It wasn't much to look at, nor did it taste all that good, but it was hot and filling. I've never been one for meat or cheese, and that night's meal was macaroni and cheese with hot dogs. * BLECH *

Movies in the lounge and a bit of alone time on our bunks ended the evening. We had to ask permission to get off of our beds to even go to the bathroom. I wasn't use to this kind of militant life.

The next morning we got dressed, made our beds and went to breakfast. It was a bit better as we had waffles, eggs and fruit. After our meal, we cleaned the dining hall and then headed to school.

Walking into the classroom, I noticed Miss Dalent sitting at her desk with a kind of confused smile adorning her beautiful face. She really was a lovely woman with tan skin, short dark hair that framed her face and a perfectly white, straight smile that she wasn't afraid to share. I don't think she was a day past twenty-five.

She handed out the day's lessons to all the girls except for me. When everyone was working on their assignments, she asked me to step outside. I was a bit worried because I had always done well in school. I thought maybe my tests showed I was behind the normal levels of children my age.

"Maggie? Why are you here?" Miss Dalent sat on the top of the steps leading to our classroom as I stood in front of her. She pulled out a cigarette from her pocket and lit it. Oh my goodness, it smelled amazing. We were not allowed to smoke there.

"I'm here because, um, because... Well, honestly? I have no idea. I guess I messed up somewhere, and this is what they decided to do with me." I wanted that cigarette so badly. I almost reached for it.

"They?" She flicked the ash from the end of her cigarette.

"Yeah, they, as in the court, social worker, my mom... All of them." I reached for the cigarette without thinking. She pulled her hand back and smiled at me.

"But what did you do?" She repeated herself.

"I cut myself and was sent to a hospital. When it was decided that I wasn't suicidal they sent me to juvie where I did just over three months, had court, and they sent me here." I stood with my hands at my side.

"You didn't do anything else? You didn't steal anything? Hurt anyone other than yourself? Run away? Nothing?" She looked shocked.

"No Ma'am, I would never do anything like that." I was actually a bit hurt that she would think that of me. "Well, I did steal a bit in my foster home, but I only took the things I needed like shampoo and tampons because they wouldn't buy them for me. I'm really sorry, but how did they know? I never got caught." My eyes were filling with tears.

"Oh, Maggie, please, don't cry." She looked around, making sure we were alone, and handed me the cigarette, now almost burnt to the filter. She lit another one as she did it.

"Miss Dalent? Why am I here? Do you know something that I don't?" I took two drags off the cigarette, and it was gone.

"I know that you tested in third year college levels and are the most intelligent student I've ever had the honor of teaching." She handed me the second cigarette.

"What? Really? I was afraid I had tested poorly and was in trouble." I slowly inhaled as to enjoy every bit of the treat in my hand.

"Not at all, Maggie. It's not that I don't believe you, but I need to look at your records to find out why you are really here. It just doesn't make sense to me." She took the cigarette from my hand and took a couple drags before she handed it back to me.

"Will you tell me what it says, please?" I smoked the last of it and butted it on the ground, picked up the cigarette end and threw it in the trash can to my left.

"Yes, of course." She watched what I did with the cigarette butt, and she looked amazed that anyone would be considerate enough to throw trash in the can instead of leaving it on the ground. "I just don't understand..." Her words trailed off as she stood up, and we went into the classroom.

The rest of the day went the same as the day before had, except instead of doing laundry, I was assigned to cleaning the dorms. Chores changed daily unless you were assigned to kitchen duty. When you worked in the kitchen, it was for a week straight, and I looked forward to it because I loved to cook.

I was excited to wake the next morning, so I could get to school. I was sure Miss Dalent would have some information for me. Plus, I really wanted a cigarette.

"Maggie? Can I speak to you outside again, please?" I followed her out the door and behind the small building that housed our classroom. She immediately took out two cigarettes, lit them and handed one to me.

"I looked at your files last night and even called your social worker this morning. I just don't get it, Maggie. You have no business being here, but they're leaving you here." She took a drag from her own cigarette.

"What do you mean? I don't understand." I stopped smoking and looked at her.

"From what I can see and what I was told, you haven't done anything wrong. You need help, not discipline. You should be in a home with people loving you, not in a work camp." She smiled so sweetly at me.

"Then why am I here?" I felt faint.

"In my opinion, you are here because they didn't know what else to do. Make me a promise, Maggie? Don't turn out like some of these girls. Don't let this place make you someone that you're not. You are strong, intelligent and capable. I look forward to our next three months together and getting to know you better." Miss Dalent hugged me and we finished our cigarettes. "Do your best, and I will make sure you have a cigarette or two every day, as long as you keep it a secret. I shouldn't do it, but I think you're being punished enough. One more thing? If you ever feel like hurting yourself again, please, talk to me or to someone that can help you?" I promised her I would do my best and I would keep our secret. She handed me a piece of mint candy before we went in, to cover the smoke smell on my breath.

Once again, there is no need to go into detail of the three months that followed this. It was the same thing every day except the weekends. Monday through Friday it was wake up, eat breakfast, clean, go to school, lunch, back to school, dinner, chores, movie or alone time and bed. Saturdays and Sundays consisted of the same schedule except we didn't have school. Instead, we went on hikes and had sing-a-longs around a campfire. If any of the girls misbehaved they were made to cut wood, all day, with a hand saw. I never got in trouble... Ever. It wasn't because I didn't want to cut wood. Heaven knows, I did enough of that as a younger child and was quite good at it, but more because I didn't want to let down Miss Dalent or myself.

On the last day of school, Miss Dalent pulled me aside. She told me she had never had a student like me before, and it was a pleasure to have me in her classroom. She said I would go far if I just remembered I was worth everything good that was coming my way.

What was this feeling deep inside of me? Could it be? Is it? Oh my God! It was self worth. I felt good about myself for the first time ever. I liked it... A lot.

So, in order to graduate, we had to complete two major tasks. The first would be happening that weekend, the weekend of my sixteenth birthday. We had to perform a solo camp, of three days and two nights, in the middle of the forest. Now mind you, I was born in early spring, and there was still snow on the ground.

We were given a tarp, a gallon jug of water, a tin camp-set that consisted of a bowl, a cup and spoon, a ten foot piece of rope, a mummy sleeping bag, six meal packages, three matches, twenty sheets of toilet paper and a multi-tool that had a hatchet on one end and a shovel on the other. We were allowed to bring one change of clothing and a book, if we desired. Of course, I brought my copy of "The Scarlet Letter." It was my favorite book.

Our counselors took each of us, individually, into the middle of the woods and left us there. We could not see or hear anyone, and we had to survive... No problem. I thought back to my first few days in Minnesota, and how I had learned to build a fort. I started with that. I knew it was important to have a warm place to sleep.

I used the hatchet part of the multi-tool to cut the rope into eight pieces. There were two, twenty four inch pieces and six, one foot pieces. I then went into the woods and found a long, thick, straight branch and six shorter ones. I hoisted the long branch up between two trees, and using the longer ropes, I tied each end to a tree. Testing that it was strong enough to hold weight, I then secured the smaller branches to it, putting three on each side, with the one foot lengths of rope.

Journeying back into the forest, I gathered a few loads of pine boughs and drug them to my tent. I covered it in layers of pine, except for an opening in the front of it, and put the tarp over the entire structure. Using stones I found near the trees, I weighted down the bottom of the tarp. I placed more boughs on the ground inside my tent and spread my sleeping bag out on them.

I knew I was going to have to keep a fire burning because with only three matches I couldn't afford to let it go out and risk not being able to light it again. I gathered as much fallen wood as I could find and snapped more pine boughs from the trees. I stacked it in a huge pile about fifteen feet from my tent. Clearing a large area of snow, I formed a safe place to burn a fire and placed stones around it.

I had to go to the restroom. I grabbed my shovel and walked about twenty feet from my camp site to dig a hole. I used that hole as my bathroom and covered it with a stone that was near it. I didn't want the scent to attract animals.

On the way back to my campsite, I gathered birch bark from the trees to use as kindling. I needed something to start the fire. I stuffed my jacket with as much of it as would fit.

I stacked some of the bark, smaller wood and the larger branches into the ring to look like an upright triangle. Carefully lighting the first match, I reached to light the fire and it blew out. Shit, I only had two left.

Knowing I would freeze, if I didn't start the fire, I grabbed some of the birch bark and went into my tent to light it. After getting it lit, I rushed to the fire ring and got the fire started. * PHEW *

I took my spare t-shirt out, put my food in it and gathered the ends into a knot. I peeled strips of bark from the green logs I had brought in for the fire and braided it together to form a rope. I found a thick, short branch to act as a weight and tied the rope to it. I then attached the other end of the rope to the t-shirt containing my food. I was able to throw the weight over a tree branch and pull the food up to hang from said branch. I wrapped the braided rope around a lower branch to secure it. I knew better than to leave my food down because it would also attract animals.

There was still daylight left, but I knew it wouldn't last long. I quickly went into the forest to gather as much firewood as I could before it got dark. I figured even if I didn't use it all, it would be there for the next girl that had to do this. Share and share alike, and all that.

I moved an old stump near the fire to act as a table and a large flat stone to sit on. I put the stone near the fire to heat it up. My stomach growled with hunger so I pulled my food down from the tree and began preparing my first meal of the day.

I opened the food pack with the edge of the hatchet and saw it was soup and crackers. After pulling the flat stone from the fire's edge, I put the food pack in it's place to heat. I sat on the stone and gathering the pine boughs I had placed there earlier, I weaved them together to form a door to cover the opening of my tent. There, all done... Easy peasy.

Dinner had never tasted so good. I had earned it, heated it and enjoyed every drop of it. I found some peanut butter in another pack, and I ate it with my crackers for desert. I was full, tired and lonely. I used the hand dug restroom one last time before bed, grabbed my "door" and headed for my tent.

It was too dark to read, so I just placed the door over the opening, climbed into my sleeping bag and tried to go to sleep. It was not an easy thing to do. Sounds from the forest kept me awake until my body gave in, and I simply passed out from exhaustion.

I woke up early the next morning. It was my sixteenth birthday, and I was alone in the woods. I started to feel a bit sad until I heard singing in the distance.

I slowly crawled out of my warm, comfy bed and saw my counselor walking toward me. She had something cupped in her hands and was singing Happy Birthday to me. I smiled.

When she was close, she handed me a small cupcake with a single candle in it, told me to make a wish and blow it out, which I did. I know I'm not supposed to reveal what I wished for, but it can't hurt now, right? I wished for love.

She looked around and told me she was very impressed with what I had done. She asked if it was okay to bring the other counselors around to see it. I agreed, and she set off to retrieve the staff. In the time she was gone, I stoked the fire and got the embers burning again. I took down the food pack and decided to have instant oatmeal for breakfast with a cup of hot cocoa. I was sitting at the fire's edge, with my socks and boots drying near the fire, warming my bare feet when the staff arrived.

They were all very impressed with what I had done, and one of them asked me what had inspired me. I told them the story of my arrival in Minnesota and what I had learned from my cousins and mother over the years. I went on to say the rest of it was pretty much just common sense. One of the counselors told me she wished everyone had as much sense as I did. They left me to my day after wishing me a happy birthday.

I was very touched by the sweet words of the staff and proceeded to make small gifts for them. I snapped off some small, green, willow branches and wove them together to make four baskets; one for each of them. I thought maybe they could use it for their jewelry or keys. Lunch was next, and I had chili and more crackers. It was palatable, to say the least.

I spent the afternoon reading, gathering more firewood and keeping the fire stoked. After dinner, I picked up one of the empty foil packs and cleaned it out with snow. I then filled it with more snow and sat it at the fire's edge to heat. I used the melted snow and my worn long johns to wash up. I didn't want to waste my drinking water for a bath. I pulled out the clean long johns, jeans and sweatshirt from my backpack. Feeling much better, I changed into my clean clothes and sat by the fire for a little while, listening to everything going on around me. I could hear wolves howling in the distance, an owl hooted loudly as if telling me a story, and the wind began to whip through the trees. Yep, it was going to be a cold night.

At sun set, I piled wood onto the fire, put everything away and headed for my tent. I stripped down to my long johns and crawled into bed. It was a cold couple of seconds between stripping down and getting into my sleeping bag.

I slept peacefully and awoke to the sun hanging brilliantly in the morning sky. It was time to leave. Damn, I was just starting to really enjoy this.

After eating breakfast and using the bathroom, I tore down my tent and packed everything up. I filled the hole I used for a bathroom with the dirt I had removed to create it and placed the rock back over it. Sitting by the fire's edge once again, on the stone I had just warmed up for the final time, I waited to be picked up by my counselor. When I saw her approaching, I began to kick snow over the fire and made sure it was completely extinguished before we left.

We all gathered in a small cabin not far from our campsites and talked about the experience. All of the other girls complained about how hard it was to stay warm and cook their meals. When it was my turn, I was afraid to say anything because I actually really enjoyed myself. The staff strongly encouraged me to tell my story, so I did. The other girls looked at me like I was an alien. That was nothing new for me though. I didn't care. They weren't going to take away my self worth.

We returned to the main camp and spent the rest of the weekend in the "big house" where we were able to just be kids. The big house was a building on the camp property where groups could stay to have a break from the dorms. While the others watched movies, sang, danced around and ate junk food; I wrote... A lot. When I had been on the solo camp, I thought of a horror story idea and wanted to get it written down before I forgot. When I finished writing it, I showed it to one of the staff, and they asked me to read it to everyone before bed. I hesitantly agreed.

After dinner, I read the story to the group in front of the fireplace. No one could take their eyes off of me. Even though I was used to public speaking, I was very uncomfortable because it was such a small group, and they were literally just a few feet from me.

When I finished reading the story, one of the girls accused me of stealing it from her. I was so upset. The head counselor asked her to prove it by showing her the original. Of course, she couldn't. My counselor told the group she had seen me writing it all day and was sure it was my own, personal work. The girl that accused me of stealing her story was sent to bed early, and the rest of us were allowed to stay up to watch a movie and eat ice cream.

On Sunday night, we had to go to bed early because we were starting our last task the next day. We had to complete it before we could graduate. The twelve of us girls were going on a one hundred mile hike through the forest, carrying full packs and accompanied by four of our counselors. This... THIS was going to be tough.

The next morning, we woke up before the sun did. We worked together and made pancakes, eggs and fresh fruit salad for breakfast along with hot cocoa and orange juice. We wanted to make sure we had something hearty to give us some energy before we headed out on our trek.

After we ate our breakfast and dressed in our warmest clothing, we set out on our journey. It was to last five days, and we were to hike twenty miles a day. We loaded into a couple of vans and were then taken to our drop site.

We were lining up when the head counselor announced I would be leading the hike. Thanks, nothing like putting me on the spot. I made sure the girls had their packs on correctly and that each of them had brought their two gallons of water. We headed out down our marked path.

A lot of the girls were complaining about the pace that I set, so I made sure to stop every hour for a ten minute rest period. Three hours into the hike, I picked a nice area next to a creek and we stopped for lunch. The counselors assigned jobs to each of us girls, and we set about to prepare and serve lunch.

When lunch was concluded, we packed up and set out once again. I tried to keep the pace a bit slower this time because a few of the girls had mentioned how tough it was to keep up and how tired they were getting. This was not a race. It was about achieving our goal as a group.

It took us four and a half hours to hike the rest of the first twenty miles, to include our rest periods, before we stopped to make camp. Once again, the counselors assigned us our jobs, and we completed them. We all slept in one large tent that one of the counselors had been carrying. A few of the girls put up the tent while the rest of us gathered wood for a fire and prepared for the rest of our camping needs.

When we finished setting up camp, we prepared and ate our dinner. We then sat around the campfire, talking and singing. Eventually, we all made our way into the tent and fell into a deep sleep, exhausted from the day's events.

This same routine was repeated for the next four days. When we needed water, we stopped at a stream and looked for moving water to fill our containers. There was a bit of squabbling, but for the most part, we worked as a team and achieved our goal. At the end of the fifth day, we met the vans at the same place we had been dropped off and returned to camp.

It was now Friday night. We were allowed to stay at the big house again and prepare for our graduation from camp on Sunday night. The counselors offered us the opportunity to watch movies, but we were all too exhausted. After unpacking our gear and eating, we went directly to bed.

After breakfast Saturday morning, we were allowed to retrieve our belongings that had been confiscated when we first got to camp. Well, everything except for cigarettes. We all lazed about the living room and went through our things. The girls were all talking to each other about what they were going to do when they got home. I didn't participate in the conversation, but I listened. The girls talked about going to parties, getting drunk and fucking their boyfriends. I just smiled a faint smile and shook my head a little. Had they learned nothing during their stay here? Isn't that what got most of these girls sent to camp?

Saturday night, we went into town to see a movie and have ice cream. I was truly touched by the movie we had seen. It was about four young boys that had set out on a journey to see a dead body. On their journey, they discovered new and meaningful things about one another, themselves and strengthened their friendship. I'm sure you know what movie I'm talking about. * wink *

When we arrived back at the big house, I was asked by a staff member, to re-write the lyrics to a song for us to sing at our graduation. I did it and taught the other girls the new words. We practiced it and then headed off to bed.

Sunday night was now upon us, and the girls were excited to be going home. We filed into the cafeteria to stand at the front of the room, speak about our experience at the camp and sing our song. As we did, each of the girls would look out at their waiting, proud parents and wave. Well, not all of us had parents there to congratulate us for doing such a fine job. I didn't. Instead, my social worker sat in her car and waited for me to come outside.

When the ceremony was all said and done, I grabbed the awards I had won, my personal belongings and went outside. When I got in the car, I asked Amy where my mom was, and she said that Susan was just too busy to attend. Figures...

We drove into the dark of night in complete silence as a single tear fell down my cheek. There was nothing left to say and nothing that could comfort me. I knew I was on my own from this point forward.

CHAPTER SIX

I was taken to the crisis center where I had originally started my foster care journey. I was only staying for the night because it was too late to go to the next foster home by the time we arrived in town. After going through the intake process again, I was shown my room, and I went to bed.

My mind wandered to the graduation that night. All those parents, sitting there, happy that their pain in the ass kids had made it through the camp and probably thought that somehow it would change them. I had been around these kids enough to know better than that. Here's to hoping, I guess.

The next morning, Amy picked me up, and we drove to the next foster home. I sat in solemn silence as she told me about the next home I would be living in. Home? Really? What the fuck ever...

Wrenshall was a small town, and I knew I would never fit in. Experience proved this multiple times in the past. I was too different and really didn't care. I loved my torn up jeans, multi-colored hair and heavy make-up. It had become my trademark look, and I wasn't changing it for anyone.

We turned onto a dead end street where the houses looked like they had been cut out by the same cookie cutter. The lawns were perfectly manicured, and little flowers bloomed in the front gardens. Yeah, this place was gonna be fun... Not.

Turning into the driveway of the house, my stomach filled with knots, and my breath caught in my throat. I thought to myself, "Just keep your head down, stay invisible, and you'll make it through."

After grabbing my belongings, we went to the front door and knocked. A beautiful woman answered the door with a huge smile on her face. I was a little taken aback by the warm welcome. Was she another one of "those" foster parents and hiding it behind her smile?

"Hi, Maggie, I'm Kaye, and it is so nice to meet you. Amy has told me a lot about you. Come in, please." Kaye stepped away from the door to make room for our entrance.

We sat and chatted a bit before Amy left. I was then shown to my room. It was pretty typical with a bunk bed, dresser and desk. It had white walls with light wood trim around the windows and doors. I sat my luggage on the desk and began to unpack.

"You can do that later if you like. Come on, let's sit and get to know each other better." Kaye's enthusiasm was a bit overwhelming, but I did what I was asked to do.

We sat at a table on the back patio, drank iced tea and chatted until dinner time. Kaye told me how much she liked my style and that we could go shopping the next day for some new clothes. It felt a little like a backhanded compliment, but I just blew it off.

As Kaye busied herself with dinner preparations, I put away my belongings. I barely had enough to fill two drawers in the dresser, but I didn't mind. It was better to travel light. I had just finished when Kaye knocked on my door and came in.

"Do you need any help?" She asked as she opened the door.

"No, thank you, I just finished." I smiled at her.

"Would you mind helping me with dinner then?" She smiled back.

"Sure, that would be fun." I was excited to help. I loved cooking and looked forward to any opportunity to learn.

We stood side by side in the kitchen. Kaye prepared to bake chicken with lemon pepper, and I made a salad. We chatted as we stood there, and it felt so natural. I told Kaye I was a vegetarian. She said she thought that took a lot of discipline, and she would be sure to stock up on fresh fruits and vegetables.

Kaye's husband, Cory, came home as we were pulling the chicken from the oven. "Smells good in here." Cory's voice rang through the house from the front door. He entered the kitchen, and we were introduced. He shook my hand and told me that it was nice to meet me. I was a bit startled as he was a very large man with an even larger voice.

After washing up, we all sat down to eat at the table, like a family. What the hell? We only did this in my home for holiday meals. This was new, and I loved it. I listened as the two of them talked about their day and was shocked when Cory asked about mine. I told him about unpacking, the chat Kaye and I had on the back patio and how I helped to make dinner. He then invited me to join them in the living room to watch a movie after dinner. I was so excited that I started to swing my legs back and forth under the chair I was sitting on. What a wonderful place.

That's when reality set in, and I thought to myself, "Wait, hold up Maggie, don't get so excited. These things never last. Just remember that at the first sign of trouble they will get rid of you just like your parents did." Nothing lasted... Ever. I made up an excuse of having to write a letter and excused myself from the table.

Kaye and I went shopping the next afternoon for some new clothes and other things I needed. I was happy to have a day to settle in. I was nervous about starting a new school.

It was Tuesday morning, and I was getting ready for my first day. I must admit, the butterflies were strong. I dressed in my favorite ripped up jeans, a white t-shirt and pulled my hair up into a ponytail. After putting on my make-up and perfume, I went to the kitchen to grab something quick to eat before I walked to school.

"Good morning Maggie." Kaye was standing in the kitchen, making breakfast.

I accepted the plate she handed me and sat down at the table. She had made french toast with a side of fresh fruit and there was orange juice and milk already waiting for me on the table. Wow! We chatted a bit about how I slept, was I nervous, etc. and then she grabbed her keys to drive me to school.

"I can walk; it's okay." I grabbed my bag to head out the door.

"No way, I want to take you to school, and besides, I have to register you." Kaye smiled and winked at me.

"Oh, okay." I forgot about the registering part.

After Kaye signed me up for school, she handed me a twenty dollar bill for lunch and headed off. I stood there in amazement, for just a moment, trying to take it all in. Was she for real? Then the bell rang to warn me to head to my homeroom class.

Everyone was already seated when I entered the room. Yep... All eyes on me. Oh well, I was used to this. I handed the teacher my papers from the main office, was introduced to the class and told to take a seat, which I did near the back of the class. I knew my place.

I stayed quiet through the first half of the day and then found myself in the cafeteria. Oh, how I hated this place. Cliques, teasing, "I'm better than you" thinking and acting, the cafeteria was always a place of great distress.

Um, wait, what? Each grade was sitting together? Laughing and talking? What the hell was this?

One of the girls from my homeroom class, and every other class for that matter, flagged me over to their table. I hesitantly nodded in recognition, accepted the invitation and made my way over.

"Hi, I'm Kat and this is..." She began to introduce everyone in our class to me.

"Hey, I won't remember all your names, so be patient with me as I learn them." If I'm here long enough to learn them...

"It's understandable. We only have one name to learn and you have twenty-seven." Kat smiled at me as she spoke. She appeared to be very sweet.

Then the questions started, "Where did you move from? Where do you live? How do you like it here? Where do you get your clothes?"

I answered them each, as best as I could, without giving up too much information. I was a very private person, and I didn't like to give people too much ammunition against me.

"I love the pink and purple in your hair. Would you do mine?" Diane said quietly to me. She was a skinny girl with brown hair and eyes and was very soft spoken.

"Um, sure and thanks. Just let me know when you have some time. It takes a couple of hours." I was a bit shocked.

Okay, so maybe this wasn't going to be as bad as I had earlier thought. The kids here seemed nice enough and very accepting.

I made it through the rest of the day unscathed. When the last bell rang, I grabbed my bag and started walking home, alone. It wasn't long before Kat caught up with me.

"Hi, want some company?" She was a bit out of breath from running to catch up with me.

"Sure... Hey, where can I buy cigarettes here?" I was almost out and didn't know this town very well.

"There's a store right up the block. Come on, I'll walk with you." Kat walked on and talked as though we were already best of friends. She told me about her family and how she had grown up here.

I walked into the store, bought three packs of cigarettes and two diet sodas, with the left over money from lunch. The clerk didn't think twice about selling them to me as I looked older than my age of sixteen. I walked out and handed Kat one of the sodas.

Kat and I walked home. She lived almost right across the street from me and talked my ear off the whole way. She was excited to have a classmate living so close.

We said goodbye, and I went into the house. I hesitated at the door for just a minute and almost knocked. It still felt strange to walk into someone else's house.

Kaye was there and greeted me as I walked in. She asked about my day and listened as I told her everything I could remember. I had homework, so I excused myself to my room to work on it.

Dinner, movie and bedtime... The usual stuff. The rest of the week went almost exactly as the first day except Diane started walking home with Kat and I.

We were becoming quite the trio. We did everything we could together, and that weekend we were having a sleep over at Kat's house. I found myself excited at the thought. I had never really made friends in my other foster home, and I missed it more than I would admit to myself at the time.

After I checked in with Kaye, I grabbed a change of clothes, a sleeping bag, a pillow, my make-up and hair things and headed over to Kat's. Diane was already there when I arrived.

We went directly to the basement and laid out our things. Kat put on some music and started to dance around. It was country music, and I just couldn't get into it.

"Um, Kat? I brought some music with me. Can I play it?" She smiled, grabbed the tape from me (Yes, a tape. Don't even try to play. You know they were cool back then.) and put it in the stereo.

"Wow, this is cool music!" Diane was sitting on her sleeping bag watching Kat dance around like a fool.

See, Kat was the extravert, Diane the introvert, and I was an ambivert.

I looked like I liked attention, but I really didn't. It was nice to be with people I could just be "me" around.

We spent the night giving each other make overs. Well, I did their make-up and hair coloring, and they watched as I did mine, so they would learn how to do it themselves.

Around four in the morning, we crawled into our separate sleeping bags and talked ourselves to sleep. It was an absolute blast, and I almost felt like I was home.

We woke up, ate breakfast, and after packing up my belongings, I headed back to Cory and Kaye's. They were awake and sitting on the back patio having coffee.

"You're on time, nice." Kaye spoke to me through the screen door.

"Yep, it was fun. Is it cool if I go for a walk with Kat and Diane after I do my chores? We're thinking about going to Dan's and playing basketball." I asked even though I knew they would be okay with it.

"Sure, but where does Dan live again?" Cory answered me.

"Right up the street, next to the store." I had walked over to the screen door, so we didn't have to yell.

"Yep, just be home by dark, and if you go anywhere else, call and let us know." Cory smiled at me.

"No problem, I don't think we are going anywhere else, but I'll let you know if we do." I turned to go unpack and put away my things.

When I walked into my room, there was an envelope on my dresser. I opened it and looked inside. There was a note and five, twenty dollar bills in it. The note said, "for your allowance this week." Holy shit! This just seemed too good to be true. Kaye and Cory were kind, generous, genuine and cared about me? Yeah, too good to be true. I had to watch myself to not get lost in the fantasy.

I completed my chores, met Kat at her house, and we walked up to Dan's where Diane was waiting for us. We all sat around for a bit and chatted. I was getting bored so I stood up, grabbed the basketball and started shooting hoops.

I heard Diane and Dan laughing, and I turned around to see what was so funny. I knew I wasn't a jock, but I was pretty good with a basketball. I had hoped they weren't laughing at me.

"Hey, Maggie, don't you ever shave above your knees?" Diane laughed as she spoke to me.

"What do you mean?" Yep, they were laughing at me.

"The back of your knees are hairy." Dan pointed at me and laughed even harder.

"Oh yeah, I guess I forgot." I just kind of blew it off and laughed with them, but the truth is, I was heart broken. No one had ever taught me how to shave, and I had to figure out all that stuff on my own. I guess I had never thought to shave there. I couldn't help that I didn't have a mom that taught me these things. Neither of my foster moms had shown me either. I am sure they thought I already knew that stuff.

"Don't pay attention to them, Maggie. Come on, I'll walk home with you." Kat shot the two of them a dirty look, and we walked home.

So, now is the point where I skip ahead. I don't see any reason to go into every detail of every day. Quite frankly, they were all pretty much the same, school, friends, hanging out, football games, sleep overs, music and family meals. I had been living at this foster home for over a year and was now seventeen and in my Junior year at school.

The end of the school year was quickly approaching, and they were having a dance. This was the first school dance I had ever attended, and I didn't know what to expect. I did know that I wanted to surprise everyone.

Kat and Diane came over the afternoon of the dance to get ready at my place. Did you read that? "My place..." It was home. I was finally home.

We spent the afternoon curling and fixing each others hair, and I did their make-up. It was finally time to get dressed for the dance. Kat and Diane put on pretty dresses in my room, and I went into the bathroom to change. I didn't want anyone to see what I was wearing until the last minute, and I kept it very secretive, though they tried to get me to tell them.

I walked out wearing a white, short sleeved dress with a handkerchief cut bottom. It was fitted at the top and flowed down my legs. There were no crazy colors, no tears or holes, just a simple white dress with matching white, three inch heels. I had tied my long, blonde curls on top of my head with a couple of clips and let the curls fall where they wanted to. I kept my make-up pretty tamed, compared to normal, with earth tones and a light pink lipstick.

"Oh my gosh, Maggie, you look amazing!" Kat was the first one to speak.

"I ... I... WOW!" Diane was at a loss for words.

I thanked them both for their compliments. After grabbing our purses, we went outside where Cory was waiting to drive us to the dance, though it was only a few blocks away.

"Beautiful." Cory smiled as he opened the doors for us.

I felt beautiful, and it showed in my confidence. I wanted to be remembered for more than my rebellious clothing, make-up and hair. I was sure this dress would do the trick.

We walked arm in arm into the gymnasium and stopped to admire the decor. The dance committee had gone all out with the decorations. There were white twinkle lights strewn about everywhere with white and orange streamers hanging with them. It was beautiful in it's simplicity. The stage was in the center of the back wall, and atop it sat the DJ that had been hired to host the dance. He was still setting up as we entered.

There were quite a few students there already, and a few of them approached us as we walked across the floor toward the DJ.

"Wow, Maggie, what a difference." Laura was the first to say something. She was one of the popular girls and though there weren't cliques in this school, as there were in others, there was definitely a hierarchy of the more well-to-do students.

"Thanks, Laura. Your dress is pretty." I tried to sound sincere. It had a pink bodice with a blue, kind of fru fru skirt on it. There were a lot of pleats in the bodice and rolling layers of material in the skirt. It was absolutely hideous.

Kat, Diane and I got ourselves some punch and sat down on the set of bleachers that had been pulled out. We watched as other students entered and began to mingle. The lights were turned down, and the music began to play after a brief introduction from the DJ.

The three of us put down our punch glasses and danced together to a couple of fast songs. We were getting a bit tired, so we chose to sit down once again.

This time, we sat down next to the boy I had a crush on. His name was Brad, and he was so cute. He was the tallest guy in our class, and he made me swoon every time he smiled. Okay, I didn't know what it was to swoon back then, so it was more, "giggle like a school girl", which is okay since that is what I was.

I inched my way closer to him... And then a little closer... And then even a bit closer until our fingers touched. It was completely romantic, until he stood up to walk away. Oh, hell no buddy.

I stood up quickly, "Brad? Do you want to dance?"

Brad stared at me for a moment, hesitated but then took my hand, and we walked out onto the dance floor. "Can't Fight this Feeling" by REO Speedwagon was playing as he pulled me a bit closer to him. I felt my cheeks warm, and I knew I was blushing. Thank goodness it was relatively dark in there.

Every step brought us a bit closer until I was swept up in his arms with his heart beating against mine. Our eyes locked in a nervous stare and our lips were frozen in permanent smiles. It was sweet, innocent and awkward... And it was fantastic. * swoon *

One of the boys in our class was having an after dance party at his house, and I was allowed to go. Diane, Kat and I rode with some of our other friends to James' house when the dance concluded.

His parents were gone for the weekend, and he lived out in the middle of nowhere, so we could get as loud and obnoxious as we wanted. There was a keg of beer sitting in a kiddy pool filled with ice, and a few of the kids brought bottles of hard liquor. I hadn't drank in a couple of years but gave in to the surroundings.

I was pretty well on my way to drunk and was standing around with Kat and Diane. We were talking, laughing and watching others make complete fools of themselves. It was the typical teenage, backwoods party, and we were all having a blast. Until the cops showed up...

"Shit, run!" I heard an anonymous voice yell but did as I was instructed. I ran out to the woods and hid behind a huge tree with Kat and Diane. We hunkered down and planned to wait it out until the police left. We were wrong.

Flashlight beams filled the forest and shouts of, "We found another one!" rang out through the underbrush. It was only a couple of minutes before the three of us were also discovered and brought out of our hiding place to the awaiting squad cars.

After the police officers took down our information, we were each escorted to our separate homes. I knew I was in trouble... Big trouble. Thoughts raced through my head, and I told myself that no matter what happened, to pretend like I didn't care, even though I did.

The police knocked on the door, and Kaye answered it. A look of shock crossed her face. She thanked the officers for bringing me home as I walked past her, and she closed the door. Cory was soon to join us in the living room, and Kaye filled him in on the situation. They told me we would discuss it in the morning and to be prepared to wake up early. I was a bit confused because I thought there would be screaming and yelling, but instead there was almost silent disappointment.

A knock on my door woke me the next morning. The sun was almost at it's highest point in the sky, and my first thoughts were, "I thought they said I had to wake up early."

My door opened slowly. I was expecting to see Kaye. Nope, it was Amy. "Pack your things, Maggie. You're leaving."

I knew it. Things were never as good as they seemed. Now, I know I messed up by drinking, but you would think that things would have or could have been handled differently. Well, on to the next chapter I suppose.

CHAPTER SEVEN

I spent a few days at the crisis shelter before I was taken to my next foster home. It was supposed to be a punishment for drinking, but in reality, it was a nice break. I had gotten used to being by myself and just preferred it that way. No people meant no heartbreak.

Wow, this one was REALLY out in the country. Wright, Minnesota was feeling wrong already, and I hadn't even gotten to the new foster home yet.

We drove up a long gravel driveway. The house was old and looked quite charming. There was a large garage, a barn, an outer building of some kind (I later learned it was a sauna), a garden and a lake. Wait, a lake? Fuck yeah!

The car had barely come to a stop when a lovely woman, with long dark hair, approached us. She had a full length skirt on that flowed in the breeze as she walked toward the car.

"Hi, Amy, it's so nice to see you again. This must be Maggie. Hello, my name is Willow, and I would like to welcome you to your new home." Willow opened the car door for me and took me by the hand to help me out.

"Hey, Amy, pop the trunk will ya?" Willow spoke with such a soft, yet commanding voice.

When the trunk was unlocked Willow retrieved my luggage and closed the lid. Amy started to get out of her car, but Willow told her it wouldn't be necessary, and she had things from there.

Amy waived goodbye as she backed down the driveway and out of sight. Two teenage boys came out of the house, picked up my bags and took them inside. Boys? Really? My interest was definitely peaked now. * wink and grin *

Willow took me by the hand and walked with me down to the shore of the lake. She pointed out different things to me as we walked. It was all feeling a bit odd but not in a bad way.

They had their own sign making company that Jack, her husband, ran out of the garage. Willow said he was usually very busy in there, and we children were not allowed inside without invitation. She then pointed around to the rest of the property and said, "The rest of this? This is your home. Feel free to explore, learn and most of all have fun."

We sat at the water's edge talking about the circumstances that had brought me there. She then explained the rules of their home and hugged me. I was uncomfortable at first and then I just melted into her hug.

"I've always wanted a daughter, and now, here you are. Come on, I'll introduce you to the rest of the family." We walked back up to the house, and she did as she said she would.

They had two sons, Jason was sixteen and Jack Jr. was seventeen. They were both very polite and shook my hand as she introduced us. I was then taken out to the garage to meet her husband.

Jack Sr. was a tall, lanky man with bright blonde hair that hung half way down his back. He had many visible tattoos and a really awkward smile. He was working on a sign when we walked in but stopped to talk to us.

"Hello, Miss Maggie, and welcome home. You'll see that we are kind of new age hippies here. By the looks of you, you'll fit right in." He winked at me and went back to work.

I was then shown my bedroom, which was located off the back side of the living room, on the main floor, right next to Willow and Jack's room. It looked as though it had at one time been a three season porch that had been converted into a bedroom.

There were large windows on two sides of the bedroom that had views of the lake. It was gorgeous. Willow had hung stunning white curtains on the windows. The bed's duvet cover and pillow cases matched the curtains. It was almost as if she knew that white was my favorite color. The bed sat directly under the windows, and there was a little table next to it with a lamp on it. A dressing table, with a large mirror hung above it, sat against the common wall between the two bedrooms. There were all kinds of little containers and boxes on the table for me to put my things in. It looked like a princess's room, and I felt like one.

As I walked around the room, looking at and touching everything, I started to think to myself, "Don't get lost..." but then I stopped the thought. It couldn't hurt to get lost in the fantasy for just a bit, right?

Willow came in behind me and started to unpack my things. I sat on the bed folding clothes and getting them ready to place into a dresser, but I didn't see one. That is when she slid part of the wall to the side to reveal a HUGE walk-in closet that had built in drawers. Wow, I was really excited now.

"You don't have enough clothes to fill even half of this closet, do you?" Willow put away my things as she spoke to me.

"No Ma'am, but I have what I need." I handed her the rest of my clothes.

"No Ma'am? Oh no, Darlin', that's just too formal. You can call me Willow. Come on, let's go shopping. Every woman needs a closet full of clothes and shoes." She dropped what she was doing, took me by the hand, and we headed out.

We drove into town... If you could call it a town. There was a small grocery store, a gas station, a couple of churches and a vintage clothing store. That's it, but it was completely lovely. We pulled up to the used clothing store and parked.

Willow and I entered the store, and she said, "Shop to your hearts desire."

So I did...

We walked out of the store with four huge garbage bags full of clothing and shoes. I had never owned so many clothes. Willow had picked up a few things for herself and for the boys as well. We smiled at each other as we put the bags in the back of her old pickup truck.

When we returned home, Willow and I immediately began to wash the clothes. When I went to change out the first load, I noticed that there was no clothing dryer.

"Willow? What do I do with the wet clothes?" I stood in the kitchen holding a basket of wet laundry.

"We hang them on the lines, of course." She looked up and smiled at me.

"Oh, okay." I walked outside to look for the clothesline.

I stood there at the lines, hanging the clothes and taking in my surroundings. It was peaceful, serene and beautiful. As I hung a pair of wet jeans on the clothesline, a hand covered my own.

"Here, Darlin', let me show you how to do this without leaving fold marks." Willow took down the jeans and showed me how to hang them by the legs with the clothespins.

"Okay, thank you." Really? Someone was taking the time to teach me something? Hmm... I finished hanging the clothes, as she showed me, and continued with the laundry as it finished washing.

I was in heaven. There was definitely something different about this place. The peace filled my heart and overflowed into my soul. I finally felt like I was home, and there was no doubt in my mind whatsoever.

It was summer, so I spent a lot of time outdoors with Willow. If we were both awake, we were at each others sides. She expanded the knowledge that my mother had given me about organic gardening, crocheting, sewing, canning, harvesting wild foods such as cattails and cooking. Oh, how I loved to cook with her. Also, the entire family was vegan. I had no issue switching from vegetarian to vegan.

She taught me many new things as well. I learned about different natural oils and their medicinal uses. Like, did you know that if you have a headache that lavender oil will get rid of it? Or, that tea tree oil is great for rashes? I could go on and on, but this is not the time for that.

Anyway, I soaked it all up. Everything she had to teach me, I memorized. The most important lesson? She taught me how to love and to allow myself to be loved.

It wasn't all about work either. The boys and I spent a lot of time together playing football in the mud, going on hikes and sweating in the sauna. We used to sit in the sauna until we were dripping with sweat and then run out and jump into the lake. Jack Sr. put a rope in a tree for us, with a knot in the end of it, so we could swing out and jump into the cool waters.

Jason and I had grown quite close. He had the soul of an artist, and we spent the majority of our time hiking, taking pictures, sitting on the lawn painting and laying side by side in the hammock reading to one another.

Jason and I were almost inseparable. Although he was a year younger than I, he seemed more mature. He taught me about artists and their different techniques. We spent countless hours studying random paintings, photos and sculptures.

One rainy afternoon, Jason and I were in the loft of the barn looking at a new photography magazine. He was holding one side of the magazine, and I was holding the other. We were shoulder to shoulder as we chatted about the photos, smiled and laughed... He kissed me.

His lips were soft against mine as I kissed him back. There was no thought involved. There was simply a young passion, a shared love of art and a rainy afternoon in the hay loft.

It just kind of happened, and then it was over. It's not like we wanted a relationship. We simply got caught up in our passion for the arts and let it overtake our bodies. We never talked about it; we both understood that it was just a moment in time.

I was about to start my senior year in school, and there was a lot that needed to be done. We had to go shopping, sign me up for classes, and I had to get a physical. I wasn't as nervous about starting a new school this time because I had met quite a few of the students already.

Willow took me shopping and then to the doctor. After being poked and prodded, I sat on the bed in the exam room waiting on the results.

"Congratulations." The doctor entered the exam room carrying my files in his hands.

"What do you mean?" I started to swing my legs against the end of the bed.

"You're pregnant. By the looks of it, I would say you're approximately nine weeks along." He didn't even look up at me.

I sat there in total and utter shock. Pregnant? How the hell did this happen? My mind wandered back to that rainy day in the hay loft. Fuck.

The doctor gave me some pamphlets and left the room. I got dressed and went out to the waiting area, where Willow sat crocheting.

"How did it go?" Willow put away her yarn and got ready to leave.

"Fine." I just couldn't tell her, yet.

We drove home listening to music from the 70's and chatting about what it would be like when school started in a couple of weeks. Honestly, I don't remember much of the conversation as my mind was a million miles away. I was going to be a mom, and I didn't even know where to begin.

I knew I was going to have to tell them, sooner than later. How did I tell them they were going to be grandparents? How did I tell them their son and I had shared one moment, out of our love for art, and that moment created another life? Jason was only sixteen, how was he going to be a dad?

A deep sadness crept into my life and hung like a dark cloud over my head. Willow noticed the change and tried desperately to talk to me. I assured her I was fine, but I know she saw through the facade.

It had been a week since I had received the news, and I knew it was time to talk to them. Where would I even start? Did I talk to Jason first or all of them at the same time? I waited for the perfect moment.

We were all sitting at the table, having dinner, and the boys were excitingly talking about starting school. They prattled on about sports and classes. My mind wandered away again.

"Maggie?" Willow reached to touch my hand.

"Yeah?" I jumped at her touch.

"Are you okay? You seem to be in deep thought." She looked at me with such love in her eyes.

"No, I'm not okay. I'm pregnant." The words flowed with the tears down my cheeks. So much for waiting for the perfect moment.

"Pregnant?" Jack Sr. sounded angry.

"Yes, Jack, I found out when I went to the doctor last week, but I didn't know how to tell you. I'm so sorry." I froze in my seat and braced myself to get backhanded. It didn't happen.

"Who's the father?" Jack was trying to contain his disappointment.

"Jack, give her a minute. Can't you see she's upset?" Willow took me by the hand and led me to my room.

"Want to talk about it?" We sat on my bed with her arms around me.

"No, but I know we have to." I sank into her hug and cried.

"Maggie, I know you've only lived here for a few months, but I've truly grown to love you. I hope you know you can tell me anything." Willow stroked my hair as she spoke to me.

"I know, Willow. I'm just so afraid." How did I tell her?

"I understand. I won't push you. When you're ready to talk, I'll be here." She left me alone in my room to think. I was tired of thinking. I just wanted someone else to make the decisions for me. I had plans to go to school to become a writer. I wanted to do something, to be someone. How was I going to do that with a baby hanging off my hip?

I fell asleep that night with my hand on my stomach and tears in my eyes. I knew I was going to keep the baby and find a way to make things work. Women did this all the time, and I knew I could do it too.

It was around three in the morning when Jason quietly snuck into my room. He touched my shoulder to wake me. "Maggie? Is the baby mine?" He whispered softly to me.

"Yes, Jason. I haven't been with anyone else." I took his hand in mine as I told him the answer to his question.

"What are we going to do?" He sat on the side of the bed next to me.

"I'm going to keep it." Tears filled my eyes once again.

"Okay, we'll tell my parents in the morning." He leaned over and kissed me on my forehead before leaving my room.

I laid there thinking until the sun made it's appearance in the eastern sky. Today was the day it all came out, that all of their questions were answered, and my life would take a new direction.

Throwing on my robe, I walked out to the kitchen. Everyone was already seated at the table, and Willow was serving them their breakfast. "Good morning, Darlin'. Did you rest peacefully?" Willow smiled.

"Good morning. No, I hardly slept." I sat in my place at the table.

"Maggie, we need..." Jack Sr. started to speak.

"I know, Jack." I cut him off before he had a chance to finish, and I looked across the table at Jason. "I'm about ten weeks pregnant, and your son, Jason, is the father. We didn't mean for this to happen, it just sort of did. It was only once, but once was all it took."

A hush fell over the room. No one spoke, and all you could hear was their breathing. I began to shake with nervousness. Willow reached over and touched my hand to calm me.

"We kind of figured that, Maggie. Jack and I talked about it last night, and we would like you to stay here. We want to help you raise the baby while you and Jason finish school." Willow was so calm that it almost scared me.

"Really? I don't know what to say. This is... This is just..." I broke off into tears. "I don't even know why I'm crying."

"It's all part of the beauty of pregnancy, Sunshine." Jack Sr. was now holding my other hand. "Give it some time and everything will work out. You'll see."

We spent the rest of the morning discussing details. Jason and I would finish high school while Willow and Jack Sr. looked after our baby. They knew that Jason and I had no intention of being a couple, but that wouldn't stop us from raising our child together. I would maintain physical custody of our child, and Jason would have as much visitation as he wanted. It sounded like the perfect plan. We all knew this wasn't going to be easy, but together we could achieve anything.

I finally felt like I was part of a family... A real family. This is what unconditional love was supposed to be. I felt truly blessed to be a part of this family, and I would never do anything to let them down again.

Willow called Amy to tell her what was going on, and Amy insisted on coming out the next day to talk to us. Ugh, why couldn't she just leave us alone? We had things covered. I had grown to dislike Amy, because instead of speaking up for me, she did whatever the court said to do. She allowed me to get locked up in juvie and be sent to that work camp for cutting myself. It didn't seem that she was looking out for my best interest... At all.

Willow and I were sitting in the living room, looking at material for baby blankets, when Amy arrived the next day. She didn't speak when she handed Willow some paperwork. Willow sat on the couch, read the papers and started to cry.

"Get up and pack your things, Maggie. You're coming with me, like it or not." Amy's hardened voice was void of emotion.

"What? No! We have this all figured out. I'll be eighteen in eight months. You can't do this. You can't..." I stood up and started yelling at Amy.

"I'm not the one that did this; YOU are. You and whatever guy got you knocked up. The court has decided that this is an unfit place for you, and you are to be sent to a home for unwed mothers until you are of age." Amy spoke as if she had no heart, no feelings.

I ran to my room and collapsed on my bed. Why... Why did we tell her anything? If we had just waited a while longer, she wouldn't have been able to do this. NO! NO! NO!

Willow came into my room and sat down on the bed next to me. "I'm sorry, Maggie. I'm so, so, so sorry. You have to go with her, or they will send the sheriff out here to arrest you. It's not the end of the world. You can come back here when you are released from the state's custody. We'll always be here for you."

"Oh, Willow, why? Why can't they just leave us alone?" I hugged her tightly.

"Because they do not know what love is, Maggie. They have no idea what love is. They only know their job." She stroked my hair and patted my back. "Okay, dry your tears and let's get you packed. You don't have to take everything since you'll be returning, right?"

Willow put on her "everything is going to be alright" face and helped me to pack two suitcases for the trip. She even included some of her maternity clothing from when she was pregnant with Jason. I was touched at the gesture and hugged her tightly once more.

Jack Sr. had taken the boys fishing, so they were unaware of what was happening. I walked outside, to the car, and Willow carried my luggage. I looked across the lake to try to see the guys before I left. Just a glimpse of them was all I needed, but they were nowhere to be seen. My heart sank into my stomach, and I hugged Willow goodbye.

"It's not goodbye, Darlin', it's just see you later." She kissed me on my cheek, and Amy and I left.

I stared out the window as we drove away from the only unconditional love I had ever known. I silently cursed at the trees. How dare they stand there, so tall and straight, mocking me.

CHAPTER EIGHT

"What the hell do you mean you're sending me to California? What happened to the group home for unwed mothers?" I stood across from Amy's desk fuming.

"I've spoken with your parents..." Amy looked at papers on her desk.

"What do my so-called parents have to do with this? They haven't cared about me since the day Brianna was born." I cut her off in mid-sentence.

"If you would let me finish, please. I spoke to your parents, your Aunt Mattie and the courts. We all believe that it would be in your best interest for you to go and stay with your aunt and uncle in California until you turn eighteen. A change in scenery might do you some good." Amy's spoke through her clenched teeth.

"My best interest? Since when do you care about my best interest? So I have no say in this? What about the arrangements that Willow, Jack, Jason and I made? Doesn't that mean anything?" I felt as though my world was not mine anymore or if it ever had been.

"No, it doesn't. We don't even know if Jason is the father." She sifted through her paperwork.

"What? How dare you! Of course, he is the father! Do you think I'm some kind of fucking whore?" I slammed my fist onto her desk to get her attention.

"Watch yourself, Maggie. This is why we think it is best for you. You are turning into an angry girl, and it's not healthy." Her voice dripped with condescension.

"An angry girl? Are you kidding me? You... YOU turned me into this person. You never cared about me, and I'm not the only one that thinks that. Tell me Amy, tell me why you allowed the court to lock me up when I needed help? Tell me how you slept at night knowing that I was at a detention camp when I needed emotional support and not discipline?" Though I kept my voice down, the disdain lept from my throat. I couldn't control it. Hell, I didn't want to control it. She had to know how I felt.

Amy stood up, leaned over her desk and looked straight into my eyes, "I slept just fine. How about you?"

Taking a deep breath, I calmed myself. I wanted to slap the smug look from her face. I knew, if I laid a hand on her, I would be arrested, and the state would take my baby the second it was born.

"Now, get your shit together. I'm taking you to your parents house, and your father is going to drive you to Minneapolis, where your aunt is waiting to fly with you to California. End of discussion." Amy put her papers away.

I knew, by the tone of her voice and her selection in language, I had gotten to her, but I had no choice other than to do what I was told. I hoped maybe my words would sink in and have their intended effect before another child went through what I did. Gathering my luggage, I followed her outside. She may have thought she had won the war, but her battle was just beginning.

We drove in absolute silence. There was nothing left to say between us. Well, at least nothing constructive. As we pulled into the driveway of my parents' home, I turned to Amy and said, "I would like to thank you for all of the hard work you did for me, but I would be lying, so I won't."

She didn't respond, but instead got out of the car, opened the trunk and dropped my bags on the gravel driveway. That is where, and how, our relationship as social worker and client ended.

As Amy backed out of the driveway, my father came out of the front door. We hadn't seen each other in over a year and a half. He looked older, more haggard then I had remembered. My heart raced as he approached and hugged me. I didn't know what to do, so I did nothing. I couldn't make my arms move to hug him back. He took that as a personal insult.

"Well, I see nothing has changed. You're still the hateful bitch you've always been." He stepped away from me.

"Hello, Richard. It's nice to see you too." I refused to get drawn into his nasty world.

"Come on, let's go. Everyone is waiting for us, and it's a long drive." He threw my luggage into the back of his pickup and got in.

"What about Susan and Brianna? Aren't they coming with?" I asked as I got into the truck.

"No, they don't want to see you." Spite punctuated his sentence.

"Oh, okay." I didn't know what else to say. I sat, staring out the window, holding my hands over my stomach. I sang a lullaby in my head, hoping that my unborn child could hear it, would know that it was loved, and I would protect it, not only from his hatred, but from all of the ugliness in the world.

Richard turned on the radio to drown out the silence. The song on the radio was something about, "If she seems cold and bitter, then I beg of you, just stop and consider, all she's gone through..." I thought to myself, "how apropos."

We finally arrived in Minneapolis. We pulled into the driveway of Aunt Bianca's house where Aunt Mattie had been staying and awaiting our arrival. It was just as I had remembered it.

Getting out of the truck, I heard Aunt Mattie yell, "They're here."

I grabbed my bags and stood in the driveway. I didn't know what to do. It all seemed like a bad dream. I wanted to turn around and run back to Willow's.

Aunt Mattie came running out of the house and wrapped her arms around me. "Hi, Maggie, oh my goodness I've missed you. How are you? You look fantastic."

"Hi, Auntie, I'm fine. I'm just a little tired from the drive." I handed my bags to her and started to follow her into the house.

"Tired? Why the fuck would you be tired? I did the driving." Richard walked behind us.

"Now Rich, don't start." Aunt Mattie stopped in her tracks, causing me to walk into her, as she spoke to my father.

"I'm not starting..." He knew better than to finish his sentence. Aunt Mattie was the matriarch of our family even though she was the youngest of the siblings.

We sat around the kitchen table, and I listened as everyone talked over one another, planning out my future. I realized, at that moment, I would never be in control of my own life if I lived with any of these people. As they planned my future, I was planning my escape for the moment I turned eighteen.

After dinner, we all said goodbye, and Richard drove Aunt Mattie and I to the airport. I sat in the back of the truck because I didn't want to be that close to my father. It wasn't because I hated him, it was because I loved him so much, and I knew he didn't love me.

It didn't take us very long to get to the airport. It was as if the traffic lights were working for the system and didn't want me to stay in Minnesota either. I was hoping we would miss our flight, and by some miracle, I would be allowed to go back to Wright, where I was happy and loved.

Butterflies attacked my stomach as we pulled up to the front of the airport. We were here, and there was no turning back. Fuck. I picked up my bags, jumped down to the sidewalk, and waited for Aunt Mattie to get out of the truck.

Richard got out and approached me. He tried to hug me, but I pulled away from him. I looked up at his face and saw what appeared to be pain. Not like he was in pain, but the pain of a broken heart. Bravo Richard... Bravo. Way to put on a show for your little sister.

"Listen, Little Shit, (Oh... Good job using the nickname.) I don't know what I'm supposed to say right now, so I'm just going to say that I wish you the best, and I love you." Richard turned and walked away.

"Say something to him, Maggie." Aunt Mattie's voice echoed in the fog that had taken over my brain.

I didn't. I couldn't. I watched as he pulled away from the curb and out of sight. With a sigh, I followed Mattie into the terminal, loaded the plane and stared out the window.

Six hours and one layover later we were arriving in Sacramento, California. Two hours later, we were parking in the driveway of my aunt's house in Lodi. Home sweet fucking home, I hated it already.

No one opened the door for us or came running out to greet us. Aunt Mattie sat her luggage on the front porch, unlocked and opened the front door. I followed her inside and stopped in the doorway. This? This was how they lived?

In the beginning of this book I introduced you to Mattie and her family, but let's have a little refresher course, shall we?

Mattie is my father's youngest (half) sister. She is married to Glen, and they have two children, Rhea and Robert (Rob). Rhea was a bit older than me and Rob a little older than Brianna. There, all caught up.

So, back to the way they lived. It was absolutely filthy. This was better for me than living with Willow and her family? THIS? There was stuff, for lack of better term, everywhere. Here, let me paint you a verbal picture...

Walking into the front door of their ranch style home, you walk directly into what should be the living room. To your right is an archway that leads to an eat-in kitchen and a second archway leading out of it. There is a door, off the backside of the kitchen, that leads to the garage where the washer and dryer, and a shit ton of other crap, was housed. In front of you, past the living room, is a hallway with two bedrooms on your left and a bathroom and the master bedroom to the right. Pretty basic, right?

Here's the kicker of it... There was literally wall to wall crap. Not just wall to wall, but floor to ceiling in some places. I couldn't tell if there was furniture under all that shit or not. It looked as though a hundred yard sales had exploded in their home, and dynamite was used to cut walking paths through it.

So, I walk in and see Rob sitting on a chair, surrounded with mountains of trappings. He was playing a video game on a television that barely peeked out through the chaos.

"Why didn't you open the door, Rob?" Aunt Mattie worked her way through the winding trail.

"Busy." Rob's answer was almost inaudible.

"Come on, I'll show you to your room. You'll be sharing it with Rhea." Mattie dropped her luggage in an opening in the first doorway to the kitchen.

I followed her down the hall to the first door on the left. Was it possible that Rhea kept a clean room even though the rest of her home was a disaster? And? ...Nope.

"Dammit, I told Rhea to clean up this room before we got home." Mattie started to push things aside to make room for me. "I don't know why she keeps all this junk."

Really? Did she just say that? I wanted to say, "Maybe she gets it from her mama." but thought better of it. * rolls eyes and snickers *

"Just put your stuff wherever you can make room for it." Mattie walked out, closed the door, and left me to my own devices. So, I did what I was told... And then some.

I began to clean and organize right away. I had to live here for at least eight months, and I was not going to live in this, in this... Ugh. There were no words for "this".

I picked up all of the clothes, that appeared to be dirty, and began laundry right away. After moving some boxes into the closet and making room on the floor, I was able to pull out the trundle bed and set it up against the far wall. I re-hung the curtains that had gotten pulled down under the weight of the "treasures" that sat upon them, and I tacked up the posters that were hanging halfway off the walls.

When the bedding was fresh from the dryer, I made both of our beds. I loved the crispness of the sheets as I spread them over the mattresses. They smelled so fresh and clean. I fluffed the pillows, placed them in clean cases and stacked them on the beds. I used some empty boxes, I had discovered, to make drawers to put my things in. When I was finished, I tucked them into the empty space beneath Rhea's bed.

I did not touch her belongings on the desk as they were her personal things, and I would hate for anyone to go through mine. I used more boxes and sat them next to my bed to use as a desk, night stand and dressing table all in one. Carefully, I sat out my belongings and arranged them neatly. Sticking my journal under my mattress, I looked around and saw that I was done. There, all nice and neat.

I was sitting on my bed, listening to music, when Rhea came home. I saw her walk in, so I removed my headphones, said hello and smiled.

"What the hell did you do?" Rhea looked around our room and was furious.

"I, um... Your mom said to make room for my things, so I cleaned up. I put all your laundry away, after I washed it, and stuck some boxes in your closet, but I didn't touch anything else." Oh wow, really? She was angry? I guess not everyone had the same passion for cleaning that I did.

"I don't know where any of my things are now. How dare you touch my things." Rhea began to fling her stuff from the closet to the floor.

"I'm sorry. I was just trying to help." I was almost in tears.

"Why don't you help by not being such a slut and getting knocked up. Oh wait, it's too late for that." Venomous words hung from her lips.

I didn't know what to say or do, so I just put my headphones back on, sat there and closed my eyes. I pretended to be back at Willow's where things were clean, orderly and loving. Ahh.... Better.

Needless to say, the rest of the night was pretty quiet. Uncle Glen went to work. Aunt Mattie cooked, and we ate dinner. After, I went back to sit on my bed and write in my journal.

We were supposed to be going to San Mateo the next day to visit with some of the other family, Uncle Harry and Aunt Mae. I was excited to be going because I didn't remember ever meeting them.

We made the lengthy trek to San Mateo. The three of us kids were loaded into the back of the covered pickup and were made comfortable with lots of pillows, blankets and a cooler full of food and drinks. I had my Walkman, tapes and journal to keep me occupied. Music and my journal were my only constant companions.

I had never seen such a gorgeous home as the one that Uncle Harry and Aunt Mae lived in. There was a glorious, sprawling, green lawn forming the front yard with huge palm trees in the center of it. The facade of their home was a light tan stucco. The double doors that marked it's entry were dark, solid wood and looked almost foreboding in their protective stature.

We walked in, and immediately, I was introduced to the family. Uncle Harry shook my hand and told me it was nice to meet me. He was my father's youngest surviving brother and looked just like him. Aunt Mae hugged me up in her little arms, and I could feel the love emanating from her. I loved Aunt Mae right away.

Mae had moved here from Japan and had married Uncle Harry in the process. She kept a very tidy home, and though I know we were not related through blood, I knew I got my clean streak from her.

As everyone sat in the living room, gossiping about the rest of their family, Aunt Mae snatched me up and took me to her room. She told me stories of how her life was as a young girl and how she had been training to be a geisha when she met Uncle Harry. As she told me the stories, she showed me some of her many special treasures.

Aunt Mae held a shamisen tight to her chest and told me how she had been training to play the three stringed instrument since before she could speak. She plucked lightly at the strings as she reminisced. I sat and stared at her in amazement, soaking up the stories and knowledge she had to share with me.

She took me to the kitchen and showed me how to properly eat and drink without the food touching my lips. She said she saw a dainty beauty in me that she had to nourish. Aunt Mae made me feel special and no one had done that except for Willow, so I felt an immediate bond with her.

When we were finished chatting, it was time for Auntie Mae to serve lunch, so I went outside to smoke a cigarette. Yes, I smoked when I was pregnant. No one told me not to, so honestly, I had no idea it was bad for the baby.

I was laying on the lawn, enjoying the shapes of the clouds in the sky, when Uncle Glen came out to talk to me.

"You know, you don't act like you're pregnant. Are you sure you're pregnant?" He stood over me casting a shadow.

"What do you mean? Of course, I'm pregnant. It's not like I talked the doctor into lying for me." I sat up, butted the cigarette and put my hands over my stomach.

"Well, we'll see about that. Your aunt is going to take you to the doctor on Monday." He said it as if he were about to bust me in a lie.

"That's fine. I should be seeing a doctor anyway to make sure that my baby and myself are healthy. It is the right thing to do, and isn't that why I'm here? So you and Mattie can do the right thing?" Ha, take that asshole.

"Like I said, we'll see..." Glen's words trailed off as he walked away.

How did I always seem to be thrust into these situations? Didn't he realize it was hard enough to be seventeen and pregnant? I didn't need his shit on top of it too. This was my first time being pregnant. It's not like I knew what I was doing.

So, instead of telling me that I shouldn't be smoking, or wearing tight clothes, or whatever... He tells me I didn't act like I was pregnant? Geez, thanks for the advice. (Did the sarcasm come across alright there?)

The drive home seemed longer than the drive there. I wrapped up in a blanket, put my headphones on and zoned out. These next eight months were going to crawl by.

Monday morning arrived and true to Glen's word, Mattie took me to the doctor. I was shown to an examination room, told to pee in a cup and wait.

Mattie sat in the room with me as I waited. She talked to me about how I shouldn't sit with my legs crossed on the table because it was unbecoming of a young woman. Okay, lesson learned. (It's amazing the things we write about and remember as young people.)

The doctor came back into the room, flipped through some papers and said, "Yep, she's pregnant. She needs to start taking prenatal vitamins and see me again in two months."

"SHE is sitting right here, so you can speak directly to me." I cleared my throat and spoke to the doctor.

He looked at me and then back at my aunt, "Make sure she gets these vitamins."

That's it, that's all that was said. I was treated like I wasn't even there and was given no other advice. I was cattle in their eyes.

We drove home without stopping at the pharmacy to pick up the vitamins. I went to my room, put on my headphones and wrote in my journal. Later that evening, I got a plate of food, ate it and went back to my room. School was starting the next week, and I couldn't wait. I was nervous about starting a new school again, especially one that was so large, but it would be a nice change in the monotony.

I woke up, early the next morning, and headed out while everyone was still sleeping. I walked for a ways and then got on a city bus. While watching out the window, I saw a sign at a fast food restaurant that said "help wanted." Pulling on the cord to signal to the driver that I wanted to depart, I stood up and got off the bus.

I walked into the restaurant, asked for an application, sat there to fill it out and then asked to speak to the manager. When he came out, I felt my cheeks blush. He was SO cute.

Diego, the manager, sat at the table with me and went over my application. He said he would like to offer me a job, but because I was still in school, I would need to get parental permission and have some paperwork filled out by the school. I accepted the paperwork from him and told him I would return by Friday with it filled out and ready to work. Diego told me, if I were to do that, he would put me to work the following week. I was stoked.

I did a bit of people watching as I waited on the corner for the bus. It took a little while for it to arrive, and I was happy to see it as I was getting nervous standing there. I had never seen the type of activity, or people, that I had witnessed on that street. There were prostitutes and homeless people everywhere. My small town mentality had a hard time digesting it all.

When I arrived home, Uncle Glen was sitting at the kitchen table drinking a cup of coffee. He had just got home from work and looked so tired.

"Can I fix you some breakfast?" I had to make the offer.

"Sure, where have you been?" Glen looked surprised at my offer.

"Out doing this." I handed him the paperwork and set about to make him pancakes and eggs.

"Wow, Maggie, I'm so proud of you. Really? You went out and got a job?" He sipped at his coffee as he spoke to me.

"Yep, someone needs to take care of this baby, and it looks like that someone is going to have to be me." I flipped the pancakes in the pan. "Would you sign the paperwork please?"

"Sure thing." He signed it right there at the table. "I'll take you to the school when I wake up for them to sign it as well."

"Will someone be there?" I handed him his plate.

"Yep, they're preparing for the new school year, so there should be someone in the main office." He handed me the paperwork.

"Thanks." I don't know if I was more excited about working or that he was proud of me.

"I need to take you in to register you anyway, so we'll do both." He ate his pancakes and eggs with a smile on his face.

"Thank you. After you shower, give me your uniform. I'll make sure it gets washed with the other laundry, and I'll iron it." I sat with him while he ate.

"Thanks, Maggie. You sure aren't what I expected. I'm sorry about the other day in San Mateo. I know this must be hard for you." He stopped and looked at me.

"Thanks, Uncle Glen. It's kind of tough, but there's nothing I can do about it now. It's not like I tried to get pregnant. It was an accident." I held back the tears.

"Well, some accidents are blessings in disguise." He finished eating and put his plate in the sink.

While Glen napped, I did laundry, washed dishes and cleaned up as best I could in the kitchen. Mattie, Rhea and Rob left to go school shopping. Mattie said she would pick up the school supplies I needed. She said she would take me clothing shopping later that week. I didn't care as I really didn't feel like going anyway. I preferred to stay home and play my role as the maid.

When Uncle Glen awoke, he kept true to his word and took me to school to register me and get my paperwork signed, so I could start my job. He then took me to turn in the paperwork to Diego and get my schedule.

"I'm surprised to see you back here so fast." Diego smiled at me when I handed him the signed papers.

"Well, I really need this job. I'm pregnant and need to make some money." Oh shit. Maybe I shouldn't have said that.

"I see. Does your boyfriend work?" Diego thumbed through the papers.

"I'm single and doing this all on my own." Please, please, please still hire   me.
"Oh, okay. Well, I don't have time to write out a schedule for you right now. I need you to go pick up your uniform here." He handed me a card with an address on it. "Be back here at ten in the morning on Saturday for orientation." He smiled again.

"Alright, thank you. I promise, I won't let you down." I accepted the card, shook his hand and walked out.

"Everything okay?" Glen sat in his truck and waited for me.

"Yep, I start Saturday at ten in the morning, but I have to go pick up my uniforms first. Would you take me, please?" I was beyond excited.

"Sure, then we go celebrate." We drove off to do just that.

We picked up my uniforms and then went for a drive. We drove through the most beautiful country settings I had ever seen. There were giant vineyards everywhere, and the grapes hung heavy on the vines. Orchards lined the sides of the roads and were brightly dotted with colorful fruits. Small fruit stands were scattered along the gravel throughway, and we stopped at each of them to sample their wares and buy a bit to snack on. The fresh cherries were my favorite.

With our fingers and lips stained red from the cherries, we drove on and on just laughing, talking and telling stories. It was almost nightfall when we turned around to head home. I was saddened to see the day come to an end.

When we arrived, we found a note from Aunt Mattie saying she had taken the kids out to eat because she had no idea where we were, or what we were doing. We just shrugged it off. That day started a bond between us that I would cherish my entire life. Oh, how I loved that man.

Saturday morning, I got up early and got dressed for work. I tied my hair into a bun on the back of my head, did some simple make-up and put on my freshly washed and ironed uniform. Even though it was just a fast food restaurant, I was excited to go to work. It was my first real job other than helping the neighboring farmers bring in their hay and babysitting for friends of the family.

Uncle Glen came home from work, we had breakfast together, and he drove me to my first day on the job. He handed me ten dollars for lunch, told me to call him when I was finished because he wanted to pick me up and hear all about my first day.

I walked in the side door, went up to the counter and ordered a hot cocoa. I was about fifteen minutes early, so I thought I would sit out in the lobby and observe things for a bit. I had barely sat down when Diego approached me.

"Hi, Maggie, nice to see you again. May I sit down?" Oh, that smile of his.

"Of course, I thought I would come in a little early and kind of scope things out. I hope that's okay." A shy smile crossed my face.

"It's more than okay. It shows initiative, and I like that." He sat down across from me in the booth.

We chatted for a while about the weather, how long I had lived in

California and what I would be doing there. I found out I was hired as a cashier, and I loved the idea of it. I really didn't want to be a cook there... Too much meat. I enjoyed talking to and interacting with people, so being a cashier was perfect.

"Well, welcome aboard, Maggie. Let's get you started, shall we?" Diego reached across the table and touched my hand.

"Sure." I slowly pulled my hand back and followed him to the front counter.

After he showed me around and explained how things worked, I was put directly to work. It was easy enough. I just had to remember to smile, be courteous and up-sell, "Would you like fries with that?"

I found something to enjoy in every interaction with the customers. I had to hold in my laughter when extremely obese people would come in, order four chicken sandwiches with fries and an extra-large diet coke, like that was gonna help. There were homeless people that would come in with a fist full of change to buy their first meal of the day. They would smile gratefully at me when I waved off their change, and I reached into my pocket to pay for their meal. My favorite part though, were the children that were usually very sweet, and would wait with great anticipation to see what toy they got with their little meals.

I worked for six hours and chatted with Diego on my breaks. My feet and back hurt, I smelled like french fries and greasy burgers, but it was amazing. I absolutely loved my job.

I called Uncle Glen, and he picked me up after work. He asked about my day, and I told him all about it. He warned me against paying for the meals of the homeless people. He said most of the people, around there, were homeless because they chose to be out of drug addiction. It didn't matter to me though. After all, we were all human and deserved to be treated with respect and compassion.

When we got home, I cleaned the bathtub, grabbed my pajamas and took a long, hot bath. It was so nice to just relax amongst the bubbles with my music playing in my ears.

When I finished, I rinsed out the tub and did a load of laundry. I found a note on my bed from Aunt Mattie saying she wanted to take me shopping for clothes the next afternoon because school started on Monday. I worked Sunday afternoon but hoped she could take me in the morning.

"Aunt Mattie, I work tomorrow afternoon, so can we go shopping tomorrow morning?" I approached her in the kitchen.

"I'm sorry, Maggie, I have plans tomorrow morning. Maybe we can go Monday after school. I'll let you know." She didn't even look up at me.

"Oh, well, that's okay. I have enough clothes for now. I get paid a week from Friday and will just pick up whatever I need then." I went out to the garage to switch over my laundry from the washer to the dryer. I didn't understand the sudden change in Mattie's attitude toward me, but I knew I had to accept it because it seemed like there was no changing it. Maybe she was just having a hard time with something personal in her life. All I could do was wait and see.

The next day at work was pretty much like the first. Diego wasn't working, but he came in to have lunch with me anyway. He said he just wanted to check on his new favorite employee. It made me feel special. I had the biggest crush on him, and I think he was crushin' right back.

Diego gave me a ride home after work and asked me if I would like to go out sometime. He said it was against company policy, but it would be okay if we kept it a secret. I told him it would be fun, and I was good at keeping secrets.

It was Monday morning, and my heart felt like it was leaping out of my chest. As I said before, I was nervous but excited about starting school. I had only witnessed schools, as large as this one, on television and couldn't wait to experience it.

I rode to school with Mattie, Rhea and Rob. Mattie was a music teacher there and also helped with the drama classes when she could. We dropped Rhea off at her first day of college classes on our way to school. Today was Rob's first day at the high school, as well. He was a freshman and seemed to be almost as nervous as I was.

I found my way to my first class, second class and so on. It was now lunch time, so I made my way to the cafeteria. Mmm, the smell of nachos hung in the air, so I made my way to the nacho bar. I piled my plate with chips, cheese and hot peppers. The cravings made it hard to be vegan while I was pregnant, so I stuck to vegetarian.

I looked around but didn't see any faces I recognized from class, so I just sat at the first empty table I could find. This was nothing like the smaller schools I had attended. No one sought me out or sat to ask me questions. I sat alone in a sea of unfamiliar faces. I didn't mind it though. It was cool to sit there and just people watch. There were students singing and dancing on top of tables. Cheerleaders bounced around in their uniforms and practiced their cheers. Jocks sat at tables together, punching each other in the arms and laughing loudly, and the stoners huddled in the darkest corners. I saw Rob sitting with a group of his friends, but I thought it best not to approach him.

Lunch was over, so I went to my next class. The health class was in an outer building that sat behind the school. There were about twenty students in there, all of them girls.

"Why is it just girls in here?" I asked one of the girls sitting by the door.

"We're all pregnant." Really? I walked out and went to the library. There was no way I was attending that class and later made changes to my schedule to avoid it.

My final class of the day was art. It was also housed in an outer building behind the school. There were about forty students all together, and they sat in groups of four around tables. I found an empty table and sat down.

The teacher was late getting to class and introduced himself as he walked through the door. He told us that he ran his class differently than any other teacher, and he didn't care what we did just so we were creating. We were each assigned a small cubicle and told to put our names on it. He then unlocked and opened the doors to the supply cabinets and told us to have at it.

I waited until all the students gathered their supplies and sat back down before I approached the cabinets. I surveyed what was left and chose to make a plaster sculpture. Grabbing a handful of newspaper, I sat back down at my table and began to carefully tear the paper into different sized strips. I was very methodical in my creativity.

I had barely finished tearing the paper when the final bell rang. Gathering up the pieces of torn newspaper, I placed them into the cubicle that was assigned to me and headed out of class.

Mattie told me she was going to have to stay after school, so I walked home alone. I cut across a field and through a giant culvert. There were kids in there smoking cigarettes and weed. One of the guys approached me and asked if I wanted to get stoned. I told him no thanks because I was pregnant, but I stayed to smoke a cigarette and talk to him. I had never smoked weed before, and I wasn't going to start now.

They were a fun group of guys, and I recognized a couple of them from art class. I found out they met there every day. I told them I would meet them there and hang out when I could, waved goodbye and finished walking home.

I worked that afternoon as well, but because it was a school night, I was only allowed to work until nine at night. When I was finished with work, Diego was there and offered to drive me home. He was as sweet as he was cute.

This schedule went on for the rest of the week. I had met the guys in the culvert, every day, for lunch and after school. I also completed the wire base of my sculpture in art class and was going to start wrapping it in newspaper and plaster when we had class on Monday. I had made a set of hands holding a heart. I wanted to sit it next to my baby's cradle eventually, so that my baby always knew how much I loved it. My art teacher told me he was impressed with my skills and creativity.

It was now the weekend, and I didn't have to work. I was tired and needed the break, so I didn't mind at all. Diego called, to see if I could go out, and Mattie said it was fine as long as I was home by ten.

Diego was four years older than me, so he had graduated high school a few years ago. He took me to his former school to watch a football game. He bought me popcorn and a diet soda. We sat in the bleachers, cheering on his old school, even though they were playing against my current one. I felt a little like a traitor, but I didn't really care. After all, I had only been attending it for a week.

After the game, we went for a drive around the city, so he could show me around. Lodi was much larger than I had remembered. We stopped in at a bowling alley so he could have a beer. I had another diet soda and we talked until nearly ten. Oh shit. I had to get home. I used the pay phone (yes, the pay phone.) at the bowling alley to call home and let them know I might be a little late. Uncle Glen answered, told me it was fine and to be home by 10:30. I thanked him and hung up.

Diego drove me right home, and we sat outside talking in his car until it was time for me to go in. He kissed me on my cheek and said goodnight. I got out of his car, watched as he pulled away and then pulled into a driveway two houses down from where I lived.

"What are you doing?" I shouted down the street.

"Just saying hello to my mom before I head back to my place." He laughed as he yelled back his answer.

Wow... His mom lived two houses down from me? This was awesome. I walked into the house as if I were walking on clouds. Uncle Glen was sitting at the kitchen table and asked me about my date. I told him all about it, kissed him on the cheek, went to write in my journal and tuck myself into bed.

Willow and Jason filled my every thought that night. I missed them terribly, but I realized that I may never see them again. I mean, why would I leave California? I had a job I loved, was doing fine in school, had plans to go to college and had just been out on the most amazing date, with the most amazing guy ever. Sorry guys... Don't miss me too much.

CHAPTER NINE

It was December. I was over six months pregnant and really starting to show. My belly was getting round, and it was beginning to cause issues at school. For whatever reason, they did not like pregnant teens attending school there once they started showing. I was told I would be transferred to a school for unwed, teen mothers. Fuck. I really liked the teachers and the environment at my school. I just didn't see the point in changing to a different one, but I didn't make the rules, so I had no other choice. I was to switch schools after Christmas break.

I finished my last two weeks of school. On my last day, I turned in my books and said goodbye to my teachers. Aunt Mattie met me at the main office to take me out of classes and to get my transcripts for the next school. We were going to enroll me in the new school after Christmas break.

I hadn't gotten very close to many of the students at school, except for the group of boys that hung out in the culvert. On my way home, I stopped in to tell them about my transferring schools. They were sad to hear I wouldn't be coming around anymore, but they understood and wished me well.

During the first few days of Christmas break, I busied myself cleaning up the living room and setting up the Christmas tree along with the other decorations. I hadn't decorated the tree yet. I always thought that was something that should be done as a family.

I took the outdoor lights and decorations outside, set them up in the yard and hung the lights around the front porch. There was no snow in Lodi, so I used sheets of white batting to cover the small yard to give it the appearance of snow. I then set out a small sleigh with reindeer and placed Santa next to it.

I waited patiently for everyone to get home, but Rhea and Rob had no interest in helping me to decorate the tree, so I waited for Aunt Mattie and Uncle Glen. I was happy when they came home and agreed to help. We turned on some Christmas music and started right away.

Aunt Mattie's attitude with me had changed quite a bit, and we were all getting along much better. Whatever had been going on in her personal world seemed to be resolved, and she was back to the fun loving and sweet woman I had known my entire life. She couldn't walk past me without rubbing my tummy. I guess it was good luck or something.

Aunt Mattie made hot cocoa with peppermint sticks in it for the three of us while Uncle Glen and I took out the ornaments. We sipped at our hot cocoa and hung the ornaments until we finished decorating the tree. When we finished, we stepped back to admire it. The tree was beautiful. We had decorated it with lots of lights and all of the decorations they had collected over the years.

I started to pick up the storage boxes from the decorations when Aunt Mattie pulled a small, square box from her purse, handed it to me and asked me to open it.

Inside, was a stunning sterling silver ornament. It had my name and the year etched into it. It was a little girl, on her knees, praying in front of a Christmas tree. I clutched it to my heart, started crying and thanked her for it. Uncle Glen cleared a spot on the front of the tree, and I hung it there. I was so happy; I couldn't stop crying.

I went to sleep that night feeling like I was in the right place at the right time. As much as I needed them to take care of me and help me along, they needed me too. Maybe that was the reason I ended up there... Maybe.

The next morning, Aunt Mattie and I went shopping for gifts for the family. It was nice to have my own money for once. I bought gifts for my aunt, uncle and cousins, brought them home and wrapped them. I knew what I wanted to get for Diego, but I wasn't going to find it at a big box store, so I asked Uncle Glen to take me to a sporting goods store that afternoon. He said he would.

Diego was a Chicago Bears fan, and I wanted to get him a stadium jacket. I didn't hold it against him, but how the hell could he like the Bears when we lived in California? I had been a Forty Niners fan since I could remember. Football was a big thing to both of us, so I thought it would be the perfect gift. I found what I was looking for, purchased it and left.

I asked if I could invite Diego for Christmas dinner, and they said it would be fine. I called him right away to ask him. He had met my aunt and uncle already, and he gladly accepted the invitation. He said his mom had invited me as well, so we made plans to spend time with both families. Aunt Mattie and Uncle Glen were fine with that. I think they knew that Diego and I were getting pretty serious.

Christmas Day arrived, and we had dinner with my family. After dinner, we all exchanged gifts around the tree. My aunt and uncle had even gotten a gift for Diego. They had picked up a nice set of new seat covers for his car. I was as surprised as he was.

I handed Diego his gift from me and watched as he opened it. His eyes lit up, and a huge smile crossed his face as he pulled the jacket from its box. He stood up, tried it on right away and then hugged me with the biggest hug I had ever gotten from him. I couldn't help but to giggle; I was so happy.

Everyone finished exchanging gifts and thanking one another. Diego didn't give me anything, but he had picked up a really nice coffee maker for my aunt and uncle and sweatshirts for my cousins. Oh well, it wasn't about the gifts. I just figured he had run out of money, and I was happy that he was able to get gifts for my family.

After we helped clean up the mess from the wrapping paper, we went to Diego's mom's house. I sat on the couch with Juanita, his mom, and talked to her and his two little brothers while his step-dad and him went outside for something. I had a hard time keeping up with all the questions. This was the first time I had met any of his family.

"How's it going in here?" Diego and his step-dad, Carlos, came in from outside.

"We love her Diego. She's a keeper." Juanita stood up and hugged Diego.

"That's good to hear, Mama." Diego sat on the couch next to me and kissed me on my cheek. He then looked at me, smiled and dropped to his knee on the floor in front of me.

"Maggie, I believe in fate. Fate brought you back to California; fate brought you into my restaurant, and fate is the reason we are here. I love you, and I want to spend the rest of my life with you. I cannot ask you to marry me yet, because you are not eighteen, and I must get permission from your uncle first, but will you please, accept my promise ring as a token of our great love and intention to be man and wife someday?" He pulled a small box from his pocket, opened it and showed me the tiniest diamond ring.

"Of course, Diego, I love you so much." I dropped to the floor with him, hugged, kissed him and let him put the ring on my finger. It fit perfectly.

And just then, at the very moment he put the ring on my finger, I felt my baby kick for the first time. "Oh my God. I just felt her kick."

"Really?" Diego put his hands on my stomach. "How do you know she's a she?" She kicked at his hand.

"I just know." I put my hand over his, and we felt her kicking together.

Diego leaned in and kissed me again. It was the perfect moment in time. Our little family was almost whole.

Diego's family congratulated us, and we ate again. It was the most amazing day ever, and I didn't want it to end, though I knew it had to. When we finished eating, I helped to clean up, and Diego walked me home.

He came in with me to talk to my aunt and uncle about marrying me. They told him that it was too soon to discuss this, and that they would talk to him about it once I graduated from high school. Okay, not what we wanted to hear, but we could be patient.

When Christmas break was over, I started classes at the school for unwed mothers. It wasn't quite what I had expected, and I became fast friends with a lot of the girls that attended there. After all, we were all in the same boat just trying to stay afloat.

It wasn't as structured as a regular high school, and we spent much of our day in parenting classes. We learned different coping mechanisms, how to change diapers and make bottles. They taught us everything I should have been taught from the beginning. I stopped smoking that first day. It was a little tough, but every time I craved a cigarette, I just touched my belly and knew that it was for the most fantastic reason ever.

Diego and I spent as much time together as we could. We went to his grandparents house almost every weekend, had dinner with them and played cards. They taught me how to play a game called "Back Alley." It was a lot like spades except the trump card changed with every hand. You started with thirteen cards, eventually played down to just one and then back up again to thirteen. There were twenty six hands played in every game. Grandma Garcia and I kicked Grandpa's and Diego's butts quite often.

Grandma made sure I learned how to cook for Diego. They were a proud Mexican family and wanted to pass on their traditions. I was honored they took me in and were willing to teach me.

I spent a lot of time in the kitchen, with Grandma Garcia, learning how to cook authentic Mexican food. She often said love was the best ingredient to cook with. I loved that old woman. The first thing she taught me how to make was enchiladas. It was my favorite, so I loved learning how to make them.

We even made our tortillas from scratch. We cooked the seasoned meat, and while it was simmering, we chopped up bell peppers and onions to saute them on the stove top. She taught me how to make her secret red sauce, and to this day, I have never shared that recipe with anyone. She would beat me where I stood if I ever even thought about sharing it without her permission.

I was still working but only part time. I spent much of my time preparing for the arrival of my baby. I sewed and crocheted blankets, hats and little booties. I kept them all in neutral colors even though I was convinced I was having a girl.

Aunt Mattie took me shopping for some of the bigger things I was going to need, and we stored them out in the garage. Uncle Glen had cleaned up the garage, so there was now space to store my belongings.

They talked to me about getting my own place and how expensive it was going to be. They said I could stay with them as long as I needed. I didn't want to tell them that Diego and I had already decided to move in together once I turned eighteen. That discussion was better suited for another day.

The months seemed to fly by. I was now almost eight months pregnant. A friend of ours from work, Maria, wanted to throw me a baby shower, and I was touched at the idea. Aunt Mattie said she would host one after the baby was born, so our friends could throw one now. I thought that was a fair compromise.

Maria came over, and she and I spent the afternoon planning the baby shower. We were going to have it at the bar, that Maria's husband worked at, and invite all of our friends from work. Since it was February we decided to have it on Valentine's day.

I went to school that week and invited all of the girls from my class to the shower. We were all excited because I was the next one due. I'm not going to lie; I was nervous as hell.

The weekend was here, and the shower was off to a great start. Over fifty women showed up, and each of them brought a gift. We played games, ate food and took turns telling stories of funny child rearing moments. I must admit, a couple of the stories had me a bit worried. I swore, in my head, I would never let those things happen to my child. Like really, who lets a toddler get into the chemicals stored under a sink, has to rush them to a hospital and then laughs about it?

I was sitting at a table, at the front of the room, with Maria and a couple of Diego's cousins when the urge to pee hit me. I had just ordered my fourth iced tea, so I thought I should go before it got there. I got up to go to the bathroom, passed out and hit the floor. I woke up in a booth with Maria putting cold towels on my head.

"What happened?" I was pretty dazed.

"You passed out drunk." Maria looked very concerned.

"What? No way, I didn't touch a drop of alcohol." What?

"Well, what were you drinking then?" Maria was still holding the cold towel on my head as I sat up.

"I ordered iced teas. There is NO WAY I would drink being pregnant." I did not order booze of any kind, and anyway, I was too young to legally drink.

Maria talked to one of the servers and found out that she had been bringing me Long Island Iced Teas.

I was fuming. How dare she risk the life of my baby because she couldn't get an order right. I told everyone the party was over and thanked them for coming. Maria called my uncle to pick me up.

I called my doctor the moment I got home. I had started seeing a new doctor at the community clinic because I didn't like the one that Aunt Mattie had taken me to. My doctor was not there because it was the weekend, but I was told by the answering service to come in Monday morning, and that is exactly what I did.

Diego took me to my appointment. He was so involved in my pregnancy that people actually thought he was the baby's father, and I never corrected them. I kind of wished he had been.

I was brought back to an examination room and all of the typical procedures were done before the doctor came in. She brought an ultrasound machine with her. I was scared because there was usually a technician that did this... Not the doctor herself. She greased up my belly and started the exam.

"Do you see that Miss Reeds? That's your baby girl. She is healthy and almost ready to be born." The doctor pointed to the screen and told us what we were seeing.

Diego held my hand, and when I looked up at him I saw tears flowing down his cheeks. I squeezed his hand.

"I told you so, Sweetheart. I knew she was a girl." Tears burst out of my eyes as I spoke.

"I know, Babydoll... I know. She is going to be just as beautiful as her mama too." He squeezed my hand a bit tighter and stared at the screen.

We sat there for a moment, listening to her heartbeat and watching the picture ,of her, on the screen. She was perfect and was soon to be in our arms.

On our way home, I asked Diego if he wanted to be put down as the baby's father on the birth certificate. He pulled the car over, and I got scared.

"Are you serious? I would love nothing more." He reached over and hugged me. I cried happy tears on his shoulder. I knew I had to talk to Jason and Willow.

When I got home, I called Willow and told her about the appointment. She said that somehow she also had known I was going to have a baby girl, had been preparing some things for her and would send them out soon.

I talked to Willow, about Diego, and told her how good of a man he was. She was glad to hear I had a supportive man in my life and wished us the best. That's when I told her I was going to put Diego on the birth certificate as the baby's father. She was shocked, but she told me she understood, though she wanted me to be the one to tell Jason. She put him on the phone, and I explained the same thing to him. He agreed it would be for the best but asked that I still keep him updated about our daughter. I told him I would never keep him away from her, and he could see her whenever he wanted to. Before hanging up, I thanked them both for being so understanding and told them I loved them both very much.

It was now the weekend, and neither Diego nor I were working, so I went over to his place for a while. I needed to get out of the house, and this was perfect. Aunt Mattie told me to be home before midnight... No problem.

Diego and I were sitting on his bed watching a movie. We hadn't had sex yet. I know, I know... Shocking. Diego respected my decision, and I just hadn't been ready for it. That is, until the pregnancy hormones kicked in. I was due in a few weeks, and my hormones were raging out of control.

I told Diego about my little issue. He smiled and kissed me. As he pulled away, he sat up higher on the bed and looked at me.

"Look, Maggie, I love you with all my heart, but I would rather wait until after you have the baby and recover." He had a very serious look on his face.

"What? Why? Is it because I'm fat and ugly?" I looked at him and started crying... Stupid pregnancy hormones.

"No, Babydoll, it's because I love you with all my heart, and I don't want to see you make a decision, that you might regret later, because of how you are feeling right now with your hormone surge. I've been reading a lot about this, and I understand what is happening to your body." He pulled me onto his chest and stroked my hair as I cried.

"Really?" I looked up at him, and he kissed my nose.

"Yes, really. I promise you that is the only reason. Now, quit being silly, and remember I love you." He kissed me on my nose again. We laid there and finished watching the movie together before he took me home.

Aunt Mattie was surprised to see me home so early. She and I talked for a bit before I went to sleep. I couldn't stay up as late as before. I was getting more and more tired as my pregnancy progressed.

It was Monday morning, and I had an appointment with my doctor. Diego, once again, took me to my appointment and came in with me. We sat in the waiting room until we were called back.

The doctor performed the examination and said it was now time for me to stop working. My cervix was beginning to thin, and she wanted me off my feet until it was time to deliver.

Diego and I went to the restaurant, after the appointment, and explained to the owner what the doctor had said. He completely understood and told me my job would be waiting for me when I was ready to return. He also said he would give Diego as many hours as he could to help make up for the loss of my income. He was such a sweet guy and even overlooked the fact that Diego and I were dating.

We decided to spend the afternoon with Diego's grandparents. I called home to make sure it was okay, and Aunt Mattie said it was no problem. She just asked that I was home by midnight. I was not in school, at the moment, because I was so close to giving birth. Diego's grandparents lived only a few blocks away, so Aunt Mattie knew exactly where I was.

We arrived at their home and walked in the front door. As usual, Grandma was in the kitchen cooking, and Grandpa was in his recliner watching television. We said hello, and I kissed Grandpa on the cheek before I went into the kitchen to help Grandma prepare dinner.

The familiar smell of enchiladas filled the air. I was excited and hungry. I think Grandma Garcia liked me being pregnant because she loved feeding people, and I always had an appetite.

"Hola Abuelita. (Hello Grandma.)" I greeted Grandma as I entered the kitchen.

"Hola mi nieta. (Hello my grand daughter.)" Grandma Garcia kissed me on the cheek and rubbed my belly. "You're getting bigger every day mi nieta. Almost time, si?"

"Si Abuelita. We went to the doctor today, and she said my cervix was thinning and for me to stay off my feet until it was time." I stirred the enchilada sauce and tasted it. YUMMY!

"What are you doing then mi nieta? Sit... SIT!" Grandma pulled out a chair and helped me to sit down in the kitchen. I was so fat that I had a hard time moving on my own sometimes.

She put the bowls of seasoned chicken and cheese in front of me. As she fried the corn tortillas, she would stack them on a plate and sit them in front of me to roll the enchiladas.

I layered the chicken with the onions, bell peppers and shredded cheese across the tortillas. I then rolled them up and sat them in a deep baking dish. When I finished filling the dishes, she would cover the filled pans with sauce and put them in the oven to bake. Grandma knew I didn't eat meat, and though she didn't understand it, she always let me make some enchiladas with just the bell peppers, onions and cheese for myself.

We made re-fried beans and Spanish rice to go with the meal as well. No one cooked like Grandma did, and I felt honored to be able to help her in her kitchen. She chased away anyone else that dared to enter when she was cooking.

Tia (Aunt) Carmen set the table for the family, and we all sat around the table with Grandpa and Grandma at the heads of it. Grandma brought the food out to the loud clapping, shouts of gratitude and praise from her family. It was the same thing every week, and since we could not make it there over the weekend they had postponed it until today.

We ate as a family and listened intently to the stories Grandpa told us. He spoke of the old ways in Mexico and how they lived without electricity or running water. He talked to us of the grand gardens they grew to feed their family and of the struggle and sacrifice it took to move to the United States to become citizens. They were the same stories every week, but we didn't mind. We loved, well at least I loved, hearing the stories.

After dinner, we sat in the living room for a bit. I told Grandma I was just too tired to play cards and thought it best that I go home to sleep. She asked me to wait a minute and went back to her bedroom.

She came out holding a white box and sat it on my lap. I looked up at her and asked what it was.

"Open it mi nieta. It is a gift for the baby." She waved her hands at me to instruct me to open it quickly.

I pulled the silver, silk ribbon from the box and lifted the lid. Pushing aside the tissue paper, I saw what was inside, and my breath caught in my throat as tears sprung to my eyes. It was a christening gown, and not just any gown, but the one that each of her children had worn when they were baptized. She had made it, when they lived in Mexico, from material she took from her own wedding gown. It was hand beaded and absolutely stunning. I carefully lifted it from the box and looked at it. She had shown me this gown when I first told her I was pregnant.

After placing the gown back in the box, I stood up, hugged Grandma to me tightly and thanked her over and over for the beautiful gift. She patted me on the back, told me I was part of the family, and she was happy to pass it down to me. She said she expected I do the same for my daughter.

We said goodnight and promised to come back and visit that weekend. I picked up the box, and we headed out to the car. Diego wanted to stop by his church before he took me home, so we headed toward Main Street and St. Mary's Catholic church.

After stopping at the four way stop on the corner, Diego looked both ways and didn't see anyone coming, so he started to pull out onto Main Street. I saw bright lights approaching us at a very fast speed. Before I could say a word, I heard the crunching of metal as an oncoming car slammed into the passenger side.

The sight of swirling red and blue lights hurt my eyes as I opened them. I heard someone say something about blood pressure before I passed out again.

I woke the next morning to the brightest, white light I had ever seen. Sitting up with a start I realized I was in a hospital bed. Immediately I reached to my stomach. It was no longer round with life. WHERE WAS MY BABY?

Aunt Mattie and Diego sat at the side of my bed. Diego had a cast on his right arm. I looked at them and waited for the news. Neither of them spoke but instead looked at me with tears in their eyes.

"Where's my baby? What happened?" I cried out to them.

"You were in a car accident. You were hit by a drunk driver. Your baby is gone." Aunt Mattie took my hand as Diego got up, came to the other side of the bed and took my other hand.

Gone... I pulled away from them and laid down in tears, holding my stomach and feeling where I had once carried her life inside me. Gone... Oh, how I despised that word. Gone... She was gone...

What do I even write from there? The memory of the time that she grew inside of me still weighs heavy on my heart. It is an experience I shall never forget... Nor do I ever want to.

I fell into a deep depression, so Mattie took care of all of the arrangements. There was no funeral, no burial and no mention of her again.

I spent the next two months in bed and found solace in the darkened shadows of my room. I only got out of bed to tend to my most primitive of needs. She was gone...

I named my daughter Destiny... She at least deserved a name.

CHAPTER TEN

It was now early spring, and life was moving along at a snail's pace. I didn't mind the slowness of it though because I wasn't ready to face life head on anyway. It was hard enough to keep up with school and work.

The weekend of my eighteenth birthday was here, and Diego told me he had a surprise for me. He asked me to pack an overnight bag and to be ready at seven. We had been dating for about eight months and had yet to have sex. I was pretty sure this would be the weekend.

I told my aunt and uncle that I was staying at a friend's house from school and would be home Sunday morning. They were disappointed I would not be home for my birthday but had made no plans because I was still emotionally recuperating from the loss of Destiny, so it didn't really matter. They were just happy I was starting to get out again and asked that I check in from time to time. I agreed and headed out.

I walked down the block to Diego's mom's driveway where he was parked, threw my bag in the back seat, got in and kissed him hello. He wore a smile that cut across his face. He kissed me back and we left.

We drove south and eventually pulled into the parking lot of a little, out of the way hotel. It was beautifully quaint and had colorful lounge chairs outside of each of the hotel room doors.

Diego went inside to check us in and soon returned with the key. I smiled, got out of the car, grabbed my bag and followed him. After unlocking the door, he turned to me, grabbed me up in his arms and kissed me long and deep. I actually swooned.

We walked in and I noticed there were two beds. Hmm... Interesting. Maybe all the rooms were like this? I sat my bag on the top of the dresser and looked around. It was a very common room with a stack of towels on a shelf and sample size toiletries in a basket on the bathroom counter near the sink. There was a television on the dresser, at the end of the beds, with a nightstand between them.

I sat down on the bed closest to the window and watched as Diego put our things into the dresser. He was so sweet. I giggled to myself at his thoughtful ways.

He walked over and sat on the bed next to me. Taking my hand in his, he looked at me and kissed me again. As he pulled away from me, he lowered himself off the bed to his knee on the floor.

"Maggie, Will you marry me?" Diego pulled a ring out of his pocket and showed it to me.

I was in shock. Was this really happening? I knew we had planned to get married, but I didn't think he was going to propose right now. I rubbed my eyes and looked at him, at the ring and started to cry.

"Yes, of course I will marry you!" He put the ring on my finger, and we kissed again.

"Maggie? I know you still hurt from the loss of our baby, but there will be others. We can start a family of our own as soon as we are married." He kissed me again.

"I would rather not talk about this right now, Diego, please?" I wasn't ready to have this discussion with him or anyone.

I didn't want to sit in the hotel room, so we walked around town hand in hand, stopping to look in the windows of the small shops that lined the streets. It was a beautiful little town, and we truly enjoyed ourselves. I was getting hungry, so we looked for a restaurant and stopped to eat dinner.

We walked back to the hotel and crawled into bed to watch a movie. It was kind of our thing, and we did it every chance we got. I rested my head on his chest as we lay there.

At exactly midnight, Diego leaned down, whispered "Happy birthday, Babydoll" and kissed me sweetly on the lips. We fell asleep, wrapped in each others arms.

We spent the entire next day sightseeing. Diego took me to see some of the underground caverns, and we took a tour of them. They were incredible. There were stalagmites and stalactites everywhere. The tour guide asked that none of us touch them, but Diego managed to snap one off for me as a souvenir.

On the way back to the hotel, we picked up a pizza and decided to just hang out in our room again. Was tonight going to be the night that we finally made love?

When we arrived, we ate our pizza and decided to watch a movie. I told Diego that I wanted to shower before we settled in for the evening. I grabbed my pajamas, a white oversized t-shirt with matching cotton panties, and headed directly to the bathroom.

Diego was already in bed watching television when I returned. I noticed the blankets, on the bed by the window, had been turned down and the pillows set up against the headboard.

"What's this?" I pointed to the second bed.

"I got your bed ready for you." He smiled that sweet smile of his.

"Oh, you don't want to sleep next to me?" I was a bit confused.

"I would love nothing more than to sleep next to you, but I didn't want to be presumptuous." Again... Sweetest guy ever.

"I'm just going to call home and check in real quick." I picked up the phone and put my finger to my lips to signal to Diego to be quiet. "Hi, Auntie, just calling to check in."

"Hey, Maggie, can I speak to the parents there please?" Mattie asked as if she knew something was up.

"Um, they're sleeping." Shit.

"Look, Maggie, I read your journal. I know you're spending the weekend with Diego. You need to come home this instant." Mattie was upset.

"How dare you read my personal things." I was furious.

"It's my right as your parent. Now, come home." She wasn't budging.

"Look, Mattie, you're not my parent and never will be. I'm eighteen years old and I don't have to listen to you anymore. Keep your hands and eyes out of my personal belongings. I'll see you when I get home tomorrow." I hung up.

I explained to Diego what happened, but I wasn't going to let it ruin our night. I crawled into bed, next to him, to watch another movie, hoping he would make a move, but instead I fell asleep on his chest. We slept like that all night long. It was peacefully sweet, and I wouldn't have changed a bit of it.

I awoke the next morning to breakfast in bed. Diego had gone to the store and picked up doughnuts, fresh fruit and orange juice. He had it all sitting on the bedside table with a single rose in a glass of water.

"Happy birthday, Babydoll. How'd ya sleep?" He stroked my hair and smiled at me as he woke me from my slumber.

"Oh... Thank you, but it's not my birthday anymore. I slept very peacefully." I sipped at the orange juice.

"Good, that's what I wanted to hear. And I know it's not you're actual birthday, but I thought we would celebrate all weekend long." He ate a doughnut and handed me a banana.

We finished our breakfast, cleaned up, dressed, packed and left. We took the back roads home, so we could enjoy the scenery once again.

A couple of hours later, we pulled up in front of my house. What the hell was that? There were boxes stacked up on the front porch.

I got out of the car, walked up to the house and saw my name on each of the boxes. There was a note taped to the front of one of them.

"Maggie,

You wanted to talk to me like an adult and pretend to be one? Go pretend. You are no longer welcome in our home. Good luck in your future.

~Mattie"

Wow... Really? Well, I guess that's what I get for being so rude, but she still had no right going through my things, and she definitely had no right to read my journal. What was I going to do now? I barely made enough money to pay my own way. Well, shit.

I showed Diego the note. He was just as shocked as I was but didn't really show it. He walked up to the porch and started packing my belongings into his car.

"What are you doing?" I watched him as he put the first of my things into the trunk.

"I'm moving you in with me." He finished loading my things into his car, opened the car door for me and we were off.

Yep, it happened just like that. There was no discussion and no time to think. I just moved in with him. We had planned to do it anyway, might as well just do it.

Our first night of living together felt a bit awkward. As I said before, we had been dating for several months but had not had sex yet. I knew tonight would be the night.

I readied myself in the bathroom and dressed in my usual night clothes. I put a robe on over my pajamas and walked into our bedroom.

Diego was waiting on our bed. He had already showered and was laying there watching television. When he saw me, he turned it off and smiled.

"Do you know how beautiful you are, Maggie?" He pulled back the blankets to invite me into bed.

"No, but I like hearing it." I took off my robe and joined him.

I laid on my back against the pillows and breathed in deeply. So... This was it; this was my new life.

Diego rolled onto his side and looked at me smiling. "Are you alright?" He asked gently.

"Of course, I'm just a bit nervous." I looked at my hands.

"No need to be nervous. We love each other, and this is what people in love do." He reached to touch my hands.

He lifted my left hand to his lips and began to kiss my fingers. He looked into my eyes with each kiss. I smiled and felt the nerves leave my body as he worked his way up my arm and across my neck. His lips were warm and soft against my skin, and his breath sent chills through my body. We undressed each other under the heaviness of the blankets.

Very slowly and gently, Diego moved his body closer to mine. He began to kiss my lips as he spoke to me in a tender and loving voice. "Is this alright?" He whispered the words against my lips.

"Yes..." I breathed the word out.

His hands moved over my body caressing me as they traveled. His touches were intimate and delicate. It felt as though he were touching the energy that formed me and not my skin itself.

Diego lifted himself over me and placed himself between my legs. He kissed his way over my full breasts, stomach and down my thighs to my feet. As he moved his way back up my body, I felt him enter me.

My head rolled back with a pleasurable sensation, and my breath caught in my throat as he moved in and out of me. I was feeling things I had never felt before. I lifted my body to meet his. There were tingles in my most intimate of places, and I felt them building. What was this? What was happening? I didn't care; I just wanted it to happen.

I screamed out in pleasure and pulled him to my lips. We kissed deep and passionate kisses. He bit my lip and then my neck. My legs trembled, and the lower part of my body pulsated with pleasure. I had my first orgasm.

He finished just after I climaxed and kissed me again and again. Moving slowly off me, he laid on his side and leaned on his elbow looking at me, smiling.

"I've never felt that before." I was crying as I told him what happened.

"Please, don't cry." He wiped the tears from my cheeks.

"I love you, Diego." I rolled onto my side and laid on his chest listening to his heartbeat.

"And I love you, Maggie." He stroked my hair until I fell asleep.

By the time I woke up, Diego was already at work. I didn't have to work, so I took the city bus to school and signed myself out. I knew I would not be able to finish school and work full time too. I felt like I didn't have a choice right now but thought, once we got settled, I would go to night school to finish my high school education.

When I got home, I saw Diego sitting on the front porch. His head was in his hands and he was staring at the sidewalk.

"Hi, you're home early. What's up?" I sat next to him on the porch, pulled one of his hands away from his head and held it.

"Something horrible happened today. When I got to work, there were fire trucks everywhere. The restaurant burned down." He looked at me with panic on his face.

"Was anyone hurt?" I couldn't believe it.

"No, luckily it happened sometime after it was closed. They don't know what caused it, but they're investigating now." He pulled his hand away from mine.

"Well fuck, I don't want to sound selfish, but what are we going to do now?" So much for getting settled.

"I don't know... I just don't know." Diego stood, helped me up, and we walked into our apartment.

We spent the rest of the night going over our finances. No matter how much we cut back, we only had enough to make it another two months, and then we would be in trouble. We decided we would start looking for work the next day.

Work was not easy to come by. I hadn't graduated from high school, so a lot of employers wouldn't even talk to me. Diego had only worked at the restaurant so had very limited work experience. We spent weeks combing through the newspapers, going to the job center and applying everywhere we could think of. We were running out of options and time.

I talked to Diego about the only other option I could think of. Maybe, if we moved to Minnesota, it would be easier. We could stay with my parents until we could get on our feet and go from there. He hated the idea but hesitantly agreed.

I called Pops and talked to him. He reluctantly consented to allow us to move in. It was agreed we could live in the basement until we could find work and set out on our own again. We knew this was going to be tough, but we also knew we had to do whatever it took in order to start our life together.

We were leaving the following weekend, so we immediately started going through our things and deciding what we were going to keep and what we would put in a yard sale. It took us about a week to get it done, so we were cutting it close.

The yard sale was successful. When it was done, we donated the things we couldn't sell. It made me feel good to help others.

It was going to be hard to say goodbye to his family. They had all been so kind to me and accepted me into their family as one of their own. I felt very blessed to have such amazing in-laws.

Juanita and Carlos invited us over for dinner. We accepted their invitation and joined them after we cleaned up the yard sale Saturday afternoon. We stopped and bought flowers for Juanita and a special cigar for Carlos.

The familiar scent of menudo met us as we stepped into Diego's parent's home. Juanita was a good cook but not as good as Grandma. I couldn't stand menudo. It was a soup that was made from beef stomach, in a clear broth and had lime, chopped onions, chopped cilantro, crushed oregano and red chili peppers in it. Grandma had taught me how to make it, but she had converted the recipe to use corn instead of the beef stomach.

I looked at Diego and made a face. He knew I didn't care for menudo, and he squeezed my hand to let me know he would take care of it. I had converted back to vegan after I lost Destiny.

We said hello and hugged everyone. After presenting them with their gifts, we sat down to talk for a while. Carlos told us about work, and that it was going well. Juanita talked about her volunteer position, at the church, and how they were planning a carnival to raise money for the Sunday school class to go on a trip to a convention in Florida. It appeared like they were staying busy.

Diego's little brothers came into the living room and brought some of their toy cars with them. He got up, sat on the floor with them and played. Juanita and I went into the kitchen to finish preparing dinner.

"Mi hija (my daughter), Diego told me you don't eat meat, so I bought you stuff to make a salad. It's in the refrigerator. Go ahead and get it ready." Juanita started making fresh tortillas to go with the soup.

"Thank you, Mama." I was so relieved that I didn't have to say anything to her about not eating the soup.

We set the table and served dinner. There was constant chit chat as we ate. The boys were full of energy and told us stories about school.

Continuing the after dinner tradition, the men cleared the table, and Juanita and I washed dishes. We stood side by side at the kitchen sink working in silence but smiling. I adored my mother-in-law.

The guys were watching television in the living room when we finished cleaning up the kitchen, so we joined them. When the show ended, the boys were told to get ready for bed.

After they changed into their pajamas and brushed their teeth, they came out to the living room and hugged us goodnight. Diego and I took them to their room to tuck them into bed. I stood in their doorway and listened as Diego knelt next to the bed, with his little brothers, and prayed. "Dear God, please watch over my little brothers in my absence. You know how much I love them and how special they are..." Diego spoke softly as he prayed.

My eyes welled up with tears, and when they were done praying I went in to kiss them both goodbye, told them I loved them and would see them again when we could. They were upset, but they were too young to understand. Closing the door behind us, we went back to the living room.

The four of us adults talked about our move to Minnesota, and what we hoped to do once we got there. Diego's parents offered us some advice and then prayed with us to ask for guidance and protection. It was a very sweet moment.

When we stood up to leave, Carlos reached into his back pocket, handed Diego a sealed envelope and told him to put it away and open it later. We all hugged and tried to fight back the tears, but they flowed anyway.

Juanita and Carlos stood on the porch and waved to us as we drove away. I knew this was hard for Diego, so I reached over and held his hand to remind him that it was going to be okay.

We didn't talk much that night. Diego was in deep thought, and I was scared that he might be having second thoughts. I didn't know what to say, so I said nothing. I just stayed at his side supporting and loving him. We fell asleep that night, on opposite sides of the bed, for the first time since we had moved in together. When I woke up in the morning, Diego was curled up around my body with his hand over my heart. I knew we were going to be alright. * smile *

It was Sunday morning. I quietly scooted myself out of Diego's arms and went to the kitchen to make him breakfast. I made all of his favorites, waffles, scrambled eggs with chorizo, crisp bacon, fresh squeezed orange juice and coffee. I set it all on a tray, grabbed the newspaper from the front porch and brought it in to him. I sat it on the bedside table, crawled back into bed, behind him, and wrapped him up in my arms.

"Baby? Are you awake?" I whispered into his ear. He didn't move. "Baby? Are you awake?" I whispered a little louder, and he still didn't budge. "Diego!" I yelled and then laid back down and pretended I was asleep. * giggle *

Diego jumped a bit as he woke up and turned over to look at me. He poked me in my forehead with his finger and asked if I was awake. I tried to pretend to be asleep, but my smile told on me.

"Good morning." He gave me a kiss and lingered there for a moment.

"Good morning, Baby." I kissed him back and smiled.

"Mmm... Just the way I like to wake up." Diego kissed me again.

"Oh, yeah? And how's that?" I knew what he was thinking.

"Come here." He pulled me into his arms, and we made love.

When we were both exhausted from our morning exploits, I pointed over to the tray on the bedside table. Diego looked in the direction I was pointing and smiled. He thanked me for breakfast, sat up and started eating. I warned him that it was cold, but he didn't care. We shared the orange juice and spent the entire morning in bed just cuddling, talking and laughing. It was nice to take a break from all of the stress.

Shit, it was Sunday. The realization of it hit me again. We had to go to Grandma and Grandpa Garcia's house for dinner, cards and goodbyes.

I jumped out of bed, picked up our dirty clothes and threw them in the hamper. We showered together and then scrambled to get dressed and out the door, so we wouldn't be late. They hated it when we were late. I think they looked forward to our visits more than we did, and we loved our Sundays with them.

The moment we walked through the door, we heard Grandma yell from the kitchen. "You're late."

"Lo sienta Abuelita." (I'm sorry Grandma.) As always, I took off my shoes, said hello to Grandpa, kissed him on the cheek and headed to the kitchen.

Grandma was making tamales. Mmm... My second favorite food that she made. She had the dough, fillings and corn husks all laid out on the counter in preparation for my arrival. I thought it was sweet of her to wait for me.

Diego went out to the yard with Grandpa to help him mow the lawn. Grandma and I sat in the kitchen preparing the tamales. We spread the dough in the corn husks that had been soaking in warm water and were now sealed up in a plastic bag to keep them moist. Once we readied all of the husks with the dough, we put the filling in them. Grandma made black bean and bell pepper filling for my tamales and beef for the rest of the family. We wrapped the husks around the filling stuffed dough and placed them in the steamer to cook for about an hour and a half.

Grandma and I sat out on the back porch sipping tea and chatting. I reached into the shopping bag I had brought in with me and handed her the box with the christening gown in it. She wouldn't take it from me.

"Mi nieta, put that away. That is yours to keep. There will be other babies." She patted my hand as she spoke.

"Gracias Abuelita, but I don't know that there will be." I tried to fight the tears back and couldn't look at her.

"Si mi nieta, there will be. Come, come..." She took me by the hand, and we walked over to her flower garden. "Kneel before Mother Mary, and let's pray."

"Dearest Blessed Mother, I ask that the saint watch over Maggie, heal and guide her life. Send a guardian angel to watch over Maggie and Diego. Take their pain; they've mourned long enough. Help them to let go of their loss and remember the love they shared with their baby for the time she was growing in Maggie's body. We kneel before you in gratitude and love... Amen." We both made the sign of the cross over our chests and head and stood up.

I hugged Grandma and cried a healing cry. She knew what I was feeling and hugged me back as though she were taking my pain from me. Have I mentioned how much I loved this old lady? I truly did.

It was just the four of us for dinner that night. We listened to the same stories from Grandpa and smiled as he told them. He didn't repeat the stories because he had nothing else to share with us; he told us the stories so we would remember the old ways and learn lessons from them.

We played cards and, as usual, Grandma and I kicked their butts. Grandpa jokingly said he thought we were cheating. He didn't like to lose, but Grandma and I were good. * wink *

It was getting late, so we needed to head home. We planned to get up early to pack the car and head out before noon. I helped Grandma to clean up the snacks from our card game, while Grandpa and Diego went into the back of the house.

Grandma had packed a huge cooler of food and drinks for us for our road trip. I kind of knew she would do that. She was always feeding us. Have I mentioned how much I loved her? Yeah? I thought I may have.

Grandpa and Grandma Garcia walked us outside to our car. We hugged, kissed and said goodbye. I promised them I would take good care of their grandson and told them how very much I would miss them and loved them. It was a harder goodbye than when I left my foster home with Willow.

We stopped by Diego's church on the way home, so he could say a little prayer and light a candle. It made him feel better, and I was at his side to support him in whatever he needed to do in order to feel whole.

When we got home, we stood in the open door for a moment, and Diego wrapped his arms around me as we looked around our mostly empty apartment.

"We're going to be fine. This is going to be a good thing." He whispered into my ear.

"I know, Baby." I twisted around in his arms and kissed him.

After we got changed and tucked ourselves into bed, Diego told me why he and Grandpa Garcia had gone into the back of the house. He had given Diego a gift for the two of us. Once again, it was in a sealed envelope, and he was told not to open it until we had gotten home. Wait a minute... A sealed envelope? Where was the one that Carlos had given us?

We jumped up and started frantically looking around the entire apartment. Since everything was packed, it had to be out somewhere in plain sight. Wait... The hamper. It was in Diego's jeans in the hamper. YES!

We sat on the bed together, and each of us opened an envelope. We pulled the contents of the envelopes out, placed them on the bed and just stared. In front of us were fifty, one hundred dollar bills. Diego's family had given us five thousand dollars. We just looked at each other and smiled. We were going to be just fine. * phew *

We slept in each others arms, one last night, in that bed, in that apartment, the one we had started our lives together in. We came from humble beginnings and were moving on in love and gratitude. I knew we would love each other forever.

Waking early the next morning, Diego ran out to get us some breakfast while I packed the last of our things. We were leaving a lot of stuff behind, but we were giving the neighbors the keys to the apartment when we left. They were going to come in, get the last of our belongings, keep what they wanted and give away the rest.

Breakfast was eaten, the car was packed, the neighbors were given the keys, and we headed out on our journey. We had decided, that even though we were given this amazing gift, we would still stay with my parents for a while until we could find our own place. This was definitely going to be an adventure...

CHAPTER ELEVEN

"I always knew you'd marry a *N*" (I can't even type the word). Pops looked at Diego and then at me.

"Take another look Pops, he's Hispanic." I was mortified.

Yep, I'm not kidding, whatsoever. Those were Pops' first words when I introduced him to Diego. We had just pulled into the driveway after a four day trip across half of the United States, and this is how we were greeted. What had I been thinking? I should have known that nothing would have changed.

I would like to be able to tell you that things went well, and we lived happily in my parents basement, but that would be a lie. It took less than two weeks, and we were moving out. No need to get into detail. Let's just say that egos, bigotry and a frying pan to the back of my head were the catalyst to send us packing to Duluth.

Diego and I found a one bedroom apartment in the west end of Duluth. We paid six months rent up front, so the landlord would rent to us. She had reservations about it because we had just moved into town and weren't working. It took almost the remainder of our money, but we didn't care. We knew we would be okay as long as we worked together.

You know how they say everything for a reason? Well, there was a reason we were supposed to move to Duluth. I needed to finish high school, so I enrolled in adult education classes.

While I attended school, Diego found employment with a local cleaning company. It was not an ideal job, but at least it was employment for now. Diego told me that he wanted me to focus on my schooling, and he would take care of everything else.

We spent our evenings taking walks together and getting to know the city. I had been there a couple of times as a kid with different foster parents, but was not all that familiar with it. There was so much to see.

Duluth was a sea port city on Lake Superior, and it had a park built around the port where gigantic ships would come through for the loading and unloading of cargo. The park was called Canal Park, and you could walk out on the sides of the port to a lighthouse to watch the ships come in under the Aerial Lift Bridge. It really was a sight to be seen. As a ship approached, a siren on the bridge would sound to warn traffic to stop. The operator of the bridge would then hit the controls, and the bridge would literally lift up to allow for the passing of the ships. It was spectacular. We spent many nights down there watching the ships coming and going.

During the day, there was a free maritime museum in Canal Park, and we spent a lot of time there learning about the history of our new home town. They had an extensive collection of interactive displays that were lots of fun and a schedule of all of the ships that were due into the port daily. There were a couple of kitschy little restaurants there as well. We usually stopped for a bite to eat at least once a week.

We walked hand and hand on the beach at Park Point and would skip rocks. Once in a while, there would be a group of people there partying around a bonfire, and we would be asked to join them. Most of the people we met in Duluth were very kind. If I remember correctly, they called it "Minnesota nice."

"The Depot" was the main museum in town. We had made friends with someone that worked there as a custodian at night through the same company that Diego worked for. He would let us in after hours to check it out. We would sneak into the antique trains and even made love in them a few times.

Enger Tower Park was another of our favorite places to hang out. Enger Tower was a five story tall tower situated in the middle of a multitude of different themed flower gardens. You could walk up the stone steps inside the tower and have a three hundred and sixty degree view of the city and Lake Superior. It was absolutely stunning.

We had lived in Duluth for nearly four months when I finally finished school. I received my General Education Diploma in October of 1989. I knew it wasn't the same as finishing high school and earning a high school diploma, but I was proud of myself nonetheless.

I felt the need to get out into the community more and meet people. I often volunteered at a local soup kitchen and was fortunate to meet a lot of incredible people there. Chris, the head cook, was one of them.

Chris was an older man and lived alone in a little house up on a hill in Duluth. He was jovial and kind with some pretty amazing stories to tell.

When all of the patrons were served and the kitchen cleaned up, we would often sit around with Chris and listen to his stories. He told us about some of the former patrons, their struggles and how he himself had struggles that he had overcome.

Chris had been married for almost fifteen years to the love of his life, Tiffany. He spoke of their wedding day and how beautiful his bride had been. Tiffany had worn her mother's wedding dress, and they were married at a small Baptist church in her home town.

They moved to Duluth, not long after they were married, to start their lives together. He worked as a chef at a local diner, and she was a homemaker. They had tried for years to have children, but every time Tiffany got pregnant she lost the baby. They had given up hope and decided they would be happy with just the two of them.

That's when it happened. Tiffany became pregnant and carried to full term. Three years after they had been married, on the first day of spring, Tiffany gave birth to a beautiful and healthy baby girl. They felt their lives were complete.

After twelve years of working at the diner, Chris and Tiffany were offered the opportunity to purchase it, and they did. They worked hard to remodel it and make it their own. They spent their days and nights cleaning and painting it until it was like new.

Chris reached into his wallet and retrieved a newspaper clipping to show us. It was a picture of him, Tiffany and their daughter, standing in front of the diner. They were all smiling and pointing to the new sign. Below the small article, announcing the re-opening of their restaurant, was a larger headline. "Local Business Owner and Daughter Killed in Robbery Attempt."

Tiffany and their daughter, Donna, had been at the diner late the night before the grand re-opening while Chris ran some errands. A man entered the restaurant and tried to rob them. When he discovered that there was no money in the register, he shot and killed Tiffany and Donna, leaving them there to die on the floor.

Chris, returning from his errands, was the one to discover them. The man that shot them had gotten away and was never found. They only know it was a man because a worker, from the clothing store next to them, had seen him running from the diner.

Chris' smile faded as he carefully folded up the paper and put it back in his wallet. It had been twenty one years that he carried that clipping with him.

Chris sold the diner to a developer that tore it down and built a parking garage. Every day, he would place two daisies at the entry to the parking garage in memory of his girls.

I couldn't help myself. I stood up and hugged him tightly. I felt him submit to my hug as he lifted his arms and hugged me back. Tears fell from my eyes as my heart broke for him.

Diego, Chris and I spent a lot of time together after that. We took him out for coffee, went to the train depot museum and went for walks by the lake whenever we could. We knew Chris had to get out, and we enjoyed listening to his stories.

One night, as he was dropping us off, he asked if we would like to come to his home for dinner the next night. We gratefully accepted his invitation, and he said he would be by after work to pick us up. I quickly ran upstairs and began the preparations for his favorite dessert, cheesecake.

Chris picked us up as he said he would. I had the cheesecake in a box, and he was curious as to what it was. I told him it was a surprise, and he would have to wait and see. He seemed to be in good spirits.

As we drove up the hill, he told us of the state of his home. He said it was a true bachelor's pad and not to be shocked when we saw it because it had been years since it had been cleaned properly. I told him it didn't matter to us, and we were just happy to share this night with him.

That is, until we walked through the front door. Though I tried to keep a smile on my face, my stomach churned at the sight of his home. The entire living room was covered in a fuzzy layer of dog hair. As we walked through and turned the corner into the kitchen, my stomach lurched into my throat. The pungent odor of mold attached itself to my face and wouldn't let go. All I could think was, "you're going to cook for us in here?"

I'm not sure what happened in my mind, but I pushed past Chris and started cleaning. I washed dishes, scrubbed counter tops and cleaned the garbage can. I scraped down the top of the stove and scoured it until it shined. After sweeping the floor, I scrubbed it on my hands and knees until I could see my reflection.

Diego and Chris had gone into the living room to watch television. When I finished the kitchen, I then cleaned and disinfected the bathroom. I just couldn't stop cleaning. I was saddened that such an amazing man was living in complete filth.

Chris was in the kitchen, prepping our meal for the night, when I came out of the bathroom. He looked at me with utter embarrassment on his face and an apology on his lips. I told him there was no need to apologize, and just let me do what I do. He thanked me, and I continued into the living room.

I knew there wasn't enough time to get it as clean as I would like, so I asked Diego to help. He vacuumed the furniture, carpet and curtains while I dusted and started to organize. It didn't take us long, and the place was starting to look like an actual home and not a dog bed.

Diego and I cleaned ourselves up and were just about to sit down in the living room when Chris brought us our dinner. He knew I didn't eat meat and had made eggplant Parmesan for me and chicken Parmesan for himself and Diego. It was delicious.

After we ate dinner, we had dessert, watched a movie and sat around chatting. I got up to wash the dishes and clean up. Chris and Diego took Chris' dog for a walk. I was all done cleaning by the time they returned.

"How much do you pay for rent?" Chris hung up his jacket.

"Four hundred fifty dollars a month plus another one hundred fifty or so in utilities." Diego took the leash off of, Bowser, the dog.

"Why do you ask?" I came out of the kitchen as they were coming in.

"Well, I was thinking that I have all that space in the basement, and maybe the two of you would like to move in here instead? I would just need a little money to help pay utilities." Chris asked as if he thought we would say no.

"Are you sure? That would be amazing." Oh, I was excited.

Obviously, we accepted his invitation. We moved in that weekend and made ourselves right at home. I finished the cleaning I had started, painted the main rooms of the house and started to work in the yard. Diego and Chris began building a bedroom and living room in the basement. There was already a laundry room and bathroom down there, so it didn't take them much to finish it off.

I was not allowed into the basement until they were finished. Diego and I slept on the pull out couch for over a week while they worked in the basement. I have to admit, I was a bit concerned. I knew they could do the construction part of it, but it was that "homey" feeling that worried me.

The front yard was looking gorgeous. I was in the middle of planting the last of the flowers when Diego came out to get me to come in and see the finished basement.

At the top of the stairs leading to our new home, Diego blindfolded me and carefully lead me down the steps. I held his hand with one hand and touched the wall to steady myself with each step.

When we reached the bottom, Diego removed the blindfold and told me to open my eyes. I did, and as I looked around I couldn't believe what I was seeing. It was beautiful. There was a large open room directly in front of me that served as our living room. To the right was a door leading to our bedroom, and to the left was our bathroom and the laundry room. They had painted everything with the left over tan paint and added white trim to brighten up the entire thing.

They had brought in our furniture from the garage and had it all set up. They did a really nice job, and I was so grateful for the work they had put into it. All it needed was some curtains and art. I hugged them both before I set out to make the curtains and do a few paintings.

Life progressed beautifully. Diego was still working for the cleaning company, and I was starting college. We had planned our wedding for right before I started classes in September.

Our plans were shattered when Diego lost his job. We decided we had waited long enough and went to the courthouse to get married. It was quick, simple and done. We were happy just to be Mr. and Mrs. Garcia. We didn't have the money to spend on wedding clothes, so we got married in blue jeans. Diego wore a nice, white, button down shirt with a blue tie. I wore a blue, long sleeved, corset shirt that buttoned down the back and had laces up the front of it. It was casual but still beautiful. We stayed one night in a hotel in Canal Park for our honeymoon.

Diego carried me over the threshold and kissed me as he sat me down. He turned to close the door, and when he turned back around I was standing at the side of the bed. He just stopped and stared at me, smiling.

"You really are beautiful, Maggie. I am such a lucky man." Diego walked over to the dresser and picked up the bottle of complimentary champagne. He removed the cork and poured us each a glass.

"Thank you, Diego. The love we share makes me feel beautiful." I felt the blush raise to my cheeks. I accepted the glass of champagne from him and took a sip.

Diego smiled slyly at me over his glass of champagne. I sat my glass down on the bedside table, giggled and ran to the other side of the bed.

"Diego, behave yourself!" Even though this was obviously not our first time together, I was a bit nervous.

"Come here Mrs. Garcia. I'm going to claim what is mine." Diego placed his glass on the dresser and came around to the other side of the bed where I was standing.

I hopped up on the bed. "Come and claim me then Mr. Garcia... If you can catch me!" I jumped off the bed and ran toward the bathroom.

Diego ran around the bed and cut me off at the door. He stood in the doorway to the bathroom with one hand on the threshold and the other reaching out to me. "I said come here Mrs. Garcia."

I reached to take his hand. As he pulled me tight into his arms, he looked into my eyes and told me he loved me. I stood on my tippy toes to kiss him and tell him that I loved him as well. He kissed me back a long and loving kiss that made my knees weak.

"I do love you, Maggie. I love you more than anything in this world." Diego reached to stroke my cheek.

"And I love you, Diego. More than I can even find the words to tell you." Our eyes locked in a loving stare as he kissed me once again.

Wrapped up in his arms, Diego reached behind my back and methodically unbuttoned my corset. I felt the softness of his fingers on my skin as he lingered with each button. Chills ran up my back, and my body was covered with goose bumps.

He held me close, with his hand on my now exposed back, and stepped forward, forcing me to walk backwards toward the table next to the bed. He reached around me and turned on the radio. A slow, love song was playing.

"Perfect." Diego then placed his other hand on my bare back and swayed with me to the music.

"Every newly married couple has to have their first dance." He whispered softly into my ear.

I rested my head on his shoulder and just got lost in the moment. It could not have been more perfect if it had been planned. I didn't miss the big wedding or reception. I was happy in that moment... That perfect moment.

Were you hoping for another sex scene here? HA! Like I would actually share the intimate details of our honeymoon. I know in the beginning of this book, I said I was going to share all the juicy details with you, but I have to keep some of them for myself. * wink and evil grin *

Waking before Diego the following morning, I rolled onto my side and rested my head on my hand. I watched the shadows that were cast on his face by the sun shining through the blinds. They moved as the shades danced in the light breeze that wafted through the open window. How did I get so lucky?

I lay there watching him until he roused from slumber. He opened his eyes and smiled at me.

"Good morning, Mrs. Garcia." He yawned, stretched and kissed me lightly on my forehead.

"Good morning, Mr. Garcia." I kissed him back, got out of bed and dressed. Well, I didn't get out of bed right away. Diego gave me multiple reasons to stay there for a while longer. * wink *

We ordered room service and enjoyed our breakfast in front of the open window that overlooked Lake Superior. We watched the sunshine sparkle over the waves that crashed against the shore. Yep, this was perfect.

After breakfast, we packed our things and headed back to Chris' house. He was staying at his parents for the weekend, so we would have the house to ourselves. We spent the remainder of the weekend curled up in bed and living in the love we were creating.

It wasn't long until Diego found work again. It was at a fast food restaurant, and though he hated it, he worked hard to take care of our family. He had a hard time in school, had barely graduated and found it difficult to even fill out a job application. I was proud of him for doing everything he could to take care of us. Life was good.

I spent the next few month putting in a garden, working in the yard and fixing up the house even more. When Chris and Diego weren't working they would help me as well. Our home was becoming quite the little showcase.

It was now almost autumn, and I was about to start college. I had already registered and taken care of my financial aid. Every day I grew more and more excited about going back to school.

On my first day of school, I awoke to the smell of breakfast being made. Diego had gotten up early and cooked for me. He really was the sweetest guy.

I wandered upstairs, still sleepy eyed, kissed him good morning and got myself a cup of coffee. We ate breakfast on the back porch and talked about how excited I was.

Diego cleaned up his mess from cooking while I got dressed for school. I grabbed my backpack, and we headed out the door. Diego drove me to school, kissed me and said he would be back later to pick me up when I was finished.

College was amazing. I loved every moment of it. The professors, the books, the studying and the socializing. I knew I had made the right decision.

I had so much fun in school that the months just flew by. Before I knew it, I had made it successfully through my first year. I couldn't believe that it went by that quickly.

It was now summer break. Though I loved school, I was happy for the time off. I was constantly tired and just couldn't seem to get enough sleep. I was so concerned that I made a doctor's appointment.

Pregnant? What? YAY! Diego and I were going to have a baby. The doctor gave me a prescription for prenatal vitamins, and I picked them up and started them right away. A baby... A second chance to be a mom.

I went home and told Diego right away. He hugged me tightly and then pulled away as if he were scared.

"What's wrong?" I was confused.

"I don't want to hurt the baby or you." He touched my stomach.

"You can't hurt me or the baby by hugging me." I giggled a little and pulled him into my arms.

We started immediately building a nursery in the basement. Diego and Chris put up another wall in the living room to section it off for the nursery. It sat directly outside our bedroom door, so we could always hear our baby.

Diego painted the nursery a light green color, and I painted a garden scene on the walls, so our child would be surrounded by flowers, butterflies and life. We got a crib from a second hand store and painted it bright white. I made a bumper and sheet set for the crib in a bright yellow material and started crocheting a matching blanket. We kept everything neutral because we didn't know the gender of our child yet. I was only eight weeks pregnant.

We spent the next four weeks talking about names, going window shopping for the things we needed and saving money to get them. We could not have been happier or more content.

I was working in the garden when it happened... Cramps, blood and tears. I knew what was happening, and I didn't want to believe it. I screamed for Diego as I crawled toward the back door of the house.

Diego scooped me up, put me in the car and drove me to the hospital. Three hours later, after a D&C we left, just the two of us.

Our hearts were broken. The worst part is that we couldn't figure out why it happened. The doctor said that sometimes it just happens, and we could try again, in a few months, after my body had time to heal. At that point, I didn't know if I wanted to try again.

We stored the baby things in the garage and painted the nursery back to the tan color. After a couple of months, I turned the room into a home office and sewing room. All physical traces of a nursery were covered, but the emotional scars were still there.

I went on birth control because I just couldn't face losing another baby. I had convinced myself that I wasn't meant to be a mom. It was easier that way.

I went back to school that fall, and life went on as normal. Well, almost normal. Diego became very withdrawn and moody. I thought it was because of us losing our baby and tried to be as supportive as I could, but it didn't seem to be enough.

He had quit his job. We were now living on the money I made from my part time job at the college and what was left over from my school grants and student loans. Diego began to drink daily and became more and more withdrawn. Again, I tried to be understanding and supportive, but he was making it very difficult.

I came home from school the Tuesday of Thanksgiving break to find him passed out on the couch. I put my books away, changed my clothes and headed upstairs to start cleaning. I washed the dishes, swept and mopped the tile floors, dusted the living room and was starting to vacuum when he came upstairs screaming at me.

"Bitch, I was fucking sleeping, have some respect!" He slammed the basement door shut behind him as he came storming into the living room.

I turned off the vacuum and looked at him. I was completely shocked. Diego had never spoken to me like that before, and I didn't quite know how to react.

"I'm sorry, I just wanted..." I wasn't able to finish my sentence before he slapped me across the face.

I stood there for a moment holding my face and trying not to cry. Diego turned around and went downstairs to go back to sleep. I sat quietly, in the corner of the couch reading, afraid to make a sound.

Chris came home and saw the welt on the side of my face. He asked what happened, but I was afraid to tell him. I just shrugged it off, told him his dinner was in the oven, and I was going to bed. He and I never spoke of it again.

Thanksgiving came and went. As usual, I went all out for dinner. Even though I was vegan, I still made the full meal for Diego and Chris. Diego seemed to be in a better mood, but he never apologized for slapping me. It was just kind of forgotten... Kind of.

After break, I went back to school. My friend Patrick and I were in a few classes together and hung out between and after classes. His boyfriend attended school with us, and we all belonged to the same study group. Patrick asked me how vacation was. I don't know what came over me, but I broke down and told him what had happened.

Patrick held my hand and let me cry. He told me no one should ever be abused and that I didn't have to take it. I told him Diego was not like that most of the time, and I think us losing the baby, and Diego not working, were pulling him into a deep depression. I went on to explain that I had forgiven him for what happened. Patrick warned me it would happen again. He told me something I'll never forget, "First time shame on him, second time shame on you. Please, Maggie, don't let there be a second time."

CHAPTER TWELVE

The next two years went by pretty fast. Diego worked on and off at whatever job he could find for however long he felt like working. Chris was still cooking at the soup kitchen and had started to teach a class to the clientele about cooking on a budget. I was about to receive my Bachelor's Degree in Art History. Yep, I went from G.E.D. to Bachelor's Degree.

The four years it took me to earn my degree seemed to fly by. Patrick and I planned a party together to celebrate our graduation. We were going to have it in the backyard at Chris' house and invite everyone we knew.

We strung lights through the branches of the birch trees, set up card tables for games, picnic tables for food and groupings of chairs for people to sit and chat. There were two kegs of beer, each sitting in large plastic bins full of ice, with stacks of plastic glasses sitting next to them. We hired a friend of ours to act as a bartender to make the mixed drinks for our guests. He was also in charge of switching the tapes for the music. Patrick and I spent hours and hours making mixed tapes, so the bartender just had to flip them over or switch them around for the party.

Chris and I did all the cooking. He took care of the barbecued food and potato salad while I made the coleslaw, fresh fruit salads and veggie trays. We set up a giant buffet table, and Chris ran an extension cord out the kitchen window to plug in all the crock pots so the hot foods would stay hot. All in all, it was a beautiful set up.

The party was jumpin'. People were eating, drinking, talking and congratulating Patrick and I for our hard work and for receiving our degrees. There was a table full of gifts for Patrick and I, and we were so thankful to everyone.

Some of our neighbors even wandered over and joined in the festivities. When everyone finished eating, we pushed the tables aside, still leaving room for people to sit, and cleared an area for dancing.

Patrick grabbed me to dance. He knew how much I loved it. We were having a blast... Until Diego saw us.

He had been drinking pretty heavily and did not like that Patrick and I were having such a fun time. He walked out to the dancing area, grabbed me by the arm and pulled me into the house. I looked behind me, as we went through the back door, to signal to Patrick that it was alright.

Standing in the living room, Diego yelled at me about my behavior and how inappropriate I was behaving. I explained to him that I wasn't doing anything wrong; I was just dancing. He wasn't hearing it, and instead of listening to me, he grabbed both of my arms and started shaking me. I yelled for him to stop, and that's when he punched me. I fell to the floor and he kicked me in the stomach. I hunched over and curled up in a ball. It didn't stop him. He continued to kick me a few times and then pulled me up, by my hair, until I was standing in front of him.

Just as Diego was raising his fist to me again, Patrick burst through the back door, came into the living room and grabbed Diego by the back of the shirt. He pulled him away from me and dragged him through the living room, down the stairs to the basement. I followed them, begging Patrick not to hurt Diego.

Patrick slammed Diego against one of the support poles in the basement and told him, "I don't know why Maggie loves you so much because God knows she deserves better. If you EVER lay another finger on her in anger, I will tie you to this pole, I will fuck you in your ass, and you WILL enjoy it... Got it?" He then threw Diego to the floor and went back out to the party.

I rushed over to Diego to help him up. He hugged me tightly and started to cry. Diego told me he felt like he had lost a part of himself when we lost the baby, and he blamed me even though he knew it wasn't my fault. He said he realized what he was doing was wrong, and he would never hit me or hurt me again. We stood there crying together.

When the party was over and everything was cleaned up, Diego and I went to bed and cuddled all night. We hadn't been that close in a long time. He kissed my forehead and told me he loved me.

I woke up early the next morning and made Diego and Chris breakfast. I wanted to do something nice to thank Chris for all of his hard work on the party and show Diego that I wasn't upset about what had happened.

While I was cooking, I phoned Patrick to tell him about Diego and I working things out. Patrick reminded me he had told me there would be a second time. We talked, and Patrick expressed his concerns about it happening again. I told him I was sure it would get better, I loved him for helping me, and I hoped we would always be friends. He assured me, no matter what happened in life, our friendship would always be a part of it.

Diego and I lounged around all day. Neither of us had much energy after cleaning up from the party. Chris went to visit his parents, so we were home alone.

"Want to go to the casino?" Diego nudged my leg with his foot.

"Um, sure!" I LOVED the casino.

We got dressed and headed out. The casino was about a half hour south of us, and it was a nice drive too. We pulled in, valet parked and went inside with high hopes.

Diego loved the black jack tables, and I played slots. I changed out my cash for quarters and started walking around looking at the machines.

I dropped a few quarters here and there, but I didn't really hit anything worth staying for. I played my favorite machine, the red, white and blue stars, won fifty dollars and thought to myself, "well, at least I doubled my money."

Drinks were free, so I sat down at a machine I had never seen before and ordered a rum and coke. I dropped a few quarters in and played while I waited. It was kind of a cool machine with rows of fruit all over it and was called "The Super 8 Line."

My drink arrived, so I sipped at it and just watched everyone around me. I loved people watching at the casino. There was always some old ladies playing penny slots like their lives depended on it and young couples basking in the hopes of hitting it big.

Finishing my drink, I dropped the last eight quarters, of my open roll, into the slot machine and hit the spin button. Oranges started lining up across the screen and all of a sudden bells and sirens started sounding off. I had won the jackpot... $10,000.00..... Oh my God! Oh My God! OH... MY... GOD!

I jumped up screaming and waited for an attendant to come and pay me. I took the little piece of paper I was given to the counter, and I watched with delight as the cashier counted out the one hundred dollar bills. Scooping up the money, I thanked her and skipped away looking for Diego.

He was sitting at a black jack table and didn't look very happy. I walked up behind him and put my hand on his shoulder.

"How ya doin'?" I held back my delight.

"Not so good, you?" Diego was concentrating on the dealer.

"I did alright." A smile crossed my face but he couldn't see it.

"Yeah?" He was standing up to leave as he had just lost the last of his money.

"I won a bit." I pulled the cash out of my pocket and showed him.

Diego scooped me up in his arms, swung me around and kissed me. We walked hand in hand out of the casino... Happy.

After retrieving our car and heading out, we decided to stop for breakfast and talk about my winnings.

"Maggie? There is something I've been wanting to talk to you about. Now that you're done with school, I was thinking maybe we could move back to California." Diego sounded hopeful.

"Well, I guess this would be the time to do that, huh?" I replied with a smile.

We went home, told Chris about our winnings and plans and started packing. Chris was saddened to see us go, but he knew it would make us happy to return to California.

It took us less than a week to pack, and we were on our way. Packing our car with everything we could carry, we left the rest for Chris. We hoped that maybe he could rent out his basement if it were furnished. There were a lot of college kids in the area that were always looking for cheap places to live.

The drive to California was spectacular. We took the northern route across North Dakota, Montana, down through Idaho, Oregon and into California. We stopped along the way to see the sights and make memories.

I did most of the driving. Needing to take a break, I saw a beautiful rock formation in the distance and pulled over. I lit a cigarette and walk toward it while Diego slept in the car.

As I got closer, I noticed some of the rocks were moving. Now, I knew I was tired, but I was also sober... So what the hell?

FUCK! BUFFALO! I turned tail and ran back to the car. Crawling on the hood of the car, I sat there and watched them graze. They were so majestic and wild. It was absolutely stunning.

Deciding that I had seen enough wild life for the moment, I got back in the car and drove until I found a diner. I woke Diego as I was pulling in, and we ate a light breakfast before heading out again. This time he drove and I slept.

The rest of the trip was pretty uneventful. Well, except... Naw, I don't know if I should tell you. Okay, okay, you don't have to twist my arm.

It was around two in the morning. Diego was fast asleep, and I was driving. I had just made it past the border of northern California when all of a sudden there was a really bright light in the sky, and my car stalled out. FUCK!

I sat there for a moment, watching this light, attempting to start the car and trying to wake Diego. He wouldn't wake up, and the car wouldn't start. I watched as this light darted across the darkened sky, stopped and hovered and then dashed away. Reaching to try the ignition one more time, the car started, and I drove on.

Now, I'm not going to say it was aliens, but I'm not going to say it wasn't. Whatever it was, scared the piss out of me, and I'm happy to say that was the closest it got to us. Maybe it was looking for intelligent life, and it realized it wasn't finding it in our car.

We pulled into Lodi with hope in our hearts. After visiting with family, we set out to find an apartment. We checked ourselves in to a cheap hotel and began the search.

It didn't take us long to find one. We discovered a beautiful, one bedroom apartment, not far from where we lived when we first met, and we rented it right away.

We spent the next week buying furniture and unpacking. Our little home was looking wonderful. I hung curtains, arranged furniture and set up our kitchen. I loved being a home maker.

It didn't take us long to find work this time. We were both hired as security officers at a club on the east side of town. It was a bit scary to work at because a lot of the local gangs hung out there.

Here's where Bryce comes into the story... Yeah, Bryce. He was our supervisor at the club and thought of himself as a police officer. Let me tell you, this man was delusional, to say the least.

Bryce stood over six feet tall and was really out of shape. He used to tap his round belly and say he wasn't fat; he was solid. I half jokingly told him he was only solid because he was full. Okay, I wasn't even half joking, but I had to make it seem that way.

Have you ever met someone that's done it all? I mean, like every time someone says they've done something or seen something, so have they? Yeah, that was Bryce. He had been a cop, a fire fighter, was in the Air Force, was an attorney, climbed mountains, wrangled steer, rode in rodeos, was a descendant of Thomas Edison, was a shaman for his tribe, (even though this man was so white he glowed.) had lost family on the Trail of Tears (that he swears Lewis and Clark lead.), he invented weight loss techniques and anything else you can think of. Did I mention he was delusional? Yeah? Okay, let's move on then.

I was assigned to the front door. My job was to search everyone as they came in to check for weapons. I didn't mind it at all. I got to pat down all of the handsome men as they arrived. I realize I was married, but that didn't mean I couldn't enjoy my job. One of my favorite sayings is, "Just because you're on a diet, doesn't mean you can't look at the menu."

Diego worked inside the club. He was to make sure there was no underage drinking or other illegal things going on. We were never to get involved, only observe and report.

There were two main gangs in the area. I would rather not put their names out there, because quite frankly, they don't deserve to be recognized. Let's just call them gang A and gang B.

Members of gang A showed up at the bar for a quinceanera (that is the Latin celebration for a girl's 15th birthday). Everything was going just fine... Until gang B showed up. They knew that they would be patted down, and weapons would not be allowed through the front doors, so they made arrangement for some of their members to sneak weapons in through the bathroom windows.

I was at the front door when I heard screams coming from inside. As I stepped through the door, I told the people in line they would have to wait, and I locked the door behind me. Walking through the vestibule, I noticed the members from gang B, coming out of the bathroom, with knives in their hands, and there were already some in the dance hall.

I ducked into the bar and called the police. After all, as previously stated, our job was to observe and report. After removing my uniform over-shirt, I snuck out and began to look for Diego. I was worried about his safety.

As I walked through the door into the dance hall, I saw Diego being pinned up against the wall by one of the guys from gang B. He had a knife to his throat and was yelling at him. Oh HELL NO!

I acted without even thinking. I grabbed the guy by the back of his shirt and slammed him into the locked metal door to my left. The door lead into the vestibule, and when the dirtbag hit the door, it flew open, and he fell to the floor. I didn't stop there either. My boot fit real well over his neck, and I left him pinned there until Diego was able to cuff him. I knew our job was to observe and report, but NO ONE was going to put their hands on my man and get away with it.

That's when the shit hit the fan. All of a sudden, members from both gangs filled the foyer, and they were fighting. I mean really fighting... Knives, closed fists and brass knuckles.

Diego and I were trying to get through the crowd and into the bar to escape the chaos. Bryce, being the total idiot that he was, closed and locked all three doors that could have been our escape. As if that weren't bad enough, he then proceeded to unload an entire can of mace into the crowd. You know, the crowd we were a part of? Yeah, Bryce was a special kind of stupid.

We were all gasping for breath and trying not to rub our eyes when, thankfully, the police started pounding on the door. I struggled to get to the door, fumbled for my keys and unlocked it.

The police came in and took control of the situation. It was quickly resolved, and the appropriate people were arrested. Needless to say, Bryce, Diego and I lost our jobs.

We weren't too worried about it. We still had plenty of my winnings to live on until we could find employment again. Diego and I continued to look for work, and it wasn't long before we found employment with a different security company. So much for my degree.

I worked the swing shift as a security officer at a convenience store a few blocks from our apartment. Diego worked the same shift at a doughnut shop just down the street. Yes, I realize the irony in that.

We were enjoying our life. Diego hadn't hit me since my graduation party, and I no longer feared it. He kept his promise.

When we weren't working, we had people over for barbecues, played board games, had small parties and went out a lot. We were "that" couple and loved every minute of it.

Diego and I celebrated our fifth wedding anniversary by taking a weekend trip to San Francisco. He had set it all up in advance, and it was a complete surprise. We spent the weekend doing all the touristy things, like taking the Alcatraz tour, going to the wax and interactive science museums, eating at every restaurant on the wharf and enjoying the street artist performances. It was magical.

At night, we rode the street cars up and down the hills, held hands and just talked. Diego showed me a side of him I hadn't seen in a while. He was sweet, romantic and compassionate.

It was Sunday night, the actual day of our anniversary, and we decided to stay in for the night and order room service. Diego and I cuddled in bed, ate dinner and watched a movie. It was sweet.

When the movie was over, Diego sat up, took my hand and looked into my eyes. I smiled at him and waited to hear him say something charming and flirtatious.

"Maggie, there's something that I need to tell you, but I don't know how." His voice was uneasy and shaky.

"Just tell me, Diego. We've always been able to talk about everything." Oh boy, I was getting worried.

"I'm gay." He almost spit the words out at me.

Yep, just like that, and nope, he wasn't kidding. I wasn't mad. I couldn't be mad. I was a firm believer that people had to be who they were. It was just that simple… But boy had Patrick been right about his threat to Diego! * laughing *

CHAPTER THIRTEEN

Our divorce was simple. We had no children or property to worry about. We split the few bills we had, I kept what was left of my winnings, and he kept the car. Fair is fair.

So here I was, twenty four years old, newly single, living on my own in a small studio apartment, a bit jaded and bored as fuck. What do I do? I take dance lessons, of course!

I had always loved to dance, and I had taken ballet and tap when I was younger. Now? It was time to learn salsa.

There was a dance studio on the same block where I lived, so I went to check it out. It was exactly what I was looking for. Upbeat music greeted my ears as I opened the door, and I saw the most exquisite man, dancing by himself, in front of a wall of mirrors. I walked in and watched him for a moment before I introduced myself.

His name was Antonio, and he was beautiful. He took me by the hands and spun me around as he looked at me.

"You have the eyes and hips of a dancer." His accent sent chills up my spine.

"Thank you." I felt the blush raise to my cheeks.

Of course, I signed up for classes immediately. I mean, who wouldn't? Antonio was sexy, charming and WOW could he dance. I decided to start with the salsa lessons and go from there.

I was still working at the convenience store, but I looked for other work in my spare time. I had this amazing degree and was doing nothing with it. What did a person do, other than teach, with a Bachelor's degree in art history?

The thought of self evolution haunted me at every turn. I couldn't take it any longer, so I cut my long, blonde hair short and dyed it red. Most of my "wife" clothes found their way to charity shops, and I purchased an entire new wardrobe of jeans, corsets, t-shirts and tank tops. I was young and wanted to feel it. Next step? Why a tattoo of course.

I shopped around for a credible, clean tattoo shop and made an appointment. I'm not going to lie; I was nervous as hell. People had told me that the upper arm was the easiest place to get one, so that's what I wanted.

The appointment was for three in the afternoon, but I showed up early because I wanted to see their clean room and autoclave. I was shown around and was impressed with what I had seen. Yep, I was definitely going to do this.

I showed the tattooist the art I wanted and was brought back to the artist's area. I sat there for just a bit while he drew up the stencil and readied for the tattoo.

He cleaned and shaved my upper arm, put some gel on it and then placed the stencil. After a couple of minutes, he peeled the stencil from my skin and told me to check it out in the mirror. I loved it.

After changing his gloves, he inked up the needle and got started. It stung a bit at first but then it felt like he was just drawing on me. It didn't take long, and he was finished with the outline. He rinsed my skin, and I checked it out in the mirror while he set up for the coloring.

Okay, so the outline wasn't all that bad, but the color? Yeah, the color hurt a bit more. He used a large set of needles so that it would cover more skin at once. About an hour later, he was finished.

It was stunning! After checking it out, one last time in the mirror, he wrapped my arm with plastic wrap. I paid him and was on my way out the door. I now had the most gorgeous lily and butterfly on my arm, and I could not have been happier.

My newest obsession? Tattoos! I wanted to become a tattoo artist. Why not put my degree to good use?

Now, usually a person would get tattoos from their favorite artist, hang out at the shop when allowed, work for free as a shop bitch for a couple of years and then MAYBE be allowed to start learning. I didn't have that kind of time, so I offered to pay the artist that did my tattoo to teach me, and he agreed, but only after he saw my drawing portfolio and was convinced I had the talent to do it.

Kyle had been a tattoo artist for just over ten years, and I was honored that he was going to take the time to teach me. He helped me pick out and order the machines and supplies I would need to start and had me purchase a bag of oranges. Oranges? Maybe it was because he wanted snacks.

Nope, it was to practice on. Now, I'm not going to go into all of the details here because I know there are a lot of people out there that want to be tattoo artists. It's not that I don't want them to, but I do want them to go about it the right way. Let's just say that oranges were my only clients for quite some time.

Between work, dance classes and tattoo lessons, I kept myself quite busy and wasn't concerned with dating. That is, until I got asked out. Kevin was a regular patron at the convenience store I worked at, and he would often buy me coffee and chat with me while I was on patrol.

He was six foot five inches tall, had really dark skin, a white smile and arms that could crush me if given the chance. He had gorgeous tribal tattoos covering his upper arms that made him look even tougher than he was. This was, of course, before tribal tattoos became over-popular.

My twenty fifth birthday was fast approaching, so I told Kevin he could take me out for my birthday the following weekend. He agreed and asked me where I wanted to go, and I told him to surprise me. I liked doing that, so I could see what kind of an imagination a man had and how much he paid attention to the things we talked about.

Thursday nights were my favorite nights, DANCE NIGHT! Oh my gosh, I LOVED dancing with Antonio. He made me feel feminine, alive and sexy.

I booked private dance lessons, for two hours, every Thursday night. Antonio and I had been dancing for about six months, and I was getting pretty good, even if I do say so myself. I always dressed as though we were in a competition, sparkly, form fitting and in classic black.

Close your eyes and picture this... Oh wait, I take that back. If you close your eyes you can't read this. Okay, read this part and then close your eyes and picture it.

The lights are low, the music starts, and the most beautiful man in the world walks across the room to you, and he wraps you up in his arms. You sway back and forth to the music as you look into each others eyes, and then the tempo picks up. He twirls you around, matches you step for step, and he pulls you back into his arms. Pushing you away from him again, your only contact is your finger tips, as your hips swing to the beat of the music. Just as quickly as he pushed you away, he brings you back into his arms with your back against his chest.

You feel his breath against your neck, and you get lost in the moment. Yeah, it was like that.

SWOON * Ahem * Oh yeah, okay... I'm back with you.

Yep, I LOVED dance nights. I not only learned to dance, I got some amazing exercise, and I was able to be close to Antonio. He made my knees weak.

At the end of our lesson, I went into the back to the changing rooms and changed back into my street clothes. Tonight was the night I was going to ask him out. I wondered to myself, how many women asked him out after dance class.

I walked out of the back full of confidence when I stopped dead in my tracks. Antonio was standing at the front reception area and was kissing a man. Why were all the good men either gay or taken?

Clearing my throat, I stepped toward the couple. Antonio pulled away from the man, and both of them began to blush.

"Oh, Maggie, um, this is my boyfriend, Rico. Rico, this is Maggie." Antonio looked embarrassed.

"Nice to meet you. Are you guys busy? I thought maybe we could go catch some dinner?" Oh well, at least we could still have dinner.

"That would be nice, sure!" Rico was pretty enthusiastic with his answer.

Dinner was enjoyed by all. Antonio and Rico told me about how they met in the eleventh grade and had been together ever since. They were such a sweet, loving couple, and we became fast and forever friends that night.

I drove them both back to their car at the dance studio and said goodnight. Antonio hugged me and told me he looked forward to our next lesson and to have fun on my date that coming Saturday. Oh shit... MY DATE! What was I going to wear?

After stopping by the office to check my schedule, I saw I didn't work again until that following Monday. Good, I would have time to go shopping and get my hair done before Saturday. I called Rico to see if he wanted to go with me, and he gladly accepted the invitation.

Rico and I spent all day shopping, getting manicures, having our hair styled and eating lunch. We had a blast and it was nice to have some time to get to know him. Antonio had become a big part of my life, and I wanted to know Rico as well.

Saturday night, I was dressed to impress. I had considered getting dressed up in my finest of clothes but decided to go casual wrapped up in a bit of sexy.

I wore blue jeans, a white tank top and black hip boots with six inch heels. I flat ironed my cropped, red hair, so that it laid smooth against my head with full short bangs that sat just over my ice blue eyes. Just as every other day, I put on heavy black eyeliner and mascara. I completed my look with ruby red lipstick that matched my hair.

I was pretty excited to be going out. This was my first date since my divorce, and I hoped it would be special. Kevin and I talked so much, and I really hoped he had been paying as much attention as I had.

Seven o'clock, I heard his truck pull up... Base hit. Then I heard the horn beep... Strike one. I walked down stairs, and he didn't get out of his truck to open my door... Strike two. What happened to being a gentleman, coming to the door to pick up your date and opening a door for a lady?

Kevin told me I looked nice, and I returned the compliment. We drove for quite some time and then pulled into a steak house. Really? A steak house? Well, at least they had a nice salad bar.

We were seated right away and ordered our drinks. The conversation started out well. He talked about his daughter and how fantastic she was. She played volleyball and was a straight A student. He seemed proud of her, and I liked to see that.

The server came back to take our order. I asked for the salad bar and another rum and coke. Kevin ordered a forty dollar steak and a double scotch.

Our meals were served, and we ate through the small chit chat. It was a bit awkward and slow moving, but I didn't mind. We had been talking at my job for almost four months, so we knew quite a bit about each other already.

When we finished with our meals, the server asked if we wanted dessert, and we both declined. He gave us our check. The little folder sat on the table, so I reached for it and opened my purse to pay. Kevin didn't flinch. I slid a hundred dollar bill inside and handed it back to the server, telling him to keep the change.

Is it just me, or was that a bit weird? Kevin asked me out. I didn't mind paying for my part, but I had a twelve dollar salad and a couple of cheap drinks. He had a forty dollar steak, two very expensive drinks, and he didn't even offer to pay for part of it? Hmm...

Kevin asked me if I would like to go for a walk on the beach after dinner. I politely declined and made the excuse that I needed to get home because I had things I needed to do before work.

When we pulled up to my front door, Kevin leaned over to kiss me. I just couldn't be polite any longer.

"Look, Kevin, you're a nice enough guy, very handsome and smart, but you're not my type." I kept my voice as calm as I possibly could.

"That's fine. You're a snooty bitch anyway." Really? REALLY? Did he just say that?

I looked at him for a moment and stepped out of the truck. "Here's a little bit of advice, if you want it or not. When you take a lady out, come to her door to get her, and don't sit out here in your broken down, rusty truck honking the horn. Be a gentleman, open a door for her and pay at least your part of the check. And for goodness sake, don't take a vegan to a fucking steak house." I slammed his truck door shut without giving him the chance to answer me. Needless to say, I didn't go out with Kevin again. Oh well, at least I got that first "after divorce date" out of the way.

Were you hoping the date was going to work out, and he would be "the one" for me? Come on. We all know better than that. That seldom happens. Most everyone needs a rebound date.

I had my last class with Kyle. He said that I was a natural born tattoo artist, and it was time for me to do what I did. I was touched that he had so much confidence in me.

Kyle allowed me to tattoo his calf as my first official tattoo on a person, other than myself. He asked me to tattoo a Celtic cross, with intricate knot work in it, and though I was a bit nervous, I did what he asked me to do. It turned out wonderfully. I was impressed with how well I did because of his instruction. It was time for me to move on.

So, remember Bryce? Yeah, I know, how could you forget him. Well, here is where he enters the story again. I would like to extend my sincerest apologies.

Bryce moved to Colorado, started a new security company and asked me to join him. I thought about it for a little while and decided to do it. I know, I know... But it was a chance for a new start, and that was exactly what I needed.

I had my final dance lesson with Antonio, and I took him and Rico out to eat. They surprised me with a small going away party with some of our friends. I was so touched.

I put in my notice at work and finished working those last two weeks. I had to have time to start going through my things, deciding what I had to take, what I could get rid of and start packing. I gave away or donated the things I didn't want, and I packed up most of the rest. I left out only the things I needed to live until the day I moved. My tiny apartment was full of boxes, my bed, a television and a few kitchen and bathroom items. It looked empty, but it was with purpose.

It was Saturday night, and my last night in town. I was leaving the next day, so I decided to stay home and rest a bit before the long road trip.

Tears fell down my cheek, as I sat in my bed watching a sappy romance movie and finishing off my second bottle of wine. I was SO lonely and actually missed Diego quite a bit. The almost empty apartment made it seem even worse, so I tried to call Antonio and Rico to see if they wanted to go out, but there was no answer. Well, shit. There had to be someone... And that's when I remembered something Rico had told me, "The best way to get over an old guy is to get under a new one."

I picked up my phone again and dialed a familiar number. "Hey, Kevin? I know we ended on a not so good note, but I'm moving out of state, and I think you should come over here and fuck me goodbye." Yep, I was that blunt.

"On my way." He hung up before I could respond.

Kevin lived about a half hour away, so I knew I had a little time to ready myself for his arrival. I grabbed my things and headed to the shower for a quick wash and shave. After jumping out, I wrapped up in a towel, combed my hair and brushed my teeth. I ran into my apartment, from the shared bathroom, and almost slipped on the hardwood floor, but I caught myself right before I fell. The towel fell off, but I didn't care. Hurriedly, I threw on some make-up, my fake silk robe, picked up the towel, threw it over a chair and sat on the bed to wait.

I heard his truck pull up, so I jumped up and poured him a drink. Two fingers of scotch over ice, I remembered, then I drank it, and I poured him another one.

Kevin knocked on my door, and I opened it slowly with a smile on my face. He tried to speak to me, but I covered his lips with my finger to quiet him. After handing him his drink, I walked over to my little bar and poured myself another one.

I slammed mine back, and he followed my lead. Sitting on my bed, I pulled him toward me and unbuttoned his shirt. I remember thinking how surprised I was that he was wearing a button down shirt and not a sloppy t-shirt. He had actually taken a moment to get dressed before coming over.

OH... MY... DAMN. His body was more ripped than I had imagined. Even though he was a total tool, I was a lucky girl... At least for a little while.

Kevin took me by the hands and helped me to stand in front of him. He reached down, slowly untied my robe and let it fall open. Stepping back, he looked at my body, smiled and licked his lips. I reached to unbuckle his belt and jeans all the while looking into his eyes.

As his jeans fell to the floor, Kevin grasped my ass and lifted me to him. I wrapped around him and kissed him deeply. His tongue darted in and out of my mouth as if it were playing peek-a-boo with my tongue.

Kevin turned, pushed me against the wall and set me down. Using one hand he pinned my arms above my head and slowly suckled at my neck, my collar bone and over my breasts. Pulling my hands down to my stomach, he kept them locked there with one hand and used his other to separate my thighs. I felt the warmth of his breath against my tender skin as he tasted me.

I wrestled my hands away from his, and I gripped his bald head to hold him where he was. I didn't want him to stop because it just felt that good. It had been so long.

My legs quaked with pleasure, and he stood again to kiss me. Dropping to my knees, I returned the favor. The hardness of his body against the softness of my lips turned me on even more. His fingers wrapped in my hair and kept rhythm with my movements.

Letting go of my hair, he backed away from me. Kevin took me by the hands and beckoned me toward the bed. Laying on his back, I moved my body over his and slid him inside me. It was a perfect fit. I started to slowly move as his hands found their way to my hips, and he directed me to flow to his cadence.

Sweat ran down my neck and between my breasts. He raised his mouth to my body in order to taste it's salty sweetness. My fingernails dug into his chest as I climaxed again.

Kevin's arms wrapped around me as he rolled me over to my back, never leaving my body. He moved himself in and out of me, and I locked my legs tight over his, as to not let him move away from me until I climaxed again.

He laid tight to my body and breathed into my ear. I felt his heart beat faster and heard his breath quicken as he erupted inside me. We stayed there until our heartbeats slowed.

Kevin rolled over and pulled the blankets up over his shoulder.

"Oh no, Kevin. This isn't a sleep over. Thanks for the fun, but it's time for you to get up, get dressed and go home." Nope, wasn't having this.

"What? Really?" Kevin asked, puzzled.

"You heard me." I wasn't giving in.

Kevin did as he was instructed and left with a sad puppy-dog look on his face. I smiled at him, locked the door and fell into a blissful sleep.

The sun peeked through the bare windows and woke me up early Sunday morning. It was time to pack the car, give the remainder of the furniture to the neighbors and leave for Colorado. Ugh, this was going to be a long day.

CHAPTER FOURTEEN

Most people would have taken the northern route from Lodi, California to Colorado Springs, Colorado because it is a bit shorter, but I am not most people. I decided, since this was my first road trip alone, I wanted to make the most of it. I hopped on the southern route, so that I could go through Vegas.

I spent Sunday morning packing my car and a small tow behind trailer. Once it was packed, I met Antonio and Rico for a 'see ya later' breakfast, and I headed out.

The traffic was cooperating with me as I headed south on 99. That is, until I hit Bakersfield and then it was as if the flood gates opened. Why the hell was there so much traffic on a Sunday? Oh well, I coped with it and made it through.

I had planned to get to Vegas in about ten hours, counting stops, but it took me a bit longer. Sixteen hours later, at almost four in the morning, I was pulling into a cheap, little hotel just on the outskirts.

After checking in, I grabbed my overnight bag, went to my room, showered and collapsed into bed. I didn't move until I woke up early that afternoon. I was exhausted.

I wanted to check out the strip, so I showered again, got dressed and headed out. There was so much to see and do. As I told you before, I was a slots machine kinda girl, and I was ready to gamble.

Even though it was the middle of the afternoon, the Strip was completely lit up. I remember looking at the lights and thinking how I would hate to have to pay the electricity bill there.

I stopped in a few casinos and dropped twenty bucks at a time. In total, I won almost sixty-eight hundred dollars, and I had an absolute blast. I had never been in such an energetic environment before.

I had no desire to take in the shows and other things that Las Vegas had to offer. I simply walked the strip, gambled, ate a couple of meals and took in the entertainment that the street performers had to offer. It was so much fun that I lost track of time and didn't get back to my hotel until 6:30 in the morning. I had to be up and out by eleven so it was time to hit the hay.

My wake up call came in at ten. I was in such a deep sleep, they had to call me twice to wake me. After hanging up I showered, dressed, threw my stuff in my bag and headed out.

Eight hundred and twenty miles to go to Colorado Springs. I figured it should take me about twenty hours all together with stops. That is, if I had gotten a decent night's sleep, but since I didn't, I planned to pull over at a rest area and catch a nap somewhere along my journey.

Radio blasting, windows down, coffee at my side and a cigarette in my hand, I drove for almost eleven hours straight, except for fuel and food stops, to Grand Junction, Colorado. It looked like a good enough place to sleep.

Remembering some of the horror stories about crimes committed at rest areas, I decided it would probably be in my best interest to stay at a hotel again. I pulled into another cheap hotel, just off the interstate, to sleep for the night.

When I saw the clerk, I wasn't sure if I had made the right decision. He smiled at me with an almost toothless smile, and he looked like he hadn't showered in a month of Sundays. He licked his lips as he asked me for my information, and he had a strange look about him. I was relieved when he told me my room was at the other end of the hotel. The more space between us the better.

I gathered my things from my car and went up to my room. It was surprisingly clean, but I laid my sleeping bag out on the bed anyway. Better to be safe than sorry; I suppose.

After I made sure the door and windows were locked, I turned on the air conditioning, full blast, and went to take a nice, long shower. It felt so good to wash the road grime from my hair and body.

Wrapped in a towel, I lit a cigarette before turning on the television. There was a knock at the door, and my first thought was the clerk.

"Just a minute." I threw on my clothes, almost falling over in the process, and picked up my pocket knife.

"Who is it?" I was looking out the peephole in the door, but all I could see was dark hair.

"It's your neighbor." A deep, manly voice answered me.

"Um, what do you want?" Like I was dumb enough to open the door to a stranger.

"Just had a question for you." Same voice.

Leaving the chain lock on, I opened the door and peeked through the small opening. There stood the second most gorgeous man I had ever laid eyes on. Thick, dark, curly hair framed his face and accented his deep green eyes. His lips formed a smile over his perfectly white, slightly crooked teeth, and his black t-shirt was tight enough to show the ripples of his very fit upper body.

"Um, hi... Yeah, I know this is strange, but I saw you come in, and I was wondering if you smoke pot?" He smiled as he spoke. Why did I have such a soft spot for smiles?

"Can't say that I do... Why?" All I could think was, "YUM."

"Well, I've been on the road for quite some time, and I could use some company. Don't worry, I'm not a murderer or pervert. I just want someone to talk to. I thought I would offer you a joint or a drink, and we could chat." Yep, sure... That's what all the perverts say.

"Look, I'm not going to let a total stranger into my room, but I've been on the road too, and I could go for a nice conversation as well. Give me a few minutes, and I'll meet you at pool side. Cool?" WHAT WAS I DOING?

"Yeah... Sure... Great. ... Um, what do you drink?" He lit up like the Vegas strip as he nervously shifted on his feet.

"Don't worry about it. I have my own bottle. By the way, I'm Maggie, and you are?" I reached my hand through the opening in the door to shake his hand.

"Oh right, my name is Adam, but my friends call me Blaze." He shook my hand.

"Blaze, huh? Alright, I'll meet you in a few minutes." Again, what was I thinking?

"Awesome!" Blaze left, and I closed the door.

Before I continue, I would like to remind you that I was not in my right mind. Hell, I wasn't in my left mind either. I was divorced from a man I thought I would love forever, and I had lost my daughter and had a miscarriage. I lived as though I had my shit together, but in reality, I was an emotional mess. Don't judge me on what you are about to read, okay?

I finished getting dressed. I didn't plan to swim, so there was no sense in putting on a swimsuit. I changed into a pair of torn up, light blue jeans, a black lace bra and my white cotton tank top that had lace over the breast and around the bottom. I then threw on my black kicks. Of course, I had to throw on something else black so it looked intentional. Yeah, yeah, I know... What was I thinking?

My short, red hair looked cute either way, combed or not, so I decided to go with the bed head look and leave it messy. Thick black eyeliner, black eye shadow, heavy black mascara and blood red lipstick finished off my look. I hadn't changed my make-up style since I was in high school, except for the color of my lipstick. It worked well for me, so why change it?

I wasn't sure if alcohol was allowed in public, so I shoved my bottle of tequila and two plastic glasses, from the side of the bathroom sink, into my oversized purse, put on my sunglasses and went down to the pool. Blaze was sitting there smoking a joint. He looked up as I approached and smiled a sexy smile.

Even though there were other patrons at the hotel, we were the only two at the pool. I pulled up a lounge chair next to Blaze, looked around and took out my bottle of tequila, the two plastic glasses and sat them on the table.

"So, tell me, Blaze, what brings you here?" I poured each of us a large shot and handed him his.

"I graduated from college last June, and I have been traveling ever since. I'm on my way to Seattle to start work with an advertising firm next week." He drank the shot, set the glass down and took a toke from his joint before he offered it to me.

I declined the joint, and we made more small talk while draining the bottle of tequila.

"Well, fuck. I'm nowhere near drunk enough, and I don't know this town well enough to go looking for a liquor store." I knew I should have bought more than one bottle.

"No problem, I've been here for a few days and know where there's one. I'll be right back." Blaze got up to leave.

"Here, let me give you some cash." I reached into my purse.

"No, I got this. Still be here when I get back?" He touched my hand to push away the money.

"Nope, I'll be in my room. Join me?" I think the tequila had temporarily stopped the common sense part of my brain.

"Sounds like a plan. Need anything else?" Oh there was that smile again.

"Sure, why don't you pick up a pizza?" A pizza? Really? I had been vegan for years. Oh well, one night, right?

The minute Blaze left to go to the store, I picked up the empty bottle and went to the front desk to extend my stay for another night. I had a feeling I would need another night to recover after this one.

Opening my hotel room door, the logical side of my brain was screaming at me, "What are you doing? You don't even know this guy!" My body was saying something completely different. *wink*

There was nothing on television, so I ran down to my car and snagged my portable stereo and CDs. Yes, I actually upgraded from tapes to CDs. It was part of my self reconstruction. Music had always been an integral part of my life, so I felt that it was worth the investment.

I set the stereo on the floor in front of the dresser and stacked the CDs next to it. I popped in a CD I had purchased in Las Vegas that was a compilation of 70's rock bands. It was one of my favorite eras for music and reminded me of Willow.

Finally, sitting on the bed, I lit a cigarette. Wait, did sitting on the bed seem too brazen? I quickly moved to the chair by the window and then thought better of it. I didn't want to look like I had put any thought into this, so I plucked up the ashtray, my cigarettes, lighter and sat on the floor in front of my stereo. I was sitting there, thumbing through my collection, when Blaze knocked on the door.

I jumped up to let him in, and just as I reached the door, I stopped, took a deep breath and put a smile on my face. I knew how to do this. Dropping my gaze to the floor, I opened the door and looked up at him with the sexiest grin and most innocent eyes I could muster.

FUCK. It wasn't Blaze. It was the creepy hotel clerk.

"Yeah?" ICKY... Why was he here?

"You forgot your receipt when you extended your stay. Can I come in?"

"Um, that would be a no, thanks." I grabbed the receipt from him and slammed the door closed.

A few minutes later, there was another knock on the door. This time, I wasn't so presumptuous and asked who it was. Blaze answered me back and I smiled.

I stepped behind the door as I opened it and once again produced my sexiest "come in and fuck me" look. He met my gaze, smiled and handed me the pizza box. He bent to pick up another small box that was sitting on the sidewalk containing two bottles of tequila and a twelve pack of beer. Wow, he was prepared to party.

"There's nothing on TV, so I was listening to some music." I cracked the first bottle of tequila and took a drink right out of the bottle.

"Awesome, I'm a music junky. Whatcha got?" He accepted the bottle from me, took a shot, sat on the floor where I had just been sitting and started looking through my music collection.

"I don't have a lot. I'm only now starting the transition into CDs." We passed the bottle back and forth.

"That's cool. I'll be right back. I got some shit you might like. Oh, um, is it cool if I bring a couple joints?" He stood up and stopped at the door.

"Sure." I didn't know what else to say. I had never smoked pot before, but there was a first time for everything, right? I tossed him the hotel key and told him to let himself in when he returned.

There was a light tap at the door and then I heard the keys in the lock, so I knew it was him returning and not the creepy clerk guy.

"Here, check these out." Blaze handed me a stack of CDs and lit a joint. His collection was mostly alternative rock bands, so I popped one in.

"Thanks, Blaze." I took another shot of tequila and opened a beer.

"Hand me those beers, and I'll put 'em in the fridge." He stuck the beer in the refrigerator and sat back down on the floor next to me. "Whatcha think?"

"Oh, I'm diggin' this. I'll have to write these bands down, so I can pick them up later." And yet another shot of tequila with a beer chaser.

"You can have those, Maggie. I always buy two copies when I get new CDs. I don't know why, just something I do." He set the joint down in the ashtray and cracked open a beer himself.

"Really? What do I owe you for them?" That was SO cool of him.

"How 'bout a kiss?" Blaze smiled and looked at me out of the corner of his eyes. Leaning over, I kissed him on the lips. Goose bumps covered my skin, and I began to blush. "Thank you, please, don't think of me as a pervert, but I've been wanting to do that all afternoon. You have gorgeous lips." Blaze blushed a bit himself.

"Nope, I don't think you're a pervert, but don't go thinkin' you can buy me with some CDs." I giggled and winked at him.

"I would never think that about you, Maggie. 'Class' should be your middle name." Smiling, he winked at me.

"Okay, you can stop with the flattery now." I winked back. I didn't care if it was a line or not. I was eating it up.

We continued to drink, eat pizza and listen to music until the sun disappeared into the moonlit sky. Blaze had picked up a few other munchies along with the pizza.

"This is the best pizza I've had in a long time. As a matter of fact, this is the first pizza I've had in years." I reached for another piece.

"Really? Why's that?" Blaze was on his third piece.

"I'm vegan." The words didn't feel right coming through lips that had just had pepperoni and cheese pass through them.

"Wow, why'd you ask for pizza then? I could've picked up something else for you." He seemed a bit shocked.

"I just felt like it. Besides, what goes better with beer and tequila than pizza?" I laughed.

"Guess you're right." He opened another can of beer.

"Hey, you got another joint?" Stop it, Maggie. SHUT UP BRAIN!

"Yeah, sure." Blaze reached into his pocket to pull out another joint. "Are you sure about this? Thought you said you've never smoked."

"I haven't, but there's a first time for everything, right?" Um, hadn't I just said that to myself earlier? Yeah, that's what I thought too.

I took the joint from him and lit it. I coughed a bit as I inhaled and then tried it again. Ooh... it tasted so good. We shared the rest of it in between more shots and more beer.

Now, as previously stated, I had never smoked pot before and wasn't sure how I would react to it, but I had enough booze in me to not really care. All I know is that I was starving. Blaze and I finished off the pizza and ordered another one. It wasn't long before it was delivered. We sat there, for what seemed like hours, laughing, talking and eating everything we could find.

I noticed the early morning sun starting to peek in the windows from behind the blinds, and I knew our night was coming to an end. Dammit.

"Hey, Blaze? How long are you staying here?" I asked him with hope in my voice.

"I was supposed to check out tomorrow morning, but I extended my stay one more night... You?" He sounded just as hopeful.

"Same here, um, do you want to sleep here tonight?" Here I go again.

"Sleep wasn't what I had in mind." Blaze winked at me as he passed me another joint.

Smoke encircled our heads as we kissed again. He was such a good kisser. Is it just me or is kissing a huge turn on? It's just yummy when it's done right. Anyway...

I didn't have a lot of sexual experience, and I remember thinking to myself, "You're never going to see this guy again, just have fun... Be wild." That's exactly what I did.

I laid on the floor and poured tequila into my belly button. Blaze leaned over and slowly sucked it out.

He started to kiss my stomach and lightly bite my skin. I arched my back to meet his lips. He wrapped his arms around me and lifted me toward him. Now, sitting face to face, our lips locked in an aggressive and deep kiss.

"Let's take a shower." I whispered into his mouth.

Without any further discussion, Blaze picked me up and carried me into the bathroom, turned on the water and literally slammed me into the shower, clothes and all.

Joining me, he pulled at my wet tank top, ripped it from my body and followed suit with my bra. His strong arms lifted me to him, and he buried his face in the wetness of my breasts. I slid down his body, and our lips found each other's again. Gripping the back of his head while biting his lip, I slid my free hand down the front of his pants and felt what he had to offer me. Oh... My... GOD.

I quickly worked to unbutton his jeans, and I pushed them from his body as I sunk to my knees in front of him. I pulled him fully into my mouth to experience all that he had to give me... And I do mean ALL.

I looked up into his eyes and watched him watch me. It was like nothing I had ever experienced before. The water ran over our bodies and steamed up the bathroom. He tasted salty against my tongue, and I felt him grow even larger inside my mouth.

Blaze latched onto handfuls of my hair and pulled me up to meet his lips once again. "Slow down, Maggie. We have all the time we want." He kissed me hard and stripped me of my jeans. "My God, you're beautiful..." His words ended against my lips.

Our naked bodies evolved into one, complete organism. We ensnared each other in a shared grasp, and it was difficult to tell where I started and he ended. He lifted and pinned me against the wall of the shower with my legs wrapped around his waist. He had yet to take me fully, as we were enjoying the sensation of our naked, wet skin against each other and the taste of our lips combining.

Lifting me away from the shower wall, Blaze reached, turned off the water with one hand and used his back to open the shower door. He carried me, still wrapped around his waist, to the bed and dropped me on it. I grabbed at him to pull him on top of me.

"Not so fast, Maggie. We have to be safe." He reached for his wallet and put on a condom. "Now... Now we can do this right."

His body, heavy against mine, pinned me to the bed as he cupped my full breasts with his hands. The heat of his breath danced across my skin, and he kissed his way down my body. I moved against his mouth, directing him to his destination.

Blaze, now kneeling on the floor, pulled me to the edge of the bed, slipped his hands under me and lifted my hips to meet his mouth. Oh yeah, this man knew what he was doing.

He slid his face between my thighs and devoured me. I cried out with an orgasm that shook me from the inside out... And then he went back for more. I begged him to stop as my body heaved in frenzied spasms. He wouldn't stop, so I pulled away from him and sat up on the bed. He knelt in front of me and kissed me again. I tasted sweet on his lips.

Sitting, he pulled me closer to him, told me to sit on his lap and wrap my legs around his waist. I did as he asked and felt him plunge inside me. Our bodies, still wet from the shower, undulated together, as our lips answered our carnal need to kiss one another. We moved in a silent rhythm as if we were dancing to our own choreographed routine. We scratched each other's backs, drawing blood through the skin, until we mutually trembled in utter rapture.

I fell asleep on his chest with his hands wrapped in my hair. I awoke in an empty bed in the early evening. Rolling over to see what time it was, I noticed a bag of weed laying on the night stand with a note...

"Dearest Maggie,

Smoke this and remember me with the fondest (not foggiest) of memories. I know, I shall never forget you. Not to sound cliche, but thanks for the memories.

Fondly Yours,

Blaze"

Smiling, I re-read the note and held it close to my heart as I thought about the events of the last day and night. I showered, dressed, rolled and lit a joint. Packing up my stuff, I headed out to finish the last leg of my journey to Colorado Springs. I didn't care that I had paid for a night I wouldn't use.

I still have that note.

CHAPTER FIFTEEN

Three hundred miles never felt so long. It took me almost six hours to drive the rest of the way to Colorado Springs. As soon as I got there, I was tempted to turn around and go back.

Remember how I told you that Bryce was delusional? Yeah, I should have reminded myself about that before I moved to Colorado. Everything he had told me was exaggerated.

Bryce had told me that he had a cabin, and there was plenty of room for me and my things. What a liar! Okay, in all fairness, it was a cabin. That wasn't the problem. The problem was the amount of space. He lived in a miniature, one room cabin that had a tiny bathroom off of one side of it. Not my idea of "enough space."

The security company he started? Yeah, he had one client, and it was a parking garage at night. Yep, I should have known better.

I didn't waste my time arguing with him. Over the years I had learned it wasn't worth my energy. Bryce lived in a make-believe world that he created, and he preferred it that way. But, I still considered him my friend.

Well, since I was here, I had to figure out where I was going to live. I checked into a hotel for two nights and started looking for an apartment. I had saved up some money and had my winnings from Vegas, so I wasn't too worried.

On day two, I found a really nice one bedroom apartment in downtown Colorado Springs. It was well lit, spacious, and I could afford it. After talking the landlord into renting to me, without a job, I paid three months rent up front, along with the deposit, and moved in.

I really loved my new home. The front door sat off to one side and entered into the main living area. Directly in front of you, past the living room, was a two story tall wall that hid the galley style kitchen from the rest of the apartment. There was a dining area to the left with sliding glass doors that opened to a small private back yard with a patio. A set of stairs leading to the loft bedroom and master bath sat to the right of the front door. There was a half bath and large storage closet built under the staircase. The loft bedroom had a cut-out window overlooking the living room. The entire apartment was painted a soft beige and had lightly stained wood trim and base boards. The floors were all hardwood except for the staircase and bedroom which had a nice, plush, beige carpet on them.

I had brought everything with me except furniture. I headed out and found a thrift store where I purchased a futon, a coffee table, a console table, an entertainment center, a dresser and a dining table with four matching chairs.

I didn't want to buy a second hand bed. Instead, I found a relatively inexpensive furniture store, purchased a queen size bed and had it delivered. That way I wouldn't have to haul it up the stairs myself.

Once all the furniture was in place, I set out to unpack. I knew I was going to be exhausted by the time I was finished, so I started with my bedroom first. I made the bed, put the clothes away and put my small TV on top of the dresser. There... done.

The master bath was pretty simple to unpack as well. I then found my way down the stairs to set up the dining area. I set the table and hung the art. It looked really pretty. I then proceeded to unpack three bottles of beer into my belly. * Wink *

I was tempted to call it a night at that point, but I knew the way my mind worked. I would never be able to get to sleep knowing I had so much to do. When I finished the last of the three beers, I unpacked the kitchen and arranged the living room. There, all done. * phew *

I fell into bed that night and don't remember moving a muscle. I was exhausted and probably snored loud enough for my neighbors to hear me. When I woke up the next morning, I did a little grocery shopping and then started to look for work.

I was driving down one of the main streets in the west end of town when I passed a tattoo studio. Hmm... maybe? It couldn't hurt, right?

Grabbing my portfolio from the back seat, I went inside. The place was pretty busy, so I sat in the lobby and patiently waited for the owner to have time to talk to me. When he finished with his client, he asked me back to his office.

Tango, the owner, looked at my portfolio and told me I was a talented artist. He said he was concerned because I was so new at tattooing, but was willing to give me a shot as an apprentice.

Working out the details of my employment, we decided I would pay a fifty percent chair rental, and he would supply the needed gear. A clause was added stating that either of us could walk away from the contract with a two week notice without reason. Satisfied with the arrangements, we shook hands to make it official. I was to start work that weekend.

I felt like I had fallen into paradise. In just a few day's time, I had found a nice apartment and a great job? Yeah, I was stoked! Time to go out and celebrate.

There was a club right up the street from me called "Roundup." It was a country bar but on Wednesday nights it was ladies' night, and they played dance music. Ladies got in free, which was awesome. Wine, wells and drafts were free too, which was even better. * wink *

I dressed in my usual attire and headed out around ten o'clock. As I pulled into the parking lot, I could hear dance music playing and saw a line of people waiting to get in. Damn, I hated lines.

Deciding to leave my purse in the car, I grabbed my driver's license and cash. I knew it wasn't safe to leave my purse in the front of my car, so I locked it in the trunk and went to stand in line.

One of the bouncers, from the front door, was walking the line and picking people to go in. He approached me, smiled and said, "You, go on." I was excited, but I played it cool.

After the bouncer at the door checked my identification, I was handed free drink tickets and walked in. It was dark, loud and crowded. I had never seen anything like it but couldn't wait to experience it.

I went to the bar, got a rum and coke and tipped the bartender. He smiled and said the next drink would be better. I winked at him before I went to sit down.

Now, where to sit? The tables and booths were all full. I looked around and saw two women sitting by themselves, so I approached them.

"Hi, can I sit here?" I hoped they didn't think I was hitting on them.

"Sure, want a shot?" The slimmer of the two handed me a shot of tequila.

"My kind of women. My name is Maggie. I just moved here on Monday from California. What's your names?"

They introduced themselves. Chloe was petite and had dark hair that she wore short around her very pretty brown eyes. Sara was a healthy sized girl with long, light brown hair and green eyes. They both had pretty smiles.

Sara stood up to let me slide into the booth. I hate to say it this way, but she had the biggest breasts I had ever seen! I mean, I was pretty well built myself, but this girl... Holy shit!

In between dancing, the three of us talked quite a bit. They were both students and were going to school to become medical assistants. I told them about my new job and how excited I was to start working that coming weekend. Chloe said she knew a lot of people that wanted tattoos, and she would send them my way. I expressed my thanks because I needed to start building a customer base.

When the club closed, Sara and Chloe wanted to go out to eat. They said they had gotten dropped off by Chloe's boyfriend, so I volunteered to drive. We went to an all night restaurant and had breakfast.

I gave them a ride home, we exchanged phone numbers, and I left. My gas tank was almost on empty, so I stopped to fill it up and buy a pack of cigarettes before I headed home.

I slept in late Thursday morning. I had one hell of a hangover, and I hadn't even really drank all that much. I thought maybe I was dehydrated and decided to take it easy for the rest of the day.

Getting bored with just resting, I got out my tattoo machines and got them tuned up and ready for work. As I said before, Tango was supplying the ink, caps, needles, tubes and such, so I didn't have to worry about that, but I wanted to use my own machines.

I hadn't seen Bryce since I moved in, so I invited him over for dinner. He really liked my new place and even talked about moving in with me. Oh hell no buddy! That will NEVER happen!

I made vegan tacos, and he swore up and down that they were meat. I laughed and just let him believe what he wanted to. I guess that says a lot about my cooking skills though. When we were done eating, we watched a movie, and he went home.

After cleaning up the kitchen, I took a long, hot bath and went to sleep. I didn't have to be to work until two in the afternoon, but I wanted to be bright eyed and bushy tailed for it.

Waking up early Friday morning, I got my clothes ready for the day. I had always loved the pin-up look, so I decided to go with that for my first day. I wore a pair of dark blue jeans rolled up to my calves. I then put on a short sleeved, red and white checkered shirt. With my hair pinned in curls to the top of my head, I wrapped a matching red and white checkered scarf under the back of it and tied it on the top. Make-up, perfume, and I was ready to go. Now, what was I going to do for the rest of the day? It was only ten in the morning.

After turning on some music, I dug out my easel and oil paints. It had been quite some time since I had an opportunity to paint. I had always loved abstract art, so I moved the paint over the canvas according to the way the music made me feel. It was soft and sensual. When I finished it, I hung it on the empty wall in my dining area and cleaned up my mess.

I wasn't sure what was available in Colorado Springs as far as take-out vegan food, so I thought it best I make my own to bring in. A small salad and a home made veggie burger would do just fine. I whipped up a blender full of fresh fruit smoothie, dumped it in a thermos, packed up my food, and I was out the door.

"Hey, Maggie, you're early." Tango looked up from his desk when I walked in.

"I was up early and didn't have anything to do, so I thought I would come in. Is that alright?" I put my food in the fridge in his office.

"Yeah, but I was going to order in food for us tonight." He looked disappointed.

"Oh, that would have been nice, but I'm vegan, and I didn't know what there was around here, so I brought in my own food." I felt bad, but I loved being vegan and wasn't changing it.

"So am I." Tango was vegan? That was awesome!

"Wonderful! How about we share what I brought in and next time it's your treat?" Yay! Another vegan!

"Sounds incredible, thanks, Kid." He winked at me and stood up.

Tango showed me around the shop and got me acquainted with everything. He then went into his office to catch up on some paperwork while I did a bit of basic cleaning. He kept a really clean shop, but no one cleaned like I did. * wink *

There were three appointments that day, and Tango was going to do them. They were intricate pieces, and he wasn't sure that I was ready for them. He asked that I watch the front, and if any walk-ins came in, I was to let him know, and he would decide if he wanted me to tattoo or not.

Around seven that evening, a guy came in looking to get a dragon tattoo on his shoulder. I asked him to wait in the lobby while I took the art back to Tango. He looked at the art, and gave me the go ahead to do the tattoo. I got a price quote, okayed it with the client and drew up the stencil. After setting up my area, I asked the client to come back. Once I cleaned and shaved his arm, I covered the area with gel and placed the stencil.

The client was pretty nervous, so I turned on some music to take his mind off of things. I removed the stencil, cleaned him up again and started the tattoo. It wasn't all that difficult. I made sure to do my absolute best because I not only wanted the client to like it, but I wanted to show Tango just what I was capable of.

When I finished the outline, I poured the color ink and got to work on filling it in. The client took it all pretty well and was relieved when I told him I had finished. He looked at it in the mirror, paid me the set price and tipped me sixty dollars. He said he would be back for more, and he would be bringing some friends too. Before he left, he poked his head into Tango's area, told him he thought I was really talented and would be back. Yep, I was beaming with pride!

When we cashed out, Tango handed me two hundred dollars. I was shocked. "I thought I paid fifty percent chair rental? This is more than half of what I earned." I tried to hand him back some of the money.

"You earned it, Kid. I've never seen this place so clean. I have some things to do tomorrow, so I won't have the shop open. I'll see you on Monday." He smiled and walked me to my car.

Since I didn't have to work the next day, I headed home and called Sara and Chloe to invite them over. They said it sounded like fun and were going to get a ride to my place.

We were going to have a sleepover. Movies, popcorn, beer, and a few joints were on the agenda for the evening. Tango was a pot head, so I was able to get a little weed from him. I didn't know if Chloe and Sara smoked pot, but if not, that was okay, just meant more for me.

Damned Blaze got me hooked on this shit! * laughing *

I didn't have much in my place for non-vegans, so I thought it best that I order in some food. The girls showed up at my place just as their pizza did. They walked in carrying it. They had met the delivery guy outside.

"Wow, Maggie, this is a nice place." Chloe sat the pizza on the kitchen counter.

"Thanks, I like it. It'll be cooler when I can finish decorating it." I handed them each a beer.

"What do you plan to do?" Sara cracked open her beer.

"It needs some color, lots of color." We grabbed the rest of our food and drinks and went to the living room to set it down. I then gave them a quick tour of the rest of the place and told them to make themselves at home.

We changed into our pajamas, settled into the living room and turned on some music. We decided to save the movies for later. I dug out a bottle of tequila to go with the rest of it.

"You gals smoke pot?" I had to ask.

"Sure do." Chloe was usually the first one to speak.

I rolled a joint and handed it to Sara. She lit it, took a hit and passed it to Chloe, and in turn, Chloe passed it to me. We sent it around the circle until it was gone.

Now, I don't know how many of you have smoked pot, but I am assuming that quite a few of you have. You know how it is when you get the giggles? Yeah, imagine the three of us, stoned out of our minds and laughing at nothing. So of course, we had to start taking shots. * wink *

We talked a lot throughout the night and didn't even get to the movies. Chloe showed me a picture of her two little girls. They were gorgeous. Chloe was Korean, her boyfriend was African American, and wow, did they make pretty babies! She told me that her boyfriend was a cosmetologist, and if I ever needed his services, she would loan him to me for a while. Yeah, that got us laughing all over again.

Sara was normally a quiet woman, but when she had smoked a little pot and had a couple of shots, she really opened up. She talked about her past and how every guy she had gotten with was only into her tits. Yep, we all burst out laughing again. How could we not? Her breasts looked like two watermelons that were barely contained by a rubber band!

I told the two of them about my marriage, divorce and school. We talked about my new job and how much I loved it there, and that's when Chloe asked for a tattoo.

"Chloe, I don't know if that's such a good idea right now. I'm pretty lit." I was being honest.

"Oh come on! Who gives a fuck? Let's do this!" Chloe was really excited.

"Really, Chloe, not a good idea right now. I would be more than happy to give you one tomorrow when we're all sober." I was trying really hard to postpone this.

"Alright, fine." Chloe was actually pouting. It was kind of cute.

"So, are you dating anyone, Maggie?" Sara found a way to change the subject.

"Nope, I haven't met anyone worth dating, although, there was this guy I met in Grand Junction..." I told them all about Blaze and our little adventure. Again, we couldn't stop laughing.

"I know this guy from school; he might be your type." Sara was the first to stop laughing.

"Sara, you're always trying to fix people up. What's that all about?" Chloe playfully slapped Sara on the shoulder.

"I just love to see people happy." Sara looked down at her drink. I think her feelings were hurt.

"Um, sure, Sara. I would love to meet your friend. I'm not really looking for a relationship, but it could be fun." I hadn't thought about dating since the fiasco with Kevin.

"His name is Jared, and he's a really sweet guy. He won't be back around for a month or so. He's out visiting his mom on the east coast, but when he gets back I'll set it up." Sara seemed excited.

Chloe turned up the music, and we danced around like idiots. I taught them a few of the salsa steps that Antonio had taught me, and we had an absolute blast. We drank, ate, smoked pot, ate some more and finally collapsed into an oblivious sleep sometime as the sun was coming up.

When we woke up the next afternoon, I gave Chloe a small tattoo of a butterfly on her hip. She loved it, and so did I. I hated to tattoo out of my dining room, but she was a friend, so I let it slide. I still had my sonic cleaner, autoclave and the rest of my gear, so I was able to keep things sterile.

When I finished her tattoo, we cleaned up, dressed, and I took the girls out to eat before I dropped them off at home. I needed to get a cell phone, so I went shopping. After picking one out and signing up for a plan, I headed home to sleep some more. I was exhausted.

I woke up later that evening and decided to check out a different club. Sunday night was ladies' night at a place called "Reeds'." Of course, I had to check it out because that was my last name.

This was back in the day, when smoking was still allowed in bars, so when I walked in, the air was heavy with smoke. I scanned the crowd, got a free drink and sat at the bar. I kept looking around as if I were waiting for someone.

That's when I saw him. He was dressed to impress and had a smile that lit up the darkness of the club. Again, what was my deal with smiles?

"Hello, my name is Dwayne. May I sit here or are you waiting for someone?" Oh, that smile.

"Hi, nope, not waiting for anyone; have a seat." I smiled back and twirled the ice in my drink.

You know how this kind of thing goes. We had a bit of a conversation, danced, drank a few more drinks, and before I knew it, we were heading out the door to my place.

Please, don't think that I was easy because that couldn't be further from the truth. I was lonely. Dwayne made for good company and great sex. Okay, so maybe I was a little easy, especially for a guy with a smile like his.

Yeah, we fucked. We fucked like animals! Our clothes were dropped up the stairs to my bedroom as if we were leaving a trail of breadcrumbs to find our way back to reality.

It was the first time I woke up next to a guy that I wasn't in a relationship with. It was a bit awkward. I quietly got up, showered and dressed. When I came out of the bathroom, Dwayne was sitting on the side of my bed.

"Hey, you hungry?" Still awkward.

"Yeah, want to go out for breakfast?" There was that smile again.

"Naw, I was thinking I would make us breakfast while you showered." I had to put that shower thing out there because it was truly needed.

"Sure, thanks." He looked surprised.

"I left some towels for you on the counter, help yourself." I went downstairs to start breakfast.

I made bagels, a fresh fruit salad and coffee. We sat on the patio and ate breakfast together. The conversation was light and fun. He got up to go home, so I walked him to the door.

"Can I call you sometime, Maggie?" He kissed me at the front door.

"Sure, that would be nice." I grabbed a piece of paper off of the console table by my front door and scribbled down my cell phone number for him. "Look, I'm not really looking for a relationship though."

"That's cool, neither am I." Dwayne kissed me again and left.

I spent the rest of the day cleaning house, washing laundry and doing a bit of grocery shopping. I needed to get things done as I worked all week.

Monday was a slow day at work. Tango said it was usually like that. I wasn't having it, so I called Chloe, told her we had openings for tattoos, and if she got a few friends to come down to the studio, I would give them a ten percent discount. Before I knew it, four of her friends were there, with Chloe at their side. Tango was impressed with me again.

We each did two of the tattoos and made seven hundred dollars between us. After we cleaned up for the day, Tango gave me two hundred fifty dollars. I reminded him, once again, about the fifty percent chair rental, but he wasn't hearing it. He told me that I earned it and to shut up and enjoy it. I laughed and offered to take him out for a drink.

Tango insisted on paying for our meals and drinks. I thanked him and told him I would see him at work the next day. I went home and watched a movie.

There was a knock at my door. Who the hell was knocking on my door after midnight? I thought maybe it was Bryce, so I threw on my robe and went to the door.

It was Dwayne. He had been at the club and was really drunk. He said he was afraid to drive all the way home because he lived on the north side of town. I let him in and told him he could sleep on the futon. I gave him a blanket and headed up to bed. I locked my bedroom door because I didn't want him to think he could just crawl in bed with me.

The next morning, I, once again, made us breakfast and coffee. I had to wake him up because I had some errands to run before work, and he was not staying at my place when I wasn't there. He thanked me for breakfast, and we made arrangements for him to come over after work because he said he needed to talk to me.

I went to a print shop to have some business cards made. I wanted to hand them out at the clubs to help boost business. They said the cards would be ready in a week, and they would ship them to me.

Tuesdays at work were our days for inventory and ordering. Tango showed me how to do the count and place the order. I picked it up quickly and took care of it while he did a couple of tattoos. Once again, at the end of the day, he handed me some cash even though I hadn't done any tattoos. Tango said he knew the day he met me that he and I would make a great team. I was really starting to love this guy... In a platonic kind of way, of course.

Tango asked me if I wanted to go out to eat, but I explained that I had something to take care of. He told me that he had booked an early appointment and needed me there at noon the following day. I hugged him and left.

Dwayne was at my door when I got home. I was a bit nervous because this seemed to be urgent. I hoped he wasn't there to tell me he had some disease. I mean, we were safe and used a condom, but ya never know.

I made a pot of coffee and sat down on the futon with Dwayne. I didn't think either of us had to be drinking. He had quite a bit the night before, and I had to get up early for work.

"So, what is it? Let me have it." I handed Dwayne a cup of coffee.

"I don't even know where to start." He looked upset.

"The beginning is usually the best place." Fuck, now I was really worried!

Dwayne explained that he was losing his apartment because the building had been sold, and he didn't have enough to rent another place quite yet. He asked if he could stay with me for a month or two, until he could get on his feet. I let him move in but told him that it was only for a month. I also set a couple of ground rules. There was to be no one in my home unless I was there and that included him. I told him that he would not be bringing people into my home, whatsoever. He agreed, hugged me and left. He was going to start bringing some of his things over when I got home from work the next night. Yeah, it was probably a stupid move on my part, but I just couldn't say no to him. He had that smile... That damned smile. It was only going to be for a month. I was sure it would be fine.

I got to work a little early again and helped Tango set up for his appointment. When it was all set up, he explained that I was the one that would be doing this tattoo, and it was going to be an all day kind of thing. Um, wow!

Tango had a friend that wanted a full back tattoo done all in one sitting. Now, normally this kind of thing would be done in a few sittings, but I guess it was important to her to have it all done at once. The tattoo was of a caterpillar turning into a butterfly, and it was to be surrounded with flowers. All in all, it would take me about six hours. This was going to be tough, but I knew I could do it.

Tango's friend showed up, and we got started right away. As soon as the tattoo was underway, Tango excused himself saying he had some errands to run. He put up a "be back later" sign and locked the front door.

We were about five hours into the tattoo when Tango came back. He checked the work I was doing, told me I was a natural born artist, and he no longer thought of me as an apprentice. I couldn't stop smiling.

When the tattoo was complete, I sprayed down her back with some witch hazel to help with the swelling and stinging. I told her she could relax for as long as she needed. Tango called me into his office while she was resting on the tattoo bed.

"Maggie? I have something for you, so I'm going to need you to stay after for a little while once Tina leaves." He was smiling a huge smile.

"Okay, Tango. You didn't have to get me anything though." I was shocked.

"Oh, yes I did." He asked me to go wrap up Tina, get paid and send her home.

When I finished cleaning up, I went back into Tango's office. He was sitting in his chair waiting for me.

"Here." He handed me a black box with a red ribbon on it. "Open it."

I pulled the ribbon from the box and took off the lid. Inside sat the most beautiful tattoo machine I had ever seen! It was in the shape of an "M" and had little hearts surrounding it. Oh... My... GOD!

I sucked in my breath, hugged him tight and thanked him for the amazing gift. He had it handmade for me by one of his friends in the industry. It was beyond amazing!

We locked up the studio early and went out for dinner and drinks. Tango was like the father I had always wanted, and I was so proud to call him my friend. I could not have asked for a better employer or friend.

Dwayne showed up shortly after I got home. He didn't have much stuff, so I emptied my storage closet in the living room to make space for his things. I reminded him, once again, of the rules, and I headed upstairs to go to bed.

"Maggie? Um... I was thinking..." I knew what he was going to say.

"You can stop thinking, Dwayne. I'm not saying it won't ever happen, but it's not happening tonight." I shut off the lights and went to bed.

The next few weeks were pretty uneventful. I worked, came home, shopped, worked some more and hung out with Chloe and Sara. I went out on the nights that I didn't have to work the next day, passed out business cards and enjoyed myself. Life was good and I was happy.

CHAPTER SIXTEEN

"Has anyone ever told you that you have beautiful eyes?" He smiled.

"Hello, Jared." I was sitting at a table at the club when he approached me. "Has anyone ever told you that's an old line and doesn't work on smart women?"

"Oh, beautiful and feisty. I like that. Hi, Maggie, it's nice to meet you. Can I buy you a drink?" Jared sat across the table from me.

"That would be nice. How about a round of tequila?" Oh, he was cuter than Sara had said.

"Sara has told me a lot about you. You're a tattoo artist?" Jared signaled for the server to come over and placed our order.

"Yes, I am. I've only been in town about two months now, but I'm loving it. She said that you're a student. What else do you do?" Sara had already told me, but I was trying to make small talk.

"I'm a tour guide at Garden of the Gods. I only work part time because right now school is more important." He handed me a shot.

"That's awesome. I haven't made it out there yet. Maybe you can give me a personal tour sometime?" Yep, I was diggin' on him already.

"Sure, do you have anytime this weekend? Weekends are best for me since I don't have school." Jared drank another shot.

"Yep, I don't work on Sundays." I drank my second shot as well.

"Wonderful, why don't I pick you up Sunday morning, and we make a day of it?" Jared was charming to say the least.

"Sounds perfect." I smiled at him and asked him to dance.

We spent the rest of the night talking and dancing. We didn't drink much more after the first few shots except for a couple of beers. I told him I had to drive home and didn't want to get sloppy drunk. He agreed that was a good idea.

When the club closed, he offered to follow me home, so he knew I got there safe and would know where to pick me up on Sunday. I agreed and we left.

He was pulling in behind me when I was getting out of my car.

"You have a lead foot, Maggie." Jared laughed a little as he got out of his car.

"You're not the first person to tell me that." I giggled a schoolgirl giggle.

"Here, put your number in here if you don't mind." He handed me his cell phone, and I put my number in it.

"I would invite you in, but I have a temporary roommate that sleeps in my living room." Yeah, I had broken my own rule and let Dwayne be there when I wasn't home.

"It's cool. I understand. Anyway, we just met." Jared was a gentleman too? How did I get so lucky?

"I had fun tonight. I'll see you on Sunday?" I stepped close to him.

"Sure thing. I had fun tonight too." He leaned in and gave me the softest of kisses. "I'll call you tomorrow night if that's okay? What time do you get off work?"

"That would be great. I am usually home by eleven or so." I shifted on my feet. I had to pee but didn't want to go in quite yet.

"I'll call around eleven thirty then." He kissed me again and left.

I walked into my apartment to find Dwayne sitting on my futon with some guy. "What the fuck, Dwayne? I thought we had an agreement." Yeah, I was a little upset.

"Oh hey, Maggie. This is my cousin Matt. Don't worry, we didn't steal anything from you." He was drunk.

"That's not the point, Dwayne. Say good night to your cousin. I have to get up early tomorrow." Oh, the nerve!

"You can't order me to do anything, Bitch." Bitch? Oh hell to the no!

"I'm going to write that off as you being drunk. You have five minutes to say goodnight ,or you can both leave. This IS still MY place." I went upstairs to change into my pajamas. When I came back down, Dwayne's cousin had left, and he was laying on the futon. "Don't let that happen again, Dwayne. I'm doing you a favor, and I deserve some respect."

He didn't say a word to me. I got my lunch ready for work and went to bed. I locked my bedroom door behind me.

Dwayne was already gone when I woke up the next morning. That was probably a good thing because I didn't want to deal with his shit. He had already overstayed his welcome, and it was time for him to leave. I decided that I would talk to him about it when I got home from work that night.

Work was pretty busy. We were getting more and more clients every week. Tango teased that it was because everyone wanted to come in and see his sexy co-artist. I would just laugh it off whenever he said things like that. He had a special way of making me smile.

I was inking an average of ten tattoos a week and making decent money. Tango and I closed up shop a bit early and he asked to see me in his office again.

"Hey, Tango, you wanted to talk to me?" I was a little nervous. It seemed like every time I was enjoying something in my life, something happened, and it ended.

"Yes, I did, Maggie. Sit down." Tango motioned to the chair on the other side of his desk.

"Is everything okay?" Now, I was really nervous.

"It's better than okay, Maggie. I've never made as much money as I have since you started working here. I want to make you a partner in the shop. We'll split everything down the middle, fifty-fifty. How's that sound?" Tango pushed some paperwork across his desk.

"Really? Are you fucking kidding? Tango, that's amazing! I don't know what to say!" I picked up the papers to look at them.

"Say yes, and take that paperwork to an attorney to have him go over it with you." He smiled at me.

"I don't need an attorney. I know you're a fair man. Oh, thank you!" I jumped up and hugged him.

"Well at least read it all before you sign it, Kid. It's the smart thing to do." Tango winked at me.

I had no doubt, whatsoever, that it was all legit, but I took it home to read it anyway. I bet that a more excited and thankful person could not have been found that day. I couldn't wait to tell my friends about it.

Though I was out of my mind thrilled, I was downright exhausted when I got home. I was hoping that Dwayne wasn't there, but I saw his car when I pulled into the driveway. Dammit...

As I walked up to my door, I could smell a really strange odor. What the hell? That better not be coming from my apartment. Shit, it was.

I walked in to find Dwayne and his cousin sitting on my futon smoking CRACK! Oh, I was beyond livid.

"What the fuck are you doing, Dwayne? Get your shit, and get the fuck out of my apartment!" Oh hell to the no. I didn't care about pot, but crack? Hell to the fuck no... Again!

"I ain't going anywhere you fucking cunt!" What? No he didn't!

"I said get the fuck out! You can come by tomorrow, and get your shit." I was not going to back down from this.

I started to walk toward the kitchen when I felt something hit me in the back of the head. I fell to my knees and grabbed my head; I was bleeding. Dwayne had thrown a beer bottle at me.

I turned around and started to yell at him to get out, or I was calling the police. He and his cousin were standing right there behind me. As his cousin grabbed me by the shoulders and held me, Dwayne slugged me in the face with a closed fist.

I managed to wiggle my way out of his cousins grasp and ran toward the stairs. I barely made it to the first step when Dwayne tripped me. I fell to the floor.

Every time I tried to stand up, Dwayne would hit me again. As Dwayne was beating the shit out of me, his cousin grabbed my purse and took all the cash I had out of my wallet. After a few more punches, I just stayed on the floor and pretended to be knocked out. I didn't have the strength to fight them both.

I laid there for quite some time before Dwayne and his cousin left to go to the liquor store. The very second they left, I got up and called the police. They were there within minutes. I showed them Dwayne's pipe and bag. They looked at my face, took pictures and my statement. The two officers waited, out of sight in my kitchen, until Dwayne and his cousin returned.

"I see you're awake, Bitch. Make us some..." Dwayne didn't have a chance to finish his sentence before the police officers came out of the kitchen and arrested him and his cousin. Take that assholes!

The officers warned me he could be released that night because the jail was full. I was scared. They told me there would be a restraining order put in place, but I knew it was just a piece of paper and wouldn't protect me.

As the officers were taking Dwayne and his cousin outside to finish reading them their rights, my phone rang. It was Jared calling. I answered the phone and told him what was going on. He hung up without saying a word. I guess I scared him off. Who in their right mind would want to get involved with a woman that had this kind of drama in her life?

A few minutes later, there was a knock on my door. I figured it was the police needing more information. I saw the lights from their cars through my curtains, so I knew they were still out there.

I opened the door. It was Jared. He had raced over to be at my side. Wow, what a great guy! He had gotten there before the police even had Dwayne in the squad car. Dwayne was putting up a fight, and the officers had him pinned to the ground.

I let Jared in and closed the door. He hugged me, walked me to the kitchen, started cleaning up my cuts and putting ice on my bruises. The police left a few minutes later.

Jared helped me over to the futon and sat with me. I explained everything that happened in great detail. He sat there and listened to every word I said. I started crying, and he pulled me gently onto his lap and let me cry.

After I felt a bit better, I called Sara and Chloe. I didn't want to be alone in case Dwayne got released. They took a cab to my place right away.

Sitting in my living room, we talked about what happened. I told them I had no idea that Dwayne was a crackhead. I was just as shocked as they were.

It was getting late, and I knew there was no way I could go into work the next day. I called Tango, got his answering machine and left a message. I knew he would understand.

I was absolutely exhausted and wanted to go to bed. I asked the girls to sleep with me because I didn't want to be alone. They agreed but only if Jared stayed the night too. I said it was okay with me, if it was okay with him. He said he would feel better if he were there anyway. We all went up to my room. The three of us girls slept across my bed, side by side, and Jared slept across the foot of my bed. Wow, what a gentleman.

When we woke up the following morning, the girls made us breakfast. It was nice not to have to cook and to have someone take care of me for once. I was in so much pain that I could barely breathe, let alone cook.

Jared sat on the patio with me while I smoked a joint. I usually didn't smoke in the mornings, but like I said, I hurt bad, and I knew it would help. I offered some to Jared, but he said he only smoked on the weekends.

"Don't you have school today?" I sipped at my coffee.

"Nope, well, yes, but I'm not going in. You need me more." He reached over and held my hand.

"Really, Jared, I'm okay. Go to school." I tried to smile at him.

"You're not a good liar, Maggie. Unless you're kicking me out, I'm not going anywhere until you're better." Again, what an amazing guy. Sara wasn't kidding when she told me he was sweet.

Chloe and Sara had to go to school. They both had tests they couldn't miss. I let Sara take my car, so they wouldn't be late. They said they would be back that evening.

Tango called to check on me. He said to take off as much time as I needed, and if there was anything he could do to just let him know. I thanked him for his kindness, and I assured him I wouldn't be out long.

While I was on the phone with Tango, Jared packed all of Dwayne's belongings and set them next to the stairs. He said he didn't want me to have to worry about anything. He checked around the apartment to make sure that nothing was forgotten.

Jared and I lounged around and watched television. He made lunch for me and even cleaned up his mess. I didn't really feel like eating, but because he cooked for me I ate what he made. He made vegan chili for me and it wasn't too bad.

I took a nap on the futon with my head in his lap while he watched a movie. He stroked my hair gently until I fell asleep and was still doing it when I woke up. I sat up and smiled at him.

"How are you feeling, Maggie? Can I get you anything?" Jared was the kindest person I had met in a long time.

"I'm better. I need to get out of here for a while though. Want to go for a walk?" Fresh air would do me some good.

"Sure, but let's take it slow. You're pretty banged up, and I don't want you to wear yourself out."

After I showered and dressed, we left on our walk. We walked around the complex and then around the block. We stopped at the convenience store to get a newspaper and cigarettes. There was no mention of what had happened in the paper, and I was relieved.

When we got back to my place, Jared and I played cards until Sara and Chloe returned. We ordered in some food and watched a movie. Chloe said she had to get home to see her boyfriend and girls, so Sara drove her home in my car.

A little while later, Sara came back, dropped off my keys and asked Jared to drive her home. He did, and while he was gone I soaked in the tub. I gave him my apartment keys, so he could let himself back in when he returned. I was happy that he was staying another night. The police had called and said that Dwayne and his cousin had been released that morning, so I definitely didn't want to be home alone.

Just as I was getting out of the bathtub, there was a knock on my door. I ran downstairs and asked who it was. A voice said it was the Colorado Springs police department. After checking through the peephole, I opened the door. There stood an officer with Dwayne. He had come by to pick up his belongings. I motioned toward his things that were packed and waiting for him by the stairs.

They were just leaving as Jared was returning. Thank goodness that was over. I hoped, except for court, I never had to see Dwayne again.

Jared stayed at my place through the weekend but had to go back to school on Monday. We hung out almost every night after school. We slept in the same bed, but nothing ever happened. We were taking our time to get to know each other. Plus, I think Jared knew I needed some time to just breathe.

Tango stopped by to check on me and pick up the partnership paperwork. He got absolutely irate when he saw the bruises on my face. I made a joke about it and told him he should see the other guy. It took me two weeks before I was ready to return to work. I didn't want to be seen with bruises. Tango understood completely and was able to manage without me.

I painted a lot when I wasn't working. Most of it was abstract art, but I did a few pieces of tattoo art as well. Tango hung four of my pieces in our studio. I had gotten a few compliments on them and even sold one of the pieces to a bail bondsman in the area.

One night, after work, I invited Jared to go with me to meet Bryce. I warned him about Bryce's make-believe world to try to prepare him. Nothing I could ever say could prepare him to meet Bryce, but I tried nonetheless.

We had dinner at Bryce's and listened to his stories all night. I swear, the man didn't breathe. He could talk non-stop. He would have been great if ever in a situation that called for a filibuster. * laughing *

After thanking Bryce for dinner and saying goodnight, we went back to my place. Except to get clothes, Jared hadn't been home in almost a month. He said he wasn't worried about it because he had a roommate that took care of the place when he wasn't there.

The next day was Sunday, so we finally went to Garden of the Gods for the tour he had promised me when we first met. I was healed now, so it was a good time to go. We packed a picnic and planned to make a day of it.

I had never seen anything as beautiful as Garden of the Gods. The rock formations were absolutely stunning! There are no other words to describe it. My favorite was called "The Kissing Camels." Go ahead, search it on the internet. I'll wait for you. * wink *

Welcome back to the story. Beautiful, right? Now, do you see why I fell into instant love with the place? I thought so.

Anyway, we spent the entire day hiking, taking pictures and stopping for our picnic. I could tell Jared really loved that place. He knew every inch of it.

It was October, so the sun was setting pretty early. We hiked up to a stone overlook, and Jared held me in his arms as we sat there watching the sun set over the canyon. It was really romantic and could not have been a more perfect ending to our day.

We got back to my place just in time for me to shower, change and head out to the club. We hadn't been out since the whole incident with Dwayne, so I was looking forward to it. I dressed in my sexiest clothes. Jared had gone home to shower and change. He said he would be back to pick me up by nine thirty.

Jared showed up as I was finishing my make-up. I liked that he was so punctual. He knocked on my door like a gentleman. He just kept getting better and better.

We met Chloe and Sara at the club. They were already sitting at a table when we arrived. We ordered a round of drinks and caught up on what had been going on since the last time we had all hung out.

A slow song started, and Jared asked me if I wanted to dance. I accepted his invitation, and he took me by the hand to lead me out to the dance floor. He wrapped his arms around my waist and pulled me close to him.

The singer sang something about, "Making plans to be together. Wanting this to last forever and ever."

I whispered into Jared's ear, "If only it could be that easy."

"It can be." He answered back.

I buried my smile in his shoulder. I didn't want him to see it. I think I was afraid of falling in love with him but knew it was too late. I already had.

When the song was over, we went back to the table and hung out with Sara and Chloe a bit longer. I wanted to be alone with Jared, so I made an excuse that I had a headache. We said goodnight and Jared drove me home.

Jared unlocked the door to my apartment and opened it for me. We barely made it through the door, when I turned around and kissed him. I pulled away from him for a moment and smiled. He locked the door, dropped my keys on the console table and wrapped me up in his arms. This time, the kiss was long and deep. It made my knees weak.

We found our way to the futon and continued to kiss each other. His hands traced my body as if he were trying to memorize it, and our lips only separated to allow us to breathe. This had been a long time in the making, and the passion that was expressed proved it.

Jared was laying fully over my body, and I could feel how much he wanted me. I struggled to stand up. Grasping him by the hand, I took him to my room.

We slowly undressed one another and took just a moment to admire each other's bodies. He was a stunning specimen of a man. His stomach and legs were tight and muscular. My body craved his.

"Maggie, are you sure about this?" He stepped close to me.

"Yes, I am, Jared. I've thought about this moment for quite some time." I put my arms over his shoulders.

"As have I, Maggie... As have I." Jared leaned down to kiss me once again.

As he kissed me, he slowly lowered me onto the bed. He knelt in front of me and starting at my toes, he kissed his way up my body. It was hot and sexy, and I wanted more. When he reached the apex of my thighs, he lingered for just a moment and then worked his way down my other leg.

When he reached my other foot, I giggled a bit and pushed myself further onto the bed. I was very ticklish. Jared stood up and joined me.

Satisfied whispers filled the air, as our bodies entangled in the soft sounds of love. We made love until the sun came up. When we were both completely satisfied, we fell into a deep and peaceful sleep.

I woke late that morning to the scent of freshly brewed coffee. I put on my robe and went downstairs. In the kitchen, next to the coffee pot, was a note...

"Dearest Maggie,

I had an amazing night last night. I had to go to school, but I wanted you to start your day knowing that I am very much in love with you. Good morning, Maggie. I'll see you when you get home from work.

Always,

Jared"

CHAPTER SEVENTEEN

The crisp, cool nights of autumn were upon us. It was wonderful to have someone to cuddle with. Jared and I were an official couple. Except for school and work, we never left each other's sides.

Business was going exceptionally well at the tattoo studio. Tango and I were booked six days a week and seldom had space for walk-ins. We decided we would set one day a week aside for people that did not make appointments, on a first come first serve basis. It worked out well for us.

With working six days a week and spending so much time with Jared, I seldom had time to paint anymore. I was really missing it, so I took the week of Thanksgiving off from work. I was hosting dinner that year and had invited all of my close friends, so I needed time to prepare as well.

I called Jared and explained my compulsion to create, and I told him I needed a night alone. He understood. Even though he and I had not had a night apart since the whole Dwayne episode, he still kept the apartment he shared with his roommate. Jared asked if he could stop by the next day when he was finished with school and work. I told him that would be great and looked forward to seeing him.

I asked the manager if it was okay to paint my apartment, and she agreed as long as I painted it back to beige before I moved out. I don't think that what I was about to do was her idea of painting though. Oh well, that's what the deposit was for.

Oil paints were usually my first choice when I created, but I always kept some acrylics on hand for when the mood struck. I dug out my acrylics and a tarp from the storage closet. After spreading the tarp out on the floor near the wall I wanted to paint, I set the paints on the tarp.

I turned on some slow, sensual music and sat on my futon with a bottle of red wine. As I drank straight from the bottle, I stared at the blank living room wall in front of me. What to do... What to do... What to... YES!

I got up and checked to make sure my door was locked. After checking that all the blinds and curtains were closed, I stripped naked.

I wanted to feel this piece of art.

Picking up the bottles of brown and orange paint, I squirted some onto the wall and then added a bit of red and purple. I used my hands, in horizontal strokes, to move and blend the paint. I pushed some of it vertically up the wall and felt the coolness of the paint against my breasts.

Stepping back to survey my work, I decided that highlights were needed. I put white paint on my fingertips, and barely touching the wall, I added the accents in the same horizontal movement.

The bottom of the piece was lacking in shadows. Mixing black and brown paint in the palm of my hand, I sat on the tarp and rubbed the paint on the bottom of my feet. I shimmied, back and forth, along the tarp using my feet to spread the paint on the lower part of the wall.

When I finished the shadows, I wiped the paint from my feet using my hands. Out of habit, I wiped my hands across my thighs to remove as much of the dark paint as I could. Picking up the red, orange and yellow paints, I again filled my palms.

Pressing my body against the wall, I reached as high as I could and smeared the paint in a circular motion. With very little paint left on my hands, I moved them away from the circle in a horizontal stroke.

Wiping the blended colors onto my stomach, I removed them from my hands. Using blue, white and lavender paint, I filled the spaces between the red, orange and yellow streaks I had just created.

Again, I stepped back to study my progress and was not yet satisfied with it. I stood over the tarp, picked up the bottles of paint and squeezed each of the colors onto different parts of my body. I covered as much of myself, front and back, as I could reach.

I approached the area closest to the front door and pressed the front of my body to it. I stepped slowly to the right, and I kept my body tight to the wall as I moved. Being very careful not to break contact, I raised my arm over my head and turned until the left side of my body was flush against the art. Again, I took a few steps and turned until my back made contact. I repeated this pattern down the entire wall until I reached the corner and then turned and followed the same path back to where I started.

Carefully stepping away, making sure to stay on the tarp, I looked again. Yep, it was perfect! It was exactly what I had envisioned. I wiped my feet on the tarp to make sure I wouldn't track paint through my apartment and ran up the stairs to shower.

After changing into sweats, I cleaned up my mess. When I finished, I grabbed another bottle of wine and sat down on the sofa to take in what I had just created. It really was perfection.

Feeling pretty lonely, I picked up my cell phone and called Jared. I wanted him to come over and see what I had done. He answered his cell phone right away.

"Hi, Baby, whatcha doin'?" I was feeling a little tipsy from the wine.

"I'm at the club with some guys from work. What are you doing?" I could hear the music in the background.

"Oh, okay. Still going to see you tomorrow?" Yeah, I was a bit disappointed.

"I was just going to give Mike a ride home. Feel like company?" Oh Yay!

"Sure! I miss you." A huge smile crossed my face.

"I love you too." Jared hung up.

Wait, what? Did he just tell me he loves me? * SWOON *

It had been not quite two months that we had been dating, but like I said before, I had fallen in love with Jared. I didn't care that this seemed fast because it felt right.

I finished my second bottle of wine. (You know, I kind of sound like an alcoholic in this book. Hello, my name is Maggie and... * giggle *) There was a movie playing in the background, but I was focusing my attention on the art I had created. I wondered if Jared would see what I saw? I fell asleep on the futon waiting for him to come over. I wasn't worried because he had his own key to my place. I knew he would wake me when he came in.

The sunshine was trying to peak in through the curtains when I opened my eyes the next morning. Jared wasn't there. My heart jumped into my throat. I picked up my phone and frantically dialed his number. Please be okay... Please be okay... PLEASE.

"Hello?" Jared's sleepy voice was the most amazing sound I had ever heard.

"Oh my God! You're okay. I was so worried." I exhaled the breath I had been holding.

"Maggie? I'm so sorry! I came home to get something to eat, and I passed out on the couch." He sounded hungover.

Jared explained everything to me and said he would be over in a little bit. He had fallen asleep with chicken in the oven, and it burned to a crisp. He had to clean up his mess before he could come over. I was relieved he was alright.

I ran upstairs to shower and dress before Jared got there. Sara and Chloe were coming over to help me start preparations for Thanksgiving dinner. We were going all out this year. Turkey with homemade stuffing, collard greens, cranberry sauce, green bean casserole and pies. We were making every bit of it from scratch, even the bread for the stuffing. Well, all of it except for the tofu turkey I was making for Tango and I. It was something new on the market, and I couldn't wait to try it.

I was laying on my bed, putting on lotion, when I heard the key in the lock downstairs. Jared called out my name as he came in. I yelled downstairs to tell him I was in my room.

He came upstairs with the most apologetic look on his face. I smiled at him as I stood to hug him. I wondered if he remembered telling me he loved me?

"You're naked. Is this for me?" He took me by the hands, stepped back and looked at me.

"It's all yours." Of course, I hadn't planned it, but it worked out well.

Jared's hands felt cool against my warm skin as he touched my waist and kissed me. He moved his hands down my body until they were firmly on my butt cheeks. As he lifted me off the ground, I wrapped my legs tight around him.

"You smell so good." His words whispered across the skin of my neck.

After laying me gently on the bed, Jared stood and undressed. I loved looking at his body. He was exceptionally well built.

He pressed my body into the thickness of the blankets as he laid fully on top of me. My hands roamed the contours of the muscles on his chest and arms. I held my breath as his right hand moved over my breasts, down my stomach and stopped between my thighs.

Jared looked into my eyes to see the pleasure he was creating with his touch. He kissed me again and with every kiss the passion shared between us grew. I couldn't take it anymore, I needed him inside me.

"Make love with me, Jared. Please?" I begged him.

He moved himself between my thighs, and my body naturally lifted to invite him inside. He started slowly as to allow me to feel every inch of him. The waves of pleasure began to wash over my body, and I felt myself imploding with orgasm. I screamed out his name and dug my long fingernails into the flesh of his back.

Jared buried his face into my neck and bit me hard. Feeling his teeth penetrate my skin, I climaxed again. He then pulled away from me and flipped me onto my knees.

Entering me slowly at first, his pace began to quicken. Keeping one hand on my hip, he slid his other hand up my back and into my hair. Clutching a handful of my hair, he pulled back to lift my face toward him and kissed me. My knees gave way from the resulting trembling, and we fell flat onto the bed. Jared didn't stop. Instead, he reached his hands under me and lifted my hips, slightly off the bed, to meet his slowing strokes.

"Flip back over, Maggie. I want to look at you." Jared pulled away from me.

I did as he directed, and he lifted my legs over his shoulders. He thrust deep inside me and bit at my right leg as he did. Closing my eyes, my head lifted off the pillow as waves of pleasure crashed over my body once again.

Jared dropped my legs to his sides and laid down on me. He kissed me as he moved inside my body. "Open your eyes, Maggie. I need to see your eyes." He kissed me as he whispered into my ear.

I did as he asked, and our eyes locked in a loving stare.

"I love you, Maggie." Jared's hand was on the side of my face.

"I love you, Jared." I whispered those three little magical words.

Our bodies were so close that daylight could not be seen between them. Jared moved slowly inside me. My toes curled and just when I thought I couldn't take it anymore, Jared's pace quickened again, and we both climaxed. My muscles pulsated around him as we lay there in the afterglow of our escapade.

"Anyone home?" Chloe's voice echoed through the bedroom window.

"Shit, I forgot to lock the front door." Jared started to laugh, so I put my finger against his lips to quiet him.

"Be right down." I answered Chloe. We hurriedly got up and dressed.

We raced down the stairs to find the girls in the kitchen. They were putting away the groceries they had brought over.

"Your door was unlocked, so we let ourselves in." Chloe handed each of us a beer before putting the rest in the fridge.

"Why is your neck bleeding, Maggie?" Sara grabbed a paper towel, wet it in the sink and placed it on my neck.

"Oh, um..." I couldn't think of an excuse fast enough.

"We caught them fucking." Chloe was almost as blunt as I was.

Laughter filled the kitchen. We finished putting away the food and then smoked a joint. This was going to be fun. We had a huge meal to prepare, and I was glad that we had a couple of days to do it. I liked to have most everything ready before Thanksgiving Day, so I wasn't rushing to get it all done.

"Where are your girls, Chloe?" I handed the joint to her.

"At home with Jeremy." She took a hit and passed it to Sara.

"Are they going to be joining us for dinner?" I had to ask. We had been friends for months and I had yet to meet her daughters or boyfriend.

"Nope, he's taking them to his mom's." Chloe answered as though it were nothing.

"Oh, okay." I didn't understand, but it wasn't up to me to pass judgment.

"Maggie? This is stunning!" Jared yelled from the living room.

"Thank you, Baby. That's what I did last night with my alone time." I joined him at his side.

"It's us at Garden of the Gods, right?" He was staring at the wall I had painted the night before.

"Yes! Wow, I wasn't sure if anyone would pick up on that." I was happily shocked.

"How could I not see it? You are truly talented." Jared kissed me.

The girls joined us in the living room, and we opened a couple of bottles of wine. We talked about the painting and how I created it.

"I think I see a boob mark." Chloe was not known to be tactful.

We laughed again, finished the wine and went to the kitchen to start cooking. We began with the bread. I showed the girls how to knead the dough, so it formed a smooth, elastic ball. When it was done, I placed the three balls of dough into greased bowls, covered them with damp towels and set them on the top of the stove to raise.

My cranberry sauce recipe was very simple. One cup of granulated sugar, one cup of orange juice and a pound of fresh cranberries. I asked Chloe to combine the sugar and orange juice in a pan. It had to be cooked down until the sugar dissolved. As she stood at the stove stirring the sauce, Sara and I started the pie crusts. We worked well as a team of three. Jared was not allowed in the kitchen.

I asked Chloe to add the cranberries to the sauce, and to cook them until they started to pop. Sara and I rolled out the pie crust and placed them into the pans. We were making pumpkin, apple and pecan pies with the crusts we had just made. Jared loved chocolate, peanut butter pie, so we were going to make that as well, but that needed a graham cracker crust.

When the bread finished raising, we punched down the dough, formed it into six loaves and put them in greased bread pans to raise again before baking. I used a knife to cut crisscross patterns in the tops of two of the loaves, so they would be pretty on our table.

The cranberry sauce was done, so we stuck it in the fridge to cool and started working on the pie fillings. Chloe made the apple, Sara the pecan, and I took care of the pumpkin pie. Once they were all in the oven baking, we cleaned up our mess and started working on place cards and the table setting. I wanted this to be the perfect meal.

Is it just me or did you just get hungry too? Maybe we should move away from the food for now. No need to get into every detail.

Jared was playing a video game, so we joined him in the living room and all took turns playing. The game consisted of stacking different colored and sized bricks to form large rows of them. I was great at this game!

We opened more wine and smoked more pot. Getting a little tired of losing to me, everyone decided to shut off the game and watch a movie. It was our typical night of hanging out together.

It was getting late, so the girls unfolded the futon and made their bed. Jared and I headed upstairs to get some sleep as well. We had another long day in front of us tomorrow. It was the last day before Thanksgiving, and we had a lot to do.

We slept in late Wednesday morning. I think we were just really tired. Naw, who am I kidding? It was the wine.

Jared and I showered, dressed and went downstairs. The girls were still sleeping, so we put on our jackets and had our coffee on the back patio. The air was crisp and we could see our breath as we spoke.

"Ya know, Maggie, I've been thinking." Jared sat his coffee on the table.

"You shouldn't do that. You might hurt yourself." I giggled at my joke.

"Haha... What do you think about us moving in together?" His question came out of nowhere.

"Um, I think that would be amazing!" I jumped up, sat on his lap and hugged him.

"Really? My place or yours?" He kissed my cheek.

"Mine, you have a roommate, and I think we should live alone." I didn't even have to think about that one. I had met his roommate, Finesse, one time and I couldn't stand her. She was a stripper with two kids and seemed to have no concern whatsoever for her babies. That's just my humble opinion though.

"I completely agree. When should we do this?" Jared looked at me full of hope.

"The sooner, the better, yes? I mean, you pretty much live here already." I stood up and took Jared by the hand to pull him to me. I hugged him tightly.

"Good, because I already started packing." He laughed.

"That sure of yourself, huh?" I playfully slapped him.

"Nope, I'm that sure of how much we love each other." He smiled and kissed me deeply.

"Do the two of you ever stop?" Chloe opened the sliding glass door.

"There is no stopping when you're in love." Jared answered her.

"In love? I knew it!" Chloe clapped her hands together. "Sara, wake up! You did it! They're in love!"

"Yay." Sara's sleepy voice barely carried across the living room out to us. "Where's the aspirin?"

We all started laughing. I made breakfast for everyone, and we told them about our plans to move in together. The girls were happy for us and offered their help.

"I was thinking, that while you ladies were cooking today, I would start bringing my things over, cool?" Jared was putting his dishes in the sink.

"Sounds perfect." I finished my breakfast and cleaned up the mess.

While Jared was gone, Sara, Chloe and I worked on drying bread for the stuffing. We cut up vegetables for a snack tray and made homemade dip as well. Of course, we had to sample the pies while we worked. It probably wasn't a good idea for us to be smoking pot while we cooked. * Wink *

We were done with everything, except the turkey and tofu turkey, by the time Jared showed up with the first load of his things. We weren't baking the main courses until tomorrow. I wanted our home to smell like Thanksgiving on the actual day.

The girls and I helped Jared to haul his things into our home. I was surprised at how much he could fit into his little car. He had a 1976 Chevette, and it was packed to the brim.

The four of us spent the rest of the evening moving Jared in. Sara took my car and went with Jared to his place, so it would go faster. It took three full trips, with both cars, to finish. He didn't bring any furniture, he only owned a bed and a dresser, and since I had what we needed, he left it for his former roommate.

The bedroom, bathroom and living room were cluttered with Jared's things. Knowing we had company coming the next day, I pulled out three bottles of wine, rolled a blunt, and the four of us put everything away. There was plenty of room, almost like it had been planned from the moment I moved in and bought the furniture.

It was one in the morning when we finished unpacking. Bryce and Tango were supposed to be there around noon. We took turns taking showers and went to bed.

Jared wrapped me up in his arms, and I fell asleep on his chest listening to the sound of his heartbeat. There was something about knowing he lived there that brought me peace. I wanted to sleep like that, every night, for the rest of my life.

Thanksgiving morning came early. We all stayed in our pajamas while we finished cooking. I stuffed the turkey, covered it with honey infused butter, tented it with aluminum foil and put it in the oven to bake. The tofu turkey wasn't going to take long to bake, so that would go in the oven with the sweet potatoes and green bean casserole.

It was ten in the morning, and I needed to start getting dressed. I wanted to look the part. Ya know, the whole homemaker thing. I had purchased a new black, fifties styled dress that had white polka dots on it. It was fitted at the waist and had a matching belt. It was adorable, and I knew I was going to rock this look!

My hair had grown out quite a bit from when I had it cut in California, but I kept it dyed deep red. I used a large barrel curling iron to put big drop curls in my hair. After combing them out, I parted my hair down the middle. Taking half of my hair at a time, I rolled it into glory rolls and pinned them to the sides of my head. I then curled my bangs under and pulled them apart a bit so that the sides touched the rolls. I finished off the style by taking the ends of the rolls and tying them up using a ponytail holder with a bow that matched my dress.

Make-up was next. Sticking with my usual style, I put on black eyeliner, mascara and black eyeshadow with white highlights at my brow line. A bit of foundation and deep red lipstick finished my look. There, all done! * smile *

I put on pantyhose and a pair of six inch, black heels that had straps around the ankles and headed downstairs. I couldn't wait to see everyone's reactions. As I said before, I loved the pin-up look, but this was the first time that I had gone this far with it.

Sara, Chloe and Jared were all in the living room, waiting for me to finish dressing, so they could get dressed themselves. As I walked down the stairs, Jared stood up and met me at the bottom.

"You are stunning, Maggie, absolutely stunning." He took my hand in his and kissed it.

"I didn't know this was a formal dinner." Chloe sounded upset.

"Yes, you did. She told all of us a week ago. Anyway, why do you think we made place cards?" Sara spoke up.

"Well, I need to go home and get different clothes then." Chloe always did things like this, so I kind of expected it.

I gave Chloe my car keys, so she could go home to change. Sara headed up to my bedroom to get dressed, and Jared followed me into the kitchen. He was like a puppy following at my heels.

"Maggie, you're always beautiful, but today you look spectacular." Jared wrapped his arms around me and whispered into my ear as I stood at the kitchen sink.

"Thank you, Baby." I smiled and turned to kiss him.

We stood there making out until Sara came downstairs. We just couldn't get enough of one another. Isn't that how it always goes in the beginning though? * wink *

Jared went upstairs to change his clothes. Tango and Bryce showed up just as Chloe was coming back. Everyone was there, and I made the introductions.

Our guests were sitting in the living room, drinking wine and chatting. I was taking the turkey out of the oven and putting in the remainder of the food that needed to bake, when Tango came into the kitchen.

"Maggie, I was just checking out the piece you painted on your living room wall. You used your body, didn't you?" He handed me the tofu turkey to put in the oven.

"Yes, I did. Why do you ask?" I closed the oven door and turned to face him.

"That is one of the most unique and emotionally moving pieces I have ever seen. Would you be willing to paint a wall in the shop? I would pay you of course." How could I say no to Tango?

"Of course, what did you have in mind?" I couldn't say no, and I didn't want to either.

"Something abstract." He smiled.

"Sure, give me a bit to think about it, and then we can talk. You don't have to pay me though, fifty-fifty, remember?" I hugged him.

"No, I want you to just do it. I don't want to know about it until it's done. Just let me know when and how long you'll need the shop. I trust you." He hugged me tighter and we joined everyone in the living room.

We all chatted as the rest of the food baked. The timer went off, and the three of us ladies went to the kitchen to set the food on the table. When we finished, we called everyone in to sit.

Instead of praying, we took turns expressing something we were thankful for. When everyone finished, I took my turn. "I am thankful I moved to Colorado Springs and met all of you. The love and friendship that I receive from each of you has made my life complete. I love you all." I raised my glass of wine, and we all toasted to continued friendship and love. "Now, let's eat."

CHAPTER EIGHTEEN

"Deck the halls with boughs of holly. Fa la la la la la la la la. 'Tis the season to be jolly. Fa la la la la la la la la." (Admit it, you just sang that song in your head. * giggle *) Even though I've never been a religious person, I've always FREAKING LOVED CHRISTMAS!

Tango allowed me to go all out with decorating the studio. I put a huge tree in the front window and decorated it with a ton of white lights and tattoo themed decor. I used Tango's huge vintage tattoo machine collection as ornaments. After cutting out dozens of tattoo pictures, I placed them inside of clear globe ornaments and hung them in the empty spaces to fill the tree.

I'm not sure if it was the pot Tango gave me, or if I just had a moment of awesomeness, but I decided to use tattoo needles and stainless steel back stems to make a star. Very carefully, I cut off the bottom of a soda can, and I soldered needles, evenly around it, on both sides. When that was completed, I did the same thing with the back stems, except instead of making it a solid circle, I formed an asterisk on top of the tattoo needles. It really sparkled against the white lights of the tree.

Tango and I bought hundreds of boxes of candy and wrapped them, so that every client got a Christmas gift from us before they left. A jar of candy canes sat on the reception desk for people to help themselves to. I strung evergreen garland, with white lights wrapped through it, over every threshold and around every counter top. Of course, there was mistletoe in the center of the thresholds as well. It was really quite lovely.

I had figured out what I wanted to do for the mural Tango asked me to paint, but I didn't want to start it until the holiday season was over. I was going to need a few days to complete it, and this was a busy time for us. It wouldn't have made good business sense to shut down the shop for three days right now.

Our appointment book was full, every day of the week, except Tuesdays. That remained our inventory, ordering and walk-ins day. It gave us a chance to breathe at least once a week. Not that we were complaining.

Business was so good that we decided to bring in another artist. We placed an ad for open auditions and had a pretty good response. In two weeks time we interviewed over twenty-five artists, and after a lot of discussion, we finally settled on one.

Frankee had been a tattoo artist for around twenty years. Her portfolio spoke for itself. She could ink any type of tattoo and perform it with ease. Frankee's portrait tattoos were so lifelike that they looked like photographs. I knew I could learn a lot from her and was excited at the opportunity.

I called Frankee to ask her to come into the studio. She said she would be happy to come in that afternoon. I noticed Tango had a new twinkle in his eye. Hmm....

Tango had taken the day off, so I was at the shop by myself. Frankee came in as I was finishing a tattoo of a cherry blossom. I asked her to wait in the lobby and told her that I would be with her shortly.

After I cleaned up and wrapped the client's tattoo, I collected payment and received a nice tip as well. I gave the client her Christmas gift and walked her out. Because I was there alone, I put up the "be right back" sign, locked the door and asked Frankee to come into the office with me.

I asked what her expectations would be if we were to bring her in as an artist. She asked if we provided the supplies, and I told her we preferred to provide them in order to maintain consistency. Frankee said she would be cool with a seventy-thirty split and had an established customer base already. She had owned her own shop, but she couldn't keep up with it herself, so that's why she came to us. I told her we could work with that, welcomed her aboard and told her she could start on Monday.

Frankee said she still had all of her gear, and if we wanted, she would bring it in to our shop. I told her that I would have to talk to Tango about it, and I would let her know as soon as I heard anything. We shook hands, and she was on her way.

I finished two more tattoos, cleaned the shop and locked up. It was my first time locking up by myself, but I had done it so many times with Tango that it was like second nature. I had parked directly in front of the shop, so I didn't have to walk far to my car. Better safe than sorry.

A delicious scent met me as I walked into the apartment. Jared was cooking dinner. He had learned quite a few vegan recipes from the internet, and he enjoyed making them for me. He would partake of the meals with me a few nights a week but, usually, he or I cooked two separate entrees and shared the sides.

"You look tired, Maggie." Jared came around the corner from the kitchen and kissed me hello.

"I'm beat. I missed Tango today, but we hired a new artist, so it'll all work out." I kissed him back.

"Dinner will be ready in a few minutes. I made mushroom stuffed zucchini." He looked proud.

"Sounds yummy! I'm going to run upstairs and take a quick shower. I'll be right back." I turned to go upstairs.

"Dress warmly when you get out." Jared winked at me.

"Why? It's perfectly comfortable in here." What was he up to?

"I want to take you somewhere after dinner." He wasn't giving up anymore information.

"Oh, Baby, I'm really tired. Can it wait for tomorrow night?" I didn't feel like going out.

"I'm afraid that it can't. I promise, it's nothing strenuous. Tomorrow is Sunday, so we can sleep in late." He kissed me again, and I ran upstairs to shower and dress in warm clothing. I couldn't say no to him. Hell, I had a hard time saying no to anyone.

Dinner was absolutely scrumptious! I was truly impressed with Jared's developing skills. He was going out of his way to learn about and support my vegan lifestyle. I simply loved him.

We made a thermos full of hot cocoa and headed out. The drive through the foothills was beautiful. Moonlight danced over the new fallen snow and made the earth look new and clean.

Continuing up Old Gold Camp road, we headed into the mountains. I was starting to get a little worried because my car didn't have the best of tires on it. I had to take a deep breath and trust the Jared knew what he was doing.

We pulled over and got out of the car. The lights of Colorado Springs sprawled out before us. I had always loved this view.

"Maggie? Would you get the hot cocoa out of the car, please?" Jared was standing behind me with his arms around me and whispered into my ear.

"Of course, Baby. Be right back." I turned to go to the car and retrieve the cocoa and cups. There was no dome light in my car, so it took me a few minutes to find it. The thermos had rolled under the passenger side seat.

When I got out of the car, I couldn't see Jared anywhere. I thought maybe he had wandered off to relieve himself. I sat on the hood of my car and waited for him.

I heard something rustling on the side of the mountain where the headlights were shining. Oh shit! I hoped it wasn't a bear. I saw a tree move. Fuck! I jumped down to get into the car and called for Jared to warn him that we had company.

"Oh Christmas tree, oh Christmas tree, how lovely are your branches." Jared was singing. (Kind of like you probably just were in your head.)

Turning around to where I had seen the tree move, I saw Jared climbing up over the side of the mountain. He was carrying a tree that was taller than he was. What was he doing?

"It's almost Christmas, Maggie, and we've been so busy we haven't even put up our own tree. Do you remember this spot?" He was now standing beside me with a tree.

"Oh my God, Jared! That's so sweet. Yes, this is the place you brought me when you asked me to be your girlfriend. You... You are just..." My voice trailed off as tears filled my eyes.

"So, let's get this home and decorated, shall we?" He was stuffing the bottom end of the tree into the trunk of my car and tying down the trunk lid to hold in the tree.

"Yes, yes... Thank you. I love you... So much." I hugged Jared tightly as the tears still flowed down my cheeks.

"And I love you, Maggie. Now, let's wipe those tears and enjoy some hot cocoa before we go home." He took my hand and helped me back onto the hood of my car. Jared stood between my legs, sipping hot cocoa as we stared out over the city lights.

A few minutes later, we left and went back home. I didn't have any Christmas decorations of my own, so I had no idea how we were going to do this, but I knew we would figure it out.

While Jared was bringing the tree in, I used the half bath under the stairs. I could hear him digging around in the storage closet next to the bathroom. When I came out there were bags sitting all over the living room.

"What's this?" I started looking inside the bags. "Jared! You bought us Christmas decorations? You're so thoughtful!" Again, I cried.

"We're starting a life together, and I know how much Christmas means to you, so I wanted to make it special. Do you like?" He was taking everything out of the bags.

"I love it all... And I love you for doing this!" I held up a piece of mistletoe that I found in one of the bags and we kissed under it.

"Well, let's get started!" Jared was as excited as I was. He was adorable.

We set up the tree and wrapped it with strings of bubble lights. I loved how the bubbles danced up the tubes as the lights began to heat. Jared bought all antique looking ornaments. He knew that I loved the story of Santa, so he bought a mechanical, lit Santa for the top of the tree and placed it there after the tree was all decorated. It was spectacular!

We wrapped lights and garland up the rail of the staircase and hung the same lit garland over the archway that lead to the dining area. We put the small Christmas village on the console table and a set of pretty, red candles on the coffee table. Jared purchased a couple cans of fake snow, so we flocked the edges of the main living room window with it, and I cut out some snowflake stencils, put them on the windows and sprayed over them. It looked like Christmas had exploded in our home.

When all was said, done and cleaned up, we sat on the futon cuddled up watching all of the classic Christmas cartoons from when we were young. He had bought me a DVD set of them.

"Do you want to sleep under the Christmas tree?" Jared was full of surprises tonight.

"That would be incredible." I kissed him as I stood up.

Jared pulled the mattress off the futon and placed it near the tree. I went upstairs, grabbed some blankets and pillows from our bed and met him back downstairs. We made up the bed together, undressed and crawled in.

"Thank you, Jared." I kissed him goodnight and curled up in his arms. I felt like the luckiest woman in the world. I knew that Jared truly loved me, and I loved him.

I woke up alone the next morning to the smell of fresh coffee again. Where did he go now? I got up and looked for a note. There wasn't one. That wasn't like Jared at all. I poured myself a cup of coffee, sat in the dining room and waited for him. He still wasn't home after a half an hour, so I got up and cleaned the living room.

Still, no Jared. I attempted to call his cell phone, but it went straight to voice mail. I busied myself with some household chores. I had just pulled the last load of laundry out of the dryer when I heard him coming through the front door.

"Where have you been, Baby? I was worried." I kissed him hello.

"This is not the time of year to ask questions, Maggie." He smiled that gorgeous smile and kissed me back.

"Alright, alright. I'll let you off the hook this time." I figured he was out getting me a present. Oh shit! A present! I had to go shopping.

We had a late lunch together, and I made an excuse that I had to take Chloe out. I grabbed my purse, kissed Jared goodbye and headed out. The snow was crunchy under my feet, so I knew to take it easy on the drive. I really needed to get my tires changed.

I actually did pick up Chloe, so I wouldn't be lying. I finally got to meet her daughters and boyfriend. It was nice to know they were real. They were even prettier in person than they were in their pictures.

Jared loved Colorado Springs. I knew exactly what to get him. I drove to an antique store I had been in a few times. Walking in, I saw it. It was hanging on the wall. It was an antique photo of Garden of the Gods. I knew he had to have it. I looked through the rest of the art and found some photographs from when Fort Carson was first being constructed as well. I purchased the lot of them.

I don't know why I didn't tell you this before, but Jared had been a medic in the army. That's how he came to live in Colorado Springs from the east coast. He had been stationed at Fort Carson for the last part of his enlistment. He loved it here so much; he stayed.

We went back to Chloe's so I could frame and wrap everything. Jared was going to love this; I just knew it. I was excited and didn't know if I could wait to give it to him, so I left it all at Chloe's until closer to Christmas.

I stopped at the mall, after I left Chloe's, and finished up my shopping. I even picked up some Colorado t-shirts to send home to Richard, Susan, Brianna and her family. My sister was married and had a little boy. I guess God listened to the order Richard put in with him when Brianna was born. His first grandchild was a boy.

After sliding into the driveway, I parked my car and retrieved the gifts from the trunk. I carried them inside and sat them on the living room floor. Jared came downstairs and started looking through the bags.

"Hey, what are you doing? Get out of there." I was just playing.

"Just snooping." Jared jumped back.

"I'm joking, Baby. Here, help me wrap these." I handed him some wrapping paper and a pair of scissors.

We sat there wrapping and labeling gifts. Getting hungry, I left him there to finish and went into the kitchen to make us dinner. I had frozen some of the leftovers from Thanksgiving, so I pulled them out, defrosted them and made us plates.

When we finished eating, we put the gifts under the tree. We had decided we wanted to be alone for Christmas, so we were having a Christmas party that weekend for our friends.

I woke up early the next morning and took my car in to have the tires changed before I went to work. It was more expensive than I had anticipated, but I had just enough to cover it without digging into my savings.

Tango was already at the studio when I arrived. He was sitting in his office smiling. That smile usually meant he was up to something.

"Hey, Tango. How did you enjoy your long weekend?" I kissed him on the cheek.

"It was marvelous!" Tango was excited about something.

"Oh yeah? Gonna tell me about it, or just leave me wondering?" I couldn't wait to hear this.

"Well, I slept almost all day Saturday. It was nice to just chill." He was still smiling.

"And yesterday?" I knew there had to be something else.

"Frankee called me yesterday and asked me out for lunch." Tango's smile got even bigger.

"Really? That's fucking fantastic!" I was so happy for him!

"Yeah, we got along really well. We talked about how we come from the same generation, like the same music, the same sappy movies and have the same political beliefs. I'm tellin' ya, Maggie, it's almost too good to be true." Tango stood up and hugged me.

"Don't say that. Fate brought her in here for a reason." Even though my first marriage didn't work out, I still believed in fate and always will.

"You're right. Okay, let's get to work." He walked into the back to start setting up for the day.

The moment I flipped on the "open" sign, Frankee was at the door.

It was fun to watch Tango and Frankee interact throughout the day. She and Tango did two tattoos each. I had an order to put away so I left them to the appointments. At the end of the day, Frankee and Tango walked out hand in hand. Love was in the air, and I couldn't be happier. I locked up the studio and went home.

The rest of the week was pretty much just like Monday except that I actually did a few tattoos. Tango and Frankee were getting really close, really fast. It was a joy to see. I know most people would take issue with how fast they were moving, but I figured they were adults and knew what they were doing. Anyway, I loved love. * smile *

We closed the shop on Friday for the office party. Tango bought everyone new DVD players for Christmas. He had even invited Sara and Chloe. He was such a giving and caring man. We ordered in pizza and had beer to go with it. Fun was had by all.

Jared and I went home after the party and started the preparations for our own. We were having it the next day. Tango and I decided to close the shop down until after the new year. Business had slowed down since it was so close to Christmas so we weren't really missing out on much.

Jared baked a ham, and I made all of the side dishes. We were going to have a traditional Christmas dinner. Well, except for Tango and I. I picked up another tofu turkey for us because they were yummy!

We went to bed early and after making love, we fell asleep in each other's arms. I loved the way his heartbeat sounded in my ear. It was my new lullaby.

Shit! We slept through the alarm! Someone was pounding on our door! Jared threw on his pajamas and ran downstairs to answer the door. It was the guy from the liquor store delivering our order. * phew * We still had time to get dressed before everyone arrived.

Bryce was the first one to show up. He brought in a bag of gifts and placed them under the tree. I offered him a drink, and he sat in the dining room talking my ear off as I got the food out to finish preparing it.

Chloe and Sara showed up next. I was excited to see Chloe had brought her daughters with her. Jared and I had bought them gifts, and now we were going to be able to see them open them.

"Where do you want us to put these?" Chloe and Sara were holding Jared's gifts.

"Oh, um... Go upstairs and slide them under my bed. Don't let Jared see you. Wait, give me this one." I stuck it under the tree, so I had it to give to Jared Christmas Eve.

As Chloe and Sara were going upstairs, Jared peeked around the corner. "Where did the girls go?" He bent to hug Chloe's daughters, Shye and Patience.

"Oh, they just had to run upstairs for a minute. Why don't you give Shye and Patience a cup of hot cider?" That's right, distract him. * wink *

Jared took the girls into the kitchen to get them something to drink. Bryce was still talking even though no one was listening. I sat at the table with him and pretended to pay attention.

"Merry Christmas everyone!" Tango and Frankee walked in the door happy as ever.

"Hey! Merry Christmas!" I took the packages out of their hands, placed them under the tree and hugged them both. "What are you doing? You gave everyone gifts yesterday!"

"Well, Santa told us there were two little girls here that have been very good this year." Tango looked around for Chloe's daughters. He had not met them yet. I introduced them to each other, and they hugged Tango and Frankee. It was adorable.

"That is so kind of you." I was touched.

"Anyway Maggie, we wanted to get something special for you and Jared too." Tango smiled.

"You didn't have to do that, Tango. We're very happy with our new DVD player. You're too much, Old Man!" I laughed and then hugged him again. "I just love you."

"I love you too, Kid." Tango followed his nose into the kitchen and pulled Frankee with him. "Where's the food?"

"Stay out of it, Tango! It's not dinner time yet!" I laughed again.

Chloe and Sara joined us in the kitchen and dining room. Everyone was talking over each other, and it was amazing. This was exactly what I was hoping for. These people formed the family I had always wanted. We had Crazy Uncle Bryce that sat at the table babbling to himself. Papa Tango and Mama Frankee were hugged up in the corner munching on vegetables. Sister Chloe and Sister Sara were giving my nieces Shye and Patience cookies, and my man was at my side smiling though it all.

We ate dinner with the same amazing energy we had while chatting in the kitchen. Sara, Chloe, Frankee and I cleaned up after dinner. The guys took the little girls into the living room and watched the Christmas cartoons that Jared had gotten for me.

When we were finished, we all gathered in the living room. Frankee, Tango and Bryce sat on the futon, and the rest of us sat on the floor. Jared passed out the gifts but everyone waited to open them until they were all handed out.

"One, two, three... Open your gifts!" The sounds of tearing paper filled the room.

Bryce had given all of the adults a classic movie DVD set and the girls got cartoons. It was really nice of him to think of everyone.

Chloe and the girls gave everyone ornaments the girls had made themselves. I was truly touched by the gift.

Sara gave everyone gift baskets full of candy, nuts and popcorn. She put a lot of work into them. They were wrapped beautifully.

Tango and Frankee had purchased beautiful dolls for Shye and Patience. When they opened them, their eyes got huge, and they hugged them tight to their little chests.

Jared and I gave Bryce, Chloe and Sara each a sweater that we bought for them at the mall.

Shye and Patience got new roller blades from us. They loved them.

We bought Frankee a new pair of winter boots and a faux fur lined winter jacket. She was in utter shock when she opened them. I had noticed her lack of winter clothing.

Tango sat on the futon, holding his gift, with tears in his eyes. I had painted a portrait of the two of us standing in front of our shop. The original picture had been taken the day we became legal partners. He stood up and hugged me tight. "I love you, Kid... Always will."

There was one gift left to open. The one that Tango and Frankee gave Jared and I. It was a small red box with a white ribbon on it.

"Open your gift!" Tango was excited.

Jared pulled the ribbon off, and I opened the box. A set of keys? What?

"Look outside." Tango spoke softly.

Jared and I stood up, walked to the door and opened it. There sat a brand new car with a giant red ribbon on it!

"OH MY GOD, TANGO!" I didn't know what to say.

"We can't accept this. It's beyond kind." Jared spoke for us.

"You can, and you will." Tango walked over to us and put his arm around us. "The two of you are my family, and you deserve this."

Everyone put on their shoes and jackets and went outside to look at the new car. It was white with black interior. Tango remembered my favorite colors. I couldn't help it; I started crying.

"Don't cry, Kid. You deserve it." Tango wrapped me up in a bear hug.

We took turns taking everyone for a drive. I was still in shock but so happy. How do you thank someone for such an incredible gift as that?

When everyone was back inside, we sang Christmas songs, ate cookies and watched Shye and Patience play with their new dolls. Life was perfect.

It was getting late, so everyone started to leave. We said goodnight, wished everyone a Merry Christmas and told them we would see them at Chloe's New Year's Eve party.

Jared and I went to bed happier than ever. We stayed up talking about our gift for a while, and we decided to give Sara and Chloe our old cars. We knew they could use them.

Christmas Eve was here before we knew it. Jared and I called his mom to wish her a Merry Christmas. I then called Willow and did the same. With our phone calls completed, we sat down to string popcorn to put out on the patio for the little winter birds that frequented our yard.

"Do you want to exchange gifts?" Jared was like a kid at Christmas.

"Sure, but just one." I smiled at him because I knew he wouldn't take no for an answer.

Jared handed me my gift and then got his out from under the tree. We opened them at the same time.

"Wow, Jared! This is beautiful! Thank you so much!" He had gotten me a faux leather journal and had my name embossed on the cover.

"Maggie! Where did you get this? This is incredible!" He put the framed photos of Fort Carson down and hugged me.

"I picked it up at the little antique store by the mall." I couldn't help but to smile.

We spent the rest of the night cuddled up on the couch, drinking eggnog, watching the Christmas lights on the tree twinkle and talking. It was the perfect Christmas Eve.

When Jared fell asleep, I snuck his gift down the stairs and put it under the tree. There was a large red and white box there already. When did he find the time to do that? I shrugged my shoulders and went back to bed.

The next morning, we went downstairs together, got coffee and sat in the living room for a minute.

"Well, it looks like Santa has been here. You must have been a very good girl." Jared winked at me.

"Santa knows that even when I'm bad; I'm good at it." I winked back.

Again, Jared handed me my gift and retrieved his own. "Maggie, I am speechless." Jared was staring at the photo of Garden of the Gods. "Did you get this at the same place? It's... It's..." He hugged me.

"Yes, I did. I know how much you love it there, so I thought..." Before I could even finish my sentence, he was kissing me.

"Open yours." He pulled away from me and smiled.

I picked up the box. It felt empty. I took the bow off and opened it. Inside was a picture of a kitten. "What's this?" I was a bit confused.

"It's a picture of the kitten that is waiting for you to pick it up tomorrow from the shelter. I remembered you telling me about the one you had as a child." Jared sat there waiting for my response.

"Jared! It's perfect! Thank you so, so much! I love it, and I love you even more!" I jumped up, sat on his lap and covered his face with kisses.

It was the Merriest Christmas EVER!

CHAPTER NINETEEN

I named my little, four legged companion, "See-`a-tee." (Get it? C...
A... T...) She was a beautiful tabby kitten. Her markings were
sensational! She was mostly gray with white and black stripes and had
the perfect "M" on her forehead.

I always loved the legends behind that marking. There were a few
different ones, with some of them dating back to ancient Egypt. My
favorite of these was of Christ in the manger.

It is said that it was cold in the manger. This caused baby Jesus to be
fussy. Mary asked the animals to get closer to Jesus to help warm
Him, but the manger was too small to accomplish this. A little, tabby
cat heard her request and nestled in with baby Jesus to warm and
soothe Him with its purring. Baby Jesus calmed right away. The
Blessed Mother was so grateful to the kitten, she marked it with her
own initial, "M," so the kitten would always be looked upon as a
sacred animal. Sweet, right?

On our way home from the shelter, I held See-`a-tee in my jacket. I
thought of that story as she purred against my chest. I loved her
instantly.

Jared had already picked up the required necessities for a cat. There
was a litter tray, a cat bed, a scratching post, a shelf for the window
and a ton of toys. She was spoiled, and we hadn't even gotten her
home yet.

"Welcome home, See-`a-tee." The instant we walked through and
closed the door, I sat her on the floor to let her roam around. Her little
legs were wobbly as she checked out every corner of the apartment.
She eventually found her way under the futon and stayed there for a
bit.

Jared and I were sitting in the living room, watching television, when
See-`a-tee clawed her way up the front of the futon and my leg. Her
tiny, sharp claws scratched into my skin and made me bleed a little. I
picked her up and cuddled her to my chest again. She seemed to like
the sound of my heartbeat.

"I'll make an appointment with the vet to have her declawed." Jared stood up to get a wet paper towel to clean my leg.

"You'll do no such thing! Jared, do you know what they do to declaw a cat?" I picked up See-`a-tee and kissed her little nose.

"They remove the nails, right?" He was sitting next to me again, wiping the blood from my leg. It really wasn't much blood, but Jared liked playing nursemaid.

"No, they cut off their toes at the first knuckle!" I was adamant about not declawing her. I thought it was cruel.

"Oh, I'm sorry. I had no idea. Well, we still need a vet appointment, so she can be spayed." Jared was so cute.

"She's too young to be spayed right now." I picked her up and kissed at her little face again. I couldn't help it; she was so damned cute.

"Oh, right. Wow, Maggie, you seem to know a lot about this stuff." Jared was petting See-`a-tee as I kissed her.

"I love animals. It's the reason I became vegan. We will get her spayed when she's about six months old." I put See-`a-tee back on my lap. She crawled up to my chest and instantly fell asleep.

"I thought you were vegan because you didn't like meat." He looked confused.

"Nope, I can't stand the thought of an innocent animal dying just to feed my hunger. You want to know what I think the saddest sound in the world is? Try hearing a mama cow crying for her baby. The same baby that was just ripped away from her because a human wants to drink her milk, and her baby is being slaughtered for veal. That's sad." I usually didn't get into detail about why I had chosen to be vegan, but something about this whole conversation had lit a fire under me.

"I hadn't thought about that." Jared got real quiet, so I thought it best to not talk about it any longer.

We spent the rest of the day hanging out and playing with the new addition to our family. See-`a-tee loved the shelf in the window and sat up there, preening herself, for most of the afternoon. We had to put piles of books under the shelf, so she could get up to it because she was still just tiny. The shelter said she was only about eight weeks old.

That afternoon, after lunch, we went for a walk around the block. It was getting really cold out, so we kept it short. Both Jared and I loved to walk, but with winter here it became more difficult to do.

See-`a-tee was sitting on her shelf, looking out the window, as if she had been waiting for us to get home. As we walked through the door, she jumped down, came over to us and started to rub her little body around our legs. I picked her up and carried her into the kitchen. "Lunch time for the baby."

"Maggie? Have you thought about us having a baby of our own?" Jared came into the kitchen with me.

"We have a baby right here." I set her food on the counter and put her next to it. I know that a lot of people would say I was teaching her bad habits, but I didn't and still don't care.

"I meant a human baby." Jared touched my hand.

"Can we talk about this later?" I really didn't want to have this conversation. I hadn't told Jared about Destiny or the miscarriage.

"I have to tell you something Maggie. I have a son. He lives with his mom, and I haven't seen him in six years. Every time I try, she disappears again." Jared blurted out the words.

"WHAT?" I was shocked.

"I'm sorry. I wanted to tell you. I just didn't know how." He looked scared.

"Jared? I love you, but you can understand that this is a bit shocking. I need a few minutes. I'll be back." I kissed Jared, grabbed the car keys and went for a drive.

I wasn't angry that he hadn't told me. I was confused and hurt. I know I hadn't told him about Destiny, but I felt there was a huge difference in me not telling him about my stillborn daughter and him not telling me about his living son. Was I just justifying my not telling him? I knew I needed to talk to him about this, but right now, I had to have some time to just think.

Thoughts raced through my head. Jared had a son? Why didn't he tell me this before? Why didn't he try harder to see him? How old was his son? What was his name? What was he like? Had he been married to his son's mother? WHY DIDN'T HE TELL ME BEFORE? It kept coming back to that.

I drove for a while and pulled over. My tears were falling so hard I was having a hard time seeing. I wiped my tears and got out of my car. I unknowingly pulled over at a cemetery. Wow...

It was a very overcast and cold day. The clouds were hiding the sunshine, so it felt like the perfect day to be there. I walked through the gates and strolled around looking at the headstones. I knew what I was looking for. Her name had to be here somewhere.

There was a large tree on a hill at the backside of the cemetery. The branches were bare, and it looked sad and lonely. I was drawn to it. I walked up to the area where the tree was standing, and there it was... "Destiny."

I sank to my knees, touched the headstone and cried a cleansing cry. I knew this wasn't where my daughter was buried, but it made me feel close to her... I needed to feel close to her.

I sat there for about an hour, thinking, remembering and feeling. My hands were over my stomach, and I was lost in thought. I remembered what it felt like to have her growing inside me. I heard her laugh as if she were there and was letting me know she was happy. How did I know it was her when I had never heard her? I don't know, but I knew it was. I wondered what she would have looked like, and what she would have grown to be. I sat there crying until my cell phone rang. I reached into my pocket to answer it.

"Maggie? Are you okay? Please, come home." Jared sounded concerned.

"I'm alright, Jared. I'll be there soon. Don't worry. There's nothing to worry about." I hung up, kissed my hand and touched the headstone. "Don't worry, Destiny, I'll always hold you close to me."

As I stood up, I noticed the sunshine radiating through the parted clouds. I thought back to when Abuelita Garcia had prayed in the garden with me. Was this the guardian angel she asked to watch over me? A warm, fuzzy feeling enveloped me, and I knew I wasn't alone.

On the way home, I stopped and picked up a bottle of tequila. We didn't have any alcohol in the apartment except for wine and beer. Jared and I talked about it and had decided that we weren't going to drink so much anymore. I thought tonight called for a drink... Or ten.

I walked in the front door carrying the bottle. Jared was sitting on the bottom step holding See-`a-tee. He looked relieved to see me.

We sat in bed talking and drinking all night. I told him how I had lost Destiny and about the miscarriage; he held me as I cried. It felt so good to finally tell him everything.

Jared answered all my questions. His son's name was Aaron, and he was eight years old. Jared and his son's mother had never been married. He had only met his son twice, once when he was born and again when he was two years old. When Jared had joined the Army, Theresa, Aaron's mom, had gotten upset and wouldn't let Jared see his son. Every time he found her, she would move again, and the search started all over. Jared was paying child support, but it was collected through the state, so he never had an address for her. He had pretty much given up hope.

"So, Maggie, what about us having a baby of our own?" Jared looked hopeful.

"Jared, you know I love you with all of my heart, but we've only been dating for three months. I think it's just too soon. How about we talk about this when we've been together a bit longer?" I hated to let him down, but I knew this just wasn't the time.

"Alright, Maggie, I understand and agree. It was just wishful thinking." Jared pulled me close, and we fell asleep.

The next few days were very quiet. We had made it through a very emotional time, and it seemed to bring us closer, but at the same time things felt a bit awkward.

It was now New Year's Eve. We were always the hosts for parties, so it was nice to be going out for a change.

We dressed and headed to Chloe's. It was the usual crowd, so I knew it would be fun. I sat on the couch with Chloe and Sara watching the kids play.

We wanted to smoke some pot, but we never did that with the kids around. I asked Jared if he would mind taking the girls outside to play for a while. He said he didn't mind at all and would love to have some time with the girls.

"Hey, Chloe, can I take your daughters for a little walk?" Jared was putting on his jacket.

"Sure, but make sure they're dressed warm." Chloe was rolling a blunt in her bedroom.

After Jared took the girls for their walk, Chloe, Jeremy, Sara, Tango, Frankee and I smoked the blunt. I was completely stoned. I hadn't smoked for about a week, so I was really feeling this stuff.

We aired out the apartment because we didn't want Chloe's daughters to be around the smoke. We were all sitting around talking and laughing when Jared returned with the girls. They were giggling as they came into the living room.

"What's so funny girls? Did you have fun with Uncle Jared?" Chloe was helping them take their jackets off.

"Uh huh." Shye was a perfect representation of her name. She was very timid.

"Soopwise, Mama!" Patience was two years old and was just learning to talk. She was adorable.

"What do you mean Patience? What surprise?" Chloe hung up the girl's jackets.

"Maggie?" Jared was kneeling on the floor next to me.

"Yeah?" I turned to look at him.

He took my left hand in his and said, "Maggie, I love you with all my heart. Would you do me the honor of becoming my wife?" He slid a beautiful diamond ring onto my finger. I stared at it for a moment.

"Don't ask me now. I'm too fucking stoned." I was in complete shock.

"Soopwise, Mama! Soopwise, Mama!" Patience started screaming.

Everyone started laughing and clapping. I stood up with Jared. We kissed, hugged, and I said yes. We were engaged to be married.

Shye and Patience gave us all kisses and were tucked into bed. It was incredible that they slept through the music and laughter. I always found it amazing how children could turn off their ears and sleep soundly (or ignore their parents for that matter. * wink *)

We continued with our party. We danced, smoked, drank, told stories and laughed. We had a blast! Ten seconds before midnight, we stopped what we were doing and counted down the seconds.

At the stroke of midnight, we all screamed, "Happy New Year!"

"I love you, Maggie, forever." Jared swept me up in his arms and kissed me.

"I love you, Jared, always." I kissed him back.

Tango and Frankee made it to midnight, but then they headed home. Yes, home. They had moved in together and were VERY happy. When love is right; it's just right.

We kept the party going until after two in the morning. We toasted the New Year for each of the time zones in the United States. We also celebrated in between those toasts. * wink *

Having had a lot to drink, we called for a cab to go home. Sara was spending the night at Chloe's, so we gave our keys to Sara and asked her to bring our car over in the morning. We still had to give the girls their cars, but we had them serviced first. We told them their cars were ready, and they could pick them up in the morning. We all hugged before we left.

I unlocked our door as Jared paid for the taxi. I was so drunk, I fumbled with the keys for a minute but finally got inside. Just as I was stepping through the door, Jared scooped me up and carried me over the threshold.

"What are you doing?" I giggled and kissed Jared.

"Just practicing." He kissed me back. "So, when do we do this?"

"Do what?" Did I miss something?

"Get married." Jared sat me down.

"Jared, again, I love you with all my heart, but I've done all of this before. I don't want to rush anything. Can we talk about it later please?"

"Alright, I understand." Jared sounded disappointed.

Jared and I didn't talk much the next morning. Things were very tense. He was sulking, and I was ignoring him.

I had set up my easel in the dining room and was working on a painting. Jared was sitting in the living room playing video games. He got up, went into the kitchen and threw his coffee cup into the sink. It shattered and scared the shit out of me.

"Are you okay?" I turned around, not realizing what had happened.

"No, I'm NOT okay, Maggie." Jared raised his voice at me.

"Where are you hurt?" I stood up and tried to look at his hands.

"I'm not physically hurt." He yanked his hands away from me.

"What do you mean?" I didn't understand.

"What the fuck, Maggie. You say you love me, you accept my proposal and then you don't want to talk about getting married or having a baby? You ignore me all fucking day and paint in a corner?" Jared was really upset.

"Don't talk to me like that, Jared." I wasn't having this shit.

"Well, at least I got you to talk to me." He was still yelling.

"You want to talk, Jared? How's this? We've been dating for three months. Don't push me!" I yelled back.

"We've been dating long enough for you to say you love me." Jared yelled back.

"Because I DO love you, you fucking idiot!" I couldn't stop myself.

"Then why can't we talk about our wedding? You love me enough to fuck me but not marry me?"

"Go to hell, Asshole! Maybe we just won't fuck anymore!" I stormed off, ran up the stairs and slammed the bedroom door. How did he not understand that I was scared. I had been married before, I lost one baby and had a miscarriage. We had only been dating for three months. Why did we have to rush anything?

About an hour later, Jared knocked on the bedroom door. "Maggie? Are you ready to talk?" He didn't sound angry anymore.

I got up from the bed and opened the door. I stood there for a moment and just looked at him. Tears rolled down my cheeks.

"Yes, if we promise we can talk and not be mean." I stepped toward him to hug him.

"I promise." Jared hugged me back.

We talked through the morning. I told Jared all about my first marriage and how much I loved Diego. I explained how crushed I was when he told me he was gay. With tears flowing down my face, I told Jared about how my heart shattered when I lost Destiny and about the day I drove to the cemetery and cried at a stranger's grave site. Tears flowed down my face as I told him that I DO love him, but I didn't want to ruin what we had by moving too fast.

Jared told me about his own heart breaks. He told me about the woman he dated before me, how they had been engaged, and he came home one night to find her fucking his best friend, Tommy. He told me he thought he might be rushing it because he was afraid to lose me. I completely understood.

We were able to compromise on everything. We decided we would marry on our sixth month anniversary, which would be March eighteenth that year, and we would start trying to conceive on the night of our honeymoon. I gave in and agreed that we could start planning our wedding that evening, after we had a chance to recover from our first fight.

"So, isn't this the part where we have make up sex? Jared winked at me and smiled.

"I do believe you're right." I reached up and wiped a tear from his cheek.

"Wait, what did you just say? Did you just say that I was right?" He started to laugh.

"Yes, I did, but don't get used to it." I winked and leaned over to kiss him... And of course, that's when Sara and Chloe knocked on our door. They were there to return our car and pick up theirs.

Jared went downstairs to let them in while I washed my face. I put a cold washcloth over my eyes to reduce the swelling from crying. There, much better.

"Hey girls! Thanks for bringing our car back. We've signed the titles and they're all ready to go." I yelled as I walked down the stairs.

"We know. Jared just told us. Thanks so much you two!" Sara was happy to be getting my car because it was the newer of the two of them.

"Yeah, thanks." Chloe pouted. Oh well, she was getting a free car. She would get over it.

"Like we said last night, they've both just been serviced, so as long as you have the oil checked every fifteen hundred miles or so, you shouldn't have any issues." I ignored Chloe's pout.

We chatted until the girls had to leave to go home. I was happy they had no idea Jared and I had been arguing. I was a private person and felt those things should stay between us.

I heated up a quick lunch for us. I was frugal and hated seeing food go to waste, so I always made homemade TV dinners when there were a lot of leftovers.

Jared turned on some music, lit the candles on the coffee table, and we settled in to eat. We were going to start planning for our wedding when there was another knock on the door. What the fuck? Jared, once again, answered the door.

It was Jared's friend, Steve. They had been in the Army together and had remained friends. I had only met him once, but didn't really like him. I had no idea why, until that day.

"Hey, Steve, come on in." Jared answered the door. "Who's this?"

"Hi, Jared. This is my girlfriend, Mandy." Steve introduced Mandy to us as they came in.

"Your girlfriend?" I had to ask. She looked like she was twelve. Steve was thirty.

"Yep, we started dating last week." Steve had his arm around Mandy.

"Where did you meet? Her middle school recital?" I told you before, I never had an issue with being blunt.

"Haha... You're funny, Maggie." Steve tried to just blow it off.

"I wasn't trying to be funny." There I go being blunt again.

We hung out, ate lunch and had drinks. Well, Jared and I wouldn't let Mandy drink, no matter how many times Steve told us it was alright. If she couldn't show us identification to prove she was of age, she wasn't drinking in our home, and I sure as hell wasn't pulling out any weed.

We decided to watch a movie because we obviously weren't discussing wedding plans. I must admit, I was a bit relieved. I just wasn't ready.

Steve and Mandy sat on the futon. Jared and I curled up on a couple of floor pillows and settled in to watch the movie. About half way through, we heard giggling from Mandy. I turned around and saw Steve and Mandy necking on our couch. Nope, hell no and definitely not happening in our home!

"Get the fuck away from her, and get out of our home, you fucking pervert!" I stood up and yelled at Steve.

"What? We're not doing anything wrong." Steve started laughing.

"You have exactly five seconds to tell me how old you are, Mandy, before I call the police, and don't lie to me." I was furious.

"I'm fifteen. Please don't call the cops." Mandy sat up and looked scared.

"Steve, you're a fucking pervert! Look, Mandy, the only reason Steve is dating you is because he doesn't have to do anything to impress you. Going out to a fast food restaurant makes you happy. He's not into you as a person. He's into you as a conquest, ya know, someone to fuck? If you're a smart young woman, and I do believe you are, you'll dump his ass! Find someone closer to your own age. Now come on, I'm taking you home. Steve? It would be a good idea if you weren't here when I got back." I grabbed my car keys and waited by the door.

"Jared, are you going to let her do this?" Steve stood up.

"Let her? I agree with her! Get the hell out of our home, and don't come back until you get your head together." Jared took Steve by the arm and escorted him past me out to his car.

I gave Mandy a ride home and talked to her about having self worth and what older men were looking for in underage girls. I told her about my own experiences with older men. Going on, I explained how bad I felt about myself when I figured out they were just using me. By the time we got to her place, Mandy was crying. I didn't feel bad. She needed to hear the truth, and I hoped it stuck with her.

When I got home, Jared and I talked about what happened. I thanked him for supporting me, and he said that Steve was lucky that I was the one to act on the situation. Jared thanked me for standing up for what I believed in and for taking care of Mandy. I told him that I felt it was my duty in life to protect children any way that I could. He hugged me, and we finished watching the movie.

I was honestly surprised that he didn't bring up the plans for the wedding. I think he realized, after all of the emotions and bullshit we had been through that it wasn't a good time to do it. I really did have a great guy.

CHAPTER TWENTY

March was almost here already? Holy shit! Where did the time go? Jared handled most of the wedding arrangements because I was busy at work. He had quit his job at Garden of the Gods because he was going to be graduating in a few months and needed to focus on school and our wedding. Frankee and Tango got married on Valentine's Day and had left on an almost month long honeymoon, so I was running the shop by myself.

I still had to paint the mural in the shop. Tango and Frankee were due back on Saturday, and it was now Monday. I wanted to have it done before they returned. I hated to do it, but I closed the shop for a week. This HAD to be done.

Petty cash was my best friend. I grabbed a handful of cash and drove to the store. The guy at the paint counter looked at me like I was insane. Which I probably was at the time... Hell, probably? Who am I trying to kid? * laughing * I picked out twenty-four different colors of paint and asked for a quart of each to be mixed in all different finishes along with two gallons of black paint. I was feeling inspired.

Driving back to the tattoo studio, I was planning it all out in my head. I was going to need some help with this one. I needed warm blooded bodies.

Sara, Chloe, Shye and Patience to the rescue. I ordered a bunch of pizza (one vegan pizza, of course) and set everything up. This was going to be fun!

"Okay ladies, here's what I need you to do. I need you to each use every one of these colors, throw them at this wall, smear them around and just have fun. There is no right or wrong. I just need it covered with COLOR! Ready? Set? GO!" We were all wearing plastic garbage bags as smocks.

We promptly covered the main wall of the shop, along with the tarp on the floor in front of it and ourselves, with brilliant colors. There were drips and smears of color EVERYWHERE! We pressed our different body parts against the wet paint on the wall and formed extraordinary patterns. When we were finished with step one, I set up an industrial strength fan to blow on the wall and dry it. We had plenty of time to clean up, eat pizza and talked about step two while it dried.

"So, for step two, I need each of you to pose against the wall and let me trace around you. I will probably need each of you to do this a couple of times." They looked at me like I was crazy, but I was used to that.

"Auntie Maggie? This is FUN!" Shye actually spoke up.

"Thank you, Shye! I'm so happy you're having fun! Grandpa Tango and Grandma Frankee are going to be so surprised!" I kissed her on the cheek and giggled with her.

It took a few hours for the wall to dry, and the girls were getting antsy, so we took them to the park to play for a little while. It was still chilly out, but we all dressed in our warm jackets and made an afternoon of it. I loved being around these girls. They made me think of Destiny, and instead of holding in all of the love I felt for her, I was able to share it with them.

We returned to the shop and set about to draw the silhouettes on the wall. We had SO much fun! Shye and Patience posed as ballerinas. CUTE! Chloe did the splits on the floor and Sara posed with one leg off the floor, bent at the knee, over Chloe. When I finished tracing those poses, I had Sara trace me standing by the door, pretending to open it. Our next round of poses filled in the spaces in between those. This was going to be spectacular!

We called it a day after that. I was exhausted and still needed to get home to Jared to work on the wedding preparations. Oh, this was going to be a long week... * deep breath *

"Hi, Maggie! I missed you!" Jared met me at the front door with a kiss and a glass of wine.

"Hi, I'm so tired. I need a hot bath and a few minutes, then I'm all yours." I drank the wine in one swallow.

"I figured that. I ran you a hot bath. There are clean towels and your favorite pajamas waiting for you upstairs." He kissed me again and went into the kitchen. "Dinner will be ready whenever you're ready."

"I appreciate that, but I already ate with the girls." I was on my way up the stairs.

"Oh, okay. I'll put it in the fridge for tomorrow." Jared was so understanding.

I got undressed, stepped into the hot water and slid down into the bubbles. Ahh... Much better. I SO needed this. Jared was the best.

An hour had never passed so quickly. I woke to a knock on the bathroom door.

"Maggie? Baby? Are you okay?" Jared was calling to me through the door.

"Shit." I whispered to myself. "Yep, just finishing up. I'll be down in a minute. Do we have anymore wine?" I rushed to get out, slipped and almost fell.

"Yes, we do. I'll pour us each a glass." I heard Jared going back down the stairs.

I dried off, dressed and joined him. I was beyond exhausted, but I knew this had to be done.

"So, I've gotten back about sixty replies of people that will be attending." Jared handed me my glass of wine.

"Sixty? Wow! I didn't realize we invited so many people." I was happy that Jared had handled the whole invitation thing.

"Yep, we made a list, remember? Everyone from both of our jobs, and my friends from school and the Army." He looked at me with a bit of confusion in his smile.

"Oh right, sorry, I'm just exhausted." I drank more wine. I'm sure the wine didn't help with how tired I was, but it was helping me cope, or at least that is what I told myself.

"We need to get your dress from the tailor and pick up my tuxedo. There's still the cake and food too. I paid for the permit and the spot at Garden of the Gods today. Oh, I confirmed with the Justice of the Peace too. He will be expecting payment the day of the wedding." Jared prattled on. It's not that I wasn't excited. I was... Really. I was just tired.

"Great, you've been working hard at this. What do you need me to do?" I feigned a smile.

"I just need you to pick up your dress and meet me on Friday for the cake tasting." He wrapped one arm around me and gave me a quick squeeze.

"I can and will do that. I'm on it!" I reached up and squeezed his hand. I loved how involved he was with this. I couldn't let him down.

"Do you want to go with me to meet with the caterer?" Jared had way to much energy for me.

"Sure, when is the appointment?" Damn!

"Tomorrow afternoon at four." Jared shuffled through his papers.

"Okay, can you drop me off and pick me up from the shop? That way you'll have the car to do what you need to instead of taking the bus." I thought to myself, "and I won't have to watch the clock."

"Of course, have you finished your vows?" Jared looked at me.

"Yep, weeks ago!" Shit. I needed to do that! I hated lying to him, but I didn't want to upset him. I would get it done.

"Then we're set! I'll take care of the rest. No need for you to worry about a thing. I'll even pick up the flowers." Jared was super excited, and I loved seeing it.

"Thank you, Jared. You're the best!" I kissed him softly and laid down on his lap.

I don't know how it happened, but I woke up the next morning in bed. Jared must have helped me upstairs and tucked me in. I rolled over, kissed him while he slept and got out of bed. Coffee... I needed coffee. Six in the morning came way too early.

I drank four cups of coffee, got dressed in the living room, so I wouldn't wake up Jared, left him a note, walked to the corner and jumped on a bus to go to the shop. He needed to sleep in because he had a long day ahead of him. I just had to paint.

The shop was dark and spooky when I walked in. I had never been there that early in the morning. After starting a pot of coffee, I grabbed the two gallons of black paint, some paint brushes and started to paint the silhouettes. Once I had them outlined in black, it was easy to fill them in. They were going to need a couple of coats of paint. While I waited for the first coats to dry, I drank a pot of coffee and started to touch up the white ceiling from where we accidentally splashed paint on it.

I was just starting the second coats when Jared knocked on the front door of the shop. Dammit! I lost track of time.

"Hi, Jared! Just give me a minute to clean up." I dropped the paint brush in a container of water and started to go to the back of the shop to get cleaned up.

"Dammit, you knew I was coming to pick you up to go to the caterer." Jared was upset.

"Hey, lose the attitude. I lost track of time. I'll be ready in a minute." I turned to face him.

"Forget it, Maggie. I'll go by myself. Sometimes I think you don't want to get married." He turned and left, slamming the door.

I stood there for a second and then chased after him. I caught him just as he was getting into the car.

"Hey, let's not do this. Please, just give me a minute to get cleaned up. Call the caterer and tell her we're running a few minutes late, okay?" I kissed him.

"You're right. I'm sorry. It's just been a long day." He kissed me back and waited for me in the car.

I cleaned up and changed my clothes as fast as I could. When I got back out to the car, Jared was in a better mood.

We met with the caterer and okayed the menu after tasting a few samples. We then went to pick up the flowers and Jared's tuxedo. He wouldn't let me see it but said it was a perfect fit. At least things were going smoothly now.

"Maggie? The Justice of the Peace needs a copy of our vows. Did you bring them?" Jared was so on top of things. Dammit!

"Um, no I didn't. Chloe has them because I wanted her to go over them to make sure that what I wanted to say was coming across alright." Fuck, I hated lying to him.

"Okay, let's go get them so we can drop them off." Jared didn't realize I was lying.

"She's not home. She had to take the girls to the doctor." Fuck... There I go again.

"Tomorrow then?" He still had no idea.

"Sure, I'll get her to bring them to the shop tomorrow, and we can take them over after that. Is that okay?" I really had to write them now.

"Perfect." Jared drove home.

Why did I agree to write our own vows? Oh right, because I hated the part about "obey" in the original ones. Fuck, I should have just kept my mouth shut or had the Justice of the Peace skip that part. Okay, I could do this. After all, I was going to be a writer before I became a tattoo artist, right?

When we got home, Jared started to heat up dinner from the night before. I told him I needed to take a nap because I had been up so early. He told me to take my time, and he would wait on dinner until I woke up. I left him playing video games in the living room, and I went upstairs to "nap".

I locked the door, grabbed a notebook and sat on the bed. I picked up my pen, preparing to write the most amazing vows ever and... My mind went completely blank. Fuck.

Okay Maggie... WRITE! I willed my pen to write. Nope, wasn't happening. I SAID WRITE! Still... Nothing. DAMMIT! Why did I always wait 'till the last minute?

Take a deep breath. Let's start with what you love about Jared. Let's see,

1. He is the most caring and genuine man you've ever known.
2. He brings out the best in you.
3. He is compassionate.
4. He is honest.
5. He loves me for who I am.
6. He... He... He is cute as fuck! HA!
7. He is a hard worker.
8. He knows me better than I know myself sometimes.
9. He supports me in my decisions in life.
10. He has a smile that lights up the darkest corners.

Okay, I could work with this. I read what I had written, and the vows just came to me. I wrote them out and then wrote them again. When I was finished, I sealed them in an envelope and went downstairs.

"Oh hey, Baby, look what I found." I handed the envelope to Jared.

"Well, that didn't take you long. Maggie, you didn't have to lie. I wouldn't have been mad. I know you've been working hard." Jared knew all along that I hadn't written them.

"I'm sorry. I didn't want to lie, but I didn't want you to think that I didn't care." I kissed him and gave him the "puppy-dog" look.

"I'm sorry too. I've been a little out of my mind about this whole thing." He kissed me back.

"It's okay. It's to be expected. I love you." I picked up See-`a-tee from the floor, and we cuddled up on Jared's lap.

"I love you too, Maggie." He stroked my hair, and we watched television until it was time for bed.

Jared dropped me off at the shop, so he could go to school and run errands. I worked my ass off to finish the mural. Music and coffee helped me to make it through the day.

There, all done! Now, I could concentrate on our wedding. I know it probably sounds vain of me, but I absolutely loved the way this one turned out. I hoped that Tango and Frankee loved it as well.

Jared picked me up that evening, and we went out to eat. We needed the break from reality. We laughed and talked for hours. We were "us" again by the time we walked through our front door.

As always, See-`a-tee was there to greet us.

"Come on little one. It's time for bed." I scooped her up and started up the stairs.

"Maybe she can sleep in her cat bed tonight? At least for an hour or so?" Jared gently grasped my arm and gave me "that" look.

"Oh, okay. Here ya go little one. Sleep here for now." I put See-`a-tee in her cat bed.

Jared and I went up to our room and made love. It had been so long. My body hungered for his and was filled with his passion. Yep, we were back to "us" again.

When we finished, Jared got up, opened the door and let See-`a-tee in. The three of us slept peacefully all night long.

Thursday morning, and all was right in our world. Jared let me sleep in while he went to school. I woke up, once again, to fresh brewed coffee and a love note. I really did love this man.

See-`a-tee and I were lazy all day. That is until I remembered my appointment at the tailor. Fuck. I called Sara to come get me and take me to my appointment.

Sara and Chloe showed up just in time to take me. They had to pick up their dresses as well. We raced to the tailor shop before it closed. We got there just in time. The dresses fit perfectly!

The girls dropped me off at home. I hung my dress in the closet and changed back into my pajamas. This was all going to work out just fine... It had to.

Jared came home that evening, and we went over the play list for the DJ. I had forgotten all about it. At least I knew what music I wanted him to play.

With that taken care of, we settled in for a night of relaxation. I rolled a joint, and we smoked it while we chatted about everything and nothing. It was just like when we first met.

We went to bed that night with smiles on our faces. Jared took off the next two weeks from school to take care of the wedding things and for our honeymoon. He had worked so hard to get ahead in his classwork, so he could take the time off without issue.

Just as we were drifting off to sleep, my cellphone rang. Who the fuck?

"Hi, Maggie!" It was Tango. "Just wanted to let you know that we're coming home tomorrow. They are expecting bad storms here over the weekend, so we are coming home a day early."

"Okay, Tango! We can't wait to see you! Be safe! Love you!" Fuck! I had to clean the shop!

Jared and I got out of bed, dressed and went to the shop. It was past midnight, but it had to be done. It took us almost two hours to clean it completely. We drove home exhausted and hurting.

"Maggie?" Jared rolled over in bed and put his arm over my waist.

"Yeah?" I was so sleepy I could barely stay awake.

"Your mural is the most incredible piece of art I've ever seen, but if you ever do this again, can we clean it up right away instead of waiting to the last minute?" He laughed and kissed the back of my neck.

"Yes, Baby. I love you." I smiled.

"I love you too." Jared and I fell into a deep sleep.

We were so tired that we slept right through our alarm. We jumped out of bed, dressed without showering and raced over to the cake tasting. We picked out a strawberry cake with butter cream frosting, both vegan. We kept it simple with lilies around each layer and piping to match. It was going to be gorgeous.

We went home and took a quick nap. Tango and Frankee were not meeting us at the shop until that evening. It was absolute bliss to be able to take a nap with my man in the middle of the day.

When we woke up, we played with See-`a-tee for a while. I hated being so busy. It felt like we had been neglecting our precious little companion. She didn't seem to mind though. She still chased her toys all over the floor as we pulled them around for her. Whenever I sat on the futon, she would climb up to my chest and purr until she fell asleep. She was getting so big. She was turning six months in April. Just as he promised, Jared already had a vet appointment for her to get spayed. We wanted her to live a long, happy and healthy life.

At five thirty, we left to meet Tango and Frankee at the shop. I had given them explicit instructions to park in the back and not go into the shop until we were there. They were already there when we arrived.

"You're early! HI! We missed you so much!" I hugged them both. We all chatted for a bit to catch up, and I blindfolded them both and led them into the studio through the back door . We walked through the break room, and I asked them to stop so they were facing the mural I had painted, with the help of the girls. I had asked Sara, Chloe and the girls to be there, but they couldn't make it, so Jared was recording the unveiling.

"Okay, on the count of three, take off your blindfolds, 1, 2, 3!" I was beyond excited for them to see it!

They took off their blindfolds and just stood there. Fuck! They didn't like it.

"Maggie, I don't know what to say. For the first time in my life, I am rendered speechless." Tango was the first to say something.

"Well, I'm not! Maggie, this is fucking magnificent!" Frankee turned to hug me.

"Really? You like it?" I hugged her back.

"Like it? I fucking love it!" She wouldn't let go of me.

"Maggie... I... I..." Tango's eyes filled with tears.

"I love you too, Old Man." I broke away from Frankee and hugged Tango tightly. "I'm so glad you like it."

"I love it, Kid." He hugged me so tight that I almost couldn't breathe.

Jared and I had made reservations for the four of us at our favorite vegan restaurant for seven o'clock. We barely made it there in time. The host looked at us funny when we all ran through the front door.

"Barnett, party of four." Jared addressed the host. We were shown to our table right away. Nice, no wait!

The four of us talked about their honeymoon and our wedding plans. We ate too much and drank just enough. It was a completely relaxing night. Our family was whole once again.

We said goodnight and headed home. There was still so much to do for the wedding that we needed a good night's sleep and a long, stress free weekend to prepare for it. Our wedding was five days away. Thank goodness, not many people got married on a Wednesday.

You know how they say that time flies when you're having fun? Well, it also flies when you're preparing for a wedding. It was now Tuesday night, and we were getting married TOMORROW! Wow, it seemed like just yesterday that Jared and I were meeting at the club. I won't lie, my stomach was full of butterflies, but my feet were warm. * wink and a smile *

Jared and I decided that we were not going to see each other after we woke up Tuesday morning.

"Good morning almost, Mrs. Barnett." Jared stroked my cheek to wake me.

"Good morning, Mr. Barnett." I stretched and yawned.

"Um, do ya think we could..." Jared started to speak.

"Um, no, I don't think we could..." I cut him off and giggled. There was no way we were making love the day before our wedding. He had to wait.

We got up, had breakfast together, I gathered my things and kissed him goodbye for the final time as a single woman.

Tango picked me up and brought me to his and Frankee's house to stay the night and get ready for the wedding the next day. Sara, Chloe and the girls were going to meet us there the next morning to get dressed and leave together.

I had a difficult time sleeping that night. Thoughts of what could go wrong kept running through my head. I ran down the checklist of everything we had to do. We had done it all, right? Yep, I went over it again in my mind just to make sure. Then I did it again.

"Wake up sleepy head. It's time to get ready." Frankee woke me up with a fresh cup of coffee and a lily. She was the sweetest woman.

"Thanks, Frankee. You're fantastic." I sat up, took the coffee from her and sipped at it. It was really hot.

"Are you nervous?" She sat on the bed next to me.

"Yes, but not because I'm marrying Jared. I'm nervous that things will go wrong." I couldn't lie to her. I knew she could see it in my eyes.

"It'll be perfect. Just wait and see." She smoothed the hair off of my face. "Now, get up and get showered. Breakfast is waiting."

"Oh, I can't eat. I'm too nervous." I started to get out of bed.

"You will eat. No argument, or I'll tell Tango." She turned and smiled at me. "Now, hurry up, Dear."

"Yes, Ma'am." I got out of bed, showered, dressed in clean pajamas and met them in the kitchen for breakfast. Just as Frankee was making our plates, Sara, Chloe, Jeremy and the girls showed up. Yay! We could all eat together now.

When breakfast was over and all cleaned up, Tango left to go help Jared get ready for the wedding. He was not only giving me away, he was also Jared's best man.

The girls and I did our hair and make-up there. Chloe's boyfriend, Jeremy, came over and helped to do our hair since he was a cosmetologist. I was grateful for his help.

We were going to get dressed in the club room at the banquet hall, so we gathered up our dresses and loaded into Frankee's van. The drive to Garden of the Gods seemed to take forever. I swear, we hit every red light on the way. My stomach was hatching butterflies left and right!

Dressed and feeling beautiful, I waited, not so patiently, for Tango to come get me. We had to drive over to the park where the ceremony was taking place.

"He's late." I paced back and forth.

"No, he's not. It's going to be fine, Maggie." Frankee did her best to calm me.

"What if it rains? We didn't set up a tent." I still paced.

"Then it rains." Frankee stopped me and adjusted my veil.

"Who's ready to get married?" Tango knocked on the door before he entered. "Oh Maggie, my precious Maggie, you look beautiful." Tears sprang to Tango's eyes.

"Thank you, Tango. I feel beautiful. Now, let's do this." I took Tango by the arm and headed out to the car. The girls were already waiting at the park.

The music started and the girls walked in single file down the aisle. We had decided against escorts for them because we wanted to keep things simple.

Shye and Patience walked behind Sara and Chloe and dropped red rose petals with every step. It was beautiful.

The music changed to the wedding march, and everyone stood up to watch Tango walk me down the aisle. The butterflies burst in my stomach, but I held them down.

"Ready?" Tango kissed my cheek, and we took the first step, the second step, and before I knew it, he was putting my hand in Jared's.

"Dearly beloved, we are gathered here today..." I didn't hear the rest of what the Justice of the Peace was saying. I was lost in Jared's loving stare.

"Ahem, Jared? Your vows?" The crowd giggled a bit.

"Oh, um... Maggie, I've loved you from the first day I met you. You are my world, and together we will shape a life that is perfect for us. We will grow the love from the seed we have planted here today. Thank you for loving me. I shall always be grateful for your love. I love you forever and always." Jared smiled.

"Maggie? Your vows?" The Justice of the Peace turned to me.

"Jared, you are the air that I breathe. I was created to love you and only you. You've chased away the dark clouds that once kept me in the shadows. You are the light and love in my life, and today I am baptized in the love we have created. I love you, now and always." I watched as tears filled Jared's eyes. I couldn't help it, I joined him in those same tears.

"I now pronounce you, Husband and Wife. What has been joined here together today, let no one tear asunder. Jared? You may now kiss the bride." Cheers rose from our guests. At the very moment our lips met, it started to rain a soft and peaceful rain. We were truly being baptized in the love we shared.

Everyone covered their heads and ran for their cars. We all met at the banquet hall. Our guests were waiting for us and started clapping as we entered. We were all soaked, but we were happy.

The DJ began to play music and people started to mingle. The food was served buffet style so people could eat at their leisure.

Jared and I sat side by side at the head table and watched our guests enjoy themselves. People started to clink their forks and spoons against their glasses to signal us to kiss. We did every time we heard the tapping of the silverware against the glass.

On cue, the DJ started to play the music for our first dance. Jared stood, took me by the hand and led me to the center of the dance floor.

The spotlight shined on us as he wrapped me in his arms, and we began to sway to the music. I leaned my head on his shoulder and breathed in his scent.

"I love you, Jared." I whispered into his ear.

"I love you, Maggie. I told you it could be this easy." He whispered back.

"Please, join me in congratulating Mr. and Mrs. Barnett on this, their happiest of days." The DJ spoke over the song.

Mr. and Mrs. Barnett, I loved the sound of that...

CHAPTER TWENTY ONE

"As you take these next steps into your future, I hope you will look back on your experiences here with the fondest of memories. Ladies and gentlemen, please stand and congratulate the graduating class of 1998!" Mortar boards filled the air in celebration of the students great accomplishment.

Jared and I loved the hotel we stayed at for our honeymoon so much that we went back for a weekend to celebrate his graduation. Denver was a huge city and offered many forms of entertainment, but we never left our hotel room.

"Can we talk about making a baby now? Why do you keep putting it off?" Jared was laying on the bed looking at me.

"I've been wanting to talk to you about that." I joined him on the bed.

"Yeah? I'm listening." He draped his arm over my stomach.

"Yep, I think we should look for your son and then have our own baby." I wasn't sure how he was going to take that.

"Where do we even start, Maggie? I've tried this, it always comes up a dead end." Jared was discouraged.

"Leave it up to me. I have an idea." I kissed him to help calm his fears.

"Alright, I trust you. Now, come here." Jared kissed me and my toes curled. * wink *

We spent the entire weekend practicing our baby making skills. Room service, in-room movies, fresh linens and shared showers rounded out our weekend. It was definitely a celebration.

Once we returned to reality, I went back to work at the studio, and Jared began looking for work. I was so proud of him for finishing school. Now, he could work in his chosen field.

Jared secured a job at the plasma center as a phlebotomist. He loved his job and was working full time. With both of us working, we were able to put quite a bit of money into our savings and were proud of our accomplishment.

During my breaks at work, down time at home and any other spare time I could find, I began the search for Aaron. I contacted state authorities, private detectives and even talk show hosts in my efforts to locate him. Occasionally, I was given an address, but it never turned up anything. I had enough.

I sent an email to the Governor of Maryland, the last state that Aaron was known to live in, explaining our plight and asking for help. Within three hours of hitting the "send" button, I received a phone call from the Maryland State Police saying they had located Aaron and to get there as soon as we could.

Arrangements were made with Tango and Frankee. They knew not to expect me in for an undetermined amount of time, and of course, they were fine with that. They offered to purchase our plane tickets, but I assured them that we had it covered.

See-`a-tee and I waited impatiently for Jared to get home. My mind raced with ideas on how to tell him.

"Hi, Honey, I'm home!" Jared called out to me as he came in.

"Hi, Jared! We're in the kitchen." I answered.

"We?" He hung up his jacket.

"Yes... See-`a-tee and me." I came around the corner of the kitchen and kissed him hello. "Tell me about your day?"

"Same old same old, needles, plasma and clients. No one passed out today though, so that's always a good thing." He kissed me back. "How about your day? You're home early."

"I didn't go to work today, and I won't be going in for a week or two." All of the ideas I had on how to tell him flew right out the window.

"Are you alright? Are you sick?" Jared reached to touch my forehead.

"I'm fine. I have something to tell you. Let's sit down." I handed him See-`a-tee and then sat on the futon.

"Should I be scared?" He sat down with our kitty next to me.

"Nope, not scared, but maybe a little excited?" I reached over to pet See-`a-tee.

"Okay, Maggie, spill it." Jared looked intrigued.

I told him all about the email to the Governor, the phone call from the state police, and then I handed him the plane tickets. We were leaving the next day. Jared hugged me tight, and thanked me. I kissed the tears from his cheeks. He immediately called work and took the rest of the week off. They were happy to oblige.

Aaron was in foster care in Baltimore, the same city that Jared's mother lived. Perfect! We made plans to stay with his mom.

I set out my clothes and necessities for the trip, and while Jared packed them, I took See-`a-tee over to Tango's. He and Frankee were going to watch her for us while we were gone. I knew she would be well taken care of. I kissed them all goodbye and went back home.

Jared had finished packing and was sitting on the back patio when I arrived. I picked up a bottle of tequila, two shot glasses and joined him. After setting down the bottle and glasses, I sat on his lap.

"You okay?" I kissed his nose.

"It's been six years, Maggie. He won't even recognize me." He reached for the bottle and poured a couple of shots.

"Things will be perfect, and if you can't have faith in that, then have faith in me because I have enough for both of us." We toasted with our shots and he poured another. "Hey, we have to get up early. Let's take it easy."

"I know. Last one, I promise." We drank the second shot.

Sleep did not come easy that night. We both tossed and turned in anticipation. The alarm was shut off before it rang because we were already awake. Jared and I were showered, dressed and ready when Sara showed up to take us to the airport.

There were no issues with the flight, and we landed safely in Baltimore that afternoon. We drove our rental car to Jared's mom's house. She was outside waiting for us when we arrived. She looked nothing like what I had envisioned.

Mrs. Barnett was fifty-two years old when she adopted Jared. She was now in her late seventies and fit as a fiddle. She smiled a bright smile and hugged Jared as he walked through the gate.

"It's so good to see you, Son." Mrs. Barnett's loud voice boomed across the yard.

"It's nice to see you too, Mom. Mom? This is Maggie. Maggie? This is Mom." Jared introduced us.

"So, this is the white girl." Mrs. Barnett stared at me with an icy cold stare. I waited to see if she was joking... She wasn't.

"It's a pleasure to meet you, Mrs. Barnett." I reached to shake her hand. She didn't accept it.

"Well, you're here, let's go in and get you settled." She turned and went into the house.

I shot Jared one of "those" looks to let him know this was not cool. He shrugged his shoulders, picked up our luggage and stepped aside, so I could enter first. As I stepped past him, he leaned down and kissed me.

We spent the evening talking. Well okay, they talked while I listened and smiled. I knew where I wasn't wanted, so I thought it best to just keep my mouth shut unless I was asked a direct question, which I wasn't.

Sleep came early that night because we had an appointment to meet Aaron and his social worker the next day. Mrs. Barnett started to go upstairs to make our bed when Jared jumped up, ran past her and went into his childhood bedroom. She went in after him and made the bed. When we were in bed, I asked him why he had run upstairs so fast. He told me he had dirty magazines under his mattress, and he didn't want his mom to see them, so he grabbed them and threw them in the closet. I laughed so hard that his mom pounded on the wall and told us to shut up.

Mrs. Barnett had breakfast ready for us when we woke up the following morning. It was sweet of her, but she made us eggs and bacon. Jared had told her the night before that I was vegan and didn't eat anything from an animal. I wasn't sure if she was being pushy or didn't understand. I drank a cup of coffee and made an excuse that I had a nervous stomach. She seemed to buy it. * wink *

Jared and I left to go to the park where we were to meet Aaron and his social worker. Our rental car started to act funny, sputtering and spitting like it was going to die. I reached up, touched the dashboard and said, "Oh no you don't! Get us there!" The car quit acting up and got us where we were going. Jared jokingly said the car knew I would kick its ass if it didn't listen to me.

We parked under a tree where we told the social worker we would meet her. A car pulled in next to us, and Jared and I got out of our rental car. I stayed next to our car and he walked to the passenger side of the social worker's car. We had discussed with the social worker that we wanted this to be a surprise for Aaron, and she agreed. The car door opened and Aaron stepped out.

"DADDY!" Aaron ran to Jared and wrapped his arms around his waist. Jared hugged him back. There was not a dry eye between us. Now mind you, Aaron was now eight years old and hadn't seen his dad since he was two. There was no hesitation or awkwardness; he just wanted to love his daddy. Yep, here ya go... Have a tissue.

Jared introduced me to Aaron. He shyly hugged me and said it was nice to meet me. The social worker sat in her car while the three of us played at the park and had a picnic. We were allowed an hour with him. It just wasn't long enough.

Jared and I walked Aaron over to the social worker's car. I hugged him, told him I would see him later, and I had a lot of fun. He said he did too, and it was nice to meet me. I then walked around the other side to our car.

I watched as Aaron and Jared hugged one another. Aaron started crying. Jared dropped to his knees to talk to his son face to face.

"Aaron, I know things seem crazy right now, but we're going to fix that." Jared put his hands on Aaron's shoulders.

"Please don't go, Daddy! I want to stay with you!" Aaron clung to Jared's neck.

"I have to go, Son. I need to get some things done, so you can come live with us." Jared was trying so hard to maintain.

"No, Daddy! Please, I'll be a good boy. PLEASE TAKE ME HOME WITH YOU!" Aaron cried even harder.

Aaron's social worker got out of the car and told him that it was time to go. Aaron still clung to his father, crying.

"Aaron, do you trust me?" Jared had tears rolling down his cheeks now.

"Yes, Daddy." Aaron was starting to calm.

"Then you need to trust me when I say that I am working very hard to get things ready for you to come live with me and Mama Maggie, okay? Now give me a hug. I'll see you soon, I promise." Jared hugged Aaron close to him and then kissed him on his forehead.

"Okay, Daddy. I love you." Aaron said those three perfect little words.

"I love you too, Son. I always have and always will." Jared watched as Aaron got into the car and left.

Here ya go, have another tissue.

We had dinner with Jared's mom that night and then took a late flight home. There was a lot we needed to do, so we could get custody of Aaron. The social worker told us that Aaron was in foster care because his mother tried to kill herself and was in a hospital. Since Jared was considered an absentee father, we were going to have to go to court. Battle mode activated.

When we got home, Jared opened a bottle of wine, I lit the candles, turned on some music and met him on the futon. It was time to make some plans.

"Okay, Maggie, you're good at this. What's the game plan?" Jared poured me a glass of wine.

"I've been thinking about that a lot. Business is booming at the shop, and you have a great job, right? It's time for us to get a bigger place. Aaron needs his own room." I sipped at the wine.

"Sounds good. When are we going to do this?" He poured his own glass of wine.

"Now, tomorrow, as soon as possible. We have to show these people that we mean business." I leaned over and kissed Jared.

"Alright, I'll tell the center that I won't be in to work for a couple of weeks." He kissed me back.

"No, I got this. I'll start looking for places tomorrow and put a list together. We can go see them as soon as they have appointments." I was so excited!

"You are amazing and I love you!" Jared took my glass of wine, set it on the table with his and tackled me on the couch. WOW! What a night. * wink *

We woke up on the floor in the living room, sore, happy and satisfied. Jared left to go get a newspaper, and I made breakfast. We made a fabulous team.

Tango and Frankee brought See-`a-tee home just as we were having our breakfast. They joined us, and we talked about the trip. Frankee cried and hugged us. Tango offered his services in whatever we needed. I loved them both so much.

We ate breakfast on the patio and searched the classifieds for apartments. I loved living downtown, but the truth was it was not a place to raise a child. There was no yard, bars everywhere and he would have to be bussed to the nearest school. Nope, not child friendly.

The tattoo studio and Jared's job were both on the west side of town. It made sense for us to move to that area. We found four places to look at, and I called to make appointments to see them, all for today. Tango and Frankee headed over to the studio, and we headed out.

The first apartment was in an old church. It was a stunning building, and the apartment was on the first floor. There was a small yard, but it was on a very busy street. The bedrooms were small, and there was only one bathroom. We told the manager we would keep it on our list and let him know if we decided to lease it.

The second apartment had cockroaches. Nope, no thank you. I lived in California long enough to know that they weren't going away any time soon.

We made our way over to the third apartment. It was half of a duplex, and I freaking loved it! It felt like a house. It had two large bedrooms, an eat-in-kitchen, a fenced, private yard and was about four blocks from the elementary school. The only down side was it only had one bathroom. Jared didn't like that the bedrooms were not on the same floor, and there was no private parking. We talked about it and told the landlord that we wanted to think about it and would get back to her if we decided to take it.

Though we had a bit of time to find the perfect place, there was still a sense of urgency. We went out to lunch before we went to the last apartment, so we could talk about things.

"Maggie, I know you liked that last place, but please, let's not be hasty." Jared was right.

"I agree with you about the parking. I hate parking on the street too." I reached over and held his hand.

"So, ready to go? We have twenty minutes until our appointment with the next one." He was standing up to leave.

"Sure, let's go." I grabbed my to-go glass of iced tea and followed him out to the car.

A highly rated elementary school sat on the corner of the dead end street we turned on to. CHECK! The complex was two blocks up from the school. CHECK! The apartment grounds were clean, and there was assigned, off street parking. CHECK! It was a small complex compared to most in Colorado Springs. CHECK! I loved it already.

"Okay, we might have to be hasty here." Jared turned to me and smiled as we parked the car.

"I have a good feeling about this, Baby." I rolled up my window and got out of the car.

Gertrude, the manager, met us outside. She was a lovely woman with light blonde hair, big blue eyes and a charming smile. She had moved here from Germany and had a heavy German accent.

We introduced ourselves and shook her hand. She took us to the apartment, so we could look around. It was a garden level apartment. The front of it was underground, but the back of it opened out to a shared yard. We walked down a couple of concrete steps to the front door, and she unlocked it. Gertrude told us to go in and look around while she stayed outside. NICE!

When we first entered, there was a long hallway in front of us and a nice sized, boxy kitchen to our left with a pass through window to the next room. At the end of the hallway, to the left was a large room that was a combination dining area and living room. It had sliding glass doors that led out to a patio in the shared back yard. To our right was another long hallway. As we turned down the hall, there was a master suite on our right, that had it's own attached bathroom. Directly across from it there was a second, smaller bedroom. Just past the second bedroom, still on the left, was a three quarter bath with a toilet, sink and shower. At the end of the hall was a third bedroom with a fireplace and it had it's own bathroom as well.

"Jared? Please?" I was hopping on both feet like a schoolgirl.

"Yes." Jared walked up to me, wrapped me up in a hug and kissed me.

We went outside to tell Gertrude that we would take it. It was perfect! We could have the room with the fireplace, Aaron would have the other master suite, and the third room would be a nursery. The best part? It was the same price as the apartment we lived in now.

We went to the rental office where Gertrude ran our credit and background checks. We passed without issue, wrote her a check and signed a lease. With the keys in Jared's hand, we walked out happy because we knew it was supposed to be like this.

"Now we just need to get a rental truck and some help." I was prattling on at a mile a minute.

"First things first, Maggie, we need to get boxes and pack. Think we can do this before this weekend?" Jared was smiling almost as big as I was.

"Are you kidding me? I'm the fucking puzzle queen!" I winked at him and started organizing everything in my mind. Yeah, we could do this.

Moving boxes multiplied like bunnies in our living room. Sara and Chloe stayed two nights in a row to help us pack. We were determined to do this before Jared had to start work on Monday. Plus, the shop was really busy, and Tango needed me back as soon as I could get there. Frankee even came over after work to help us pack. Tango and Jared took a couple of loads of our things over to the new apartment with Tango's truck while we were packing. It was moving right along. (Pun intended.)

We got the moving truck on Thursday morning. It was loaded by lunch time. We really did have an amazing group of friends.

"Maggie, what about this wall? We don't have time to paint it." Jared was concerned about the painting of the Garden of the Gods I had done on the living room wall.

"Hold on." I dug two, one hundred dollar bills out of my wallet, wrote a note and folded the money into the paper. "Here, tape this to the wall. That should cover it. Plus, they have my deposit, and I won't be getting that back since we didn't have time to put in a thirty day notice, so it's all good."

"Are you sure?" Jared hated it when I didn't do things by the book.

"I'm sure. The landlady loves me. It'll be fine. I promise." I kissed him to seal the deal.

We put See-`a-tee in her pet taxi, locked the door and dropped the keys in a drop box at the rental office. We did it! YAY!

It took us a full day just to get the things we needed set up, so that we could function in our new place. Jared helped me unpack through the weekend, but he had to work on Monday, so I finished unpacking by myself. Everything fit so nicely in the new place. Well, everything except the futon. It was so worn out that we stuck it in the spare bedroom for an extra bed and bought a new living room set. I guess it was time to grow up and have a real living room, not one that looked like a dorm room. * wink and a giggle *

Jared and I picked out a bedroom set for Aaron's room as well. We chose a full size captain's bed with drawers under it and a nice book shelf headboard. There was a nightstand and a chest of drawers as well. Tango and Frankee bought him three sets of bedding to go with his new bedroom. Tango told us not to pay for delivery because he had enough room in his truck to haul it home for us. When we got it home, Tango and Jared put Aaron's bedroom furniture together. Frankee and I decorated Aaron's room by making his bed, hanging curtains and tacking up posters.

The new living room set was delivered on Monday. It was gorgeous. A brown microfiber couch and love seat with two end tables and a coffee table filled our living room area. Perfect!

I went back to work at the studio on Tuesday. It felt good to be back in the creative world of tattooing. I didn't realize how much I had missed it, and I had only been gone just over a week. I had three appointments my first day back. I also forgot how exhausting it was.

We had done everything that social services had asked us to do. Now, we sat and waited. Pins and needles... Pins and needles.

CHAPTER TWENTY TWO

Okay, we've done this before, and we're about to do it again. Time to press the fast forward button for a bit. Ready? We just skipped ahead two years. Sorry if it messed up your hair. * wink *

We were making four trips a year to Baltimore to visit with Aaron and to beg the court for custody. We didn't have an attorney, but we filed for a case review and custody hearing every three months. Jared and I were not going to give up... Ever! We made a promise to Aaron, and we were keeping it.

"It is the court's ruling that Aaron Barnett be returned to the custody of his mother." The judge banged his gavel, and it was over.

Our hearts sunk into our stomachs. How the hell could the court return Aaron to his mother when she was clearly not fit to raise him? She had tried to kill herself twice in front of him and was living in shared housing where they had to sleep in the same bedroom.

We were allowed another one hour visit with Aaron before we returned to Colorado Springs. It broke my heart to watch Jared and Aaron have to say goodbye again. Jared told Aaron that we weren't giving up and to remember what he had told him before. We were going to make this happen no matter what.

Returning to Colorado Springs, with heavy hearts, we set out to fight this even harder. It was time to look for an attorney. Aaron deserved to be living in a loving environment, free of his mother's drama and mental instabilities.

Our neighbor and very good friend, Alisha met us at the airport and brought us home. She had See-`a-tee with her too. I was so happy to see her... And Alisha too. * smile *

Alisha's husband, Joey, worked with Jared at the plasma center. They had two amazing little boys together, Mathew and Mark. They had moved in upstairs from us right around the time that we moved to the complex. Alisha and I became instant friends.

I was only working part time at the studio. There was so much going on in our lives that my time was needed at home. I tried to quit the partnership, but Tango wasn't having it. We did however, split the partnership three ways. I only tattooed by special appointment now and would go in on Sundays to do the major cleaning.

One night, when Jared and I were having dinner, he started to cry out of nowhere. I put down my fork and sat at his side.

"What's wrong, Baby?" I rubbed his back as I spoke to him.

"I miss Aaron. I can't stand this, Maggie. I just don't understand why they keep giving him back to her when we would be so much better for him." He wiped his tears.

"I know, Jared. I miss him too and don't get it either." I hugged him close to me.

"Maggie? What do you think about moving to Baltimore, so we could be closer to him and see him more often?" Jared had been thinking about this since the last court hearing.

"Well, I think it would be scary, but I also think we've saved enough money that we could make it happen." I dreaded the thought of moving again, but it was for our family's happiness and there is nothing I wouldn't do to make Jared happy.

"Really? You would do that for me?" Jared started to smile.

"No, I would do that for us. I'll start the arrangements." We kissed and finished our dinner. Here we go again.

Immediately, I gathered boxes, started packing and put in our notice to the rental office. This was going to be a huge move, but it had to be done. Jared put in his notice at work, and I talked to Tango about it. He was heartbroken but he understood. The partnership was dissolved.

Alisha helped me with the packing and cleaning. It took us two weeks to get everything ready. We made plans to stay in a hotel in Baltimore until we could find our own apartment again.

Alisha and I picked up the moving truck while Jared was at his last day of work. We were leaving the next day, and I could barely function. I had an awful toothache and was on antibiotics and painkillers until I could see a dentist. The neighbors banded together to help load the truck. We were truly blessed with great friends.

The only thing left in our apartment was the futon mattress on the living room floor and the television. We were going to leave early in the morning, so there was no need to leave anything else out.

I was just laying down to take a nap when my cell phone rang.

"Hello?" The call came in from an unknown number.

"Hello. May I speak to Mr. Barnett?" The caller's voice seemed familiar.

"I'm sorry, he's not in right now. This is his wife, may I take a message?" Probably some solicitor that had called before.

"This is Mrs. Johnson from the Department of Child Safety in Baltimore. It is imperative that I speak with Mr. Barnett today." My heart leapt into my throat.

"Oh, hello, Mrs. Johnson. Here, let me give you his work number." I gave her the number, and we hung up. Pins and needles... pins and needles.

A few minutes later, my cell phone rang again.

"Maggie? I have some news. Seems like we're going to have to unpack. They just told me to come pick up Aaron!" He hung up and was on his way home.

So here's how it went... Aarons' mother, Theresa, tried to kill herself again. Social Services had enough. They were aware that we were "thinking" about moving there to be closer to Aaron. They recommended to the court that Jared get full custody of Aaron, and the court agreed.

Jared hopped on a plane to go get him while I took care of things on the home front. The landlord had no issue with us staying and was even happy about it. Tango and Frankee were thrilled to hear we weren't moving and said I could still be an artist at the shop when I had time. Jared's job let him stay as well. * phew * Now, just had to unpack before they got home.

My tooth was absolutely trying to kill me. I laid down to take a nap before I started the tedious job of unpacking. I had been sleeping for about an hour when there was a knock on my door. It was Alisha, with a whole group of neighbors.

"We're here to unpack you." Alisha gave me a big hug and then just took over the job of moving everything back in. I was so thankful that I went to the nearest fast food restaurant and bought them all lunch.

Our home was now moved back in and unpacked. I don't know what I would have done without that group of people. They say that it takes a village to raise a child, and we were blessed to be living in an incredible village. * smile *

I made it to the dentist and had my tooth fixed before Jared and Aaron made it back home. Feeling much better, I busied myself making our apartment a home again. The neighbors did a great job unpacking, but I needed to decorate and clean.

The day was here. I was completely nervous. I didn't know how to be a mom, especially a mom to a ten year old boy. Memories of Willow came flooding back to me. I could do this, right?

"Maggie? We're home!" Jared's voice rang out.

"HI! I've missed you so much! Hi, Aaron! Welcome home!" I hugged them both.

"Aaron? You remember Maggie." Jared re-introduced us.

"Yes, Sir, I do. Hello, Ma'am." Aaron reached to shake my hand. What a polite young man.

"Oh, Aaron, you can call me Maggie." I took his hand, pulled him close to me and hugged him. "I'm so happy you're here."

Jared and I showed Aaron around our home and introduced him to See-`a-tee. He loved her right away, and she loved him. It was so cool to watch them get to know each other.

We had dinner in the backyard. There was a lot going on, so we ordered pizza, and I made a salad. The guys told me all about their trip, and I told them how the neighbors helped with the unpacking and such. We had a blast just hanging out.

It was time for Aaron to get ready for bed. That's when Jared told me that Aaron was sent with only the clothes on his back. I knew exactly what to do. I ran up to Alisha's and borrowed some sweats and a t-shirt from her oldest son, Mathew. That would do until morning, and then we could take Aaron shopping. There, all fixed!

Tucking in Aaron that night was a dream come true for Jared and I. See-`a-tee was curled up at Aaron's feet. I stood in the door as Jared talked to Aaron about our plans for the next day. I didn't want to interrupt their dad and son time.

"Maggie? Aren't you going to kiss me goodnight?" Aaron was the sweetest boy.

"Of course, Sweetheart." I walked over to his bed, kissed him on the forehead and wished him sweet dreams. As I turned to walk out of his room, a single tear rolled down my cheek.

Jared was in the hall waiting for me. "Maggie? Thank you, thank you so much for making this possible. Thank you for finding our son and for not giving up." … Our son. I hugged Jared tight and cried a happy cry.

While Jared unpacked his suitcase, I washed the clothes Aaron had been wearing. I wanted them to be fresh and clean for him in the morning when we went shopping. I know it's silly, but I still remember looking at his little boy clothes and just giggling. I loved him instantly.

The next morning, I made breakfast while the guys slept in. The smell must have woken them up because all of a sudden, Jared's arms were wrapped around my waist, and he was kissing my neck.

"Good morning, Beautiful. It smells good in here." Jared was happy.

"Good morning, Baby. How'd you sleep?" I turned around and kissed him. That's when I heard Aaron giggle.

"Well, good morning, Little Man. Did you sleep alright?" I stepped away from Jared and hugged Aaron.

"Yes Ma'am... I mean yes, Maggie, I did." Aaron hugged me back. It was the best feeling ever!

"Pancakes? Eggs? Bacon?" I showed Aaron what I was cooking.

"All of them, please?" Aaron licked his lips and rubbed his belly, smiling.

"Of course, Sweetheart." I made Jared and Aaron their plates and served it to them in the dining area. I sat on the couch with a cup of coffee.

"Aren't you going to eat with us, Maggie?" Aaron looked up from his plate.

"Oh, Sweetheart, I ate earlier, but I'll come sit with you." I got up and joined them at the table. Yep, I was real new to this but he was helping me right along.

We chatted and laughed. Aaron tried to share his bacon with me, so I had to explain to him that I was vegan and what that meant. He looked a bit confused, but I thought it best not to overload him with information about being vegan while he was eating.

When breakfast was over, I gave Aaron his clean clothes, we all got dressed and went shopping. Jared and I decided that this constituted an emergency, so we withdrew three thousand dollars from our savings to make sure Aaron had everything he needed. It was so much fun to shop for and with Aaron.

We shopped 'till we dropped! Aaron got new clothes for school, play and for lounging. We bought him new shoes, boots and jackets. When it came time to buy his underwear, Aaron asked that only he and his dad pick them out, so of course I agreed. While they were taking care of that, I picked out a new backpack and all of the school supplies he was going to need. Four and a half hours later, we were pulling back into our parking spot and taking dozens and dozens of bags into our home. All done... For now.

Jared and I decided to have a "Welcome Home Aaron" and "Thank You" barbecue for the entire complex. It didn't matter to us if everyone had helped or not. We just wanted to thank everyone and introduce Aaron to our friends.

We bought over twelve hundred dollars worth of food and alcohol. After okaying it with Gertrude, we set it up in the courtyard of the complex. She didn't care if we had music or alcohol as long as no one got too drunk and caused problems. She herself was going to attend.

Jake and Stephanie were good friends of ours. We had met them in the complex when we were out walking around. They were potheads and were always inviting us up to partake with them. Sometimes we would bring some, and sometimes they would host. None of us ever went without.

Jake didn't work, so he was always home making something. He had converted their second bedroom into a workshop and did a lot of restoration projects with junk furniture he would find in dumpsters or on the side of the road. He wasn't as talented as he liked to believe. His greasy, light brown hair was always held back with a bandana, and he never smiled because he had very few teeth.

Stephanie worked at a convenience store and supported the two of them. She was a short, fat woman that was bigger around then she was tall. She had long blonde hair and a crooked, dirty smile. I don't ever remember a time that she didn't have a cigarette in one hand and a soda on the table.

They were both kind people, and we grew very close with them. Jake and Stephanie had moved to Colorado from Minnesota. Though they were from southern Minnesota, it was nice to have people around from the same state that I had lived in for so long.

So, back to the party. Jake and Stephanie manned the barbecue grills while Alisha and Joey set up lawn games for the kids. Jared and I set up a bar area and had hired a bartender from a club we frequented. All in all, it was very nice.

The food was set up buffet style, so everyone could eat at their leisure. There were over a hundred people there. We had invited not only the entire complex, but people from Jared's job as well as our other friends. Tango and Frankee showed up early to help us set up, but we were already done. Tango seemed disappointed, but managed to have fun anyway. Sara, Chloe and her daughters all made an appearance as well.

When everyone had arrived, Jared stood on top of a chair and got their attention.

"Hello? Hello? Okay, quiet down for just a minute folks. Maggie and I would like to thank each of you for being here. So many of our friends and neighbors worked their fingers to the bone to help us get packed to move and then unpacked to stay, and we would like to offer our heartfelt thanks to each of you." Everyone started to clap. "Hold on, hold on... We would also like to introduce our son. This is the little man that you all worked so hard to help us with, this is Aaron."

Aaron looked embarrassed but stood at his dad's side. He nodded to everyone as they clapped. I walked over to Aaron and put my hand on his shoulder.

The party continued after that. People ate, drank and danced. The kids played games and some of the adults even joined in. There was no separating the children from the adults. We were just one big happy group. The party ended without issue, and everyone helped to clean it up. It was a complete success!

It was early September, so that meant school was starting. Jared took Aaron to the school down the street and registered him for classes. Aaron was really excited about school. We found out, through Social Services, that when he lived with his mom, he never attended school... Ever. Theresa had tried to home school him but failed miserably. He had only been in school for a few months and had been placed in the third grade when he was in foster care.

When he was tested in Colorado Springs, he wasn't even at a first grade level. The school administrators decided to start him in the second grade, though for his age, he was supposed to be in the fourth. It was going to be a long, hard road, but with us at his side and his own determination, we knew he could do it.

It was the Saturday before school was starting, and Jared had to work. It was my first day home with Aaron alone since he had come to live with us. Admittedly, I was nervous.

"Maggie? May I have a pickle, please?" Aaron had been playing outside with Mathew and Mark and came in to get a snack.

"Of course, here, let me get it for you." I went into the kitchen to get him one.

We had a gallon jar of pickles sitting on the top shelf of the refrigerator. I reached in and grabbed it by the lid. I know, I know... Stupid. As I lifted it off the shelf, the jar came loose from the lid, fell, broke against the bottom shelf and stuck straight into my foot.

"Aaron? Why don't you go ask Auntie Alisha for a snack? I'm sorry, I spilled the pickles we had, and I need to clean this up." I hollered to him through the pass through window.

"Want some help?" Aaron started to come to the kitchen.

"No! Um, that's okay, Sweetheart. I'll do it. You just go have fun." I didn't want him to see the blood. Aaron ran upstairs to get a snack from Alisha.

As I mentioned earlier, I used to be a cutter. The strange thing was that now, because of my former habit, the site of my own blood make me ill and faint. I couldn't let that happen. I didn't want to scare Aaron. I closed my eyes, took a deep breath, reached down and pulled the glass from my foot. It had gone straight through to the floor. Blood started to spurt from my foot. I grabbed a kitchen towel and wrapped it around my foot to stop the blood from getting everywhere.

I then proceeded to pick up the mess and mop the floor. Pulling the mop with me as I made my way to the bathroom, I mopped the blood up as I went. It was leaking heavily through the towel.

When I made it to the bathroom, I used my cell phone to call Stephanie to come and help me.

"Stephanie? I cut my foot. I need your..." I passed out.

A little while later, I woke up on the bathroom floor, and Stephanie was bandaging my foot. She had already cleaned it. "Maggie, you need to go to the doctor." Stephanie was taping up my foot.

"No, I'm fine. I heal fast." There was no way I was going.

"Really, Maggie, this is deep." She was persistent.

"I'll tell ya what Stephanie, I'll show it to Jared when he gets home. If he thinks I need to go in, I will." There, compromise was always a good thing.

I ended up going in. Jared said it needed stitches, and it did... Sixty of them. * sad face *

Aaron loved going to school. He was up before the alarm every day. While he dressed, I made his breakfast and packed his lunch. I was getting this whole "Mom" thing down, and I was absolutely loving it!

Jared was promoted at work. He was now phlebotomy supervisor and got a pay raise. I worked at the shop a few days a week doing tattoos and still cleaned on Sundays.

Once in a while, I would take Aaron with me, so he could see what I did. He loved being there because Tango and Frankee spoiled him. They always had new gifts for him whenever I brought him in. They had purchased a new television and video game to be set up in the break room just for Aaron. He called them Grandma and Grandpa. They ate that shit up. Neither of them had children of their own. It really felt like we were a family and had always been.

It was late fall and the weather was quite nice, so I had the back patio door open to air out the apartment a bit. See-`a-tee was sleeping in the spare bedroom, so I closed the door so she wouldn't get outside.

Alisha had a cat named Salmon that roamed freely. Every once in a while she would wander into our apartment, and today was one of those days. Aaron was sitting on the living room floor playing with her when I heard the most awful scream.

I ran out to the living room just as Aaron was ducking around the corner into his room. I saw a stray cat from the neighborhood mounting Salmon. I grabbed the broom and chased them outside.

Aaron came out of his room and asked me what was happening. He wanted to know why the stray cat had attacked Salmon and made her scream. Remember, Aaron was ten years old and a very naive child.

"It's okay, Sweetheart. That stray kitty and Salmon were just making babies. Cats get really loud when they're making babies. He wasn't hurting her." I hoped I was explaining it, so he could understand it.

With a completely straight face Aaron said, "Maggie? I think Salmon would be better off making babies by herself." I never laughed so hard as I did at that moment!

Thanksgiving dinner was amazing. All of our friends came to join us to give thanks for all of our many blessings that year. We went all out again and ate until our tummies bloated. As soon as Thanksgiving dinner was complete and our guests went home, we pulled out the Christmas decorations and got started. Aaron was with us for the first time, and we could not celebrate soon enough!

Aaron and Jared helped me set everything up. It was spectacular! We sang Christmas songs and drank eggnog while we decorated. Aaron grabbed gobs of tinsel and threw it on the tree in bunches. I didn't care that the tree was not picture perfect because our son had helped us and THAT made it better than perfect.

We bought new outdoor decorations and lights. We had purchased four reindeer with white lights on them, a snowman that had the same lights and a Santa. The Santa was lit with red and white lights and waved his arm to greet people. The three of us set them up on our back patio and plugged them into a photosensitive adapter. They would go on when it was dark and turn off when the sun started to come up. It was fantastic!

Aaron asked for a tree for his bedroom, so we made that happen too. Anything he wanted that year, he was getting, come hell or high water. We felt the need to make up for all of those years that Jared looked for him. We did just that too.

We spent the next few weeks shopping for Aaron and wrapping his gifts. We had spent almost five thousand dollars out of our savings on

Christmas, but it was worth it. We had so many people in our lives that we loved and wanted to make sure that each of them had a nice Christmas.

It was now December twenty-second.

"Maggie, it's your Aunt Sheryl from Denver." Jared handed me the phone.

"Hi! Long time no hear. How are you?" I loved Aunt Sheryl. She was my father's youngest sister. She was always so down to earth.

"Hi, Maggie. Um, I have something to talk to you about, and I want you to promise me that you will listen with a calm mind and heart." Aunt Sheryl always had a special way of talking to me.

"Okay, let me sit down." I sat down in the corner of the couch, took a deep breath and prepared myself.

"Susan and Richard are here. I told them about Aaron, and they want to come and see you. I know it's been years but maybe it's time to at least try." Aunt Sheryl's words echoed in my brain. "Maggie? Are you there?"

"Yes, I'm here. Can I call you back please? I need to talk to Jared about this." I stayed calm on the outside.

"Of course. Make it quick, please. I love you." She hung up.

"JARED!" I screamed for him.

We talked for an hour and weighed the pros and cons. They had never met Jared or Aaron. After the way my father talked to Diego, I didn't want to put Jared through the same thing, or worse. It had been years since I had communicated with them in any way. Maybe Aunt Sheryl was right, maybe it was time.

Jared told me he would support me in whatever my decision was. He had no idea what he was walking into. I called my aunt back.

"Okay, they can come visit." I forced the words from my mouth.

"They want to come for Christmas Eve and Day. They said they would get a hotel room if you don't want them to stay with you." Oh hell no!

"No, they can stay with us. We have plenty of space." I cringed as soon as the words fell from my lips.

"Want to talk to them?" Aunt Sheryl sounded pleased with our decision.

"Sure, put them on the phone." I cringed again.

I talked to my parents for a few minutes, told them how to find our home and said that I looked forward to seeing them. This was going to take every ounce of energy I could muster, but I knew I could do it.

When we hung up, I immediately went to the spare room, deep cleaned it and decorated it. I set out fresh towels, bottles of high-end lotions and scented candles. We had replaced the futon with our queen sized bed when we bought our new king sized one. It looked like a hotel suite. If they were going to come and stay with us, I wanted them to see that I was living the life they thought I never would.

I excused myself and told the guys I would be right back. I went to the nearest big box store and bought my parents gifts and a couple more things for the bedroom they would be sleeping in. I also purchased gifts for them to take home to Brianna, her husband Dick and her son from her first marriage, Clint. (Sorry that I didn't tell you earlier about Brianna's divorce and second marriage, but quite frankly I had forgotten. I was having so much fun reliving all of these memories with you... But I guess it's important to the story. Thank you for understanding. * wink *)

When I arrived back home, I gave the gifts to Aaron and Jared and asked them to wrap them. I took the other things to the bedroom and set them out. There was a new robe for each of them that I draped over the end of the bed. I then placed their new slippers under the foot of the bed, so they could easily be seen. I put together a basket with shampoo, conditioner, the lotion I had put in there earlier, two different kinds of body wash, new towels and bath scrunchies. There, NOW it was complete.

I was a nervous wreck for two days. Jared and I were in the kitchen preparing Christmas Eve dinner when they knocked on the door.

"Fuck... Jared, they're early! I'll get the door, you get Aaron." We kissed each other, and I went to open the door.

"Hello, Maggie. It's nice to see you." My father spoke first.

"Please, please, come in. We're almost ready to have dinner. Let me show you to your room." I really didn't know what to say or do.

"Thank you. It smells good in here." My mother smiled a half smile at me.

"Thanks, we made a ham with all the fixings for you. Hope you enjoy it." They knew I was vegan.

"What will you be having?" My father asked me as I led them down the hall to the dining and living area.

"I made stuffed mushrooms with quinoa. It's a recipe I found online." I took their luggage.

Just as I was about to show them to their room; Jared and Aaron joined us.

"Mom, Pops, this is Jared and our son Aaron." I was almost frozen with fear for what was to come next.

"It's nice to finally meet you both." My father reached to shake their hands. I was in complete and utter shock.

"Oh, Aaron, you look just like your father. What a pleasure to meet you." My mother hugged Aaron. I could tell that he was uncomfortable, but he hugged her back.

"Here, let me show you to your room, so you can freshen up before dinner." Jared took their luggage from me and led them down the hall to their room.

"Maggie? Do I have to like them?" Aaron whispered into my ear.

"No, Sweetheart, you don't have to like them, but you do have to be nice to them." I winked at him and hugged him. "Hell, they're my parents, and I don't even really like them myself, but I do love them. You'll understand that one day."

Aaron helped me by setting the table and bringing out the food. I couldn't believe it was going this nicely so far. No snide comments, no bigoted statements, just simple pleasantries and hollow, fake exchanges. This was SO much better than I had thought it would be.

Dinner was a success. My father even tried the stuffed mushrooms and said they were delicious. My mother took credit for my cooking skills and told stories about how I used to help her in the kitchen. Aaron laughed politely at the appropriate times. I was so proud of him.

When dinner was finished and cleaned up, we sat in the living room. My father asked what our traditions were, and I told him that we followed the same tradition as our family, one gift on Christmas eve and the rest in the morning. He got up, went to their room and brought out an armful of gifts. He handed one to Jared, one to Aaron, one to my mother, one to me and kept one for himself.

"Why don't we open our gifts tonight?" He sat down on the love seat next to my mother.

"Um, sure. That would be nice." Nothing like doing it and then asking if it was okay.

"Maggie, we had a special gift for Aaron. Shouldn't we give it to him?" Jared spoke up.

"But we only do one gift on Christmas Eve." My father cut in.

"YOU may only do one gift, but this is our first Christmas together as a family. Maybe it's time for a new tradition." Jared got up and handed our gift to Aaron. "There you go, Son. Aren't you the lucky one to get two gifts tonight."

I smiled because I loved that Jared handled that so eloquently. He was my hero. I loved him so much.

Everyone opened their gifts. They had given us each a Minnesota t-shirt. It was very kind of them to think of us like that. We had given Aaron a new stereo for his room. He loved it!

When the mess from the gifts was all cleaned up, we had hot cocoa and cookies. Aaron wanted to watch a Christmas movie, so we did and then he was off to bed. Jared and I tucked him in as usual, and then my parents went in to say goodnight. I was relieved that this night was coming to an end.

Sounds of Aaron's little snores seeped into the hallway. We knew he was sound asleep with See-`a-tee at his feet, so Jared and I brought out the remainder of his presents. There were so many gifts for him, and the rest of us, that it filled the underside of the tree. We had to stack the gifts up the corner and out over the floor. We really went all out for our first Christmas together.

"Do you think you may be spoiling him a bit?" My mother spoke up.

"Yes, and he deserves it." Jared answered her. We finished stacking the gifts and said goodnight.

I barely slept that night. I stayed awake wondering what the next day would bring. Jared held me while I laid my head on his chest. He was my rock, and I don't know how I would have made it through all of this without his love and support.

Jared let me sleep in, and he got up to make breakfast. It had become our tradition to have fresh baked cinnamon rolls, fruit, orange juice and coffee. He had it all set up when I awoke. Thank goodness my parents were still asleep.

"OHMYGOODNESS! SANTA WAS HERE!" We were in the kitchen setting up breakfast when we heard Aaron yell.

"Yes, Son, Santa was here! You must have been a VERY good boy this year." Jared and I went out to the living room.

"Can I open them?" Aaron was beyond excited.

"Why don't we wait for Maggie's parents and have breakfast first." Jared was being a party pooper.

"I don't think it would hurt for him to open a couple of them, Jared." I usually didn't contradict him in front of Aaron, but this was a special occasion.

"Oh, alright. You may open two." Jared handed Aaron a couple of gifts to open.

My parents came out to the living room wearing their new robes as he was opening his gifts.

"Well, I see that we couldn't wait for the grandparents before we started opening gifts." My mother was such a bitch!

"Richard, Susan, may I see you in the other room please?" Jared asked them to join him in the kitchen.

"We are pleased that you could join us for Christmas and are truly enjoying your company. I need you to remember, however, that this is our family and our first Christmas together. If you cannot keep your comments to yourself, I would be happy to find a hotel for you. Are we in agreement?" Jared spoke with true authority in his voice.

"Understood." My parents answered in unison.

We all ate breakfast and then opened the rest of the gifts. My parents sat in the living room as Jared and I prepared Christmas dinner. We were supposed to have our friends over, but had called them and told them about my parents. We made arrangements to have a second Christmas the following day to exchange gifts and have leftovers together. I could hardly wait.

Dinner was served at two in the afternoon, and we ate until we were full. I had tofu turkey as usual and even got everyone to try it. Aaron loved it! My father said it almost tasted like turkey, and my mother said it was palatable. I was impressed that she even knew that word.

After dinner was put away and cleaned up, we visited for a while and then helped my parents to take their things out to their rental car. We gave them the gifts to take home to my sister and her family and asked that they relay our love to them. We hugged, said goodbye and watched as they left. We had survived their invasion and came out stronger from it.

"Merry Christmas, Mrs. Barnett." Jared kissed me.

"Merry Christmas, Mr. Barnett." I kissed him back.

"Merry Christmas, Mom and Dad." Aaron hugged us.

… Mom, he called me Mom. That was the best Christmas gift I could have received. * wipes a tear from my cheek *

CHAPTER TWENTY THREE

New Year's Eve was an absolute blast! We had a houseful of friends and as tradition mandated, we toasted the new year with every time zone. The kids were all allowed to stay up and were given grape juice to toast with us.

Aaron went back to school after the holiday break. He and Mathew went to the same school, so they walked together every day. Jared was working a lot of overtime because they were short handed. I was still tattooing a few days a week and cleaning on Sundays. Aaron and Jared would often come in and help me just so we had some family time together.

It was January seventeenth and I was having one hell of a moody day. I couldn't figure out why I was in such an awful mood, so I just stayed quiet for most of the day. I didn't get off of the couch much and just laid there watching movies.

It was late afternoon. Aaron was at Alisha's playing with Mathew and Mark. Alisha and Joey had just had another huge fight, and the kids were a bit shaken up. Aaron went upstairs to entertain them and take their minds off of what was going on. Alisha and Joey fought all the time, and it was never just an argument. Joey was physically violent with Alisha and the boys. We tried so hard to get her to leave him, but like a lot of women in that position, she thought he would change if she just did better. It was a sad situation, to say the least.

I got up to get a snack, and I saw the photograph on my wall of my parents with Brianna and I when we were little. It was one of those pictures that had been shellacked onto a piece of drift wood. Remember those? Anyway, I don't know what came over me, but I got REALLY angry, took the picture down, sat it against the wall, kicked it and snapped it in half. I stared at it for a minute, picked it up and threw it away.

Jared took care of Aaron, made sure he showered and put him to bed that night. After Aaron was all tucked in with See-`a-tee, he came and cuddled on the couch with me.

"I'm worried about you, Maggie. Is there anything I can do to make you feel better?" He lifted my head, sat down and put my head on his lap.

"No, I'll be okay. I don't know what's wrong. I just feel empty." I stared at the television.

"Alright, Sweetheart, but will you let me know if I can do anything?" He stroked my hair.

"Yep." I just wanted to be quiet.

When the movie was over, Jared went to bed while I sat up listening to music. I was sitting on the floor, with my headphones on, when I saw him. I swear, my father was standing next to the entertainment center with his elbow on it. He looked at me, nodded at me with a smile on his face and then disappeared. I was a little freaked out.

Not five minutes later, the phone rang.

"Maggie? It's your Aunt Sheryl. She needs to talk to you." Jared brought me the cordless phone.

"I don't want to talk to her right now." I knew what she was going to tell me.

"Maggie, it's important." Jared tried to insist.

"I already know; he's dead." I got up and walked outside.

Jared talked to my aunt and got the details. My father had been out cutting down trees on the frozen swamp. His chainsaw got stuck, and as he was trying to free it, the tree fell on him, crushing his rib cage. His broken ribs punctured his lungs, and he had bled to death. My mother was the one to find him. His memorial service was going to be that Friday.

Jared hung up the phone and came outside to check on me. He took me by the hand, and we went to bed. He held me as I sobbed. Pops was gone, and we had just started to reconcile.

The next day, when Jared went to work and Aaron went to school, I spent the entire day cooking. I made homemade TV dinners, froze them all and cleaned the apartment from top to bottom. I was going to drive to Minnesota for his memorial service, by myself, and I wanted to make sure my guys would be okay while I was gone.

I called Tango to tell him what happened and let him know I wouldn't be coming in for a while. He understood and told me he loved me. I then called Alisha and Stephanie and asked them to come down and hang out with me.

Stephanie brought me a joint and the three of us smoked it. They listened to me tell stories of my childhood and the horrors that it contained. They hugged me as I cried, and Stephanie rolled another joint. I felt a little better by the time they left. Now, I just had to make the journey to Minnesota.

Aaron came home from school, and I talked to him about what happened. He hugged me and then went to his room to play with See-`a-tee. He understood that I needed some alone time.

When Jared came home, I told him of my plans to drive to Minnesota. He suggested I fly, but I explained to him that I needed to drive. He understood and suggested a rental car so that we didn't put that many miles on our car. I agreed with him.

We ate dinner in almost complete silence, watched a little television and then went to bed when Aaron did. I was leaving the next afternoon. Jared called into work and told them what happened. They told him it was fine to take the day off.

I hugged and kissed Aaron before he went to school. I explained to him that I would be back in a few days and asked him to make sure his dad stayed out of trouble. He laughed and said he would keep a good eye on him, hugged me and told me he loved me. It was the first time he had said that to me. I held back the happy tears because I knew he wouldn't understand them, but I let them flow once he left for school.

After Jared and I picked up the rental car, he and I spent the rest of the day just laying in bed, cuddling and talking. I was going to head out before Aaron got home from school, but I needed some time with my man. His energies filled my soul and made it possible for me to go on. I loved him so much.

Jared packed some food for me and put it all in a cooler. He walked me out to the car, put the cooler in the passenger seat and kissed me.

"Please, be safe, Maggie. Call me when you stop, and let me know you are alright." Jared held me tight against his body.

"You know I'll be fine. This isn't the first time I've done this." I looked up at him.

"But it is the first time you've done this since I've loved you. I just couldn't live with myself if..." Jared couldn't finish his sentence.

"Ssh... It'll be fine, Baby. I promise. I'll be home in a few days. I love you." I kissed him lightly on the lips.

"I love you, Maggie." Jared kissed me back.

I cranked up my music and headed out on my eleven hundred mile road trip. It would have been fun, if not for the reason I was going.

I drove through Nebraska, Iowa and into Minnesota. I only stopped to refuel, eat and stretch my legs. It took me eighteen hours, and I was there.

I pulled into the long, gravel driveway that led to my parents' house. Well, now I guess it was my mother's house. There was snow on the ground and everything looked clean and virginal. There was a car in the driveway that I didn't recognize.

I parked the car, got out and just stood there for a moment looking around. Everything looked exactly the way I remembered it even all these years later. I felt my father's presence there. Turning, I walked up to the house.

"Mom?" I knocked on the door.

"Hi, Maggie. You should have told us you were coming." Aunt Mattie answered the door.

"Oh, hi, Aunt Mattie. I wondered whose car that was in the driveway." I stepped through the front door and hugged her. "I'm sorry, I wasn't even thinking. I just drove. I knew I needed to be here." It had been years since I had seen her, and the pain of how things ended still haunted my thoughts, but now was not the time to relive those memories

"Well, you can get in your car, turn around and go right back to Colorado." My mother sat at the end of the table smoking a cigarette and glaring at me.

"Susan, I realize you're upset, but let's not do this right now." Aunt Mattie tried to calm my mother.

"I don't want her here. If she doesn't leave, I'll call the police." My mother wasn't budging on this.

"Please, Susan, at least let her rest a bit. She's had a long drive, and you're very emotional right now." Mattie tried to insist.

"What's the problem? I don't understand. We just had such a nice visit in Colorado." I was really confused.

"You killed him, Maggie. Your hate for him killed him. Don't you get it? He broke your ribs as a child, and he died the same way! Now, get the hell out of my house and off my property!" My mother threw a coffee cup at me.

"I'm out of here. I should have known better." I hugged Mattie and left.

I knew it wasn't safe for me to drive home without some sleep, so I checked into a hotel in town, called Jared to let him know what was going on and rested. I couldn't sleep, so I went to a local restaurant to get something to eat. Low and behold, Brianna and her family were eating there too. Gotta love small towns, huh?

Brianna saw me at the same moment that I noticed her. She stood up, walked over to me and hugged me in such a tight hug that I almost lost my breath. I squeezed her tightly as well. There were no words spoken between us for that moment, words were not needed.

"Oh, Maggie, it's so good to see you. I've missed you. Please, come join us for dinner. Clint's been asking about you, and you have to meet my husband." She pulled me by the hand and walked over to their table.

The four of us sat there telling stories, laughing and crying until the restaurant closed. My nephew Clint was incredible! He was now ten years old, and we got along like we had always been around each other. I had only seen him a few times when he was a small child, but he remembered me. I told him about his cousin Aaron, and we all talked about the possibility of them coming to visit over the summer.

I was sad to see the night end. It had been years since I had seen, let alone talked to, my sister. Our father's death brought us together again, thanks Dad. * sad smile *

I tossed and turned all night and was awake before I got my wake up call. After packing my things and leaving a tip on the nightstand for housekeeping, I got in my car, drove around town and headed home. Though I was not allowed to be at my father's actual memorial service, I was happy to be able to see my sister and her family.

The drive home took twenty two hours because I pulled over at a wayside rest area and napped. I don't think I was as tired as I was emotionally exhausted. Why did my mother hate me so much? We used to be close, REALLY close... I just didn't understand. I never hated my father. Nothing could have been further from the truth. I loved him, I just hated what he did and who he had become. Goodbye Minnesota, it's been, um... Real.

Jared and Aaron were waiting for me outside when I pulled into the driveway. They almost tackled me when they hugged me. We went inside and talked about the trip. Of course, I didn't say anything around Aaron about what happened. I did tell him about his cousin Clint, and they would all be coming to visit that summer. He was excited.

Aaron went upstairs to hang out with Mathew while Jared and I took the rental car back. When we were finished, we stopped by the studio to talk to Tango and Frankee. I told them what happened, and Tango crushed me with a hug. He told me that he and Frankee were the only parents I needed, and they would love me forever. Tango always knew how to make me feel better. I hated to think what my life would have been like without him in it.

The weeks moved slowly, and life went on as normal. Jared worked forty plus hours a week, Aaron went to school, and I became a full time homemaker. I had talked to Tango and Frankee, explaining that I needed to concentrate on my home life. They were sad to see me go, but they understood. It didn't change our relationship, whatsoever.

February showed up and the snow disappeared. We never really got much snow in Colorado Springs. The mountains shielded us from it. In one week, Aaron would be eleven. It was his first birthday with us, so of course, we had to do something stupendous.

I thought about it for a while and talked to Jared. We decided to have a carnival for him in the courtyard of the apartment complex. It was going to be more than amazing!

We hired clowns and entertainers out of the newspaper. Jake was going to build the game booths from the drawings I gave him. There would be a ring toss, a board full of balloons to throw darts at, a bowling game, a rubber duck race and a game where you threw little plastic balls into fish bowls to win goldfish. I was going to make a pinata too. Hopefully the weather would hold out. We figured with the games we were having, we could set it up in the apartment if the weather got bad.

Alisha, Mathew and Mark took Aaron out to a movie, the day of his party, to give us time to set it all up. The weather decided to cooperate with and was unseasonably warm. Thank goodness because I didn't know how we were going to fit all those people into our apartment. I mean, it was a nice size but with games, food and fifty people, things would have been a bit wall to wall.

Tango and Frankee brought the cake over. It was so cute! There were dinosaurs playing soccer on it. Tango said he picked it out because he knew how much Aaron was into both dinosaurs and soccer. I hugged him and thanked him.

Sara, Chloe and the girls arrived carrying bags and bags of food. We were doing the typical barbecue with hot dogs, burgers and chips. This was after all, for children. I made a jello salad and fruit salad to go along with the rest of it. We set the food out in the back yard so there would be no mishaps between the games and food. There were coolers full of soda and juice for the kids. The adult beverages were in the refrigerator in the kitchen.

We hung a giant "Happy Birthday" sign across the catwalk, between the levels of apartments, on the front of our building and placed bouquets of helium balloons everywhere. Each game booth had an adult or two in charge of it and were stacked to the brim with prizes. No matter if the child won or loss, they would walk away with a prize.

The guests started to show up, and each of the children were given a pack of twenty game coupons, so they could play each game four times. The adults were given booklets of ten coupons, so they too could join in the festivities.

Alisha called to say they were almost there, and they were going to blindfold Aaron. She made up a game so that he wouldn't get suspicious. She was going to tell him that she wanted to see how well he knew the way home, and if he could tell how close they were by the way the car moved. She was so smart!

I went out to let everyone know that Aaron would be arriving soon. I asked them to form a line across the front of the courtyard to block his view. They did as I asked. Alisha pulled up with the kids, and as Aaron stepped out of the car, everyone yelled, "HAPPY BIRTHDAY AARON!" He took off his blindfold and smiled the biggest smile I'd ever seen.

Aaron ran up to me and gave me a huge bear hug. "I love you, Mom! Thank you!" He then went to find his dad to do the same.

Fun was had by all! The kids ran from game to game collecting their little prizes. Parents joined them in their fun. We played Tag, Musical Chairs and Hide-N-Seek until the sun started to set. We then started small fires in three of the barbecue grills, so the kids, with the help of adults, could roast marshmallows and make S'mores.

It was nearly eleven o'clock when the party came to an end. Jake, Tango and Jared had already cleaned up the games from the courtyard, so all we had left to do was clean up the backyard. We were all tired, but with all of the help we had, it didn't take us very long.

I absolutely loved being a homemaker. Nothing made me happier than being there when Aaron and Jared came home. I cooked and baked from scratch and always had fresh baked goods awaiting their arrival. There was an awesome farmer's market down the street from us. I made friends with the owner, and he would sell me their bruised produce for pennies on the dollar. Cases of fruits and vegetables would be stacked up in our home and on the back patio until I processed them to freeze or can. We were never without what we needed. Through my efforts, we were able to save enough money to take Aaron on a summer trip. We were taking him to a well known theme park in Orlando, Florida to celebrate his successful completion of the school year.

With the reservations made, rental car packed and theme park tickets in our hands, we took See-'a-tee over to Tango and Frankee's. She loved staying with them because they spoiled her almost as much as we did. They had a cat tower for her and all kinds of toys. She knew it was her home away from home.

Jared had taken a week off from work and with the weekends that flanked that week, it gave us a total of eleven days for our trip. We had discussed the idea of flying, but we thought driving would be more fun because we could show Aaron more of the United States that way. We had done some internet research and had found a bunch of fun roadside attractions to stop at.

We drove east through Kansas and then dropped down into Oklahoma before we stopped for the night. Finding a cheap, little hotel right off the interstate, we pulled in for the night to eat and sleep before we headed out the next morning. We were all too excited to sleep much. We spent most of the night staying up, telling jokes and laughing at our silliness.

We had been driving most of the day when we pulled over just outside of Southaven, Mississippi. While Jared put gas in the car, I checked and filled the oil. I spilled a little on the engine and wiped it up as best I could. We paid for the gas, bought some snacks and were on our way again.

There was a bit of smoke coming out from under the hood because of the oil I had spilled. We had barely driven five miles when we heard a siren behind us. Jared looked in the rear view mirror and told us we were being pulled over by a sheriff. I wasn't too worried, he probably saw the smoke and wanted to make sure we were okay. Aaron was scared, but I told him there was nothing to worry about. We pulled over to the side of the road.

"Driver, exit your vehicle slowly with your hands up and walk backwards toward my car." The sheriff order Jared out of the car over his loudspeaker. Now, I was scared.

Jared did as he was asked. I told Aaron to keep his eyes forward while I turned to look out the rear window. The sheriff, without talking to Jared, patted him down and put him in the back of his squad car. Shit!

The sheriff then slowly walked up to the passenger side of our rental car. He knelt down next to my window and motioned for me to roll it down. I did.

"Ma'am, are you with this * N * willingly?" Yep, those were his exact words. Well, not exact, but once again, I just can't make my fingers type that word.

Now, being the smart ass I was, I wanted to tell him off. I wanted to advise him that the South had lost the civil war and there was now such a thing as human rights in place, but instead I said, "Yes sir."

He asked me what we were doing and if there were drugs in the car. I informed him that we were taking our son to Florida for summer vacation and that no, there were no drugs in the car, but if he wanted to, he was welcome to search it. He looked in the back and saw Aaron sitting there, walked away and let Jared out of the back of his squad car. He wrote him a ticket for "littering" and told him not to come back through his town. Jared got back in, and we left.

We talked to Aaron about racism and how to deal with it when he was faced with it in the future. We explained that not everyone was as enlightened as the people we knew back home. Reaching the Alabama border, I told Jared to pull over because I was driving. We didn't need anymore drama.

Jared and Aaron slept in the car as I drove down the interstate through Alabama. The car started to act up, so I pulled over to the side. The interstate was lined with thick, heavy forests, and there wasn't a gas station to be seen anywhere. Well fuck...

I woke Jared to tell him what was going on when all of a sudden there were vehicle lights behind us. Shit! I hoped it wasn't another redneck sheriff.

A little, red pickup pulled over. A couple got out of the truck and walked toward us. The woman was carrying a toddler aged girl. They asked us what happened, and I told them that the car was making a funny noise, so I pulled over.

While Jared and the man from the truck looked under the hood, I offered the little girl a juice box. Her and Aaron sat in the back seat drinking juice and eating cookies. The woman and I stood on the side of the interstate while I smoked a cigarette.

The men were able to fix the car. It was just low on coolant. I had forgotten to check it at the gas station. We were very thankful and offered to pay them for their time, but they wouldn't accept our money.

"We'll follow you until the next turn off to make sure you're okay." The man spoke to me.

"That would be wonderful, thank you." We all shook hands, and we were off once again.

We had barely gone two miles down the road when their headlights disappeared. There was nowhere for them to turn off, so we got scared. Since there was no one else on the interstate, we slowly backed down the side of the road to look for them. They were gone... Disappeared... Vanished. We knew we had backed up far enough because there was an empty juice box on the side of the road from where we had stopped. There was no way they could have turned around because there was a giant, deep ditch between the two sides of the interstate. Angels? I like to think so. * smile *

Finally, we made it to Orlando. After checking into our hotel, taking naps and getting cleaned up we headed out to see the sights. The streets were lined with shops and restaurants. We stopped in at one and ate. It was late, so we headed back to our hotel room.

We spent the next four days exploring the theme park and enjoying everything it had to offer. It was fabulous. We made some worthwhile memories there, memories that would live with us forever.

With our rental car packed full of souvenirs and the rest of our things, we made our way back to Colorado. We took a different route this time and avoided Mississippi altogether. No reason to add fuel to an old fire.

We were happy to arrive home. After unloading the car, we all collapsed into bed and slept like we had never slept before. Our summer adventure was definitely memorable, that was for certain.

CHAPTER TWENTY FOUR

School was about to start, so we were busy getting everything ready when the phone rang.

"Maggie, it's your mother." Jared reluctantly brought me the cordless phone.

"What the hell does she want?" I covered the receiver and whispered to Jared.

"I don't know, but she's crying." Jared shrugged it off and sat down next to me on the couch.

"Yeah?" I really didn't want to talk to her.

"Maggie, please, don't hang up. I'm so sorry for everything that happened. I was grief stricken and didn't know what I was saying or doing." My mother cried on the phone.

We talked for a while, and I found out that she was losing the farm. She was unable to pay the back taxes, and they were threatening to take it from her. Brianna couldn't help because her and her husband barely made enough to take care of their own needs. Not only was she losing the farm, she was finding it difficult to do all the work that was needed by herself. As I listened to my mother's plight, I started to feel sorry for her. She wanted us to move there and live on the farm with her. I told her I had to talk to Jared about it and would call her back.

"I love you, Maggie." She hung up before I could say anything else to her.

So, what do you think we did? Do you think I called her back and told her to fuck off? That would have been the smart thing to do, right? Nope, we decided to give up the life we had created and move to Minnesota. Yeah, I know... Stupid.

We had a going away barbecue to say goodbye to our friends. Most of them tried to talk us out of it, but they knew it was of no use. I had longed for my mother's love my entire life, and this was my chance to have it. We were going to rescue her. She had to love me then, right?

We told Gertrude about my mother needing us, and we were sorry that we couldn't give her a thirty day notice. She understood and said it was not a problem. We told her to keep our deposit in lieu of our rent for that month, but she wasn't having it. The day we were leaving, she handed us a check in the amount of our deposit.

On our way out of town, we stopped at the bank, cleaned out our accounts and closed them out. Taking one last look around downtown Colorado Springs, we waved goodbye, got into the vehicles and left. Jared drove the moving truck while Aaron and I, along with See-`a-tee, followed him in our car. It was a sad day but we had high hopes.

During the trip, I talked to Aaron and told him how he would be going to the same school that I had as a child. He was excited to make new friends and loved the idea of living on a farm with animals. He was such an easygoing child.

We didn't stop for any fun things along the way. School was starting the beginning of the next week, and we wanted Aaron to be there on the first day. It took us just over twenty-four hours to make the trip. We stopped for a few hours to sleep along the way.

Pulling into the driveway of the farm was a bittersweet moment for me. I had thought, at one time, I would never be returning there, and here I was, moving back in. I guess that sometimes life throws you a curve ball, and you can either hit it out of the park or strike out. We were about to see which one it would be.

With all the pleasantries and greetings out of the way, we unpacked the moving truck and put everything into the storage shed for the time being. We had to get the truck turned in because we only had a four day rental. We had used that time to load the truck and make the trip, so today was our final day with it.

Aaron came with us when we took the truck back. We told my mother we wanted to show him around town, but the truth was I didn't trust her with him. I don't know if I would ever trust her... Period.

Jared and I stayed in my childhood bedroom while Aaron slept in Brianna's. Aaron started school the week after we arrived and started making friends right away. I spent most of my time helping my mother to clean up the farm and harvesting the vegetables from the small garden she had put in earlier that year. Jared began to look for work immediately and found employment at a plasma center in Duluth. He had a forty-five minute commute each way, but he said it was worth it. Our car got great gas mileage anyway.

We paid the back taxes, along with another year's worth, so we knew there wouldn't be any issues. Twenty cords of logs were delivered and we worked as a family to cut, split and rank the wood in the unused part of the basement. We also stacked a few cords next to the barn to keep it warm for the chickens and goats. They were the only animals left on the farm. We fixed up and filled the shed that housed the feed for the animals as well. Jared and I made sure that anything that needed to be done on the farm was done and done right.

We knew things were not going to keep going well if we didn't have more privacy, so we talked to my mother about finishing the basement. She agreed, and we hired contractors to build three bedrooms, a kitchen, living room and two bathrooms down there. The rooms were going to be on the small side, but at least this way everyone had their own privacy.

It took five months for the construction to be completed. Thanksgiving and Christmas came and went as did Aaron's and my birthdays. Jared and I had gone to the casino to celebrate our anniversary. Things were still civil but no longer loving. It was as if my mother had gotten what she needed from us, so she dropped the act and was her old self again.

We moved into the basement the moment it was ready. We hadn't noticed a leak in the roof of the storage shed, and we had lost a lot of our paper based belongings to water damage and mold. Though we were sad, we knew there was nothing we could do about it. We unpacked the rest of our things and settled into our new surroundings.

We had just gotten settled into the basement when Brianna called me. "Maggie! Please, come help me! Dick beat the shit out of me." Brianna was crying on the other line. Oh hell no! No one was going to put their hands on my sister and get away with it!

I hung up without saying a word to her. Jared's wallet was laying on the bedside table in our room where I had taken the phone call. I grabbed some gas money out of it, got in our car and drove to Duluth. I hadn't told anyone where I was going.

Brianna's house was in the west end of Duluth, and I was very familiar with the area because of my earlier days of volunteering and living there. I parked my car behind her house and without knocking, I walked into her home through the back door. Clint was sitting on the kitchen floor crying. I put my finger over my lips to instruct him to be quiet, bent down and hugged him. I heard Dick screaming at my sister in the next room. I motioned to Clint to go outside quietly. I didn't want him to see or hear what was about to happen.

Walking around the corner into their living room, I saw that Dick had Brianna pinned against the living room wall by her throat. I noticed Brianna's eyes look my way, and once again I put my finger to my lips. I wanted to surprise her husband.

Stepping up behind him, I picked up the poker from the front of their fireplace and hit him as hard as I could across his lower back. He let go of Brianna as he dropped to the floor.

"Go to your son. He's in the backyard." I spoke to Brianna.

"But, Maggie..." Brianna was scared.

"I said go!" She did as she was told.

"Now, you think you're such a big man that you can beat a woman? Come here, Bitch!" I picked him up from the floor and pinned him to the wall the same way he had Brianna against the wall as I walked in.

"How's it feel, Dick? Do you feel your heart beating faster? Do you feel that fear? Are you scared yet?" My hand closed tighter, and my nails broke the skin of his neck.

"This is how it's going to work. You are going to go, wherever you have to, for a couple of days, and give me time to move my sister and her son out of this house. Then, you're going to give her the divorce she will be asking for. You can keep the house, but you will pay her alimony because you are such a piece of shit that you need to pay penance for your sin. Do you understand me? Blink three times if you understand me." He blinked three times.

"Good, now, when I let go, you're going to go upstairs and pack ONLY what you need until you are allowed back in this house, understand me? Blink again if you understand and agree." He blinked again.

I let him go, and he sank down the wall to his knees, trying to catch his breath. He looked up at me, and I saw the color starting to come back to his face.

"Go." That's all I had to say, and he was on his way up the stairs to do what I told him to do. I waited until he left before I went outside to talk to Brianna.

I asked Clint to go play on his swing set while I talked to Brianna about what happened and what was going to happen. She hugged me tightly and cried like I had never seen her cry before. I assured her that everything was going to be okay, and we went into the house with Clint, packed enough stuff for a few days, along with any valuables, and I drove them home to the farm.

When we pulled into the driveway, Jared and my mother came to the car to greet us. They were surprised to see Brianna and Clint. I stepped out of the car to explain to them what had happened. Jared helped to take their things inside and put them in the bedrooms in the upstairs part of the house. We were one big, kind of happy, family again.

When Aaron returned from school, he was happy to see his cousin. They spent the entire afternoon playing outside together. I made sure Brianna was settled in and left her in the care of our mother. I had to go to the basement and catch my breath.

Jared joined me in our living room, and I told him everything that had happened. He pulled me close, and I cried with relief. He told me Brianna was lucky to have me for a sister. That's when I told him the story about the day of her birth and how I promised her that I would always be there for her. I also told him about the times I got in trouble concerning her and how it had been beaten into me that it was my job to take care of her. I took that duty seriously, and I still do to this day.

Things progressed well. School was now out. Though Clint was a couple of months younger than Aaron, he was a grade ahead of him in school. They both successfully completed their school year and were advancing onto the next one that fall. Summer was here, and we had a lot to do. Before we started that work though, we had to do something to celebrate the end of the school year.

Clint was a country boy, and Aaron was quickly becoming one. We thought the best thing we could do was to have a good, old fashioned bonfire. There was a burning ban because of the drought we were in, but we went into town and got a special burning permit.

We plowed up the back field and ran the water hose out there. We left it running for two days and three nights straight. It was a good thing we had a well and didn't have to pay for water. Yep, we were making mud.

The day of the bonfire was upon us, so we stacked a huge pile of branches over a bunch of cardboard boxes and got it ready to light that night. All of Aaron and Clint's friends from school were invited along with their parents. We had a barbecue set up with a ton of food and drinks.

The kids had fun playing in the mud. They played foot ball and Tag until they were so covered in mud that you couldn't tell one child from the next. When the sun started to set, we called the kids up to the back yard and hosed them off. Jared started the bonfire, and everyone gathered around it. We roasted marshmallows, sang songs and told stories. It was an awesome time!

Everyone went home around midnight. Brianna took the boys inside and made sure they got ready for bed. Once they were in bed, she joined us outside to help put out the fire. We waited for awhile, after we kicked dirt on it, before we went in.

The next morning, I awoke to a rancid smell in the air. I threw on some clothes and ran outside to check the fire. Black smoke filled the air. I ran around the corner of the house to find Clint out there throwing tires and tar paper onto the fire. Stopping him from putting anything else on it, I told him to go inside. I once again, put out the fire, this time making sure it was out. If anyone had reported us we would have been in big trouble.

I went into the house and told Brianna what happened. She yelled at me saying I had no right to discipline her son. I told her I had not disciplined him and had only told him to go into the house. She kept yelling at me. I told her if she didn't watch it that Clint would become a devil child, and then she would really be sorry. Not wanting to argue anymore I went to the basement.

On Monday, Aaron and Clint were invited by some of their friends to swim at the lake, so Brianna and our mother took them into town. Jared was at work, and I was busy in the garden. I heard a car coming up the driveway. It was the deputy sheriff. What the fuck was it now?

"I'm looking for Maggie Barnett." The deputy got out of her car.

"I'm Maggie." Oh no, please, don't tell me that something happened to Jared or Aaron!

"This is for you. You have ten minutes to vacate this property. You are not allowed within five hundred feet of this property, Susan Reeds, Brianna Taylor or Clint Hanson. You've been served." The deputy stood there while I read the papers. I had been served with a restraining order.

"Wait a minute. My son and husband aren't here. I don't have any way to leave." As I spoke, Brianna pulled into the yard with our mom and the boys. "Well, my son is here, but my husband is at work in Duluth. We can't leave until he gets home."

"If you are refusing to leave than I am afraid I am going to have to place you under arrest. Please, step to the side of the car, and put your hands behind your back." The deputy wasted no time.

"Wait, what?" I couldn't believe this was happening.

"Officer, it's okay. I'm going to leave with my mom and son. She can have two hours to get out." Brianna spoke up.

"Alright, Mrs. Taylor. If she has not vacated the property at that time, please call us back for assistance." The deputy got in her car and followed Brianna out of the driveway.

"Come on, Aaron, we have to pack, hurry." Aaron and I ran into the house to start packing. I called Jared at work to let him know what happened. He thought I was kidding at first and then quickly realized I wasn't. He said he was on his way.

Aaron and I packed everything we could in the time allotted us. We heard someone pulling into the driveway and went out to see who it was. Jared had rented a moving truck and was parking it at the walkout entrance to the basement.

I hugged him, and without speaking, we quickly loaded the truck with everything we could. We were able to get almost everything into it. As we got into the moving truck and began to pull out of the driveway, Brianna, our mother and Clint were just coming back. I couldn't help it, I flipped them off as we passed.

Yep, moving there was the worst decision we had ever made, hindsight and all that good stuff. We were on our way to Duluth to figure things out from there. A single tear fell down my cheek as I stared out of the window at the trees that pointed the way to our uncertain future.

We checked into a hotel, so that we had a little time to figure out what we were going to do. We had to sneak See-`a-tee in. After getting Aaron settled in front of the television, Jared and I stepped right outside the door to talk about things. He told me he really loved his job and wanted to stay in Duluth. I knew it was the best thing to do, so we agreed that I would start looking for an apartment the next day. He held me as I cried. How was I so stupid as to believe things would have been any different. We had less than five thousand dollars in our savings because we had spent almost eighteen thousand fixing up the farm and remodeling the basement. There was nothing we could do about it now. We just had to hold our chins up and move on. At least Jared had a good job, and we were in a town that I was familiar with.

I was able to find a nice, two bedroom apartment right away. I think it was because the landlord thought Aaron was so cute. It was in the west end of Duluth, just down the street from Dick. I laughed when I saw him pass by as we were moving in. He looked scared.

We moved in across the street from a youth activity center. Aaron became a member and spent almost every afternoon there. They took the kids on field trips and had different activities for them to participate in. Aaron made friends instantly with a lot of the kids in the neighborhood, and there was always a group of children in our home or yard. We became the "it" place to hang out.

Summer was now over. We immediately registered Aaron for school. He was doing so well with his scholastic journey that there was no way we were going to let him fall behind.

Jared and I made fast friends with our neighbors as well. Since their children were at our house all the time, we thought it was important to get to know them.

There were two women on our block that I absolutely adored. Joy lived right next to us in a beautiful home. She had two children. Bobbie was a few years younger than Aaron, but they were good friends and Amy was her youngest. She was just two years old and had the prettiest little smile.

June lived kitty corner across the street. She had three sons. Jory was nineteen and living on his own. Michael was Aaron's age, and they went to school together. Neil was four years old and was always at his mom's side.

June and Joy spent a lot of time at our place. We worked on crafts and baked whenever we could. We also smoked a lot of pot when the kids weren't around. It didn't take us long to develop a deep and meaningful friendship.

One afternoon, after the ladies had left to tend to their own homes, I was sitting on the couch with See-`a-tee when the phone rang.

"Maggie? She's dead... I can't believe she's gone." Tango was crying as he spoke.

"What? What happened?" I couldn't believe what I was hearing.

"She had a simple surgery to straighten her toes. The doctor gave her pain pills, and they didn't mix with her other medications. I got up early this morning to go to the shop. When she didn't call me by noon, I went home to check on her. I thought she was sleeping, but when I touched her she was ice cold." My heart broke for Tango. Frankee had been the love of his life.

I stayed on the phone with him for over an hour. He needed me to be there for him, and I had to be. It was my duty as his friend and adopted daughter.

When we hung up, I called Jared at work to tell him what happened. He asked if I needed him to come home, but I told him I would be okay and would see him when he got home from work.

Aaron came right home after school. I sat him down and told him what happened. He started to cry, so I held him until he felt better. He asked if he could go over to the activity center, and I said that would be fine. I knew he had to be around his friends right now.

I was feeling really depressed, so I got online and signed into my messenger service. They had lists of groups on there, so a person could talk to like minded people. I signed into one that was for adult survivors of child abuse.

Instantly, I was talking with people that had been through the same things I had lived through. It was nice not to feel so alone. I was chatting with a man by the name of Dominick. He and his wife, Heather, lived in upstate New York. He seemed like a nice enough guy. I instantly felt better, so I got up and started dinner. Life had to go on.

When Jared got home from work, we talked about how alone Tango must feel. We decided to invite him to move in with us. We simply could not allow him to be alone. I called and told him what we had talked about. He agreed, so we put things into motion. He was going to sell the shop and house. We were going to find a house to buy. It was just that easy.

I flew to Colorado to be at his side when Frankee was buried. I helped him to go through her things and donate what he didn't want to keep. We made arrangements for me to come back once a month for the next couple of months, so we could take our time to clean out and organize his house and shop so they could be sold. It was a lot of work, but it had to be done.

On the flight home, I thought about the curve ball that life had thrown at us... It had worked out. Though Frankee was gone, we were in a place that we were happy and now Tango was able to join us there. Guess we hit that one out the park.

CHAPTER TWENTY FIVE

I had been house hunting for a couple of months. I hadn't found anything in the price range we were looking. Jared, Tango and I decided that maybe we would just rent a place until we could find one to buy.

Joy came over one afternoon, when I got back from one of my trips to Colorado, to tell me that she and her husband had found a new house and were going to sell theirs. I couldn't believe what I was hearing. This was perfect! I knew their house well and knew they had taken good care of it.

"Sold!" I jumped up and hugged Joy.

"What?" Joy looked at me with a puzzled look on her face.

I explained to her everything that happened. It was as if fate had stepped in, and for once in our life, things were going to be easy. I called our bank to make an appointment to get a loan for the mortgage.

Jared and I went to the bank. They ran our credit and told us there were a couple of things we had to pay off before they could give us a loan. We had forgotten to pay the utility bills we had left in Colorado Springs. We got them taken care of and were given our loan.

It took two months to close on the house. I remember what it felt like to walk into the broker's office and sign that paperwork. We had done it. We were homeowners.

Joy and her family needed a week to move into their new home. We paid an extra month's rent because we wanted to do a bit of remodeling in the house before we moved in.

The house was the typical Victorian styled house. When you walked in the front door, there was a closet to your left and a staircase that led upstairs to three bedrooms and a bathroom. Two of the bedrooms were huge, but there was a tiny one that was of no use to us as it was.

Standing at the front door, there was an archway to your right that opened into the living room. Another archway, at the end of that room, led into the dining area. There were two doors off the dining room, the one on the left was to the main floor bedroom and the other led into an eat-in kitchen. To the left of the kitchen was another door way that opened to stairs to the walk out basement and a back door that opened onto a huge deck. It really was a nice house, but we wanted to make it ours.

I called Tango to tell him we had gotten the keys to the house and were going to start some remodeling. We had planned to move him in with us once we were done and settled in. He said he had sent us a gift, and it was in our bank account. He had sent us money that way before to pay for the flights. I was curious. I thanked him, hung up and called the automated number for our bank to check the amount. Fifty three thousand dollars. WOW! Tango had given us fifty thousand dollars as a house warming gift! He had received the life insurance payout from Frankee. I called him back to tell him it was too much, but he said that Frankee would have wanted us to have it. I told him I loved him and would see him soon.

We began remodeling right away. Jared had to work, so I was in charge of it. I hired a contractor to put a bathroom in the eat-in-kitchen and connect it to the main floor bedroom. We didn't need an eat-in-kitchen because we had a formal dining room. I then had them open the archways in the living room. They were no longer rounded but instead were boxed openings to the ceilings. We tore out the main floor coat closet and turned it into a small sitting area with benches and a coat rack. The work on the main floor made it feel more open and inviting.

Upstairs, we had the smallest bedroom added on to the one that sat next to it, so it would be an office for Tango. It didn't take a lot to make all of that happen. We moved in. Now, we just had to do the basement.

We knew we were going to need extra space for company, so we had two bedrooms built into the basement along with another bathroom, living room, kitchenette and laundry area. All in all, the construction took three months. How did we get it done so fast? I hired enough contractors and laborers to do it. Plus, I rolled up my own sleeves and worked with them. When it was all done, Aaron, Jared and I painted the entire inside of the house. We even recreated the mural I had done on the shop wall in Colorado Springs on the walls of Tango's office.

School was out, so the three of us flew to Colorado Springs to move Tango to Duluth. He had sold his shop but kept all his gear. He said he had plans and not to worry about it just now. We still had to sell his house, but we said we would do that once he was moved in with us.

We packed the moving truck and were on our way. Jared drove the truck, and Aaron rode with him. I drove the rental car with Tango as my passenger. See-`a-tee sat in his lap and purred. She had hated the flight there, but was content in Tango's lap. He would have had it no other way.

Once we got back to Duluth, unpacked and got Tango all settled in, we simply moved on with life. Our home was full of life and love. We had never imagined that life would turn out this well. We had done it. We were finally settled somewhere. * smile *

Tango's house sold right away. We used the money to buy a second car and to get new furniture and electronics for the entire home. The remainder of the money was put into a college fund account for Aaron.

Joy came over to see the house and what we had done with the remodeling. At first, it was difficult for her to embrace. It had been her home for so long, and to see it so different made her a bit emotional. After a while, she started to like it.

Spring was here and we had a lot to do. The house sat on a double lot, so we were going to put a fence around the entire thing. We also planned to plant a big garden in the second lot along with a fire pit, hammock and a tire swing. Some of the neighborhood kids were going to help me. Here, let me tell you about these amazing kids...

Lily was the oldest of them all. She had just turned nineteen and was a college student. She had the prettiest, blonde hair, blue eyes and whitest smile I had ever seen. She always sported a nice tan and was the most creative one in the bunch. I felt an instant connection with her because she and Destiny had the same birthday.

Mia was the next oldest, but probably the most mature. She was a natural born problem solver and was always thinking. She had lush dark hair, olive skin and deep brown eyes. She was as pretty as she was smart.

Zoey was next in line. She was a goofball and boy crazy, but then again, weren't most young teenage girls? She had pretty blonde hair and a smile that would soften even the hardest of hearts. Her family life was a little rough, so she spent a lot of time at our house. Aaron had the biggest crush on her!

Last, but certainly not least, there was Hope. Her giggle was intoxicating.   No matter how you were feeling, the sound of her laughter brightened your day and made everything all better. She too, had long blonde hair, blue eyes and a contagious smile. She was as brilliant as she was beautiful, and I always knew she would go far in life.   Her family life was so fucked up that I talked her mom into giving us custody of her. She had two older sisters, and it didn't take much for her mom to allow her to come and live with us. Our family felt complete now.

Aaron and Hope took over the bedrooms in the basement. They liked it because they had their own space down there. They each had their own bedroom and shared the rest of it. The family room in the basement was set up just for them. They had their own television, video games and DVD player. They always had friends over to hang out and have fun.

Tango lived in the upstairs, and we used the extra bedroom as a guest room. Jared and I had the master suite on the main floor, so we could keep an eye on things. See-`a-tee made her rounds and slept at the feet of someone different every night.

So, back to the happenings. The girls and I marked out the spots for the fence posts, and Jared along with June's oldest son dug the holes. We all then tarred the bottoms of the posts, filled the holes with quick drying concrete and set the poles in place. Once they were set, we added the cross beams and then the pickets. We decided to install a privacy fence. When the entire fence was built, we as a group painted it white, so it would pop against the bright yellow of the house and go with the trim. I guess I got my white picket fence after all. * smile *

Our family dug the area for the garden by hand. It was back breaking work, but we knew it would be worth it in the end. We had to have a load of top soil brought in because there just wasn't enough dirt for the garden. While Hope and I planted the garden, Jared and Aaron hung the tire swing and dug out the fire pit. It took us three full weekends to complete our projects after the fence was built. Hanging the hammock in the trees was the most rewarding part. We took turns laying in it and enjoying the sight of our hard work.

To celebrate the completion of our yard, we invited everyone over for a barbecue. As usual, we went all out. Food, beverages, music and lots of games for the kids. Joy and her family joined us. That was the first time I met her sister Avani. She was stunning. Her and Joy looked a lot alike, but Avani was a bit more exotic looking. She had a son as well, named Ricky. We hit it off right away.

June and Joy were in the kitchen cutting up watermelon while Avani and I played in the yard with the children. Though it was the middle of spring, it was quite warm, so we started a water fight. The guys manned the grills but occasionally got caught up in the battle. Jared grabbed the water hose and got us all soaked! We laughed and laughed until it was time to eat.

The adults sat on the deck to eat while the kids sat in the yard. Of course, a food fight ensued, and the kids had a blast. We had to hose down the kids before they could go into the house, there was so much food!

The night ended with all of us sitting around a fire, roasting marshmallows and singing camp songs. We enjoyed ourselves so much we decided we would do this once a month. Joy suggested it be potlucks from then on, so we were not carrying the load ourselves. I loved Joy; she was always so caring.

Summer seemed to hit us out of nowhere. Aaron did well in school and was soon to be in the sixth grade. We were so proud of him. There wasn't going to be a vacation this year because we had spent so much remodeling the house that we had to work on building up our savings again. We did, however, allow Aaron to have a bunch of friends over to camp in the yard. They had fun, of course.

Hope was about to start the fifth grade. She did brilliantly in school and wanted to have a girl's weekend of camping and fishing. I couldn't say no to her, so I took her and the rest of the girls to a lake just south of us and had an incredible time. Fishing was the only thing I did that wasn't vegan. I couldn't help it, something about it truly relaxed me. I only fished the "catch and release" method. Unless, of course, the fish was hurt. Then I added to the girls' stringers, and they went in our freezer. The choice to be vegan was mine, and I did not impose it on anyone else.

Joy, Avani and June were at our house almost every weekend to hang out, work on crafts and bake. I crocheted, Joy knitted and Avani and June hung out with us. We smoked a little pot while the kids were outside playing and just enjoyed each other's company. We were each other's therapists and sounding boards. Tango always found a way to join in. He loved hanging out with us women and flirting. He had a thing for June. It was quite cute.

Summer progressed, and it was now early fall. We all worked to harvest the garden and prepare the produce for storage. Joy, Avani and June helped with all of it, so we made sure they took some home as well. Our community was thriving and we were the center of it.

"Maggie, do you ever miss the tattoo shop?" Tango sat with me on the back porch one morning.

"Yes, I do. I miss the creativity of it. Why?" I poured him a cup of coffee as we chatted.

"Well, as you know, I still have all of the equipment from the shop, and now that things are settled, I was thinking we should open a new one." He surprised me. I hadn't thought about all his gear for a while. It was in a storage unit up the street.

"Really, Tango? That would be awesome. Jared and I don't have the money for it though. We barely have our savings back up to where it should be." My excitement faded.

"I have the money." Tango explained how he still had money left from the life insurance policy, and he had been saving it for a rainy day. Since it hadn't rained, he thought it was the perfect time to use it.

"Let's do this then!" My excitement returned. Aaron and Hope were old enough now that they could be home alone, our home was done, and things had settled into a steady flow. Now was the perfect time.

W.T.F. Ta2z was created and legal! It took us less than two months to set it up and open the doors to the public. We were back in business. * happy dance *

We had a grand opening on August first and offered fifty percent off on your second tattoo. Our acceptance into the community was outstanding! We were doing amazingly well from the get go.

It took me a little while to get used to working again and figuring out how to fit it into my homemaker role as well. Joy, June and Avani were a huge help with that. June kept an eye on the kids and would check in with them throughout the day while I was at work. Joy and Avani made dinner occasionally and would bring it over to the house to feed my family when I worked late.

Jared was promoted to assistant manager at the plasma center and was working long hours. He loved his job and the people there. He bought lunch for the center every Friday to show his appreciation to his employees. Jared was such a good man. That is, until I no longer had the time to do everything I used to do for our family.

Jared and I started arguing constantly. He was upset that I wasn't home as often as I was before, and instead of stepping up to help me, he complained about it. I didn't understand what the problem was because it wasn't as if this was the first time I had worked.

I tried my best for two months to make things better. Tango and I hired two more artists to help out at the shop, so I would have more time at home. I cooked every weekend and made homemade, individual frozen dinners, so that when I wasn't home, Jared, Aaron and Hope could just heat one up and have a healthy meal. I baked and loaded the freezers with goodies as well. Most of the time, I only slept four or five hours a night because I would stay up late cleaning and doing laundry to make sure that our home was always immaculate. I was running on fumes, and it still didn't seem to be enough.

"I'm so sick of this shit, Maggie! You're never home." Jared was in the kitchen yelling at me, once again.

"I'm sorry, Jared. What do you want me to do, quit my job? What haven't I done now? Our home is clean, food is cooked, and I make time for us at least two nights a week." I was holding back the tears.

"We don't fuck anymore. I don't understand why you have such a hard time. Candy does it all, and she's a single mom." Candy was a woman that Jared worked with.

"What do you mean we don't fuck anymore? We make love two or three times a week. Grow the hell up, Jared! This is what happens when people have a family and work." I was angry now. How dare he bring someone else into this argument.

"Candy said this is why she divorced her husband. They never had time alone." He kept bringing her up.

"Well, maybe you should divorce me and marry that bitch instead, and then she wouldn't be a single mom!" I walked out of the kitchen, into our bedroom and slammed the door. I was done with this shit.

"Maggie, open this door right fucking now!" Jared was pounding on the bedroom door. I put my earphones on and ignored him. We needed time to cool down. Thank goodness the kids were at school.

I got on the computer and signed into my messaging service.

Dominick was online, so I talked to him about what was going on. He and his wife, Heather, had become my personal therapists when it came to this kind of stuff. He gave me some advice on how to handle this and eased my anger.

After signing off with him, I went out to talk to Jared. He was sitting in the living room watching television.

"Jared, this isn't us. We need to fix this." I sat next to him and tried to speak calmly as Dominick had advised.

"I know, Sweetheart. I just get angry sometimes and take it out on you." This was Jared's normal excuse, but I accepted it every time.

"How do we fix this?" I cuddled up on his chest to show him I wasn't angry anymore.

"There's nothing to fix. Married couples fight sometimes." He reached up to stroke my hair.

"Not like this, Jared. It scares me." I started to cry.

"There's nothing to be scared of. I love you. Now, come here and let me show you how much." He pulled me on top of him.

"Not here, Jared. The kids should be home from school any minute." I stood up, took his hand and walked into the bedroom. We had great make up sex, just like we did almost every time.

We made it through the next month without arguing. It was now November and time to start getting ready for the Holiday season. I was in my absolute glory this time of year. I loved the cooler weather and the compassion that this time of year brought out in people.

This was our first holiday season in the new house, and it had to be spectacular. I wanted to do something to thank all of our friends for helping us this past year, and thank the neighbors for putting up with all of the noise from the construction. I decided to bake bread for everyone.

I called all my girls and asked them to meet me at the house. Lily, Mia, Zoey, Joy, Avani and June all came over to join Hope and I in the kitchen. I had purchased three, twenty pound sacks of flour and was about to teach them all how to make homemade bread.

I wrote recipe cards, for each of them, with explicit directions. It was my own recipe I had created over the years and had never shared with anyone, though I was asked many times. I put the cards into recipe boxes I had decorated with each of their names, so they could start their own recipe collection.

We all gathered in the kitchen, and I gave them their gifts. They loved them, and we started baking right away. There was flour everywhere by the time we put the bread up to raise, but we didn't care. They younger girls all went with Hope to the basement to watch music videos, and the adult women retired to the living room to smoke a little pot while we listened to our music. Laughter and music filled every level of our home.

When the bread had raised, we punched it down and formed loaves. Rolling some of it out, we used Thanksgiving themed cookie cutters to make decorations for the top of the loaves. The kids painted the cut outs with food coloring, and we attached them to the loaves before they raised a second time. When they were done raising, we baked them all, four at a time and left them to cool.

With all of the bread baked, we wrapped the gift loaves in colorful cellophane, put bows on them and addressed them to each of the neighbors. The kids had a blast delivering them while the adults smoked a little more pot and ate a loaf of bread.

Baking bread for our neighbors became a tradition. We enjoyed each other's company and had fun creating new designs for the bread. Our neighbors loved it too.

Since it was our first Thanksgiving in our new home, we invited all our friends to join us. As always, I went all out preparing dinner. Turkey and all the fixings, along with a tofu turkey, adorned our table. There were eighteen people total, and we all sat around one huge table in our dining room. We had to put together two tables to make it happen, but we did it. Tango stood at one end of the table and led everyone in prayer. It was touching when he asked God to tell Frankee we all loved her and wished she was there.

With Thanksgiving dinner over, our friends all went home to spend time with their own families, and I took a nap. When I woke up, Jared, Tango, Aaron and Hope had put away and cleaned up the mess from dinner and had all of the Christmas decorations out and ready to put up. I was so touched by their gesture that I cried.

Tango, Jared and Aaron took all of the outdoor decorations outside and put them up while Hope and I put up the Christmas tree. We didn't decorate it though, we just set it up. We busied ourselves with the indoor decor and making hot cocoa for all of us.

When the guys came in, we had hot cocoa and decorated the tree together. Jared and I wrapped it with lights, and then we all hung the ornaments on it. We had an ornament for every year we had been together and told the kids the story of each one. That's when we gave Tango and the kids their first Christmas gift that year. We had an ornament made for each of them with their names and the year on it. They loved them and proudly hung them on the tree. I couldn't help but to think back to when Mattie had done the same for me. Tears sprung from my eyes as I thought about Destiny.

"Maggie, this is for you." Jared handed me a small box.

I opened the box and inside was a small angel ornament with Destiny's name engraved on it. I couldn't believe that he had done that for me. I cried, hugged him and hung it on the tree next to the rest of the family's ornaments. It hangs on the Christmas tree every year to this day.

CHAPTER TWENTY SIX

Our children were now teenagers. Goodness, that made me feel old. They loved school, and Aaron had actually caught up a bit and was now only behind by one grade! We were so proud of both our children.

While the kids were at school, I decided to paint our front porch. I had grown tired of the white accents and decided to add a pop of color with dark red. I was busy scraping the porch when I heard the front gate close. I looked up and there she was.

"Hi, Maggie. It's been a long time." Brianna was standing on my sidewalk holding a small boy. I could tell she was pregnant again too.

"How did you find us?" I was shocked.

"I looked in the phone book. Can we talk?" She set the little boy on the lawn and walked up to me on the porch.

"Yeah, I guess so." I couldn't believe she was at my house. It had been years.

"You know the restraining order is up, right?" Brianna stood there staring at me.

"I really didn't give it any thought. Who's that?" I nodded toward the child playing on the lawn.

"That's your nephew, Dakota. He'll be two next week." She smiled and touched her stomach, "And this is your nephew, Austin. He's due to be born any minute. Clint is living with his dad. He got in some trouble at school, and we thought it was for the best." She rubbed her stomach as she spoke. "Mom is in the car, and we have someone else we want you to meet."

"You understand that this is all a bit overwhelming, right?" I stood up and faced her.

"Yes, and we were going to call, but we were afraid you would say no." She turned to wave our mother over.

"I would have. You're here now though. Might as well talk a bit." I sat down on the porch swing.

"Hi, Maggie." Mom stepped up onto the porch. "You have a nice house."

"Thanks, Susan. We worked hard to make it happen." I couldn't call her Mom.

"I want you to meet someone. He's your new step dad." She waved at the man in the car. He got out and walked up to us on the porch.

"How the fuck did she snag you? You're fine as hell!" The words just fell out of my mouth.

"Hello, Maggie. You're exactly as your mother described you. My name is Dan. It's nice to meet you." He bent to hug me.

"I'm sorry, Dan. I didn't mean to be disrespectful." I stood and hugged him back.

"It's alright. You weren't disrespectful, just bold, and I appreciate that." Dan had a nice smile.

I made everyone lunch and showed them around the house. I was thankful that Jared and Tango were at work. This was a lot for me to handle, let alone them.

Dakota and I played in the side yard while they checked out my garden and the rest of the yard. We then all sat around talking until early afternoon. I found out that Susan and Dan had bought a new house in the same town we grew up in. Brianna was remarried and living on the farm with her FOURTH husband. Yep, she had married, divorced and married again in the time we had not spoken.

It was getting late, so I told them that it was nice seeing them, but I had things to do. We talked about seeing each other again sometime soon. I told them I would call them when we had some time. I knew we couldn't rush this. It had to be done in baby steps.

We said goodbye, and they were on their way. I cleaned up my mess on the front porch and went inside to start dinner. I had to work the next day, so I made sure to make enough that there would be leftovers.

I felt stabbing pains in my lower stomach. I raced around the corner, through the bedroom and into the bathroom. I was bleeding. I called Jared at work and asked him to come take me to the doctor.

"Maggie, I'm sorry. You had another miscarriage. We need to do a hysterectomy. We need to schedule the surgery soon. Please, see the nurse on your way out." His voice was sullen as he told me the results.

Jared stood up and took my hand. I couldn't help it; I burst out crying. Doctor Jennings apologized and left us there so we could gather ourselves..

The surgery was scheduled for Friday. There was no way around it. It simply had to be done. I was absolutely terrified. I had my gallbladder removed about ten years earlier, but that was a relatively simple surgery compared to this one.

I had just a few days to prepare my family before I went in for surgery. I cooked as much as I could. I made individual meals and froze them all. In between cooking, I cleaned the house from top to bottom. I think doing all of this was more about keeping my mind busy than anything else.

June drove me to the hospital for my surgery Friday morning because Jared had to work. Yeah, I know. He couldn't take the day off for whatever reason. I still think it was just too hard for him to deal with.

I was prepped and brought into surgery. June stayed at the hospital the entire time. I was truly touched by her friendship.

"Huh? Where am I?" I was in my hospital room coming out of the anesthesia.

"You're in the hospital Maggie. You just had surgery, and you're doing fine." June's voice echoed through the fogginess that had taken over my brain.

I stayed in the hospital for four days in recovery. Doctor Jennings wanted to make sure that everything was working fine before he released me. I was released Tuesday afternoon. June was there to pick me up. Jared hadn't come to visit, but he did call on Saturday morning to check on me.

Joy and Avani were at my house when I came home. They, with the aid of June, helped me into bed. I had strict orders, from the doctor, that I was not to get out of bed for anything other than to go to the bathroom and to walk around the house a bit for the first two weeks. After that, I could get up and move about the house, but I was to do no housework or heavy lifting for six weeks total. I was to see him in six weeks for a checkup.

Jared came home from work and popped in to say hi. I was so drugged up with pain medication that I could barely speak. Instead of sitting with me, to comfort me, he made an excuse and went to the bar.

See-`a-tee was my constant companion. She didn't leave my side except to eat and use the litter box. She laid next to me and purred all day and night long. Jared was sleeping on the couch because he said he didn't want to disturb me. I was heartbroken that he didn't want to be around me. I needed his love to comfort me, but instead he ignored me unless people were around.

Hope helped to bathe me when June couldn't come over. She was such a trooper. She kept up with school, did most of the housework and also did most of the cooking. The meals I had made only lasted the first week.

Tango brought me fresh flowers every day to cheer me up. He sat and talked to me about the shop. He assured me that everything was fine and that I was missed.

Aaron was busy with his own life. He made time for me a few nights a week and would come in to watch movies.

Week three, I was able to get up and sit in the living room a bit every day. I was starting to get my strength back. Joy, Avani and June would come hang out and smoke a joint or three. They cleaned house and cooked, so Hope didn't have to do it all herself.

Brianna brought Dakota to visit with me one afternoon. We sat and talked and it felt like old times again. It was nice to be working on our relationship. I had missed her so much.

My girls, Lily, Mia and Zoey came over to spend time with me as well. We watched movies and just hung out. They did their best to keep my spirits high.

At the beginning of week four, I started to venture out to the front porch. It was nice to be able to get some fresh air and watch as the world went by. It was the middle of October, and the air was starting to get crisp and cool.

Week five found me getting very antsy. I had a hard time doing nothing. I had crocheted so many stocking caps that everyone would be getting two of them for Christmas that year.

Finally, week six was here! I went to the doctor for my checkup and was told I could go back to my normal activities as long as they didn't cause me pain. If I started to hurt, I was to stop immediately and rest. If I started bleeding, he wanted me to go to the emergency room without hesitation.

After my appointment, I drove down to the shop to see Tango and the guys. They were happy to see me. I told them to make sure they got things nice and clean because I would be returning to work the following Monday. They all laughed as I left.

I called Joy, Avani and June and asked them to come over and have a celebratory joint with me. We sat in the living room smoking and talking like old times. Joy had made me a lap blanket while I was recuperating and gave it to me. I cried and thanked her. She was a beautiful woman, and I loved the blanket. It was my favorite color, white.

The kids would be home from school soon, so I excused myself, walked the ladies out and then started dinner. It felt amazing to be cooking for my family again. I had planned to have a sit down dinner with everyone that night.

Aaron and Hope came home from school and were delighted to find me in the kitchen. I told them what the doctor had said, and they both hugged me. They went to their rooms to do their homework while I finished dinner.

As I was finishing, Jared walked in the door from work. I ran up to him and told him what the doctor had said. I hugged him tight to me.

"You know, it's been a long time, and the doctor did say I could resume ALL normal activities. How about you and I play a little catch up before dinner?" I winked at him and tried to kiss him.

"Not right now, Maggie. Maybe later. I have some paperwork to catch up on." He pulled away from me, went into our room and locked the door. I stood there with tears in my eyes.

Wiping away the tears, I went into the kitchen and made dessert. I wanted tonight to be special, and nothing was going to stop me from doing that.

Tango came home and set the table. Hope helped me bring the food out, and we all sat down to eat. As I sat to the right side of Jared, I looked around the table and gave a silent thank you to the Universe for bringing us all together for that meal. I smiled as I told everyone to dig in. I loved the sound of the forks scraping against the plates, the chatter of the kids and the laughter from the shared stories. Things would soon be back to normal, and I couldn't have been happier.

As I was washing dishes, after dinner, the phone rang.

"Maggie, it happened again. I just don't know what to do." Alisha called me to tell me what had happened. She told me that Joey had broken her nose this time.

"Alisha, you know I love you, right? The truth is, it breaks my heart when you call me and tell me these things. I have to practice tough love with you this time. It's time you stood up on your own two feet. Don't call me again until you've left him. I love you." I hung up the phone and cried for her. I didn't know if I had just said goodbye to one of my best friends, for the last time, or if I were a catalyst to a healthy life for her and her sons. I hoped it were the latter of the two.

I threw myself into our home and work. Days melted into weeks and weeks into months. Thanksgiving, Christmas and New Years all came and went. We celebrated them all in our typical fashion, except this time, Brianna, her new husband Bill and their two sons joined us for Thanksgiving. They also joined us for Christmas along with our mother and new step dad as well. It was a really nice time.

It was now mine and Jared's anniversary, so I sent the kids to stay the night at their friend's houses and asked Tango if he minded staying in his room for the night. I made him a nice dinner and brought him a cooler full of snacks and drinks. He had the upstairs to himself, so he was happy to do what I needed him to.

I spent the afternoon making Jared's favorite dinner and dessert. After setting the table and making the dining room beautiful, it was time for me to do the same for myself. I soaked in the bath, shaved, put on lotion and then perfume. My make-up and hair were flawless, and I was wearing my prettiest lingerie. I sat in the dining room waiting for Jared to come home. When he was an hour late, I opened the bottle of wine. When he was two hours late, I finished it. Three hours late, I was well on my way to drunk, and four hours late, I went to bed. I gave up.

Jared came home a few minutes after midnight. He smelled like beer when he fell into bed.

"Where the fuck were you?" I woke up.

"I had to work late." LIES!

"Until midnight and drinking beer?" Oh hell no, he wasn't getting away with this.

"No, until ten, and then I stopped at the bar." He was getting angry.

"Happy Anniversary to you too, Jared." I got up and went to sleep in the spare room. See-`a-tee slept next to me all night. I don't know what I would have done without my little fur ball of a companion.

I woke up the next morning to a rose on my pillow and the smell of freshly brewed coffee. Nope, this wasn't going to fix anything. It was time to just not speak to him... At all.

"Good morning, Sweetheart. I'm so sorry. I forgot, and then I worked late and stopped at the bar and..." Jared was rambling.

I didn't acknowledge him. I went above and beyond to make our anniversary nice, and he forgot. After all of the fighting and bullshit... He forgot.

The silent treatment lasted for three days. Hope was at a friend's house. Aaron and I were watching a movie in the living room when Jared came in. He stood in front of the television and blocked it.

"Aaron? Guess what? I'm divorcing your mom." He said it so "matter of factly".

"Okay, I'm staying with Mom." Aaron shifted so he could see the movie.

"Did you hear me, Aaron? I'm divorcing your mom." Jared repeated himself.

"Yes, did you hear me? I'm staying with her." Aaron seemed like he didn't care.

"What the fuck are you talking about Jared?" I stood up to walk into our bedroom hoping he would follow me... He did.

"I'm done, Maggie. I can't even go out without you getting mad." Jared was trying to play the martyr role.

"Really, Jared? You have threatened me with a divorce, at least once a month, for the last five years. You want to go? Then fucking go. I didn't get upset because you went out last night. I got upset because it was our anniversary, I worked my ass off to make it nice, and you didn't bother to show up." I pulled out a suitcase and started packing his clothes.

"Oh, I didn't say I was leaving. I said I was divorcing you." He put away his clothes as I packed them.

"No way, Mother Fucker. If you're divorcing me, you're leaving." I yanked the clothes out of his hands and re-packed them.

"Fine, if that's what you want, then I'll fucking leave." He pushed me away and packed his suitcase.

"No, Jared, it's not what I want. It's what you want. It's what you've wanted, so just fucking go." I started to cry.

Jared slammed down the lid of the suitcase and walked out of the room. He got in his car and drove off. I was hoping he just needed some time, but I wasn't sure this time. At least he didn't take his suitcase.

I got online again and talked to Heather this time. She said she didn't want to say anything until we knew what was going on, but reminded me, that no matter what happened, I was a strong and capable woman. I was so tired of being strong.

When I shut off my laptop, I drove down to the shop. Tango had just finished a tattoo and met me in our office. I cried as I told him what happened. He hugged me and told me, no matter what happened, he would always be at my side. It made me feel better knowing that Tango, Dominick and Heather were all truly in my corner. I managed to smile. Tango opened the bottom drawer of the desk, pulled out a bottle of tequila and poured us each a shot.

Aaron called to tell me Jared had returned home and was looking for me. Poor kid, he was caught in the middle of this. I thanked him, hung up and drove home.

Jared met me on the back deck as I was walking up the stairs. "Maggie, can we talk please? I'm so sorry. I know I fucked up and hurt your feelings. I didn't know how to handle things or what to do, so I made it about you." Jared held my hands as he spoke.

"I don't know, Jared. This is all getting to be too much. How about we sleep on it and go from there?" I pulled away from him.

"Maggie, please? We've been married for so long. We can't just throw this away." Jared pleaded with me.

"I'M not the one throwing it away. YOU did that." I walked into the house and locked myself into the spare room.

Jared and I didn't talk for almost a week. It's not that I was trying to punish him, I just wanted him to think about what he had been doing and make a decision one way or the other about us. Enough was enough already.

At the end of that week, we kissed and made up. Things were quiet and awkward, but at least we were trying again. You know what they say about the couple that goes through everything that is meant to tear them apart... Sometimes it brings them closer together. I was really hoping this was one of those times.

There was always something about the start of spring that made me want to get out of the house. I do believe it's called spring fever. I asked Hope, Lily, Mia, Zoey, Joy and Avani if they felt like going camping and fishing. They said they would love to, so we packed up and headed out to our favorite spot. I loved being in the middle of nowhere with my girls.

It was almost the end of March, so it was still quite chilly out, but that didn't stop us. We were true Minnesotans and nothing could keep us down.

Joy, Avani, Mia and Lily set up the tents. We had an eight person tent that we all slept in and a second smaller one that we used to store our gear. We loved staying up late together and laughing until we fell asleep.

Zoey set up the grill over the fire pit. She never complained and always did what she was asked to do. She was a people pleaser and did amazing work with some direction.

Hope and I started to gather wood for the fire. When Zoey was finished, she helped as well. The three of us gathered a pile of wood big enough to last the entire weekend.

When we were finished, Lily started dinner for us. She had amazing "mom" qualities, and I just knew she was going to make a fantastic mother some day.

Mia was stoking one side of the fire to make coals for Lily to cook on. She was a brilliant young woman. I had no doubt that she was going to go far in her life. The way she liked to point out right from wrong and was able to stick to her own set of ethics, I suspected she would be an attorney.

Hope was my quiet one. She hardly spoke unless she had something important to talk about. Like me, she was a math geek. She was amazing with numbers, and I was sure she was going to be an accountant or something in the math arena. No matter what she chose to do, I knew she would be successful. Her drive and determination knew no end.

Then there was Zoey. She loved life and loved love. She reminded me so much of myself that I was scared for her. She saw the good in people even when no one else could. She was whimsical and girly but could take down a grown man if called upon to do so. She was my wood nymph and frolicked around in the trees catching fireflies and laughing.

Each of my girls were special in their own unique way, and I loved them for it. Though they didn't always get along, they always respected my love for each of them. If there were issues, we talked about them until they were resolved. I was proud to know that each of my girls were going to do something fantastic when they grew up. No matter how big or small, EACH of them would make a difference.

When we were done eating the yummy dinner Lily put together for us, we sat around the campfire talking about nothing and everything. Zoey would chat about her "boy problems" and Mia would offer her advice. Lily talked about whatever new art project she was working on and explained it in great detail. Hope paid attention to it all and laughed. Oh, how I loved her laughter.

Joy, Avani and I told the girls stories about our lives. We didn't hide the details from them either. We wanted them to learn from our experiences, be they good or bad. We hoped, that if the girls heard what we had lived through and done, it would influence them to make good decisions.

By the end of the night, all seriousness was dropped, and we all shared funny stories or jokes until we collapsed into bed. The sounds of nature acted as our lullaby as we drifted away into deep sleep... Until Zoey started snoring. * wink and a fond smile *

Saturday morning and it was time to go fishing! Avani, Joy and I were up early making breakfast for our gaggle of girls. Lily was the only one to join us. I still think it was the "mom" in her that made her wake so early and help.

"Five minutes 'till breakfast girls." I yelled at Zoey, Mia and Hope as they slept in the tent.

They didn't wake up. The four of us ate our breakfast and packed up the rest of it, so the girls could eat on the shore when we were fishing.

"Ten minutes until we leave girls. Don't get left behind." They knew my rule. If you weren't in the car when I was ready to leave, you would be left at the camp. Nope, wasn't having that this time.

Now, remember, this was almost the end of March, so it was still cold in the mornings... Really cold! I grabbed our water bucket, filled it with water from the creek we camped next to, snuck into the tent and doused them with it. Yep, that did the trick!

All three of them changed their clothes and came out to warm themselves by the fire. Zoey and Hope hung up the sleeping bags, so they would dry by the time we got back. Ten minutes later we were leaving to go fishing. Though they were a bit upset with me, when I first threw the water on them, they laughed about it as we drove to our fishing spot. Honestly, if it had been me, I would have been pissed too.

We fished all day and had a ball! Zoey had to go to the bathroom, so she walked into the lake until she was waist deep in water. After she shit, she rocked back and forth in the water to clean herself. We all laughed with her as she did it. Zoey was something else.

A couple hours later, I cast out in that general direction and caught a huge crappie! None of us could breathe through our laughter! Get it? She crapped in the lake, and then I caught a crappie? Yeah, we still laugh about that to this day.

A little while later, we decided to have lunch. We had packed sandwiches and a watermelon. Um, we neglected to bring a knife to cut the watermelon. Forgetting that I had a filet knife in my tackle box, I picked up the watermelon and smashed it against some rocks to break it open. We ate it, cave-woman style, and loved every bite of it.

There weren't any fish on the stringer at the end of the day. It didn't bother anyone, especially me. We didn't go fishing to catch fish. We went fishing to make memories, and we definitely did that. We packed up and headed back to camp.

Again, Lily started dinner with Avani and Joy's help. The rest of us cleaned up the fishing gear and packed it away. We tried to get a jump on things because we had to leave after breakfast the next morning. Mia, Zoey and Hope had school on Monday.

Dinner was delicious. I was always impressed with what could be cooked over an open wood fire. The food just tasted better. The girls all had hot dogs, and Joy made a nice potato and bell pepper side dish. I ate the potatoes and peppers. It was so yummy! You could taste the wood smoke in it. Joy was a fantastic cook. Lily and Avani even figured out how to make cupcakes on the wood fire. Again, I was truly impressed with their skills. I didn't eat the cupcakes because there were eggs in them, but the other girls all seemed to love them.

We threw our paper plates into the fire when dinner was over. I brought out the cooler full of beer, wine coolers and tequila. The adult women enjoyed their beverages while the younger gals stuck with their sodas.

We adults were pretty tipsy. You know, that's girl code for drunk. We had music playing on a portable stereo, so we all got up and started dancing. I swear, if anyone had been watching us, they would have thought we had lost our ever loving minds. We laughed so hard that the coyotes answered us with their call. That sent all of us running to the tent screaming as if the tent offered us protection from wild animals.

Mia, being the most logical of us, went back outside and put out the fire before she joined us in the tent. We stayed up telling ghost stories and laughing until we couldn't laugh anymore. Did I mention how much I loved my girls? Yeah, I thought so.

Sunday morning, we packed up and headed home. It was always a little sad when our camping weekends were over. We drove back to reality with heavy hearts.

"Hope, what do you want to do for your birthday? You name it, Kiddo, and we'll do it." I asked her on the way home.

"Really? Anything?" Hope was sitting next to me in the front seat.

"Well, anything we can afford to do." I knew I had to clarify my earlier statement.

"I want a tattoo. That's all I want. I don't need a party or gifts or anything, just a tattoo! Please, Maggie?" Hope was so excited she was actually clapping her hands.

"I'll tell ya what, Kiddo, even though I have custody of you, I think I need to talk to your mother about this one. If she says it's okay we'll tattoo you, BUT I get to throw you a party too. Deal?" I glanced over at Hope and saw her smile.

"Deal!" Hope continued to smile the entire way home.

I had to do a bit of sweet talking, but I eventually convinced her mother that it was okay for Hope to get a tattoo. I had a way of getting people to agree with me when I wanted something bad enough. I wanted this for Hope. The legal age in Minnesota, to get a tattoo, was sixteen as long as you had parental permission, so there was no problem with that since Hope was turning seventeen.

On Hope's birthday, I took her to the shop and inked her with the tattoo she wanted. It was beautiful, sweet and innocent, just like her. We tattooed the Japanese Kanji symbol for "hope" on her ankle. She made a good choice.

We had her party the weekend after her actual birthday. I invited all of her friends, along with our normal group of girls, to a fashion party. Lily styled their hair, I did their make-up and Mia did photo shoots with them. It was so much fun! When we were done with the photos, they did what teenage girls are supposed to do. They camped out in the living room, watched movies and talked about boys. * big smile *

I would like to add a personal note to end this chapter. I want to thank my girls for being who they are and never letting anyone sway them from their own realities. Each of you made me proud to not only call you one of my girls, but to call you my friend and daughter as well. There is a light in my heart that is kept alive through you girls, and I wouldn't be who I am today without the yesterdays that we shared. I love all of you, more than I could ever promise, and want to remind you to love me when I'm gone. You all know what that means. I love you.

CHAPTER TWENTY SEVEN

I wasn't tattooing very much anymore. I busied myself, instead, with the day to day operations and management of the studio. Tango, Cam and Jordy did the majority of the tattoos.

I missed the creativity of tattooing, but Tango needed me to run the shop. I only did tattoos by special appointment. Tango knew I wasn't feeling fulfilled, so he suggested I do another mural in the waiting area.

This time, I did a more realistic mural with a picture of Tango doing a tattoo. It turned out really well, and he loved it. When the mural was finished, we hung open shelves over it and invited local artists to display and sell their wares. Before we knew it, the shelves were full. It felt rewarding to be promoting the art from our local people. I even did a few pieces myself to display and sell.

I spent more time at home then I did at the shop. I was trying hard to keep my family together and happy. The kids loved it that I was home when they came home from school. Jared wasn't himself no matter what I did.

I was home making dinner one evening when the phone rang. "Maggie?" It was Alisha.

"Oh my gawd! Are you okay? It's been so long! I've missed you and thought about you and the boys every day." I was so happy to hear her voice. It had been years since we had last spoken.

"I am better than okay, thanks to you." Alisha explained to me what had been going on. Not long after we talked the last time, she had left Joey and moved to New Jersey. Her and the boys were doing amazingly well, and she wanted to touch base with me. We talked for over an hour, told each other we loved one another and hung up.

Aaron was turning eighteen. It was hard to imagine it had been eight years that he had lived with us. This was a big birthday, and we were ready to do anything he wanted. We asked him what he wanted, and he said he wanted a big tattoo on his back and to go to the casino. His wish was our command.

The day of his eighteenth birthday, Tango and I closed the shop. We wanted Aaron's first tattoo experience to be something special. Aaron was into "death metal" music so when he got there, we cranked up the tunes, drew up the stencil and got it ready. He wanted an eighteen inch Koi fish, swimming up his back, and that's exactly what he got.

Let me tell you, this kid was a trooper! Aaron was always a slender kid, and though he had put on about fifty pounds in the years he lived with us, his spine looked like it was nothing except skin pulled tightly over bone. I would have had a hard time getting this tattoo, and I had over a hundred of them at this point.

I peeled the stencil from his back, washed him down and asked if he were ready. He said he was, so I got started. I tattooed a thin black outline starting at the bottom of the Koi and then worked my way up. I felt his muscles clench every time the needles touched his skin, but he didn't flinch. I was impressed.

When I was done with the outline, I started the color. I had offered him a break, but he said he just wanted to keep going. I was really proud of him. A grown man would have wanted a break at this point.

When I finished with the color and highlights, I washed him down with witch hazel and left it sitting on his back, for a few minutes, while he laid on the tattoo bed. There was a bit of swelling, but it really wasn't too bad. It was done. Our son was a man.

We were saddened that Hope couldn't join us at the casino because she was only seventeen. She made plans to stay the night at a friend's house. I told her I would pick her up the next afternoon.

Tango, Jared, Aaron and I drove to a casino that was about twenty miles south of us. It was the only one around that was age eighteen and up. We walked through the front doors, the security guard checked Aaron's identification, and we were allowed to pass.

We walked around looking at all of the machines. Aaron found one he wanted to play and sat down at it. Reaching into his own pocket, he pulled out a twenty dollar bill to put in the machine.

"Oh no, Aaron, tonight's on us." I reached into my purse, pulled out eighteen, twenty dollar bills and handed them to him. "Happy birthday, Son. There's one for each year. Enjoy yourself. We love you."

Tango stayed close to Aaron to keep him company while Jared and I walked around a bit more. After playing a few different machines, we decided to go back to where Aaron was. We all played for a few hours. Jared and I lost a hundred dollars between us. Tango won thirty dollars. Aaron won eight hundred; what a great birthday gift! That's when we all thought it was best to leave.

On our way home, we talked to Aaron about the odds of that happening again. We warned him against the trappings of gambling and told him he had to be careful about becoming addicted. He said he understood and would remember what we had taught him. Yep, I was truly proud of this kid, oh um, I mean young man. * smile *

Jared and I managed to fake our way through Aaron's eighteenth birthday, but truth be told, we were not doing very well as a couple. We argued more and more as the years passed. I swear, it was at least once a week, I was online with either Dominick or Heather talking to them about it. They both thought I should just walk away, but understood that I couldn't. I loved Jared with all of my heart. They gave me advice, when they could, and listened to me cry when they didn't have anything to tell me that would help. Dominick and Heather became great friends. They were like second parents to me though we only knew each other over the internet.

Business at W.T.F. Ta2z was going as good, if not better, than it did in Colorado Springs. We were booked almost every day and even brought in a fourth artist. I now had more time for our home life. It didn't help things though.

Jared was working a lot of overtime. He was paid by salary, so I couldn't tell by his paycheck if he were really working overtime or if other things were keeping him busy. My friends suggested he was cheating on me, but I told them that there was no way he would ever cheat. I thought that maybe he just didn't want to come home after work, and was maybe going out with his friends or going to the park for some alone time. No matter, I had to figure out a way to fix things.

Jared and I hadn't been away, alone together, since our honeymoon. It was definitely time to make that happen. Maybe that was exactly what we needed.

Brianna called and said she needed to talk to me. I told her I was busy, but she could come up the next day. She said that was fine and hung up.

We had been spending quite a bit of time with my mother and step dad. I absolutely loved Dan. He was kind, genuine, compassionate and generous. I still didn't know why he was married to my mother.

When Jared came home from work, we all had dinner. After dinner, Tango and the kids busied themselves in their rooms. It was time for me to talk to Jared about our anniversary.

"Jared? I've been thinking. I was hoping we could go on a vacation, just the two of us." I sat near him on the couch.

"This is kind of short notice, Maggie. I don't know if I can get time off from work but I'll try. What did you have in mind?" He put his hand on my knee.

"I don't know. That's why I wanted to talk to you. I guess it would depend on how much time you can get off from work." I put my hand over his.

"Like I said, I'll check. Can we talk about this when I get home tomorrow night?" He turned on the television.

"Sure." I slid down on the couch and laid in his lap while we watched a movie.

I was dragging ass the next morning. I had fallen asleep on the couch, and Jared didn't wake me when he went to bed. My back hurt, and I was bitchy, but I still got up and made breakfast for everyone before they left for school and work.

Brianna showed up right before lunch. It was so nice to see her, Dakota and Austin. They had grown so much.

"Maggie, things aren't working out with me and Bill. I think we're going to get a divorce." Brianna was crying.

I talked to her about what was going on. Bill was in the Army and was seldom home. Brianna was having a hard time handling everything on her own and there was just constant drama.

We spent the day playing with the boys. Just as she was getting ready to go home, the phone rang. It was our mother and she was screaming at the top of her lungs.

"What? Slow down, Mom. What happened?" Brianna was on the phone with her. "WHAT?"

I took the phone from her. "What's going on, Mom?"

"The trailer is on fire! The fire department is there now. Dan and I are on our way out there." Mom said she would call us when they got out there and knew what was going on.

I hung up the phone and hugged Brianna. Everything she owned was in that trailer. She wanted to leave, but I wouldn't let her.

"What am I going to do, Maggie?" She sat on the couch sobbing.

"You're going to move in here until you can get on your feet again." I had to offer it, she was my sister. "Just be glad you weren't home when it happened."

Mom called a couple hours later and told us the fire department said it was caused by a faulty hot water heater. It was a total loss. Everything was gone.

Brianna cried for hours. Mom and Dan came by to pick up the kids, so she could have a break and figure things out. I called Jared to tell him what happened, and Brianna would be staying with us for a while. He said he was fine with that and to tell her he was sorry.

I got Brianna settled into the spare room upstairs and gave her a few changes of clothes out of my closet. She had finally fallen asleep when the kids came home from school. I explained everything to them, and they said they would do whatever they could to help. They got snacks and went to their rooms to do their homework.

I went down to the shop to talk to Tango and explain what happened. He said that though he was sorry for what happened that it was perfect timing.

"Maggie, you know I love you as though you were my own daughter, right?" Uh oh, this didn't sound good.

"Of course, Tango! I've never questioned it." I waited to see what he had to say.

"I think it's time that I move in to my own place. I love living with you, don't get me wrong, but I am still young enough that I would like to start dating again and maybe find a special someone to settle down with." He had tears in his eyes.

"Oh, Tango! As much as I hate the idea of you leaving, I completely understand. I'm gonna miss seeing you every day though. Do you have a time frame?" I bent to hug him.

"As a matter of fact, I do. I already found a place and plan to move out this week. Please, don't get upset. It's right down the street, and we'll still see each other all the time, I promise." He hugged me tight.

"Why didn't you tell me about this before? It feels so sudden." I cried into his shoulder.

"You had so much going on, and I didn't want to cause you more stress." He hugged me even tighter.

"Okay, Old Man. Let's do this." I kissed his cheek and left him in his office.

Jared was already home when I got there. He was sitting on the couch with his arms around Brianna comforting her. When they saw me, they pulled away from each other.

"Maggie, can I talk to you in our room, please?" Jared stood up.

"Sure, are you okay, Brianna?" I started to follow Jared into our room.

"I will be." Brianna smiled a little smile.

"Is everything okay?" I closed the bedroom door behind me.

"That's what I wanted to talk to you about, Maggie. I think we should postpone our vacation and use the money to help your sister get on her feet instead." Jared was sitting on the bed.

"I completely agree, Sweetheart. That's so kind of you to think of her like that." I sat down next I'll take some money out of savings tomorrow and take Brianna shopping for her and the boys. Mom is keeping the boys for a few days. Um, Tango is moving out next week." I had almost forgotten to tell him.

"What? Really? What brought this on?" Jared pulled away from me.

"He said he wants his own place and maybe find a woman to settle down with." I told Jared what Tango had told me.

"Oh, okay. Well, that works out alright then because Brianna and the boys can have the upstairs now. She told me that her and Bill are getting a divorce, so she's going to need us even more now." Jared stood up.

"Yep, works out all the way around." I stood up and kissed him. "We can do this, Sweetheart, I know we can. It's not going to be easy but we've been through worse."

"You're right, Maggie. None of this is going to be easy, but it'll work out in the end." He kissed my cheek and we went out to tell Brianna what we had talked about.

The next day, I took five thousand dollars out of savings and took Brianna shopping. We bought her and her boys brand new wardrobes, toys, books, curling irons, blow dryers and everything else she needed or wanted. We bought a new bedroom set for the boys with bunk beds and dressers. New televisions, DVD players and DVDs were our last stop of the day. We made arrangements for everything we couldn't fit into my car to be delivered the beginning of the next week after Tango moved out. None of it could replace the personal things she had lost, but it was a start.

We had it planned that Brianna would take over Tango's room and the boys would have the spare room. That way she would have the office with her room and have a little getaway space of her own. She was excited even through all of her loss.

"Thank you, Maggie. I don't know what I would have done without you and Jared." She gave me a giant hug when we got home.

"You would have done just fine. You're a tough woman." We walked into the house smiling.

We spent the rest of the week helping Tango pack. When the weekend arrived, we all helped him move into his new apartment. It was a very bittersweet day. I was happy for him but was going to miss him tremendously.

"Maggie, I have to tell you something. Watch your sister. Something's not right." He whispered into my ear as he hugged me goodbye.

I looked at him with a puzzled look on my face, and he winked at me. I knew not to say anything out loud because he had whispered it to me, meaning it was not something to talk about in mixed company. I told him I would call him later to check on him, and we all left. Well, all of us except for See-'a-tee. I decided she was better off with him. He needed the company, and she loved him almost as much as I did. It broke my heart to leave them there, but it was time to move on.

Jared helped Brianna to get a job at the plasma center. She had gone to school to become a medical receptionist, so it was a perfect fit. I was so happy she was moving on with her life.

It had been a couple of months since the fire. Brianna had filed for divorce, and we were all getting along well. I loved having my nephews in our home and spent as much time with them as I could. I babysat them while Brianna was at work.

The months flew by and Aaron's graduation was right around the corner, so it was time to plan for it. It took me a few weeks, but I managed to get it all planned and taken care of. I reserved four rooms at a hotel, with and indoor water park, and sent out invitations. This was a huge day for him, and I wanted it to be extra special.

And of course, before I knew it, the big day was here! We attended his graduation ceremony at school, and I cried as he walked across the stage to receive his diploma. It seemed like it had only been yesterday that he was moving in with us, and here he was, a grown man.

After Aaron's official graduation, we all went to the hotel. All of our friends showed up, and the party ensued. It was spectacular! Aaron had a blast with all of his friends. They swam and played at the water park until it closed. We let him and his friends have the hotel rooms, and the rest of us all went home. I told Aaron I was proud of him and would be back in the morning to pick him up. He had become an incredible young man.

Hope and I dropped off Tango on our way home. Brianna and her boys rode with Jared. They had become very close over the months they had been there, and I was happy to see it. It seemed as though she really had changed and grown into the woman I always knew she was. Now, that she had been working full time for a few months, I suspected she would be moving out soon. I looked forward to helping her find her own place and decorating it with her. It would be so much fun!

It was an early night for everyone as we were all exhausted from the day's happenings. Jared and I said goodnight to everyone and went to bed. I set my alarm, so I could get up in the morning and do what I had to before I had to go and pick up Aaron.

I woke up and made breakfast for everyone. Brianna fed the boys and then laid them down for their morning nap. Jared was watching television, so I asked Hope if she would like to go with me.

We picked up Aaron and then dropped him off at his friend's house. He was going to stay the weekend there, so they could look for an apartment together. They were going to be starting college together that fall and decided to find a place close to campus.

On our way home, we decided to go shopping. I called Jared to tell him, so he wouldn't worry. We got halfway to the store when I realized I had forgotten my purse. Fuck! I turned around and drove back home. I parked the car in the front of the house, instead of pulling into the garage in the back, and stepped up onto the porch. Brianna and Jared were watching a movie because I could hear strange noises coming through the open window in the living room.

"Hey guys, I forgot my..." I walked around the corner, into the living room, and there was Brianna fucking my husband on the couch.

"What the fuck? What's going on here? Jared! Brianna! How could you... Why would you..." I was at a loss for words.

"Maggie, it's not what it looks like." Jared scrambled to get out from under Brianna and pull up his pants.

"Fuck if it's not! What, Brianna, you didn't get enough of my hand-me-downs when we were kids? You had to take this one too? How long has this been going on? Never mind, I don't want to know. You both sicken me." I wanted to beat them both but knew better than to touch them.

"Maggie, it just kind of happened..." Brianna started to speak.

"I don't want to hear it. The two of you and your boys had better be gone before I get home or there will be serious hell to pay!" I turned around, grabbed my purse and stormed out the door, slamming it behind me.

When I got in the car, I started crying and told Hope what had just happened. She leaned over and hugged me tight. After I cried for a few minutes, she told me to switch seats with her because I was in no shape to drive. Hope started the car, and we drove around for a couple of hours until I gained my composure. There was no way they were going to get away with this.

Hope drove back home. We walked in to an empty house. Good, they listened to me. I called my girls, and they all came over. We sat up all night talking about what happened. Brianna and Jared were called every nasty name we could think of as we passed around a joint between the adults, and then another and another until I was so stoned I couldn't think straight.

June and Joy had to get home to their families. They both said they hated to leave me like this, but they didn't have a choice. Avani had brought her son with her and he was sleeping in my room... My room. I couldn't stop crying.

How could they do this to me? I know I wasn't perfect, but my husband and my sister? I wouldn't have believed it if I hadn't seen it with my own two eyes.

After I calmed down again, I called Tango. He told me that had been his suspicion all along. We talked for a while and hung up.

Avani, Lily, Mia, Zoey, Hope and I all fell asleep in the living room that night. I was so happy to have their presence in my life. I slept until the sun peeked through the window.

Avani and the girls had to go home. I understood and thanked them for staying with me. Hope went to shower and change. Her and I had to talk about what we were going to do. While she showered, I called Tango. He was about to go to the shop, but told me that Hope and I were welcome to come and stay with him as long as we needed to.

I knew I couldn't afford the house payments and everything else on my own. I talked to Hope, and we decided to move in with Tango until we could figure out what we were going to do.

Jared called to talk to me. Though it shattered my heart into a million little pieces, I told him to give me a week to move out, and he could have the house. I wanted nothing from him except a divorce, my personal belongings and my half of the checking and savings.

I went to the bank and took half of the money out of our accounts. I then deposited that money into a new account in my name. Like I said, I didn't want anything that wasn't mine.

Hope and I packed our things and put most of them into storage before we moved in with Tango. While Hope was at Tango's unpacking the things we brought with us, I went to the house to do a final walk through. After making sure we hadn't left anything behind, I walked out the door and through the gate. I shut the gate on my white, picket fence for the final time. It was over.

CHAPTER TWENTY EIGHT

Tango's place was a one bedroom apartment, so Hope and I slept in the living room. Tango had tried to give up his bedroom to us, but I wouldn't allow it. He was already being so kind to let us stay there that I didn't want to be anymore of a burden.

I got online and told Dominick what happened. He told me he knew I was hurting, but it was a good thing it happened. He said for me to remember everything he had taught me over the years, and that it was time I stood up on my own two feet. Heather got online with me after that and chatted for a while. I felt better, every time, I talked to the two of them.

I went to the courthouse and picked up the packet of divorce papers. Eleven years... I had spent eleven years with this man and never thought he would have done this. Not wanting to go back to Tango's yet, I drove to a park, sat in my car and filled out the paperwork. I could barely see the ink through my tears, but I managed to finish filling them out. Now, I had to get them to Jared, so he could do his part and we could file them. I kept true to my word. I didn't ask for anything except the divorce.

I pulled up in front of our house, I mean, his house and got out of the car. As I was about to walk up and put the papers in the mailbox, Aaron ran out to me.

"Mom!" He jumped over the gate and hugged me.

"Aaron! I've missed you!" I pulled him closer to me and hugged him tightly.

"Mom, I'm so sorry. Are you okay? Are you staying with Grandpa Tango? Is Hope with you?" Aaron didn't let go of me.

"I'm fine, Sweetie. Yes, Hope and I are staying with Grandpa Tango until we figure out what we're going to do." I stepped back from him. "Do me a favor? Give these to your dad? It's the divorce papers."

We talked for a little while. He told me he and his friend had found an apartment and were moving out the beginning of the next month. He promised to stay in touch with me, hugged me again and went inside. My heart broke all over again.

When I got back to Tango's, I called Alisha to tell her what happened. She was almost as shocked as I had been... As I was. Alisha told me about Mathew starting college, and she had an extra room. She suggested that Hope and I move to New Jersey and stay with her until we could figure out what we wanted to do. Hmm... New Jersey? I told her I had to talk to Hope, and I would get back to her.

"YES!" Hope was excited about the prospect of moving to New Jersey.

"I think it would be nice to get a fresh start. We have to talk to your mother and get her permission." I was getting a little excited myself.

"Why do we need her permission? You have custody of me." Hope didn't understand.

"Because she can revoke my custody of you anytime she wants. We don't want that to happen, so it's best to play by the rules." I tried to explain it as best I could.

"Gotcha. When do you want to talk to her?" Hope got up and sat next to me on the couch.

"I guess the sooner the better. Why don't you call her, and see if we can meet her somewhere to talk." I put my arm around her, pulled her close and hugged her.

We met with Hope's mom at the park down the street from her apartment. I explained what had happened between Jared and I. I went on to tell her about us living with Tango and how we were doing alright. Finally, I told her about the possibility of us moving to New Jersey.

Hope's mom told me she would never have thought Jared would have cheated on me. I replied that seemed to be the consensus. She went on to talk about how much she appreciated me taking care of Hope, and she knew her daughter was loved. Finally, she said yes.

Hope jumped up and hugged her mom and then me. I thanked her for sharing her daughter with me and for trusting me to take care of her. I promised I would take good care of her, and we would stay in touch. I left Hope with her so they could visit and told her to call me later to pick her up. Now, I had to go talk to Tango.

I drove down to the shop and waited for Tango to finish with his appointment. He met me in our office when he was done. I didn't know how I was going to tell him this one.

"Tango? Hope and I are moving to New Jersey." It fell out of my mouth before I could think of a way to break it to him gently.

"New Jersey? Wow, Maggie. When?" Tango was visibly shaken.

"I'm hoping by this weekend." I reached across the desk and held his hand.

"That soon, huh? What are we going to do about the shop?" He squeezed my hand.

"It's yours. Your idea and money started it. All I did was name it." I didn't want anything from him.

"No, Maggie, we started this. It's OUR shop. You have to let me buy out your half of it. You're going to need some money to get started with anyway." Tango reached into the drawer, pulled out his personal checkbook, wrote me a check and slid it across the desk.

"Forty thousand dollars? Tango! I can't take this much from you!" I slid it back to him.

"You can, and you will, Kiddo! Now take the Goddamned money and make an old man happy knowing that you will be safe." He pushed the check back at me.

I hugged Tango tighter than I had ever hugged him before. Tears rolled down my face and fell onto his shoulder.

"I love you, Tango. Thank you for always taking care of me." I picked up the check, stuck it in my purse and turned to leave.

"I love you too, Kiddo. Do me proud." He busied himself with some paperwork.

I went to the bank and deposited the check into my account. They said it would take three days to clear. It gave me enough time to get some things done before we left. The first thing I needed to do was get a new vehicle.

I went to the same car lot that I bought my car from. I talked to them, traded in my car and bought a brand new jeep. Because of the amazing gift from Tango, I was able to pay cash for it (well, I wrote them a check in the full amount) and got a great deal. Driving that jeep off of the lot made me feel, oh I don't know... New? Yeah, new would be a great way to put it. It was time to start over... Completely over.

Hope called, so I went to pick her up. I parked directly in front of her as she sat on the stone wall that bordered the park, but she didn't move. That's when I realized that she didn't know it was me because of my new vehicle. I got out, called her name and waved. A surprised smile crossed her face when she saw it was me. She asked about the new jeep, and I told her what happened.

"When do I get to drive it?" Hope was more excited than I was.

"Right now." I tossed her the keys and got into the passenger side.

Hope got in, put on her seat belt, adjusted the mirrors and started her up. Yes, even though our new vehicle was a jeep, she was a girl. We named her "Dawn" because she was the dawning of our new days.

We drove around Duluth for a while until we got hungry. Hope and I decided to stop and pick up Aaron to take him out to eat. When we pulled up in front of his house, Brianna was in the front yard watching her boys play. Hope honked the horn, and Brianna looked up at us. Her eyes turned instantly green with jealousy. I smiled and fought back the tears.

Aaron came running out to us, stood at the passenger side and asked about the new jeep. I made sure I spoke loud enough for Brianna to hear and told him about Tango buying out my half of the shop. I went on to tell him about us moving to New Jersey and that being the reason I bought the jeep. Brianna picked up her sons and went inside. HA! Take that bitch.

Hope, Aaron and I went out to eat at a buffet style restaurant. We talked until the place closed. Something in my heart told me this would be the last time I saw Aaron, and I didn't want the night to end. He was starting college and moving into his own place with his friend. I told him how proud I was of him, and I was honored to have been his mom for as long as I had been allowed. He told me he loved me, and he wouldn't be the man he was if it hadn't been for me.

I let Aaron drive to his house. When we pulled up, I got out and hugged him tight. Memories of him growing up flooded my brain. I tried not to cry, but it was to no avail. The tears flooded my eyes as I stood there hugging him and telling him that I loved him. He cried too, told me he loved me and then walked away.

I got back into the jeep and sat there for just a moment, looking at the house we had built a life in. Had it all been a lie? How could this have happened if it had been built on true love? There was no time to think of these things now. We had to start packing, see our friends and get the hell out of town. It was time to move on.

Hope and I decided, the best way to see everyone and say goodbye, was to take everyone camping again. It's what we did. My girls and I loved being in the great outdoors.

Since it was summer, we went camping in the middle of the week. The campground was deserted except for the couple that ran it. They were happy to see us pull up, and as we checked in, they told us how much they loved it when all of us came to camp there. I explained to them how this would be the last time and why. They didn't charge us and said they were sad to see me go. They were such a nice couple.

We all performed our usual tasks. Our camp was set up in no time, and we were now able to kick back, relax and enjoy ourselves. Starting with a drink or three for the adults.

Avani tossed Joy and I each a beer while she and June had wine coolers. This was the first time that June had been able to go camping with us. I was excited to have her along. Usually, her family duties kept her home when we camped, but her oldest son stayed with her younger ones, so that her husband could still go to work.

Mia got the campfire burning hot. It was so hot, we all had to move our chairs back from it. The flames must have reached ten feet into the air! We were doin' it big this time. * wink *

I rolled a joint, lit it and passed it around the adult women. As I sat there, I watched my girls talking and laughing. A sense of peace came over me because I knew they were all going to be okay, maybe even better than okay.

Lily, as usual, started dinner. Zoey and Mia helped her, and it wasn't too long before we were all eating another delicious meal prepared over a campfire. My girls knew how to cook, that was for sure.

We didn't go fishing our first night. It was more important for us to spend time together and talk. I told my girls about what it was like for me growing up and how I never had much of a childhood. I warned them to slow it down. They were all in their early twenties now and in so much of a hurry to grow up. It saddened me to think of them as adult women. Not because they weren't going to be amazing women and contribute to society, but because I didn't want them to lose their giggles. Does that make sense?

It was late, and the mosquitoes were trying to carry us away, so we all tucked ourselves into the tent to sleep. Of course, sleep didn't come right away. We had to stay up telling ghost stories and jokes until, one by one, we each faded away, surrendering to our dreams.

The next morning, I was the one that was woken up by a bucket of cold water! They thought it was funny to get even with me for all the times I had done it to them. All I could do was laugh, until I got up.

We camped next to a river that ran off of the lake we fished at. One by one, I pushed each of the girls into the river. All of them took a "swim" except for Lilly. That would teach 'em. * wink *

Mia and Zoey made breakfast while the rest of us hung up the sleeping bags and clothes that had gotten wet. Joy, Avani and June couldn't stay with us another night, so Joy took them home to Duluth. I promised to see them before Hope and I left for New Jersey. It was just me and my girls now.

As tradition mandated, we went fishing. It was a glorious day to be outdoors. We went to our normal spot. There were two lakes there, one on either side of the road, and they were connected via a gigantic culvert that ran under the road. It was private and serene, with good fishing.

Hope wasn't as much of a fisher as the rest of us, so she would spend her time laying on a blanket reading while the rest of us fished. As we all sat there, a large crane flew over our heads and landed in the culvert. He tried to take our line of fish! Mia chased him away, but he kept coming back. We started to feed him the fish that had swallowed the hook but were too tiny to keep. He stuck around all afternoon waiting for more fish. We named him Fraiser. He was a pretty cool bird.

We got back to camp and celebrated our last night together by having a giant bonfire. I even broke my vegan vows and had a hotdog with the girls. They teased me relentlessly about it.

We all put on our pajamas and danced around the fire like a bunch of idiots. It was a blast! I pulled out my cooler of beer and cracked one open.

"Hey, Mama Maggie, toss me one of those." Lily spoke up. She was of age, so I didn't think twice. She had taken her first drink with me a couple of years ago on her birthday. Of course, it was a shot of tequila.

"What about the rest of us?" Mia asked loudly.

"I guess it couldn't hurt. Hope is the youngest one here, and I have custody of her so ya know..." I tossed each of the girls a beer. Oh, get your panties out of that bunch in your ass, it was our last night together and except for Hope, they were all of age!

We had a couple of beers together and talked and talked and talked some more. We talked about everything and nothing. They helped me to forget and to heal. Have I mentioned how much I love my girls? Yeah, I thought so, but it doesn't hurt to say it again... I love my girls.

Even though we had foggy heads and giant headaches the next morning, we managed to have breakfast and pack up. I stopped and realized this was the last time we were ever going to do this. It wasn't that I would never see any of them again. I just knew they were growing up and would soon have their own lives. I stood there for a moment and just took it all in. I pushed the thought from my head and smiled. We had made some amazing memories that would last a lifetime. * smile *

When we got back to Duluth, I dropped off each of the girls, hugged them and told them I loved them. Hope and I were leaving the next day, and it was easier to say goodbye now.

Hope and I went home and took a short nap before we woke up and finished packing. Tango was at the shop, so we went down there to spend some time with him.

When we walked in, no one was there except for Tango.

"Where is everyone?" I walked into the back with Hope at my side.

"I sent them home. I had a feeling you'd show up." He was sitting at his tattoo station.

"Why? What are you doing?" I sat down in his tattoo chair to talk to him.

"I'm getting ready to tattoo you. In all these years, Maggie, you've never gotten a tattoo from me." He picked up a piece of art and showed it to me. It was a picture of two angels dancing together.

"What's that?" It was gorgeous.

"It's you and your Mr. Right. He's out there, Maggie and this is to remind you to never give up until the two of you are dancing together for all of eternity." He set the stencil back down on his table.

"Thank you, Tango, thank you." I held back the tears as he shaved my upper arm on my right shoulder, washed it and placed the stencil.

An hour later, I had my tattoo. Out of all the tattoos I had, this was my favorite. He had put a lot of thought into it, and I wore it proudly.

"Now, it's your turn to tattoo me. I want the same one. Frankee was my soul mate, and though I will love again, I won't ever love anyone the way I loved her."

I gave Tango his tattoo on the same arm, in the same place. We were bonded for life now. I was gonna miss that old man.

When we were done with our tattoos, I put another one on Hope. It was of a treble clef on her other ankle. We did it in solid red ink with a few black music notes around it. There, now we all had new tattoos to take that next step into our new lives.

Tango invited us out to dinner. He surprised us by having Avani, Joy, June, Lily, Mia and Zoey meet us at the restaurant. Everyone I loved was there to wish us well. It could not have been more perfect. We enjoyed our dinner, and when it was over, we said goodbye. I was going to miss them all so much.

Tango, Hope and I went home to spend our final night together doing nothing. While they watched television, I snuck off to the bathroom to call Jared.

"Maggie, I'm sorry things turned out this way. It was only the one time. We're not a couple or anything. Please, please reconsider this?" Jared was crying.

"It only took the one time, Jared. I called to make sure you filed the divorce papers like you said you would." I was holding back the tears. Everything in my heart said to run to him, but my head wouldn't allow it.

"I took them to the courthouse this morning. I love you, Maggie." Jared's voice cracked through his tears.

"I loved you, Jared, but that love is gone now. I hope you get everything in life that you deserve. Goodbye." I hung up and cried. When I was done, I wiped my tears, washed my face and joined Tango and Hope in the living room.

"You okay, Kid?" Tango put his arm over my shoulders.

"I am now." I looked up at him and smiled.

"Tomorrow is a new day. Let's just enjoy tonight." Tango kissed my forehead, and we finished watching the movie. When it was over we went to sleep. We had a long day in front of us, and we needed some good sleep.

The sun burst through the blinds to wake us up the next morning. Tango was up making pancakes.

"Up and at 'em ladies! We have to eat and get your jeep packed!" He hollered from the kitchen.

"We're up! We're up! Quit yelling, and you better have coffee in there!" I yelled back at him.

"When have you ever known me to not have coffee ready in the morning?" Tango laughed.

"You guys and your coffee. Don't you know, it'll stunt your growth!" Hope joked with us.

"Shut up, Kiddo!" I threw a pillow at her before I went into the bathroom to shower and get dressed.

When I was done, Hope went in to shower and change. We all ate breakfast, loaded up the jeep and made sure everything was in working order.

"Come here, Kid." Tango pulled me close and hugged me tight. "You know I love you, right?"

"Yes, I do, Old Man. You know I love you too, right?" I didn't want to let go.

"Yes, I do. I've never doubted it." He kissed my forehead, opened the jeep door and smiled at me. "Call me from the road when you stop and when you get there, so I know you're okay."

"I will, I promise." I blew him a kiss.

"Come here, Hope, give this old man some love." He hugged Hope and kissed her on the forehead before he opened the passenger side door for her.

"I love you both! Please, be safe!" He waved as we pulled out of the driveway.

"Well, here we go, Kiddo! On to our new life! New Jersey better watch out because we're on our way!" I reached over and held her hand for just a minute. Yep, we were on our way.

We arrived in New Jersey three days later. We stayed with Alisha for a couple of days until we got our own apartment. We spent the rest of the summer figuring out our way around Princeton.

I enrolled Hope in school. It was her senior year. I couldn't believe how fast time was moving. She would be off to college before I knew it. What would I do then?

We still had quite a bit of money left, but I needed to find a job. I applied at a few tattoo studios but had no luck. Finally, I saw an ad online. A children's activity center, like the one I used to live across the street from, was looking for an art teacher. I sent them my resume, they called me in for an interview, and I got the job!

There ya go, we were all settled in. We had a home, Hope was in school, and I had a job. What more could we want? I touched the tattoo on my shoulder that Tango had put on me. Oh right, that's what "more" I could want. Mr. Right was out there somewhere, right?

CHAPTER TWENTY NINE

Alisha and I went out almost every weekend. We found a new bar or club to go to every time, so we were always meeting new people. This weekend was no different.

We went to a bar called "The Nest." There was a band playing that night, and they were supposed to be pretty good. We thought we would check it out.

Sitting at the bar on the side facing the band, we ordered drinks and settled in to be entertained. The band was set up in a tiny corner of the bar. They barely had room to play, which was alright, since they were only mediocre at best. They were the typical seventies rock cover band and had no originality to their music, whatsoever.

Alisha and I went outside to have a cigarette. We were sitting on a bench when the bass player from the band approached us.

"Hey, you ladies enjoying the music?" He stood in front of me and lit a cigarette.

"Um, yeah. You guys a new band?" How could I tell him that they had no style?

"No, we've been playing together for years. Hi, I'm Keith. I'm the bass player." He reached to shake my hand.

"Hi, Keith. My name is Maggie, and this is my friend Alisha." I shook his hand.

We talked while we smoked and then went back in to watch their second set. Again, nothing special. Just a bunch of middle aged men reliving their younger years through played out music. Don't get me wrong, I loved music from that era, but come on... Do something with it other than mimic it.

During their next break, we again went outside to smoke. Keith followed us out.

"Hey, Maggie, can I get your phone number? Maybe take you out one of these nights?" Keith was cute enough. I didn't see any harm in it.

"Sure, here, give me your phone; I'll put my number in." I took his phone and inputted my number. "Don't call me during the day. I'll be at work."

"Where do you work?" He put his phone in his pocket.

"I'm an art teacher at a youth activity center in Hamilton. I just moved to Princeton a couple months ago." I put my cigarette out and got up to go back in.

"Don't let her fool you. She's not just an art teacher; she's a tattoo artist too." Alisha never could keep her mouth shut.

"Oh yeah? I have some work that needs to be finished. Maybe you can hook me up?" Keith trailed after us as we went back in.

"Maybe." I took my seat at the bar.

Alisha and I watched a few more songs and left before their third set was over. It was getting late, and I wanted to get home to Hope. She was at Alisha's watching Mark. We had barely spent any time together that week, and I wanted to hang out with her.

When we got back to Alisha's, I picked up Hope, and we went home to watch a movie. I told her about the night's events, and we laughed.

Just as I was getting into bed, my phone rang. It was Keith. "Hey, you left early. I was going to take you out to eat when the bar closed." He sounded disappointed.

"Hey, you should have said something and not just assumed. Goodnight." I hung up smiling. Maybe he would get the hint that I wasn't one of his groupies.

Hope loved her school and made quick friends with a small group of girls there. They would come over to the activity center after school and hang out with me in the art class. I was only working part time, but it was enough for now. I had a blast with the kids and hoped it would eventually turn into a full time job.

Keith called me almost nightly. We started talking on the phone for hours on end. There was more to him than his music, thank goodness. He was a computer programmer for some major company during the day and a wanna be rocker at night. I teased him about their taste in music. He would always fire back that he had tried to get them to upgrade their musical choices, but they didn't want to, and he didn't care because he just wanted to play music. I understood what he was saying, but I jokingly called him a sell out for not doing what he believed in.

Keith and I had been talking on the phone for about a month when I finally agreed to go out with him. Well, not exactly go out with him, but I invited him over for dinner. I made Abuelita's enchiladas and a nice side salad. Keith knew I was vegan and said he was vegetarian, so I was sure he would like the black bean enchiladas.

Hope went over to hang out with Alisha and her son, Mark, for the evening. I dropped her off and then hurried home to get dressed for my date. I was actually kind of excited about it.

I was about to put the food on the table, when I got a text from Keith saying he had to work late and would be here in an hour. Well fuck... I almost told him not to bother, but at least he sent me a message. I put the food back in the oven to keep it warm until he arrived.

I was sitting in the living room, drinking a glass of wine, when he showed up. When I opened the door, Keith handed me a bottle of tequila, apologized and smiled. Well, okay... That's better.

We sat at the table and had dinner. He raved about the food, told me that he cooked too and would like to have me over to his place for dinner, as well. He said that he seldom had people over to his place because it was his fortress of solitude and had some pretty bad experiences with women. He talked almost non-stop about the women he had dated before. I was a bit taken aback by the whole conversation, but I continued to listen as it seemed important for him to tell me.

After dinner, we sat in the living room and had a glass of wine while we talked. He asked about the tequila, so we opened it. A few shots later, and we were both more comfortable around one another. Tequila has a way of doing that.

My phone rang. It was Hope. She was wondering if she could just spend the night at Alisha's because it was getting so late. I told her that was fine and I loved her before I hung up.

"Your daughter?" Keith sat next to me on the couch.

"Yes and no." I explained how I had custody of her.

We talked about his children. He had two boys that lived with their mother, and he hadn't seen them in quite some time. He told me he didn't think he was a good influence, with everything he had going on in his life, and thought it was better that he not be around them just yet. He went on to say they lived in southern New Jersey near his parents.

I poured more tequila, got up and turned on some music. Instantly, the conversation switched gears, and we were now talking about music. There, that was better. It turned out he did have more of a range than the covers his band played.

We drank even more tequila and started making out on the couch. Wow, he was a great kisser! He had me melting almost instantly. I had to watch myself because there was no way I was fucking him on our first date.

Okay, maybe I spoke too soon. His hands were all over my body, and I needed this. I stood up, took him by the hand and led him into my bedroom.

Without going into too much detail here, let's just say he knew his way around a woman's body. He made my toes curl more times than I can count! Damn!

We fell asleep for a little while. I woke up as he was getting dressed.

"Hey, I have to get going. I have to get home and get ready for work. I'll call you later, okay?" He bent down and kissed me.

"Okay, I'll walk you out." I got up and threw my robe on. It was Saturday morning, so I planned to go back to bed when he left.

I walked him to the door. When we got to the door, he wrapped one arm around my waist and kissed me. My foot popped off the floor. It surprised me. I usually didn't react in this way.

"I'll see you later, Maggie." Keith smiled and left.

I locked the door and went back to bed. I could still smell him on my pillow. Tucking my pillow under my arm, I smiled and went right back to sleep.

It was the middle of the afternoon when Hope came home. Alisha had brought her over, and she let herself in. I woke to the smell of fresh brewed coffee. After dressing, I wandered out to the kitchen to find Hope there making herself lunch.

"Hey, Kiddo. Thanks for the coffee." I poured a cup and stood there with her.

"I saw the tequila bottle and figured you might need some." She giggled as she spoke.

"Yep, it was one of those kind of nights. Glad you're home." I gave her a little hug and then went into the living room to see what was on television.

Hope and I hung out the rest of the weekend. We talked about school and my date. I helped her with some homework, and by Sunday night we were both exhausted.

I picked Hope up from school Monday afternoon, we did a bit of grocery shopping and went home. There was a large manilla envelope waiting for me in the mailbox. I opened it when we got in the apartment. It was the final divorce papers.

"I need a drink." I went into the kitchen to get a glass of wine but decided to finish off the tequila instead.

"I'm sorry, Maggie. I know how much you must be hurting." Hope hugged me tight and cried with me for a few minutes.

"It's okay, Kiddo. It is what it is. I knew it was coming. Time to move on." I smiled at her to let her know I really was okay even though I wasn't.

"Well, I have homework to do." Hope picked up her backpack and went to her room.

I called Keith, told him about getting my divorce papers and how I didn't want to be alone. He said he would come over after work. I asked him to bring another bottle of tequila.

When I hung up, I took the last shot of tequila and then busied myself getting ready for his arrival. I cleaned up the apartment and then showered. I dressed in a t-shirt and shorts, pulled up my hair and threw on some fresh make-up. Feeling a bit better, I waited in the living room for him.

I got online and talked with Dominick and Heather for a bit. I filled them in on everything going on, and we chatted until Keith rang the doorbell. After telling them I had to go, I shut down my laptop and answered the door.

Keith stepped in, wrapped me up in his arms and kissed me.

"Here ya go." He handed me the bottle of tequila and tried to kiss me again.

"Behave yourself. My daughter is home." I whispered in his ear, pulled back and winked at him.

"Introduce us?" He took the bottle from me and went into the kitchen.

I called Hope to come out and meet Keith. After introducing them, Hope grabbed some leftovers, heated them up and took them back to her room, so she could finish her homework. She was such a good student.

"So, what's the plans for tonight?" Keith and I went into the living room.

"To get pissing drunk and fuck like animals." There went that whole blunt thing again.

"Sounds like a plan, but, um... your daughter is home." Keith poured us each a shot.

"We'll just have to keep it down. Her room is down the hall. We should be fine." I accepted the shot, drank it and poured another. I didn't want to think tonight. I just wanted to be numb.

We killed the bottle of tequila and did what I wanted to. It was sweaty, hot, nasty and exactly what I needed. Keith was an incredible lover and made sure that I truly enjoyed myself... Multiple times. * wink *

Again, he couldn't stay because we both had work the next day. Our routine worked for both of us. A little time after work, some really hot sex and a sweet goodbye.

Keith and I had been dating for a few months. Hope was doing well in school, and it was now the weekend of her eighteenth birthday. I didn't want to think about it because I knew she would be leaving soon.

"Well, Hope, what do you want to do for your birthday?" I almost hated asking her.

"I want to go to New York and spend the weekend there. Can we? Please?" She seemed so excited; I couldn't say no.

"Of course, Kiddo. I'll start making arrangements." I called Keith to see if he wanted to go with us. He said it sounded like fun and would be happy to join in the festivities. I got online, did a bit of research and made reservations.

"Okay, I reserved two hotel rooms. We leave Friday afternoon. We're going to go up to the top of the Empire State Building, see the Statue of Liberty and do all of the touristy things you wanted to do." I walked into Hope's room to tell her the plans.

"Two hotel rooms? Is Keith coming with us?" She was at her desk doing her homework.

"Yep, is that alright?" I should have asked her first.

"Of course it is! It makes me happy to know, when I leave for college this summer, you'll be with someone that makes you happy." She stood up to hug me and then went back to work on her homework. Hope was an amazing young woman.

I hadn't even thought that far ahead. Would I still be with Keith? I mean, it was fun to hang out with him, but we hadn't really gotten all that serious. I went to the kitchen, poured a glass of wine and sat in the living room. I didn't think that now was the time to talk to him about this, so I just drank my wine and watched television.

"Happy Birthday to you, Happy Birthday to you, Happy Birthday dearest Hope, Happy Birthday to you." I couldn't sing, but I woke Hope up the morning of her birthday with a song and a cup of hot cocoa. She was skipping school today, so we could get ready to leave.

"Thank you, Maggie! I can't wait to go!" Hope jumped out of bed, took the cup of hot cocoa, sipped it and set it on her dresser. She danced around the room singing, "I'm eighteen! I'm eighteen!"

"Yes, you are, but you still have to finish school, Kiddo. Don't get too excited." I stopped her and hugged her. "Now, let's pack, shall we?"

"I'm already packed!" Hope was WAY excited for this weekend.

"Okay, well, why don't you shower and dress while I pack and then we'll go out for breakfast." I left her in her room to do what she needed to do.

We had a huge breakfast at one of the diners in our neighborhood. It was delicious. After, we decided to do a little shopping because we had time to kill before Keith got out of work.

We barely made it home and were lugging our new purchases upstairs when Keith pulled into the parking lot.

"Hey there ladies. Need a hand?" Keith walked up to us, kissed me on the cheek, grabbed a few bags and helped us carry them upstairs.

"Well, we're all packed and ready to go. Did you bring your stuff?" I set the bags on the living room floor.

"Yep, it's in my truck. Can I shower here and change my clothes first?" He was still wearing his suit from work. He looked so handsome.

"Of course, I'll set out some fresh towels for you." I went to the bathroom to put out towels while he ran down to his truck to get his things.

After he showered and dressed, we left for New York. Keith drove in his truck because he was more familiar with the area then we were.

We arrived and checked into our hotel. We spent the first night walking around New York city and just taking in the sights. It was almost as lit up as Las Vegas was. Hope took pictures of everything we saw. It was a fabulous night.

When we got back to the hotel, Hope went to her room to upload the pictures to her laptop and post them on Facebook. (A bit of legalese here... Facebook doesn't endorse or sponsor my project. * giggle *) We said goodnight to her and went into our own room.

The next morning, we headed out to do all those touristy things I promised her we would. We took the ferry out to Liberty Island. I wasn't able to get tickets to go inside because they were in such high demand, but it was incredible to just be there. We took a ton of photos and hopped on the ferry back to the city. After eating lunch, we stood in line, for hours, to get to the top of the Empire State Building. We took elevator after elevator until we reached the top. There were rows of people trying to get to the edge to see out over the city. Keith grabbed us by the hands and pushed his way through the crowd. He said there was no way we waited all that time to get up there and not see over the side. Hope was beyond happy and snapped a ton more photos.

We made our way back down to ground level and stopped in at a pizza place for dinner. I, once again, broke my vegan vows and had real New York pizza with Hope and Keith. It was as good as everyone said it would be. I had to stop myself at two slices.

After making our way back to the hotel, Hope hugged me tight and excused herself back to her own room. She was excited to upload and post her pics.

"What should we do now?" Keith wrapped his arms around my waist and pulled me close to him.

"What did you have in mind?" I giggled.

"Well, there are two beds in our room. I was thinking we should get one of them really dirty and then sleep in the other." He took me by the hand, and we went into our own room. Sounded like a plan to me.

Sunday morning arrived, and it was time to go home. We had a blast in New York, and I was so happy that we were able to do that for Hope's birthday. I knew it was something neither of us would ever forget.

Hope talked non-stop about our trip on the way home. She was a giggly schoolgirl, and I loved every minute of it.

"Maggie, did you see..." Hope was still talking about everything we saw in New York.

"Shut the fuck up, Hope! I'm tired of hearing you." Keith yelled at her as he was driving.

"Keith! Don't you EVER talk to my daughter like that! I know you're tired, but you need to apologize this instant!" Oh hell no! No one was going to talk to Hope like that.

He wouldn't apologize. Instead we drove in complete silence until he dropped us off at home.

"Hope, I'm sorry. I was just tired and the traffic was bad. I don't know what came over me." Keith finally apologized.

"It's okay. I understand." Hope's feelings were hurt, but she handled it well.

"Can I call you later, Maggie?" Keith didn't get out of his truck.

"Give it a few days, Keith." I didn't want to talk to him right now.

We went upstairs, called Alisha and invited her and Mark over to see our pictures and hear all about our trip.

I pulled Alisha aside, and told her about how Keith had yelled at and cussed out Hope. She told me that it was a bad sign and to be careful. I kept that in the back of my mind.

It was a few weeks before I talked to Keith again. He had been extremely rude, and I wasn't sure if I wanted to see him. Then those stupid carnal needs kicked in, and I called him.

Things were going well between us again, and we hung out almost every weekend for the next two months. Alisha and I went to Keith's gigs and listened to him play. There were even a few that Hope was able to go to. Everything seemed normal again.

Hope was graduating from high school. The time had just flown by, and I didn't want to face reality. It was time to send her back to Minnesota, so she could get ready to start college. She had been accepted into the University in Duluth on a full scholarship. I was so proud of her.

I had hoped to be able to drive her back home, but I just couldn't take the time off from work. I bought her a plane ticket and gave her five thousand dollars to get her started in life. We spent her final night, in New Jersey, staying up all night and watching all of the girly, teenage movies she loved so much.

I drove her to the airport the next day and walked her to the security check point. They wouldn't let me go beyond that point without a ticket. I hugged her tightly and didn't want to let go.

"It'll be okay, Maggie. You've raised me well. You are the one that made me who I am today. Without you, I would have ended up on the wrong path. You came into my world at the right time and helped me achieve everything I have, with all your positivity and belief in me. Even my own family told me I was never going to get anywhere in life, and look where I am now? Above and beyond all of them. You are my inspiration and the person I look up to the most. You are an amazing person and the best mother a girl could have asked for. I love you." Hope hugged me and cried.

"Thank you, Kiddo, but YOU made yourself who you are today. You never gave up and always did the best you could... And then some. All I could do was share with you what I had been through in the hope you wouldn't make the same mistakes I made. Thank you, really, for the very kind words. You are the daughter I always wanted, and there won't be a day that goes by I won't think about you, miss you and love you." I kissed her on the forehead and watched as she walked through the security check point. My little girl had grown up and was on her way to create her own life. I missed her already.

I drove home with the music blasting and tears flowing down my cheeks. I was all alone now. What was I going to do.

Keith was at my place when I got back. "I knew today was going to be tough for you, so I thought I would come over and keep you company."

"Thank you, Keith." I melted into his arms as he hugged me. "What am I going to do?"

"You're going to move in with me. There's no sense in both of us paying rent." Keith's offer made sense.

"Really?" I looked up at him.

"Yes, really. Now, let's go upstairs, have a couple drinks and start packing." His smile made everything all better.

It took us the whole weekend to pack my things. I gave my furniture to Alisha. Hers was old, and she loved mine, so it just made sense. We packed the remainder of my belongings into Keith's truck and my jeep. With a final look back, I left to move on to my new life. It seemed so surreal.

I had been living with Keith for about a month when I got the phone call. The youth center was being closed because of lack of funding. Well fuck. Now what?

I talked to Keith and told him what happened. He said not to worry because things always had a way of working out. I started looking for work again right away. In the meantime, I was enjoying being a homemaker. I painted our apartment, re-arranged the furniture and made it feel more like "ours" and not just "his".

When Keith came home from work and saw what I had done, he told me he loved it. I had only painted the kitchen, bathroom and one wall in the living room to add some pops of color. We sat in the living room, ordered in some food and watched television. I had pretty much given up being vegan and just went with the flow of things. It was the easiest thing to do.

As was usual, I went to bed before Keith did. He always stayed up late and would join me later. He was a night owl.

"Maggie? Are you awake?" Keith snuggled in behind me.

"Uh huh." I smiled knowing what was about to happen.

"Good, I need you, Baby." Keith rolled me over onto my back and started to kiss me. His hands traveled over my skin and made my body come to life.

We were in the middle of doing what we did, and it was getting pretty hot. I always enjoyed myself tremendously with Keith.

"You know, Maggie, if you pissed or shit, while we were having sex, it wouldn't bother me. I would even clean it up." Keith stopped and looked at me.

"Um, I'll keep that in mind." WHAT? Did he really just say that to me? I knew people were into some kinky shit, (Pun intended!) but this was beyond my realm of acceptable.

I had to fake my way through the rest of it, because quite frankly, that killed it for me. We fell asleep, and a few hours later, Keith got up and left for work.

The instant he was gone, I got online and waited for Dominick to get on messenger. I told him what had happened, and we laughed about the whole thing. Keith was not the guy for me and that had just been made extremely obvious. With no job and nowhere to live, Dominick and Heather invited me to come and stay with them until I could figure out what I wanted to do next. I thanked them and took them up on that invitation.

While I packed my things, I thought about how much I had allowed myself to be changed with this relationship. We ate fast food burgers or pizza almost every night. I seldom talked to any of my friends anymore and lived for the moments that Keith and I could spend time together instead of doing what made me happy. I had to leave before I lost myself completely.

I packed what I could fit into my jeep and left a note for Keith before heading out...

"Hey Keith,

I'm sure by now you've realized that I've left. I'm sorry to break it off with you like this, but I think we both know this wasn't working out. I'm just not into the same things that you are. I hope one day you get the shit you're looking for. HA! It was what it was, and it isn't anymore. It's probably best that we forget we knew each other.

~ Maggie"

CHAPTER THIRTY

It took me six hours to get to Clyde, New York. I drove non-stop. I couldn't get out of New Jersey fast enough. I called Alisha on my way out of town and told her everything. She was sad that I had left without saying goodbye, but she understood. It was time for me to move on. My gypsy blood was boiling.

I pulled into the driveway at Dominick and Heather's. Dominick came out to meet me. He looked exactly like what I had expected. He was tall and lanky with long hair. He walked up and hugged me.

"Welcome home, Maggie. It's about time you get here." He laughed as he spoke.

"Thanks, Dominick. It was a long drive but I'm happy to be here." I pulled away and grabbed my overnight bag from the back of my jeep.

"We'll unpack everything when I get home from work tomorrow. I have to get in and get to sleep. Come on, I'll introduce you to Heather." He took my bag and we walked inside.

Heather was a beautiful woman. She was a bit shorter than me and had gorgeous, curly, light brown hair. Her eyes sparkled when she smiled.

"Hey, Shithead, this is Maggie. Maggie, this is my wife, Heather." They used the term "shithead" as a term of endearment. Dominick sat my bag down in the living room.

"Hi, Maggie! It's so nice to finally meet you!" She hugged me tightly too.

"And it's nice to meet you as well, Heather." I sat down on the couch. I was exhausted from the drive but wasn't sleepy.

Heather and I sat up all night talking. We talked about my life with Jared and everything that happened after we separated. Even though she had heard it all before online, she let me spill it all out again and just cry.

Heather reassured me that it was all for the best, and that I was now in a safe and peaceful environment. I knew what she said was the truth, but I still couldn't help but cry. I think I had held it all in for so long, and focused on being a mom to Hope, I hadn't let myself feel my true feelings.

Around five in the morning, Heather said goodnight and went to bed. I curled up, in the blankets she gave me, on the couch and slept until early the next afternoon. I guess I was more tired than I had thought.

Heather woke up just as I did. Dominick had left for work. I grabbed my overnight bag, cleaned up and changed my clothes. When I came back out to the living room, Heather brought me a fresh cup of coffee, and we chatted for a while. When we finished our coffee, she showed me around their home.

It was one of the coolest houses I had ever seen. It was constructed from giant shipping crates, but unless they told you, you never would have known. The first crate was divided into two rooms. The first half was the kitchen and the other was made into a sewing room. The crate next to that, was one large room. They had a dining area set up in part of it and the living room in the other. Another crate flanked the far end and was divided into an office, the bathroom and their master bedroom. They had another room built off their bedroom for their hot tub. There was a door off of that room that led out to an enormous, Quonset hut styled garage. The garage had a workshop in one end, a two car garage in the other and a loft above that. I was amazed with how much room there was out there!

We spent the rest of the afternoon just chatting and getting to know each other better. It was as if we had always known each other. There was not even a hint of awkwardness.

Dominick came home from work and announced that we were going out for dinner. We all piled into their van and headed out. We went to a buffet place and had a nice time. It was good to be around real people again.

We went home, watched some television and chatted until Dominick had to go to bed, so he could get up for work the next day. Heather and I stayed up late talking again. We both liked to stay up late, so it worked out well.

The next day, Heather and I were in the kitchen making dinner when Dominick came home from work.

"Hi, Shithead, I'm home." Dominick put down his lunchbox and kissed Heather.

"Hey, Dominick. How was work?" I hugged him hello.

"What's this Dominick and Heather shit? You can call us Mom and Dad." Dominick hugged me back.

"Okay, Mom and Dad it is!" That made me so happy. I felt like I was part of a real family now.

You know how some people are just natural born parents? Well that was Dominick and Heather. They had so much love to share, and they shared it with me. I was truly blessed to have them in my life.

Dad worked five days a week, so that left Mom and I a lot of time to hang out. We watched soap operas and laughed at all of the drama. Mom and I talked about crafting, and she showed me all of the beautiful t-shirts she had done embroidery on. She was a truly talented woman. She had thousands of embroidery designs for her sewing machine. It all made my head spin a bit, but I learned so much from her.

I told Mom what it was like to grow up the way I did, and how I was never really taught about what it was to be a woman. I told her the story about being teased, in foster care, for not shaving past my knees. She stepped in, right away, and gave me instruction as we went along. I know it may seem odd that I was a forty year old woman and had been doing these things all along, but I was now learning how to do them the right way. It was simple things, like rinsing the dishes before I put them in the sink and not being so quick to react with anger. She taught me how to accept people for who they were and not judge them for it. She showed me, through her actions, what it was to sit back, hold your tongue, and be a lady... Not just a woman. She was the epitome of true grace.

Mom and Dad took me on a tour of Seneca Falls. It was said that it was the city that inspired the scenes in a famous Christmas movie, my favorite one! It was incredible to stand on "that" bridge, to see the Hotel Clarence and so on. I took a lot of pictures, and when we got home, I posted them right away. I wanted my friends to see everything I was seeing.

As much fun as I was having with them, I was still lonely. I wanted to meet someone, fall in love and live happily ever after. Now, where was I going to meet that someone? Oh right, Facebook! (And let's not forget that Facebook doesn't endorse or sponsor my project.)

I signed into my account and started adding people that lived near me. I was on a mission. That's when I noticed I was already friends with someone close by. I had posted a picture of a cat and he commented on it. We had chatted a bit before this but nothing of any seriousness. Hmm...

His name was Eric, and he lived about an hour away. I wrote him a private message, right away, let him know that I no longer lived in New Jersey and was now living fairly close to him.

Eric and I chatted online for about a week before we decided to meet in person. He was vegan! YAY! That had been a huge thing in my last relationship. I had converted back myself, and it was important to me to be with someone that held the same ethics I did.

It was the Forth of July when he came out to meet me. Clyde was a tiny farm town, so we decided to stay at my place and just sit outside, getting to know each other. We grabbed some beer from a convenience store down the street and sat under a huge shade tree in the backyard talking.

He asked me about my past relationships and what I thought had gone wrong with them. I was shocked he had asked and did my best to answer his question. I told him I thought maybe I loved too much and too easily. He admitted to doing the same thing and then went on to tell me that he didn't believe there was any such thing as loving too much.

He had been married for eleven years when he discovered his wife had been cheating on him. It caused him to fall into a deep depression. I told him I knew exactly how he felt. We bonded over our shared pain.

The sun began to set into the western sky. Neither of us wanted our time together to end, so we made our way into the loft and continued to talk. We had a few more beers, and I told him the story of why my marriage ended. I started crying. Eric stood up and asked me to join him. He was much taller than me, and when he stepped toward me to hug me, I got lost in his embrace.

I tried to stop crying, but he wouldn't let me. He told me it was good to get it all out, and he had already had that cleansing moment. He said that crying would bring me into my moment of clarity and then I would be ready to truly move on with my life.

We sat on the love seat in the loft and talked. He pulled my feet up over his legs and rested his hands on them. Eric was kind and gentle. He made me feel like someone, other than my newly found parents, really cared. I believed that he did.

Twelve hours after he arrived, he took his leave. He didn't try to kiss me. I walked him out to his car and hugged him goodbye.

I went into the house and fell into a peaceful sleep on the couch. Was he the one? I guess we would wait to see.

Eric and I chatted online all week and through the weekend. We had so much in common. He loved music as much as I did. That's when I found out he was a bass player in a death metal band. Fuck... Another bass player? Okay, I wasn't going to hold that against him just because the last one turned out to be a freak.

Sunday night, we were chatting online, and Eric asked me if I wanted to come and stay the weekend with him. I excitedly accepted his invitation. I knew it was moving fast, but it felt so right.

It was Tuesday evening, and we were, once again, chatting online, and he asked if I wanted to come out early. I told him I was all packed up and ready to go, so we made arrangements for him to pick me up the next day after work. I was going to be spending four nights there and was a bit nervous. I threw a couple of extra changes of clothes into my luggage and then went into the bathroom to bathe and shave. I just had a feeling I should probably shave. * wink *

Eric was on time to pick me up. I saw him out the window. He was so sexy. As I said, he was a lot taller than me and was very slender. His dreads were tied back in a bandana, and he had a white t-shirt on with skinny jeans. He was just yummy.

When he had come out the first time, I wore shorts and a t-shirt with my hair in a ponytail... Nothing special. This time, I had gotten all dolled up. I decided to dress up in my pin-up look and go all out. I wore rolled up jeans and a white button down shirt that I tied in the front. My hair was pinned up, in curls, on the top of my head with a bandana wrapped around it and tied on the top. My make-up was flawless, and I knew I looked good.

Eric knocked on the door and I opened it.

"Wow, you look amazing!" He smiled at me.

"Thanks, I thought you might like it." I handed him my bag, and we left.

It was almost an hour's drive to get to his apartment. We talked and laughed the entire way there. We pulled over at a convenience store and picked up some beer and cigarettes before continuing on to his place.

My stomach was full of butterflies when we walked in to his apartment. I was pleasantly surprised to see that it was clean and orderly. He had told me he was a clean freak, but it was nice to see it was true.

Eric put my bag in his bedroom and went into the kitchen. He started making us dinner. Wow! Clean and he could cook too? This was just too good to be true.

We ate dinner in the living room and talked as we ate. He had music playing in the background, so we talked about the music. Dinner was amazing, and we cleaned up the mess from cooking together.

Although he had to work the next day, we stayed up late talking. We never ran out of things to talk about. It was a wonderful night. When it came time to go to sleep, he told me he was going to sleep on the couch, and I could have his bed. I told him that wouldn't do, and we could sleep in the same bed. When we got into bed, he wrapped me up in his arms, and we slept like that all night long. It was sweet and innocent.

He woke up early the next morning for work. I got up as he was getting out of the shower, and we had tea on his back patio before he left. He told me to make myself at home, and he would be back later that afternoon.

When he left, I busied myself with cleaning. He was very neat, so I cleaned his bathroom and scrubbed down his walls just to have something to do. When I was finished, I showered, changed and went for a walk.

Eric came home from work and immediately noticed what I had done. He thanked me and told me that wasn't why he asked me over, but he appreciated it. I told him I only did it to keep myself busy.

The rest of the week went just like that. We cooked dinner together, talked the night away and fell asleep with me wrapped in his arms. It was sheer perfection.

Friday night was here, so we decided to go out since he didn't have to work the next day. We walked to a local bar, had a few drinks and started to walk back to his place. We had to cross a foot bridge over a set of train tracks to get to the street he lived on. We stopped on the bridge, stood there holding hands and watching the trains move under our feet. * swoon *

When we got back to his apartment, we listened to more music and went to sleep. Again, he wrapped me up in his arms, and I felt his heart beating against my back. I had never slept so peacefully in my life.

The sun peeked through the blinds to gently stir us to consciousness. I opened my eyes to find Eric leaning on his elbow and smiling at me.

"Good morning, Maggie." He leaned down and kissed me. Our first kiss was sweet and led into our second, third and fourth kiss.

We didn't stop there either. His hands were warm against the softness of my skin. It felt natural, like we had always been together. He moved his body over mine and looked into my eyes before he kissed me again.

My hands wandered up the strong lines of his back, over his shoulders and down the muscles of his arms. Eric took my left hand and pinned it over my head as he nibbled gently on my earlobe and down my neck. It was as if there was a magnetic pull between us, and my hips lifted off the bed to be closer to him. I had to be closer to him; I needed him inside me.

Eric kissed his way down my writhing body. He suckled gently on my breasts before working his way down further. Reaching the area between my thighs, he stayed there until my legs quivered with pleasure, and I gushed with orgasm. Knowing he had pleased me to the deepest parts of my soul, he moved his way back up my body, kissing me the entire way. My nails raked down his back as he took me completely.

Again, my hips lifted from the bed to pull him deeper inside me. I felt his heartbeat race against my own and knew the culmination of our union was near. I bit my own lip as my eyes rolled into the back of my head and the intensification of pure seduction rushed over my body.

"Eric, please, please make me cum again." He didn't stop. His body moved against mine until it happened again and again. My breath caught in my throat as I felt him reach the pinnacle of ecstasy. He laid there for a moment, before moving away from me, and laying at my side.

"Oh my God, Maggie, it's never been like that before. Did you put a spell on me, or are we just that good together?" He smiled.

"We're just that good together." I smiled back, still trembling.

We got up and showered together. After dressing and having breakfast, we joined a couple of his friends to go on a hike through an old cemetery. He held my hand as we walked. Yep, it felt like we had always been "us."

That night, I was packing up my things to get ready to go home.

"Maggie, I don't want to take you back tomorrow. As a matter of fact, I don't want to take you back at all." Eric walked up behind me as I was packing, and he wrapped his arms around my waist.

"What? Eric, this is so fast. We need to talk about this." I turned to face him.

We went out to the living room to discuss what he had just suggested. I told him that I was worried because I wasn't working, and I was living on my savings. He told me that it would be fine, and we would make it through no matter. Though it was crazy, I agreed to move in with him. We went out to Mom and Dad's the next day and moved my stuff to his place.

I was sitting on the couch after we got back and had unpacked my things. Eric walked over to the couch and leaned down over me.

"Do you know what you can say now that you couldn't have said a few hours ago?" He smiled at me.

"Nope, tell me." I smiled back.

"You're home, Maggie... Welcome home." He leaned down and kissed me sweetly.

Yep, I was home.

The next few months were amazing! Eric took me out on surprise dates every week. We would go to a car show or out to eat at really nice restaurants. He was always so proud to be able to pull these things off, and I loved it! He would text me from work with a message like, "If I were you, I would get all dolled up and be ready by the time I get home." He never gave me hints as to what we were doing, just that we were going to do something.

We were sitting at home, one night, talking about life. You know, the basic, "where is this heading" kind of thing?

"I don't plan on this going any further than it is right now." When Eric spoke those words, I knew this wasn't what it seemed.

I wanted more. I wanted to be married, happily in love and to have foster children. I wanted to settle down. He wanted fun and to just live for the day. I knew at that very moment that it was time for me to move on.

"Eric, as much as I love what we have going on here, I want more than this." I looked at him as I spoke.

"I know, Maggie. It's been fun though, right?" He smiled a soft smile.

"The funnest." We both stood up and hugged. "Don't forget me, Eric."

"I could never forget you, Maggie." He hugged me tight, kissed me on the nose, and we said goodbye. I packed up and moved back in with Mom and Dad until I figured out what I was going to do next. They welcomed me home with open arms.

Eric and I spent the hazy days of summer helping each other to heal. What we had was special, and I will always hold the memories we created safe in my heart.

Now, what was I to do? My gypsy blood was boiling again. It was time to start out on another adventure!

There was a guy, by the name of Sam, I had befriended online. He lived in North Carolina. I know... I know... I guess I still had lessons to learn. A few weeks after moving back home, I was on my way out again. Mom and Dad thought I was crazy, and they were probably right, but they supported my decision and told me I would always have a home to come back to.

Once again, I packed up my jeep and headed out. The drive to North Carolina took me twelve hours. I stopped for gas and to stretch my legs, but that was it. Mom had packed me some snacks, so I was set to not have to stop to eat.

I called Sam when I was about an hour away. He lived just south of Greensboro, in a town called Eden. I loved the name of the town. What a great place to start the next part of my life's adventure!

Sam met me outside when I pulled into his driveway. We had been talking online for years, but this was our first time meeting face to face. He looked just like his pictures.

I had been there a couple of weeks, and it just didn't feel right. Hell, we couldn't even have sex, except in the missionary position, because his stomach was so fat and his, well... ya know, couldn't be seen over his stomach. We tried to have sex doggy style once, and he couldn't reach me past his stomach! It took everything I had not to laugh at him. Though as I type this, I can't help but to laugh.

Here's the long and short of it. (Again, pun intended.) He lied about almost everything else. He was truly one of those "good ol' boys" and didn't hide it once I got there.

It was all about, "Woman do this..." and, "Woman do that..." I swear, I was about to show him just what women were capable of doing, but thought better of it. He had told me not to tell anyone that my ex-husband was black because people wouldn't "take kindly" to that around there. Again, I wanted to kick his ass, but I didn't want to go to jail in "get a rope" country.

I was in the kitchen making dinner and planning my escape route, one evening, when he came in behind me.

"Skin these and cook 'em up for supper." He dropped two squirrels on the counter and walked out mumbling something about going to the bar.

Nope, I'm not kidding or exaggerating in the slightest. That's exactly how it happened. It was right then and there, I realized what I was doing. I wasn't waiting for the "right" guy. I was settling for the "right now" guy. Nope, time to move on.

I quickly gathered my things and threw them in the back of my jeep. I had gotten to be a professional at this. I didn't have much stuff anyway at this point. It was easier to travel light. I called a friend of mine in Oregon, and I told her I would be there in five days. Luckily, I still had a few thousand dollars in my bank account.

I put her address into my global positioning system and listened for directions.

"Take exit 72 to merge onto Interstate 77 North. Continue on to interstate 64 West."

I pulled over on the interstate, and I watched as the sun set into the horizon of the western sky. My mind wandered back to the day, when I was fourteen and was laying in bed; bruised, bleeding and broken. Memories of imagining what it must be like to be the sun, making itself more known in the morning sky, filled my head. I remembered thinking how it was shy and innocent at first, afraid to come out. I thought about how, as time progressed, it became more sure of itself, realizing it's own self worth and then proudly stood, at it's place, in the middle of the daylight sky. I knew it was now time for me to let my light shine. I didn't need "Mr. Right" to feel whole... to feel complete. I just needed to be me. I wasn't sure who that person was, or even if I had ever known. I had always been a caregiver in one way or another, and it was now time for me to take care of myself.

I watched as the last rays of daylight disappeared into the night sky. For the first time in my life, I was about to live for me. Though the journey terrified me to my core, I knew it had to be done.

Goodbye yesterday. Hello today. I'll see you tomorrow.

Made in the USA
Monée, IL
06 March 2020

22819214R00193